Praise for T

'Slow-burning romance, BI.   y
drama, and a country under tl   ...ᴜ ᴜᴜᴏᴏgy
does not disappoint.' – *Booklist,* starred review

'Raman has crafted a world bursting with colour and texture and kinetic energy, and a story of rebuilding a fractured family that will stick with you long after "The End." – Sara Holland, *New York Times* bestselling author of *Everless* and *Havenfall*

'Set in a richly realised world ripe with magic, *The Ivory Key* is a dazzling new addition to young adult fantasy. Featuring a broken family fumbling towards healing and a perilous expedition into the ruins of a history that never should have been lost, this is a riveting adventure by a talent to watch.' – Traci Chee, *New York Times* bestselling author of The Reader trilogy and National Book Award Finalist for *We Are Not Free*

'Everything about *The Ivory Key* is vivacious – from the enrapturing setting of opulent forts and forbidden ruins to the larger-than-life characters who will ensnare your heart with their perfect balance of heroism and faults. Brace yourself for the single best portrayal of fraught sibling relationships you will ever read coupled with a complex, multi-faceted plot that unfolds as shockingly as the twisted puzzles the characters face. You will fall into this book and never want to come out!' – Sara Raasch, *New York Times* bestselling author of the Snow Like Ashes trilogy

'*The Ivory Key* has everything I want most in fantasy. It has a world so vivid and developed, I could taste the food and feel the magic weapons in my hand. It has flawed, developed characters I rooted for and cried beside. And it has a quest steeped in lore and mystery. Akshaya Raman is a new master of the genre to watch for.' – Susan Dennard, *New York Times* bestselling author of the Witchlands series

'*The Ivory Key* is the epic YA fantasy sibling story I've been waiting for. A rich world, a satisfying slow burn romance and a main character determined to forge her own path make this series a must read.' – Adrienne Young, *New York Times* bestselling author of the Fable duology

'A rollicking adventure of royal family drama, treasure hunts and hidden histories. I loved it.' – S. A. Chakraborty, author of the bestselling Daevabad trilogy

'*The Ivory Key* is a twisty, dazzling adventure that I absolutely fell in love with.' – Tasha Suri, author of The Books of Ambha duology

'A vibrant fantasy world, four estranged siblings and an action-packed quest. *The Ivory Key* is a richly woven adventure with a tender heart. I was completely enamoured.' – Amanda Foody, author of *Ace of Shades* and *All of Us Villains*

'A secret society, a hunt for lost magic and four siblings who are each hiding their own secrets . . . *The Ivory Key* is everything I love about epic, character-driven fantasy, brimming with lushly realised settings and deliciously slow-burn romances. An immersive, unmissable debut.' – Katy Rose Pool, author of *There Will Come a Darkness*

THE CRIMSON FORTRESS

AKSHAYA RAMAN

HOT
KEY
BOOKS

First published in Great Britain in 2023 by
HOT KEY BOOKS
4th Floor, Victoria House, Bloomsbury Square
London WC1B 4DA
Owned by Bonnier Books
Sveavägen 56, Stockholm, Sweden
bonnierbooks.co.uk/HotKeyBooks

Text copyright © Akshaya Raman, 2023
Map copyright © Jared Blando, 2021

A CIP catalogue record for this book is available from the British Library.

ISBN: 978-1-4714-1126-7
Also available as an ebook and in audio

1

Design by Dana Li
Printed and bound in Great Britain by Clays Ltd, Elcograf S.p.A.

Hot Key Books is an imprint of Bonnier Books UK
bonnierbooks.co.uk

For my pillars of strength: my childhood friends, my writing community, and my families, both blood and found

Koranos
Excursion
Ritsar
Syena Fort
Simha Fort
New Border
Trisore Fort
Hima Mahal
Ithana Fort Ruins
Maravati
Lyria
Banagha Stepwell Ruins
Visala?
Inara Desert
Gauri Mahal
Jhaner Fort
Gadhor Fort Ruins
Jhaner Lake
Possible Location of Visala? See Letter from S*21
Great Library of Elendha
Sacred Scrolls "Madhvi's Lament"??
Ravas
Kastu
Gates of Savitri
Swapna
Handhar Ruins
Madhkot Fort
Moon Temple Ru
Forest
Dvar
Great Arch of Dvar
Dvar Fort
Dwaramatha
Lighthouse of Dvar
Maghgiri
Nayan Fort
Excursion #6
Nayan Island
Southern Sea
BLANDO

Mountains

s of
ala

Varaya Fort

IK Map Piece?

Yodh River

Excursion #13

Fire Temple
of Paliya

Port of Harya

Tasgarh
Fort

Rayu River

Maghya
Ruins

Vengiri
Fort

Excursion #12

Isles of
Kaanch

Elarai
Monastary

Eastern Sea

N

The LANDS of

ASHOKA

Notes from Papa's Journal

CHAPTER ONE

— VIRA —

THE DOOR WAS marked with a silver elephant.

Vira held up the magical lantern she'd rented from the merchant at the mouth of the cave. "I think this is it."

In addition to the absurd amount he'd charged for a lamp that barely illuminated five feet of space around her, the merchant's instructions had been vague at best—a series of hand waves she'd interpreted to mean that the entrance to the tavern was somewhere within the network of caves.

"You'll know it when you see it," he'd said as he closed his grimy fingers over the eight seyrs she'd handed him against her sister Riya's objections. But after nearly half an hour of wandering in the dark without proof that there was anything here besides skittering beetles and fluttering bats, she was beginning to think the man had lied.

"This *better* be it," Riya said, annoyed. "We've wasted enough time already."

This entire excursion to the Adhura province had proved to be a test in patience. It took them a whole day of questioning vendors at several different markets in the sweltering heat to get a single lead on the scholar they were trying to find. It was a miracle they'd gotten this far—and that they'd survived the day without murdering one another.

As Vira reached for the handle, her heartbeat quickened. Despite her best efforts to keep a hold on her emotions, hope bloomed in her chest. Or maybe it was desperation. She wasn't sure she could tell the difference anymore.

"This could be another dead end," Riya warned, as though she could read Vira's every thought.

Vira felt herself flush—first with embarrassment at her own transparency and then with irritation that her sister was treating her like a child who didn't know any better. "I'm well aware, thank you," she said curtly. She was the one poring over Papa's journals night after sleepless night, piecing together arcane clues and historical fragments.

There had been rumors for centuries that there were other quarries of magic scattered throughout Ashoka, purposefully hidden by the secretive and dangerous Kamala Society. In order to find them, one had to track down the Ivory Key—a legendary object said to unlock that lost magic. And Vira had found it. She'd become the first person in five hundred years to hold that secret—only to discover that the Ivory Key didn't lead to the answers she'd searched for her entire life. It led to more questions. More codes to break. More mysteries to unravel.

Papa had taught them the basics of cryptography, but the Ivory Key had turned out to be more complex than they'd expected. They needed an expert—someone who specialized in ciphers, someone they could trust to help them, because they were running out of leads and, worse, time.

That's why she was here, why she'd shirked her duties as a ruler and lied to her Council yet again, to track down a scholar she'd found mentioned in Papa's old letters. Magic. If Vira could get more magic, she could fix everything. This was her last hope, or there wouldn't even be an Ashoka left for her to worry about.

"I'm just trying to help," Riya said, a small frown creasing her forehead.

Vira forced herself to take a deep breath, stuffing down her muddled feelings. "I'm sorry. You *are* helping. I'm just tired."

It wasn't a lie. Being the maharani of a dying country was exhausting. Every day her Council brought her some new problem—news of Lyrian troop movements, a part of the border wall running out of magic, protesters gathering outside the Dvar Fort.

Ashoka was a country built on magic, a resource mined from the single quarry beneath the Dvar Palace, carefully processed by mayaka—those who worked with magic—and put into objects. Magic was what powered carriages, transported messages, and lit the city. It was what protected Ashoka from invaders; it was woven into the weapons used by the military and the walls that made up the country's borders.

Or at least it had been. As the maharani, Vira knew exactly how little was left in the quarry. Three weeks. That was all they had before the border would fully crumble, leaving Ashoka defenseless.

Finding the Ivory Key was supposed to solve Vira's problems. Instead, it had led her to disappointment after disappointment, and she wasn't sure she could handle another one, not when her heart was still too raw from what had happened during their trip to Ritsar.

What had happened after.

Her chest tightened painfully, but she pushed that aside too.

The door opened into a cramped cavern. Dim chandeliers cascaded from the high ceiling, illuminating stone walls that had been sanded down and carved with elaborate geometric designs. Low wooden tables dotted the room, each surrounded by a ring of embroidered cushions. Some were occupied by sole patrons sipping from a tankard of ale or wine. Others held groups clustered together, playing cards or talking in hushed voices. Lilting music emanated from one corner, where a sitar player seated on a rug-covered dais was strumming a lively tune.

Riya cast a furtive glance around as they approached the bar. "This doesn't look like the kind of place that many scholars would frequent."

Vira didn't respond, but she secretly agreed. She and Riya were dressed simply in cotton kurtas, without any jewelry or fine silk that would attract attention or indicate that they were worthwhile targets for robbery, but Vira could still feel gazes lingering on her. It hadn't escaped her notice that the clientele was heavily armed, talwars, aruvals, and daggers resting on the ground beside their tables. She had a talwar too—a plain curved sword that she'd brought along at Riya's insistence—but she'd never intended to actually need it.

"What'll you have?" The barkeep's kaajal-lined eyes flickered up impatiently to Vira and then back to where she was wiping the sticky counter with a dirty rag. It didn't look to be making much of a difference.

"We're actually looking for someone," Riya said. "Sharadha."

That earned them the barkeep's full attention. She dropped the rag and stared at them, one hand on her hip as her eyes narrowed suspiciously. "Who's asking?"

"Some old friends." Vira put five shiny seyrs on the counter, ignoring Riya's incredulous look.

"Sharadha doesn't have friends," the barkeep said. But a moment later she jerked her chin to the right, where a tunnel led deeper into the cavern. "Try through there."

Vira heard the roar of a crowd. They emerged in a smaller cave, where people were clustered around a table. Riya elbowed her way in first, and Vira followed, standing on her toes to look over Riya's shoulder.

It was a game of cards. On one end was a broad-shouldered young man, the heavy rings on his fingers twinkling as he rearranged his cards. On the other side was a woman who looked youthful despite streaks of gray in her long black braid. And in the middle—atop of what was surely hundreds of glinting seyrs and tolahs—was a carved wooden flute. It didn't look to be worth much, but Vira could feel the faintest hint of magic wafting from it.

Another cheer rose up as the young man set his cards on the table. Vira was too far away to make out what they were, but judging by the response, it was a good hand. A hush fell over the crowd as the woman leaned forward, waiting until the last second to flip her cards over.

The room erupted into chaos.

Vira barely dodged out of the way of someone's elbow as they punched the air above in celebration. She cast her eyes around, unsure about the result until the young man slammed his fists on the table in rage, knocking his cards onto the ground as he stormed out.

The woman rose, picked up the flute, and bowed dramatically to thunderous applause. She scraped a handful of the coins into a small cloth bag at her waist and then winked. "Remember to play nice."

That was apparently the only thing holding the crowd back, because suddenly dozens of hands dove for the money. Vira backed away in alarm, realizing too late that she'd lost Riya. She was contemplating shoving her way through the horde when Riya emerged, clutching a handful of silver tolahs.

"You went after the money?" Vira gaped at her. "Are you serious?"

"I wouldn't have if you didn't keep wasting ours," Riya said, pocketing the coins.

Vira pursed her lips. It wasn't a waste if it was actually helping them, but Riya wouldn't understand that, so she said nothing.

Riya put her hand out to stop a passing stranger. "Where can we find Sharadha?"

He gave her a baffled look. "That was the woman who won."

"Her?" Vira's brows rose in surprise. Given the letters she and Papa had exchanged, Vira expected a bookish scholar who spent her time in dusty university libraries. The woman they'd seen didn't fit that description in any way.

Vira turned back the way they'd come. And that's when she saw him. Amrit. His tall stature would have looked lanky on someone else but was filled out by his hard-earned muscles. His striking features—his jawline, his cheekbones, his long lashes. His brown eyes always full of . . .

Vira blinked, and the world around her almost seemed to change shape. It wasn't Amrit. It was a stranger. Someone who bore a passing resemblance to the former captain of her guard, former . . . *something else*. But it was too late. The floodgates in her mind had opened, and Vira couldn't stop herself from plunging headlong into the memories that haunted her.

I wish you knew that I'll always protect you.

Those words seemed to burn her from the inside out, and Vira had to stop walking just for a second, a hand pressed against her chest, as if that would somehow stop the pain. *It was a lie*, she reminded herself. Every word, every admission had been carefully constructed to pry her open—to get her to trust him. There were no hidden messages to be found in her memories, no secret promises or explanations. He'd used her and manipulated her and *left* her. He'd betrayed her in every sense of the word—taken the Ivory Key, abandoned her in the middle of the Koranos Mountains, and left with the same mercenaries who were responsible for her mother's death.

And still. After all that, she felt his absence like a bruised rib—always there, always aching. And she hated herself for it.

"Vira?" Riya turned back in alarm. "What's wrong?"

Concern laced her voice, and Vira felt irrationally angry. She wasn't a fragile vase on the verge of shattering. "Nothing." She forced herself to keep walking.

Riya's eyes lingered on Vira a moment too long, but she didn't say anything else. The tavern was more crowded now, but it was easy to spot Sharadha sitting alone in one corner, her feet up on a table, ankles crossed, a tumbler of ale in one hand. She was dressed in a simple off-white kurta and tight-fitting pants—both covered with smudges of dirt. Her sleeves were pushed up to her shoulders, revealing sinewy muscles rippling across the bronzed skin of her upper arms. A bandage was wrapped around her right elbow, the cloth stained brown with dried blood.

"I don't have what you're looking for," Sharadha said, making no effort to move as they approached.

Vira blinked in surprise at the abrupt dismissal. "We haven't told you why we're here."

"I'm not in the treasure hunting business anymore."

"It's a good thing that we're not looking for a treasure hunter then," Riya said.

Sharadha took a swig of ale. "I'm still not interested."

Vira felt panic clawing up her throat. In all the ways she'd pictured this meeting, she'd never considered that Sharadha would simply turn them away. "We have the Ivory Key," Vira blurted, yanking a piece of paper out of her cloth bag and slamming it down next to Sharadha's feet. Atop it she dropped a bag of coins that rattled as it landed heavily. "And we have money."

"What are you doing?" Riya hissed.

Sharadha's eyes went first to the bag of coins, then to the cipher, and then finally to the two of them, sizing them up like opponents in a sparring match. A crooked smile crept across her face and she dropped her feet to the ground. "Well now, you really should have led with that."

"So you'll help us?" Vira asked, ignoring Riya's furious gaze. She didn't want to hear whatever Riya had to say about not revealing their cards too early. They couldn't afford to let Sharadha slip through their fingers.

"I'll hear you out," Sharadha corrected, disinterestedly pulling the paper toward her. The change in her posture was subtle but immediate. She set her drink on the table as she leaned closer to study the cipher. "Fascinating," she murmured. "Where did you get this?"

Vira felt a surge of vindication. Sharadha—like everyone else—had underestimated her. "That's unimportant," she said, sitting opposite Sharadha. "Can you decipher it?"

Sharadha's brows rose. "I would hardly call it *unimportant*. Do you know how many have sought the Ivory Key? Forgive me if I find it hard to believe that two children found pieces of a map no one has seen in centuries and unearthed the Kamala Society's most guarded secret."

Vira's jaw tightened. She was liking this woman less and less, but she forced herself to bite her tongue before she said something she'd regret.

Riya, however, had no such qualms. "You have no idea how much it cost us *children* to get that," she snapped, fury burning in her dark eyes, and Vira was struck by how much like Amma she looked just then. "Maybe we don't need you after all," Riya said, reaching to snatch the cipher up off the table.

But Sharadha was quicker. She slammed her palm down, holding it in place. "I didn't say I couldn't decipher it. You know, your father too had no sense of humor." Their surprise must have shown, because Sharadha smirked. "You think I wouldn't recognize Ravi's children? Even if you do look just like *her*."

Vira didn't miss the way she emphasized *her*. It was the way that people sometimes spoke about Vira, as though they didn't understand what was so special about her. She'd never heard that tone applied to her mother, the former maharani. "Papa regarded you highly," Vira said. "He trusted you, and he said that we could trust you too." It wasn't exactly the truth.

8

Papa had never so much as mentioned Sharadha's name, but Vira needed her help.

Sharadha's gaze softened. "I was sorry to hear about his passing. He'd be thrilled to know it was his daughters who found the key."

Vira felt her heart squeeze just for a second. "So you'll help?" she prompted again.

Any kindness in Sharadha's eyes vanished. "For a price, of course."

"More money?" Riya asked, an edge to her voice.

She folded the paper and stood up. "A favor."

"Not interested," Riya said at once.

"You should be," Sharadha said. "Because I can't help you otherwise."

"Why's that?" Vira asked, frowning.

"Several weeks ago, my office was raided and the thieves took all my books—books that include answers to this cipher. Now I know who took it, but I can't get into their hideout alone."

"You want us to be accomplices in a robbery," Vira said.

"Come now, Vira," Sharadha said, amused. Vira bristled at the familiar address. "You're not that naive. Unearthing ancient mysteries—as much as Ravi wished it so—isn't a scholarly pursuit, nor is it a noble one. You want to find buried treasure, you're going to have to get your hands a little dirty."

As much as Vira didn't want to admit it, maybe Sharadha had a point. "Where exactly are these thieves?" she asked.

"A monastery," Sharadha said. "Up in the hills."

"I didn't realize there were many in this region," Vira said skeptically.

"I see Ravi didn't bother to teach you about the history of his own province," Sharadha said. "Long ago," she began, sounding every bit like the scholar Vira had believed her to be, "caravans of traders used to cross the mountains on foot, traveling for weeks with their wares from the ports on the western coast to the inland markets. To offer them safe passage and protection, the Adhura province authorized the creation of dozens of monasteries in the mountains, each situated a day's walk from the next one. They had altars dedicated to the goddesses, but they were basically glorified inns, offering merchants a night's rest for grain or cloth or metal—whatever they happened to be transporting. But as the roads improved and mayaka-fortified carriages became affordable, traders could pass through the mountains in a matter of days. They didn't need these monasteries anymore, so they fell to the peripheries of history, forgotten relics of a bygone era."

"The perfect location for criminals to take over," Riya added.

It was more or less what the Ravens—the bandits Riya had joined when she'd run away from the palace—had done in the Swapna Forest, setting up their camp near buildings constructed by long-abandoned settlements.

"Precisely." Sharadha looked at them expectantly. "What do you say?"

"No," Riya said. "Find someone el—"

"We'll do it," Vira cut in.

"*What?*" Riya glowered at her.

They'd come to Adhura because they'd exhausted all other options. Vira needed to know where the Ivory Key led, and Sharadha could tell them that.

Sharadha's smile was bright. "All right then. We have a deal."

CHAPTER TWO

— RIYA —

"THIS IS A bad idea," Riya said for the fifth time since they'd left the tavern. They were nearing the edge of the city, and the paved roads built for carriages were fading into dirt and gravel that crunched uncomfortably beneath their feet. Ahead of them Sharadha was walking directly toward the dark outline of the Maghgiri Mountains.

Vira—like she'd been doing all day—ignored her. "Walk faster," she said instead.

It was a hot and muggy night, and Riya could feel her clothes sticking uncomfortably to her skin. She was exhausted and sweaty and desperately wanted to be back in her own bed. But she didn't trust Sharadha, and since no amount of reason had changed Vira's mind, Riya had no choice but to go along and make sure her sister didn't end up dead in a ditch. She doubted that she'd even get a thank-you for her efforts.

Riya stuffed down her irritation and did as ordered, quickening her pace so they could catch up to where Sharadha was turning onto an empty side street lined with dilapidated buildings and thatched roof tents. The only sign of life that remained were the two stray dogs rifling through the garbage that was left behind by the old store owners.

Long ago, Riya and her brother Kaleb had passed through this region while traveling with Papa. She remembered the towns being packed with visitors, vibrantly lit and noisy through all hours of the night. It was impossible to reconcile that memory with the quiet, abandoned street before her.

But then again, a lot had changed since her childhood. Lyria, their closest neighbor to the northwest, had invaded the city of Ritsar. Without magic to protect Ashoka's borders, Vira's Council had increased taxes to fund the troops needed for defense. And with fewer coins in their purses, shoppers couldn't afford to pay for much beyond necessities. Trade had stalled and once-bustling markets were reduced to hollow shells of themselves.

It was why, two years earlier when she'd fled from the palace, Riya had joined the Ravens. Vira dismissed them as rebels, but Riya had only ever seen them as saviors. They were the ones protecting innocent citizens, stealing money back from the tax collectors for those who needed it most.

Except she wasn't a Raven anymore.

You told me you were a Raven, not a rajkumaari. So which is it?

Varun's voice rang in her head, and Riya felt her chest tighten. She'd made her choice. She just hadn't expected that doing the right thing would hurt so much.

"I hope you still think this is worth it when we both die of snakebites," Riya muttered to Vira, swatting away the moths and mosquitoes flitting around her shoulders as the two of them stumbled after Sharadha through the foothills.

"Don't be dramatic, Riya. There aren't any snakes here."

"Oh, and you're an expert on Adhuran wildlife now?"

Vira gave her a scathing look, but she didn't say anything else.

The Maghgiri Mountains paralleled Ashoka's western coast, stretching from the country's southernmost point all the way up to the capital city of Dvar. On the coastal side, the mountains were known for their beautiful port cities and picturesque villages, the cooler climate and abundant rainfall drawing Ashoka's elite in the hot summer months. But unfortunately, she and Vira were on the eastern side of the range, where centuries of dry winds had kept the land rocky, dotted with thorny bushes and scraggly trees.

It wasn't a steep climb, but the trail was faint, and even Sharadha had difficulty navigating. It felt like they'd been walking forever before she finally slowed in front of a stone archway carved into the side of the mountain. It wasn't quite in ruins, but it was clear that it hadn't been used in many years.

"In here," Sharadha whispered.

Riya tried to quell the anxious feeling knotting her stomach as they walked into the dark cave. She didn't like going into places she couldn't case first. The cave narrowed into a tunnel that Sharadha had explained would take them into the heart of the monastery, where the thieves kept their stolen wares. It wasn't a long walk, but the path curved and branched. Sharadha chose the left fork each time, something Riya committed to memory, until the passage sloped downward toward a balcony overlooking a cavern.

"Careful," Vira whispered as they peered over the edge.

Three flickering torches illuminated the large rectangular room, shrouding half of it in shadow. It would have once been a prayer hall, but the altars to the goddesses had been converted into storage areas filled with wooden crates. Shelves full of books lined one of the walls, and in the center was a table covered with piles of weapons and jewelry that two men were sorting and carelessly tossing into one of several open crates.

Riya exhaled in relief. So far, Sharadha hadn't lied to them about the layout or any details of what they could expect. She drew back. Sharadha's eyebrows rose, as if to ask, *Satisfied?*

"Let's get this over with," Riya said.

Sharadha rifled through her pockets and withdrew the crude map she'd sketched out for them at the tavern. "Do you remember what to do?"

Riya took the scrap of paper from her. "Yes." The plan wasn't that sophisticated. All she and Vira had to do was follow the directions and sound an alarm that would get the thieves to leave their post, then lock them out so Sharadha could slip in and get her books.

"Good." Sharadha looked between the two of them, as though she wanted to say something else, but she thought the better of it. "I'll see you down there." She didn't wish them luck.

Riya pulled out a small glowing rock from her pocket to illuminate the map. They retraced their steps until they reached a fork, but instead of going back the way they'd come, they waded deeper into the mountain.

Riya couldn't help speaking. "I think there's something she's not telling us."

"Maybe," Vira said. "But she's our best shot at getting answers."

"That's something Amma would say," Riya muttered under her breath. It didn't matter what it cost or who it hurt, so long as Amma got what she wanted.

"Because she knew what it took to protect a country," Vira snapped, a little too loud. It was the first real crack in the annoyingly calm demeanor she'd adopted since Ritsar, and Riya turned, surprised. But Vira's mask of indifference was already sliding back into place. "Let's talk about this later."

They wouldn't. She'd refused to engage with Riya in any meaningful way, repeatedly insisting that she was fine even though they both knew she wasn't.

Within a few minutes they were approaching their destination: a large metal door that looked too modern to belong in this ancient cave. It was latched shut with a bar that required Vira to use two hands to push it aside.

Warm night air greeted Riya as she stepped outside onto the rocky terrain. The trip wire was easy to find and even easier to tug on. As soon as they triggered it, a large metal rod hidden by magic materialized above the door and swung down on an invisible hinge, crashing into the metal doorframe with a resounding clang. They both jumped as the sound echoed through the entire mountainside.

They hurried back, locked the door again, and hid in a side corridor, their backs pressed against the wall. A good thief *didn't* trigger alarms, and purposefully setting one off had Riya on edge.

Moments later, they could hear footsteps echoing down the hall. Riya held her breath as the two men rushed past them. She waited until she heard the sound of the heavy bolt being pulled open before peering around the corner carefully. To her dismay, only one of them had ventured outside; the other was lingering at the doorway.

"Do you see anyone?" the one inside the tunnel called out. He had a hand wrapped around the hilt of a sword that hung at his hip, but he hadn't drawn it yet. The other one called back a reply that Riya couldn't make out.

She swore under her breath. They weren't actually going to find any intruders. She had to do something, or this entire plan would have been a waste of time. She moved, but Vira's hand grabbed her wrist.

What are you doing? Vira mouthed.

Riya tugged her hand free and silently snuck back down the hallway behind the thief. It was a risk, but she didn't have a choice. She was nearly behind him when the man outside caught sight of her. His eyes widened as he drew his sword.

"Look—" he tried to warn his partner.

Riya shoved the thief. Surprised, he pitched forward into his friend, and Riya used the moment of distraction to slam the door shut. They pounded on the door, but she managed to throw the entirety of her weight behind it long enough for Vira to dart forward and slide the lock back into place.

They both stood there panting as the muffled cries outside faded into silence. According to Sharadha, they had less than thirty minutes before the thieves made their way around the exterior of the hill to the other entrance they'd come in through—just enough time for them to find Sharadha and get out.

＊

When they returned to the cavern, Sharadha was nowhere near the bookshelves but rummaging through the weapons laid out on the table.

"What are you doing?" Riya demanded. "You're supposed to be finding your books."

"They're right there," Sharadha said, waving a hand toward the shelf.

"You used us," Vira said, as though it had just occurred to her that Sharadha couldn't be trusted.

Sharadha gave her a look that said she couldn't believe Vira was so gullible. "If you help me, the sooner we'll get out of here, and we'll both have what we want." She gestured toward the crates. "I'm looking for a sword. A powerful one. You'll know it when you see it."

Riya wanted to refuse or scream or maybe punch something, but they'd come this far and it would be foolish to leave empty-handed now, so she used her pent-up rage to rip open one of the crates while Sharadha disappeared into an adjoining room partially hidden behind one of the altars.

In the end it was Vira who found it. She discreetly waved Riya over to where she'd unwrapped an unassuming piece of cotton cloth. The silver hilt had a single large onyx, and the smooth metal of the blade was tapered on both sides. The magic hit Riya with full force, so strong it was almost painful to stand near it.

Vira was staring at the sword, an odd look on her face. "I think this was Chandrika's."

"That's impossible." But Riya had to admit it looked just like the one in the tapestry that hung in one of the palace's parlors.

Black gemstones were rarely used on weapons, because they were thought to bring bad luck—something Maharani Chandrika had used to her advantage. Her rule was characterized by brutal wars, and she'd ordered the creation of thousands of magical weapons to be distributed among her generals and soldiers, weapons considered so dangerous that the Mayaka Association had destroyed or confiscated them after her death. Even the royal family—who had a private vault of items belonging to former maharanis—hadn't been allowed to keep any.

"It was never found," Vira pointed out. "And people have been searching for it for centuries."

"Are you sure we should give this to her then?" Riya asked, sneaking a glance over her shoulder to make sure Sharadha hadn't returned yet. "We know nothing about her." Or what she planned to do with this.

"Yes," Vira said at once, wrapping it back up and lifting it out of the crate. "We need her help."

"Vira—"

"I'm trying to save our country, in case you've forgotten."

"So you keep saying." Riya didn't know why she still bothered to offer Vira counsel when she was determined not to listen.

"You don't think I've protected our country?" There was a sharpness to Vira's voice, as if she were in the mood for a fight.

Riya had spent the last two weeks being the levelheaded one, letting Vira have her way without argument, but she was tired. "You want to do this now? Fine. I came to you, Vira. I trusted you. We were supposed to do this together." The resentment that had been building within her for days burst out.

"We *are* doing this together."

"Are we?" Riya demanded. "Because you never talk to me. You never listen. Sharadha's a stranger and you'd rather put your faith in her than in me."

"I'm doing the best I can, Riya," Vira said, a defensive edge creeping into her voice. "You don't know how hard it is—"

"Then let me help. Let *someone* help."

"I have it under control." Vira turned away, her lips set in a straight line.

"Do you?" Riya asked. "You think I don't see the circles under your eyes? The way your clothes hang off your shoulders because you don't eat? You can hardly take care of yourself, let alone—"

"Because someone has to keep searching for answers," Vira interrupted.

"So then if I promised to spend all night combing through Papa's journals, you'd sleep?" Riya challenged.

Vira didn't respond. They both knew she wouldn't.

"You don't trust me," Riya said, realization dawning all at once.

"Stop it, Riya."

She couldn't believe she hadn't seen it. This was exactly what Amma had done—kept Riya at a distance, coddled her but refused to talk about anything important. "That's why you refuse to involve me in your planning," Riya said bitterly. "Because you think . . . what? I'll go back to the Ravens as soon as we decipher the key?"

The guilt in Vira's eyes betrayed her. "Can you blame me?" Her voice was a whisper. "Considering why you returned to the palace?"

The silence between them was horrible.

Riya had never felt so foolish—so humiliated—as she did in that moment. *She* was the one who'd recognized the Ivory Key for what it was. *She* was the one who'd made a secret copy before Amrit had betrayed them and taken it for himself. She could have gone to the Ravens with it, she could have kept it to herself. But she hadn't. She'd brought it to Vira, and this was how her sister had chosen to repay her.

"I'm not him," Riya said, anger blazing in the pit of her stomach. Anger and . . . something else. "I'm not Amrit. So stop punishing me for his mistakes."

Vira flinched. "That's not— Riya . . . I—"

But Riya wasn't listening anymore. She pressed her eyes closed, inhaling deeply to maintain her composure. She could feel something inside of her begin to shift, a spark in her veins waking after days of forced slumber. *Shit.*

This was the other reason she hadn't argued with Vira—unleashing her temper unleashed the magic that lived inside her too. It wasn't supposed to be possible. If there was one thing the world knew about magic, it was that it didn't work on living things. But it turned out that the Kamala Society had hidden more than the quarries. They'd hidden the true nature of how magic could work, and now Riya was cursed with a volatile, unpredictable power that she had no desire or use for.

"Riya?" Vira's voice was laced with alarm and fear.

"I need to sit down," she said, trying to stifle her own panic. But she wasn't quick enough. Blue light erupted around them as magic flew out of her. All Riya could do was throw her hands directly in front of her to avoid hitting Vira. And then Riya collapsed, the energy draining from her all at once. For a moment she just felt dizzy, the world spinning and blurring before her. She forced herself to take slow, deep breaths, and the room came back into focus.

Vira was beside her. "Riya? Are you—"

"I'm fine," Riya said, hating how weak she sounded—how weak she felt. "I'm—" She stopped talking as she noticed the large split in the stone wall where her magic had hit it. "Oh no." Dread filled Riya as she watched the crack spider upward.

"We have to get out of here," Vira said, following her gaze. "Now." She clambered to her feet and then helped Riya up.

"What was that noise?" Sharadha asked, rushing back into the room.

"We found the sword," Vira said, holding up the cloth-wrapped parcel. "Let's go."

"The books," Riya said, gesturing frantically toward the shelf. That was the whole reason they'd come here, and she wasn't going to leave without them.

Sharadha patted the bag slung over one shoulder, which now looked considerably heavier than before. "I already got them." She held her hand out to Vira. "Let me see the sword."

Riya's heart leapt into her throat as the crack continued to creep up toward the ceiling. "There's no time," Riya said, panic lining her voice. She grabbed Vira's hand and tugged her toward the entrance. "Let's go."

"What are you—" Sharada's eyes grew wide and horrified as stone began to break and dust rained down. "What did you do?" she demanded, sounding like a stern adult for the first time.

Riya turned before she could ask any more questions, shoving Vira and Sharadha in front of her as they fled the way they'd come. They didn't bother to be quiet this time, moving as fast as they could to outrun the crumbling mountain. There was a loud snap as the exit came into view, and Riya dove out of the way just as a large rock crashed down right where she'd been. She gasped in pain as the coarse wall scraped the skin of her elbow.

"Riya!" Vira whirled around.

"Keep going!" Riya shouted back. Her lungs were burning and she needed to catch her breath, but there was no time. She summoned a burst of energy and flung herself out of the cave just as the rock crumbled with a thunderous roar. But they couldn't stop, not when the thieves would be back at any moment. They ran down the side of the mountain, panting heavily, until they came to a stop on flat land.

Riya collapsed to the ground, hugging her knees as she waited for her breathing to even out. They'd made it out alive.

"How on earth did that happen?" Sharadha asked when she could speak again.

"It's an old cave," Riya said, not meeting her gaze. Her heart was still racing and her fingers were still trembling as she used the end of her dupatta to wipe the sweat off her forehead and neck.

"Right," Sharadha said skeptically. She looked at the two of them with some amount of wariness for the first time. She'd believed them to be children she could control and manipulate, who'd perhaps stumbled onto the key through a combination of luck and privilege.

"The book?" Vira prompted. She was still holding the sword, and the implication was clear: she wasn't going to give it up until Sharadha actually helped them.

Sharadha still looked hesitant, but either she'd decided their secrets weren't worth the trouble or she just wanted the sword too much, because she rummaged through her bag and pulled out a skinny book.

"The Ivory Key is encoded using a Niveda Cipher," she explained. "I'm not surprised you didn't recognize it. It went out of favor centuries ago."

Niveda. Riya glanced at her sister, but Vira was focused entirely on Sharadha.

"It's a simple cipher where each letter corresponds to a number," Sharadha continued. "The numbers are grouped in sets of three and refer to the epics of the great bard Rasika. The first will tell you which of her poems. The second will tell you a line. And the third a letter in that line."

"So we're turning letters into numbers and then back into . . . different letters?" Riya asked. "That seems ridiculously inefficient."

"It's why no one uses it anymore. It's easy to crack and far too cumbersome." She finally handed the book to Vira. "But the important thing is that you have to make sure you're using the *right* book of Rasika's poems."

"An edition that would have been around when the Ivory Key was created," Vira said.

"Exactly."

"Why's it called a Niveda Cipher?" Riya asked. It wasn't the first time Niveda's name had come up in relation to Kamala Society, and Riya knew by now that such things weren't accidental.

There is no such thing as coincidence, only patterns you're not clever enough to see. It was one of Amma's sayings.

Sharadha shrugged. "Niveda was a saint or goddess or something. A lot of Rasika's original songs were about her." She jerked her chin toward Riya. "You'd know better than I do, considering you're wearing that necklace."

Riya's hand jumped to the ruby pendant that had tumbled out from beneath the collar of her kurta. The gemstone was warm against her palm. "What do you mean?"

Sharadha had a strange look on her face. "It belongs to the Order of the Mayura." When it was clear that those words didn't mean anything to

Riya, she elaborated. "They're a group of magical fanatics. They worship Niveda as their goddess."

Riya looked down in surprise. "I . . . I thought it was just a family heirloom," she admitted. She'd found it in a vault that belonged to Savitri, the first maharani of Ashoka, so she'd assumed it had belonged to her. Riya didn't even know why she'd taken it, but it felt almost like it had called to her.

"I see," Sharadha said, but her eyes lingered on the pendant.

"Thank you for your help," Vira said, finally handing over the sword.

Sharadha nodded. "A word of caution, if I may," she said, sounding oddly serious. "Most people who go looking for the Ivory Key find only strife. Be sure that this is the path you want to walk."

Neither Vira nor Riya responded. They were fully aware that this journey likely wouldn't end well.

But they also knew that nothing would stop them from following it through.

CHAPTER THREE

— RONAK —

RONAK LAY IN his bed, staring up at the ceiling, where he could see a tiny black spider crawling over the smooth gray stone. He watched as it made its way across to the far wall and then disappeared into a tiny crack in the window frame—not because he particularly liked spiders, but because it was the most interesting thing that had happened all day.

Two weeks ago he'd had options. Plans. He'd even had freedom right at his fingertips. But apparently none of that mattered because somewhere along the way, everything had gone inexplicably, horribly wrong. He should have been on a ship to another country by now, starting a new life on his own terms. Instead, he was tracking the movements of insects in his room at three o'clock in the afternoon.

He sighed and pressed the heels of his palms against his eyes. There were certainly things that he *could* be doing. His mind unwittingly drifted to the note that had arrived two days earlier. He'd taken it from the messenger, dread setting in as he caught sight of Ekta's seal. And then he'd tossed it onto his desk without reading it, letting it join the unopened missives he'd received from his sister's Council and pleas from Jay asking if they could meet.

He knew he was only delaying the inevitable. He'd have to deal with the letters at some point. But he simply couldn't bring himself to care about any of it.

You don't have to protect me, Ronak. I'm not a broken boy.

Ronak dropped his hands and made himself sit up, willing himself to think about anything other than Kaleb's parting words. It was all that he'd been able to obsess over for days, his brain fixating on the moment when his brother—the brother Ronak had given up *months* of his life to protect—had walked away from him without a second thought.

He's gone, Ronak reminded himself. No matter how many times he replayed it in his head, no matter how many times he thought of some other argument he could have made that might have stopped Kaleb, it didn't matter. *He left you.*

It hurt, but not as much as the realization that there were things Kaleb had deliberately kept hidden—the desire to know his Lyrian family, to see where Papa had lived for so long . . . And Ronak had no idea why his brother hadn't confided in him.

Ronak had been angry at first—the one emotion that had broken through the cloud of nothingness in the days after they returned from Ritsar—and he'd latched on to it like a lifeline in the dark. All he'd ever tried to do was protect the people he cared about. Was that truly so terrible?

But the anger faded as quickly as it came, leaving a hollow feeling that was too raw, too bleak for Ronak to want to examine it very closely.

There was a knock at the door. "Come in," Ronak said without moving. It was probably one of the servants, back to collect the plates they'd brought in with his afternoon meal.

"Ronak?" It wasn't a servant. It was Jay.

His best friend. *Former* best friend. In the fifteen years they'd known one another, Jay had never knocked, and the oddly formal gesture felt like an insult somehow, even though he'd been the one to push Jay away.

"What are you doing here?" Ronak asked, suddenly self-conscious that he was still in bed, still in the clothes he'd fallen asleep in the night before. He clambered to his feet, but he didn't know what to do after that, so he simply stood in place awkwardly.

They hadn't spoken since the night of Ronak's engagement party, when Jay had blurted out that he'd never planned to leave with Ronak. That he actually wanted to stay in the palace, build a life with Preethi—the girl Vira and her Council decided Ronak would marry. Another mess that Ronak wanted no part of.

"You haven't responded to my notes," Jay said, shutting the door behind him. He looked around the musty room, curtains still drawn shut. "Are you ill?"

"No. I'm perfectly fine. Are you satisfied?"

Jay had an unreadable look on his face. "Is this really how you want to do this?"

"Do what?" Ronak asked. "In case you've forgotten, *you* were the one who lied to me."

This was yet another interaction he'd picked apart over and over, searching for some explanation he'd never found. Ronak had trusted Jay with *every*thing, and realizing that it hadn't been reciprocated had devastated Ronak more than he wanted to admit.

"I'm sorry." Jay shoved his hands into the pockets of his kurta. "I should have told you from the start—"

"Why didn't you?" Ronak cut in. He could hear the note of vulnerability in his voice, and he turned to walk to his desk, just to have something to do.

"I didn't think you'd take it well," Jay admitted.

"You thought I couldn't handle it?" Ronak asked sharply.

"Clearly I was wrong," Jay said dryly, "seeing as how well this is going."

"This isn't funny," Ronak said. "I trusted you, Jay. You knew exactly who I was and what I wanted, and you let me believe that we wanted the same things."

"I'm allowed to want my own life," Jay said, his jaw tightening.

"Then go live it," Ronak said.

"I'm genuinely sorry I didn't tell you, Ro. But you're still my closest friend, and why should that change even if our paths diverge?"

It shouldn't, Ronak wanted to say. He missed Jay, and he was lonely and miserable. But the words caught in his throat, and his irritation and sheer stubbornness kept them there. He turned away from Jay, resting his palms on the table and forcing himself to take a deep breath.

"Fine," Jay said finally. "You don't have to talk to me. But there's something you should know." He withdrew something from his pocket and slammed it down beside Ronak's hand. When he moved, Ronak could see that it was yet another letter with Ekta's seal. It was already broken, so he lifted the top half of the folded page to read it.

Tell Ronak to come see me within twenty-four hours. If he doesn't, he will not like what I do to his friends, and I will be starting with you.

Ronak swallowed.

"Why is she sending me threatening notes, Ronak?"

"I don't know," Ronak lied, feeling his shoulders tense.

"You told me you handled it," Jay pressed.

"I *did*," Ronak said. But he couldn't stop his eyes from flicking to the letter she'd sent him, peeking out from beneath a stack of books he'd pulled off his shelves and not bothered to put away. It was a surreptitious look, but Ronak had forgotten that Jay knew him better than anyone, except maybe for Kaleb.

Ronak lunged for it, but Jay was quicker. "Is this from Ekta?" Jay ripped the letter open before Ronak could stop him. He froze, looking at Ronak with shock. "You made another deal with her?"

"I have it under control." Ronak snatched the letter away, mentally cursing himself for leaving it out for anyone to find.

"Have *what* under control?" Jay demanded.

For a moment, Ronak wanted to confide in him. He wanted to tell him how Ekta had cornered him in this very room, how he'd lied to her and told her they hadn't found the Ivory Key in Ritsar, how he'd offered her his seat on the Council instead—a seat that he'd discovered was more difficult to give up than he'd expected, involving complicated logistics and inane minutia. He wanted to admit that he was terrified of the future, of Ekta, of getting married, of losing Kaleb forever.

But he couldn't bring himself to say any of that. "It doesn't concern you, Jay. Just let it go."

"But I can help," Jay offered. "I can—"

"I don't need your help," Ronak snapped.

Something like hurt flickered in Jay's eyes, and guilt pierced Ronak. "Fine," Jay conceded after a moment, backing off. "But if you change your mind . . ."

Ronak didn't say anything. They both knew he wouldn't.

He expected Jay to leave, but he lingered, looking around the room again, allowing his gaze to skim over the bookshelves that lined the walls of the circular tower until he landed on the easel on the far side of the room.

"You're painting again?" Jay looked surprised, raising his brows at

Ronak for permission before approaching the canvas still drying on the stand.

Ronak shrugged, even though Jay couldn't see him. He'd never been a consistent artist, preferring to follow the whims of his muse rather than a set schedule, much to the displeasure of the very expensive art teacher his parents had once hired. But painting calmed him down, gave him something to focus on when he couldn't quiet his brain long enough to fall asleep.

Ronak noticed that Jay was looking at one of the paintings he'd left leaning against the wall. Jay stood still, his mouth slightly open as he took it in. Ronak fought the sudden impulse to snatch it away, to bury the canvas under his bed, out of sight. He'd never been precious about his art, but there were some pieces—the ones he painted to process his thoughts rather than escape them—that felt too personal, too vulnerable.

It was a rendering of a memory, a futile attempt to pin down the ephemeral before it vanished forever. It was riddled with inaccuracies, he knew, but he'd revisited that moment so often in his head that it had all blurred together. He had no idea what was real anymore, which details were drawn from his imagination rather than his recollection—the intricate designs on the crumbling temple walls, the moonlight slicing through the water, the exact shade of blue light that had erupted from Riya's hand as she'd shattered the pillar into a million tiny pieces.

But the emotions . . . those were true. He'd taken his terror, his awe, his shock and confusion and tucked them within the brushstrokes—a keepsake that held a part of him now.

"It's really good, Ro," Jay said quietly. "You should consider putting this one up somewhere."

Ronak only bit the inside of his cheek. A few of his paintings, the ones Papa had particularly liked, had been framed and hung in parlors throughout the palace. But even if he wanted to, he couldn't show this to anyone. It was his memory, but it wasn't his secret to share.

"I'm not going to marry her," Ronak blurted out suddenly.

Jay turned around, surprised. "What?"

An awkward silence hung between them. Ronak didn't really know why he'd spoken. Maybe it was because he didn't want to talk about the painting. Or maybe he just needed to get this one thing off his chest and hope it would somehow fix things between them.

"I—" Ronak cleared his throat. "I'm going to tell Preethi the truth. That I don't plan to stay."

"What about the alliance?" Jay asked carefully. "Ashoka still needs her family."

"Ashoka needs magic," Ronak corrected.

Jay frowned. "That's—"

"I'll handle it," Ronak said. "Ekta. Preethi. And then I'll be gone, and your life can go back to the way it was."

Emotions flickered over Jay's face, but he turned away before Ronak could make out any of them. The quiet between them was once again full of tension and unspoken words.

For a moment it looked like Jay would say something else, but he just shook his head. "I should go," he said.

Ronak didn't stop him. When the door closed behind him, Ronak looked down at Ekta's note, which he still held tight in his fist.

We need to discuss the terms of our new arrangement.

Below it was a date, a time, and the name of the tavern she frequented on Spit Street. The meeting was supposed to have been last night, and he'd missed it, which was why Ekta had sent a more insistent message.

Ronak crumpled the note in his palm. It seemed that he could no longer avoid his problems.

✳

Ronak's hands felt a little too idle as he walked through the palace, so he found himself fidgeting—tugging on the edge of his sleeves where they wrapped around his wrists, fiddling with the simple gold chain around his neck.

It was earlier in the evening than he usually dared sneak out. He was afraid of getting caught, but he liked even less the idea of wandering Spit Street alone after dark, so he'd decided it was worth the risk.

You could still ask Jay to come with you, a voice in the back of his head reminded him. He ignored it.

He was still in his formal clothes, and he needed to change into the plain kurta he'd stuffed into the bottom of his bag under the paints and brushes he'd brought along as a cover. He knew this part of the palace was rarely used except by visitors to the library at the end of the hallway, but he still kept glancing over his shoulder as he crossed the last corridor toward the stairs that led to the servant quarters on the lower level, where he could slip out.

He was pushing back his still-wet hair from his forehead when he caught movement out of the corner of his eye. He glanced toward the library expecting to see a scholar emerging with a stack of books. But to his dismay the figure walking toward him was Vira.

She hadn't noticed him yet, but there was nowhere for him to hide. All he could do was hope she wouldn't stop him.

Of course he wasn't so lucky.

"Ronak?"

He froze at the top of the stairs, a hand on the banister. Vira was look-ing at him with confusion and suspicion, her eyes darting between him and the door at the bottom of the stairs as she closed the distance between them.

"What are you doing here?" Vira asked with no preamble. He hadn't seen her in days, not since they'd returned from Ritsar, but of course she didn't acknowledge that or ask how he'd been. Amma too had been this way.

"Painting." Ronak lifted his shoulder to draw her attention to the paint-speckled bag.

Her eyes narrowed. She didn't believe him. "What's there to paint in this part of the palace?"

"Inspiration can be found everywhere, sister. Just because you don't care to look for it doesn't mean it doesn't exist or that others don't see beauty in the mundane." He knew he was provoking her, but he had never been good at holding his tongue. And it wasn't as if she had any definitive proof that he was lying.

"I know you're investigating the Council," she announced, crossing her arms over her chest as she looked up at him.

Ronak's fingers tightened on the bag. "I don't know what you're talking about," he said casually.

Ronak *had* reopened his secret investigation, taking out all the notes he'd frantically gathered months earlier, when he'd desperately searched for the culprit who framed Kaleb for murder. There had been a dull ache in Ronak's chest when he opened the locked box under his bed, pulling out the scraps of evidence he'd gathered, the carefully constructed theories he'd never been able to prove. It hadn't mattered back then; he'd found nothing useful to help Kaleb.

There are no such things as coincidences, only patterns you're not clever enough to see. It was one of the few sayings Amma had bothered to impart to Ronak.

He didn't know why it would be different this time. Any trail that existed back then would surely have gone cold by now. But he couldn't just sit by and do nothing while Kaleb risked his life in Lyria. Kaleb had made it all too clear that he wanted a formal exoneration issued by Vira and the Council, so Ronak had gone through it all again, meticulously pinning up everything on a spare canvas, hoping that time and distance would lead him to the patterns he'd missed the first time.

"You're not that clever," Vira said plainly. "And the Council is not that inept. You're digging into their lives, and they have every right to be upset."

Of course she was on the Council's side. "I'm trying to help Kaleb," Ronak said, giving up all pretense that he wasn't doing exactly what she'd accused him of. "Or have you completely forgotten our brother now that he's not even in the dungeons?"

Vira pursed her lips. "You're acting as though you're the only one who cares about him."

"I may as well be."

"We're under scrutiny, Ronak," Vira continued as though he hadn't spoken. "We're *all* being watched closely."

When they left to search for the Ivory Key in Ritsar, Vira had told the Council they were going to Gauri Mahal to honor their father. But when the three of them returned, the Council hadn't fully bought the story that Kaleb had simply decided to stay behind for a while longer.

"Then perhaps you should have done something about it when you had the chance," Ronak said. "At least I'm trying to find the real culprit."

"It's easy to act morally upright when you don't have the weight of a country resting on your shoulders," Vira snapped, her eyes flashing in anger. "I did what any good maharani would have done."

"And what about a good sister?"

Vira turned away with a sharp inhale. She had nothing to say to that. Ronak expected that he'd feel vindicated, but he just felt empty. He was tired of having the same arguments with her. He was tired of being the only one who prioritized Kaleb's freedom.

Ronak turned away and began to make his way down the stairs when Vira's voice stopped him.

"The Council wants to move up the wedding. It'll be next month."

He didn't answer. He couldn't care less what the Council planned for his wedding. He didn't intend to be there.

CHAPTER FOUR

— KALEB —

KALEB HAD ASSUMED that palaces everywhere would be the same: opulent, colorful, living archives of treasure and history. His own home in Ashoka had been elaborately furnished with carved wooden furniture, bright tapestries, and patterned rugs, all passed down through their family for generations.

The Lyrian palace, in comparison, was remarkably ordinary.

Ordinary wasn't quite the word. There had been an immense amount of thought put into the decor, into arranging the marble statues in the courtyards just so, into carefully selecting the muted paintings that graced the walls in matching gilded frames. But it was all understated. Simple, even. And most notably, it was entirely devoid of magic.

He'd known that Lyrian culture had different attitudes toward magic. Here, it was seen as a luxury, a frivolity to showcase wealth and status rather than used in everyday objects to make life easier. But in the two weeks since he'd arrived in Lyria, he'd discovered that reading about something wasn't enough to prepare him for the reality of experiencing it.

Magic was practically synonymous with air in Ashoka. A faint prickle was always around, a phantom lingering just out of reach. Magic was synonymous with *life* in Ashoka, emanating from utilitarian objects used by people of all economic backgrounds. Kaleb hadn't realized just how much of it he'd been surrounded by until the familiar weight and comfort of magic had slipped away like a dupatta snatched by the wind. Walking through Lyria felt duller by comparison.

Walking through the palace felt *especially* dull. There was no visible sign of the skills the emperor's mayaka were rumored to possess, and without much else to keep his interest, Kaleb's mind kept wandering away from the guide leading the tour of the grounds.

Kaleb had learned from his father that the emperor of Lyria was frequently in search of scholars to work on special research projects, and to ensure that all talent was discovered and cultivated, there were stalls in all major cities where those interested could submit applications. What Papa hadn't told him was that he'd have to pass a grueling written test in Lyrian before he'd be allowed anywhere near the palace.

Kaleb's spoken Lyrian was mostly passable, but his writing skills were about as strong as a toddler's. It had been a miracle that he was one of eleven people given the opportunity to interview—or so he'd believed, until he learned that there'd been only eleven applicants in total. Kaleb's score had been the lowest by a wide margin, a mortifying fact that Hektor, the scholar who'd greeted them that afternoon, had taken great pleasure in announcing to the entire group.

His disinterest must have been obvious because Dayana, one of the other applicants—and, though she didn't know it, Kaleb's cousin—nudged him. "Pay attention," she whispered. "This might be part of the interview."

He tried to redirect his focus to where the guide had stopped in front of a cluster of statues in the center of a domed atrium. "And this, of course," the guide was saying in a monotone voice, "is our esteemed leader, Emperor Kallias, and his family. Empress Selene. Prince Elias. And Prince Lukas."

Kaleb stared up at the austere marble face of the man trying to invade his homeland. The man who was responsible for the death of his mother, the former maharani of Ashoka—a crime Kaleb had been framed for, that he'd been imprisoned for.

Sometimes Kaleb forgot that he wasn't still locked in the dungeons in the Dvar Fort. Vira had released him against the Council's wishes because she'd needed his help tracking down the Ivory Key. Sometimes Kaleb forgot that too, that he wasn't *truly* free, that his exoneration was conditional upon his success infiltrating the emperor's palace and learning about his experiments with magic.

The emperor was sculpted in full armor, but he still wore a crown, placed slightly askew on his close-cropped hair as though to lend him a touch of relatability. To his right, the empress was also in military garb, holding a short sword in her muscular arms and gazing off into the distance as her long hair flowed behind her. Behind them were the two princes, dressed in formal court attire rather than military uniforms. They had similar curly hair and sharp features, but the shorter of the two was depicted with an intensity in his gaze that caught Kaleb's attention. There was something familiar about it that tugged at the edges of a hazy memory. Kaleb *had* met the emperor once, years earlier, when he was maybe eight or nine. Perhaps there was a similarity between father and son that he was subconsciously recalling.

"Of *course* Elias had his statue updated," Dayana said, her voice low enough so only Kaleb could hear. "He's as vain as he is spoiled."

"Updated?" Kaleb turned his attention to the other prince.

"His rank as a general." She pointed to a circular patch on the sleeve of his tunic with an inscription Kaleb couldn't make out. "He was only promoted last month."

Kaleb knew that Lyria placed a heavy emphasis on military service, but he hadn't thought about what that meant exactly. Vira had been trained in combat—as had the rest of them—but that was the extent of it. Ashoka's strategy had always been rooted in defense and in magic. It was almost laughable imagining any of his siblings actually serving in the Ashokan army.

"What's he like?" Kaleb asked, trying to sound merely curious. He'd tried to learn more about the royal family beyond what was common knowledge or published in the newssheets, but he hadn't wanted to draw unwanted attention by asking too many questions.

"Elias? An insufferable ass."

"I'd keep your voice down if I were you," said Alexander—one of the others vying for a position among the emperor's scholars—with a bland smile on his face. His voice was a shade too loud, which of course drew curious stares from the rest of the group. "I doubt they'd want to hire a scholar who was bad-mouthing the royal family."

The other applicants had decided rather quickly that they didn't like either of them—Kaleb because his low score and lack of university degree made him unworthy as a candidate, and Dayana because she'd kindheartedly defended his right to be there and interview like everyone else.

Kaleb, who didn't like confrontation, stepped back, intending to ignore the taunt.

But Dayana simply returned a vapid smile of her own. "I don't need to rely on flattery to get what I want. My work speaks for itself. And besides, I've called Elias an insufferable ass to his face and I'm still here, aren't I?"

Alexander looked shocked by her admission that she'd insulted the prince, but the flicker of emotion was gone as quickly as it appeared. "Suit yourself," he said. "I was only trying to help."

None of them had known that Dayana was actually the daughter of one of the noble families—though Kaleb supposed, given the furtive glances the others were shooting in her direction, that they could certainly guess now.

Dayana waited until Alexander was out of earshot to let out a small, frustrated groan. "I shouldn't have done that."

"He deserved it," Kaleb said. He wasn't often petty, but he couldn't deny he'd enjoyed watching the smile slip off Alexander's face.

"He did," she admitted. "Not that it'll make a difference. I've known *many* men like him."

"The ones who talk over others, sure they know better than everyone around them despite having no real expertise in that area?" Kaleb asked. He knew plenty of people like that too.

"Exactly." Dayana grinned and tucked her long brown hair behind her ears. "I'm glad to have run into you here, Kol," she said, reaching out to squeeze his arm. "It's nice to know at least one person. It makes the whole process feel less daunting."

Kaleb felt a strange stab of guilt as he returned her smile. "Me too."

It was pure chance that they'd ended up there together—just like it was a coincidence that they'd met a week earlier. Kaleb hadn't planned to seek out his Lyrian family. He knew he'd have to lie to them, meet them under an assumed identity, but he'd wanted to visit Alena, his birth mother, who according to Papa had been laid to rest in her family tomb in the cemetery on the outskirts of the capital.

He'd only meant to pay his respects, but when he arrived, he found the rest of Alena's family already there. He stood frozen, watching from a distance as his aunts, uncles, and cousins paid their respects. They were virtually strangers, but he couldn't stop staring at them, desperately wanting to belong there.

He'd approached the tomb after they left, and something in the dirt caught his eye: a book. It was leather bound, with familiar gold letters glinting in the midmorning sunlight. He'd run his fingers over the fading title, a sharp pang of nostalgia and grief striking him all at once as he took in the book of Lyrian folktales. Kaleb had a similarly well-worn, battered copy on his bookshelf back in Ashoka. It had been his favorite childhood possession—the only thing he had of Alena's.

Dayana had chosen that moment to return. "What are you doing?" she'd demanded.

Kaleb hadn't heard her approach, and the unexpected interaction with his cousin caught him off guard. "Sorry," he'd said, flustered. "I . . . I just saw it lying there. It's one of my favorites."

"You've read it?" She'd looked surprised as he handed it back.

"More times than I should probably admit." He smiled a little. "It was a gift from my mother."

Dayana's eyes had softened. "My aunt." She'd lovingly traced the letters just as Kaleb had moments earlier. "I hardly remember her, but she gave it to me for my third birthday. I bring it every time we visit her."

"That sounds like a lovely tradition." Kaleb's throat was tight with emotion. He hadn't brought anything. He didn't even know what kind of flowers Alena would have liked. "Do you know where I could get a copy?" he asked. "I just moved here."

Dayana had smiled. "There's a bookstore just on the other side of the square," she said. "Tell them Dayana sent you, and even if they don't have it on hand, they'll make sure to order it."

Part of him had wanted so desperately to blurt out then and there who he was, but he'd held his tongue. Perhaps she'd be a useful ally, but he didn't know that for certain. And he couldn't risk it, not when his country—and his family—was depending on him. Vira needed to know what the Lyrian army was planning, and Riya needed him to learn what the emperor had discovered about how magic worked in people. He couldn't put his own desires above that.

He hadn't ever made it to the bookstore, and he'd certainly never expected to run into Dayana again, least of all at the palace. But he had. And she'd remembered him—stood up for him. Kaleb wasn't strong enough to turn down this opportunity to get to know his family, not when it seemed as if fate itself had intervened to give him this chance.

The group followed the guide out of the atrium and through a garden path that led to the palace. Kaleb had seen it from afar, but now that they were drawing closer, he realized just how large it was—easily double the size of the Ashokan palace. It was made of strikingly white stone, the only spots of color coming from the ivy crawling up the watchtowers and the gold trimmings around the windows that overlooked the grounds.

"Strange," Dayana murmured as the guide led them toward one of the back entrances. "We're not going to the scholars annex."

Kaleb's brows furrowed. Scholars in Ashoka lived and worked within the palace itself, so it hadn't struck him as odd. "Perhaps it's just for the interview," he suggested.

"Or maybe it's because *that's* the annex." Dayana jerked her chin toward a charred building, her eyes wide. One side of it had completely caved in, and scaffolding had been put up around it for the workers rebuilding the collapsed roof.

It was the only blemish on the otherwise pristine grounds, and it drew the attention of the other candidates as well. But the guide quickly hastened them along into the palace and down a black-and-white-checkered corridor to a room filled with rows of wooden chairs. Evidently this was the end of the tour. Hektor stood at the front. He was a tall man with sallow skin and hair and eyes so pale they looked nearly colorless. He gestured for them to sit.

"One by one, you will be called into the adjoining room and asked to demonstrate a practical use of magic," he said, his voice dry and detatched. "And at the end, three of you will be selected to join the cohort of scholars. Those who are found lacking," he said, his eyes flicking toward Kaleb, "will be asked to return home. We'll begin as soon as my associate joins us."

Now that they were actually there, Kaleb could feel his nerves returning. He had only this one shot, and after his poor performance on the written test, he had to do extraordinarily well, or coming to Lyria would have been for nothing.

Hektor abruptly straightened, a look of mild irritation crossing his face. "Prince Lukas," he said looking at the door. "I wasn't expecting you."

Whispers broke out through the room as the scholars immediately rose. Kaleb felt a little queasy as he, too, pulled himself to his feet. He hadn't expected to meet any of the royal family so soon. But when Kaleb caught sight of the figure walking in, his stomach churned for an entirely different reason. He knew the prince. He'd met him just weeks earlier in Ritsar.

But there, he'd been Lieutenant Lukas.

"I hope you don't mind that I'll be replacing Cassandra today," Lukas said to Hektor with all the confidence of someone who was higher in status.

"Not at all," Hektor said, though he didn't sound very pleased.

All the color drained from Kaleb's face as he turned to Dayana. "*That's* the prince?"

Evidently Lukas wasn't in the habit of updating likenesses of himself, because the statue was clearly several years old. There had been a youthfulness to his features—a delicateness—that was gone now, replaced by stark lines and cold disinterest.

Except his eyes. Those were the same, dark and intense as they swept over the room with a calculating glint.

"I didn't realize he was back," Dayana said with a frown.

"Why is he here?"

"He used to be a scholar," Dayana explained under her breath. "Until he became the favored to inherit the throne and then began to climb up the military ranks."

"Really?" Kaleb's brows rose in surprise. He'd assumed that Elias, the older sibling, was next in line.

Kaleb felt his heartbeat quicken as Lukas walked past him. He hastily looked down at the floor. It was unlikely that Lukas would remember him. It had been a passing interaction, a few words exchanged in a dark fort where Kaleb had been dressed as a Lyrian soldier.

But . . . Kaleb hadn't been thinking quickly enough in Ritsar. He'd given Lukas his real name. He was going by Kol now, and if Lukas *did* recall meeting him, it would look incredibly suspicious that he'd given him two different names in the span of two weeks.

He'd been foolish to think he could do this. He'd been so certain he could help Ashoka that he'd volunteered without actually assessing his skills. He was an untrained mayaka and a mediocre spy. Simply looking Lyrian enough to avoid second glances wasn't going to get him very far if he couldn't even write well enough in Lyrian to impress the scholars he was trying to infiltrate or remember to use a fake name. Kaleb needed to leave before he made things worse or embarrassed himself more. He'd met Dayana. He'd visited Alena's resting place. Maybe that could be enough.

But he couldn't move. He'd come here to try to help Vira and Riya, and he'd sacrificed too much already—his life in Ashoka, a chance at clearing his name, his family. If he failed, it couldn't be because he'd given up on himself.

Kaleb closed his eyes and took a deep, centering breath. *Show them what you can do*, he told himself, *and let them decide if it's enough*. When he opened them, Hektor and Lukas were gone—as was Alexander. The minutes seemed to pass excruciatingly slowly as Alexander returned with a smug smile on his face and the next person was called in—until finally Hektor called his name.

"It'll be fine," Dayana whispered, giving him a reassuring smile. "You'll do great."

Kaleb smiled back weakly as he followed Hektor into the adjoining room. Lukas was sitting behind a large wooden desk, slumped in his chair, looking bored as he stared out the window at the garden they'd walked through on their tour. If Hektor cared about Lukas's lack of attention, he didn't show it as he dropped into his seat and shuffled the papers on the desk.

"Kol," Hektor said, pronouncing the name distastefully. "Remind us again what university you attended?" The question was clearly for Lukas's benefit; Hektor knew full well he hadn't received any formal training.

"I didn't," Kaleb said, hoping they couldn't hear the slight tremor to his voice. "I'm self-taught. Or rather . . . my father taught me."

"Your father." Hektor said it flatly. "Well, your test results certainly do make sense now."

Kaleb gritted his teeth. "I assure you, I know how to work with magic." And he would have gotten a near-perfect score if he'd been able to write his answers in Ashokan. He wondered if Papa had faced the same kinds of comments here, if they'd judged him on his ability to communicate in their language rather than on his actual skills.

"That's for us to determine, isn't it?" Hektor gestured behind Kaleb.

Kaleb turned to see that there was another table there, this one arranged for an afternoon tea. A steaming pot sat in the center, whorls of steam lazily drifting up from the spout. Beside it was a platter with an array of Lyrian pastries: flaky phyllo layered with spinach and crumbled cheese, small hand pies stuffed with herbs and onions, deep-fried dough coated in sugar and chopped pistachios, thick slices of cake soaked in orange syrup and drizzled with honey-infused yogurt.

"Make the table disappear," Hektor said, sliding a small pouch across the desk toward Kaleb.

"Disappear?" Kaleb echoed. "That's it?" It seemed deceptively simple. He couldn't tell if this was a challenge set just for him because they believed he couldn't even do such a thing, or if the rumors of the Lyrian artificers' skills were grossly exaggerated.

Hektor didn't seem to like questions. His jaw tightened. "Yes. That's it." He motioned irritatedly for Kaleb to take the pouch from him.

Kaleb took it and stepped back. Lukas had barely spared him more than a cursory glance, and Kaleb was fairly certain that if Lukas recognized him, he would have said something by now.

He forced his shoulders to relax. This was what he was good at—what he'd spent hours doing for many years. He slipped his coat off and hung it on the back of his chair, then sat cross-legged, wincing as the stiffer fabric of the Lyrian-style pants tightened around his knees.

Then he closed his eyes and cleared his mind. It took a bit longer than usual, as his mind kept flickering toward the prince on the other side of the room. But all at once he could feel the thread of magic—the power inside that was yearning to be channeled into something. He reached out with his mind and tugged on that power.

It unspooled easily, pure energy spilling out all around him, waiting to be used. That was the thing about magic—if you knew what you were doing, it was unspeakably simple to work with. Magic was malleable, and in many cases the gentlest suggestion was enough to get it to adhere to an object permanently. The problem—and the reason that many found working with magic to be difficult—was that it didn't like restrictions. The more a mayaka wanted to control the outcome and the effects of magic, the harder it would resist.

He considered the instructions. Make the table disappear. It was vague. He could decide what that meant—turning it invisible, destroying it, send it flying to a different room. Even the use of *table* was open to interpretation, leaving it up to him as to whether that included the tea set and snacks as well.

But if there was one thing he'd learned on his tour of the palace, it was that Lyrians liked simplicity, elegance, and precision. So he coaxed the magic into the wood of the table, envisioning it slowly disappearing—but still there. All the items would remain just where they were, seemingly suspended in midair. When he finally finished, both Hektor and Lukas were watching him with interest.

"Impressive," Hektor said begrudgingly.

Lukas's gaze remained on Kaleb. "Your father trained you?" he said, speaking for the first time.

Kaleb nodded. "My written communication is . . . poor," he admitted. "But I'm capable of doing anything the emperor requires of his artificers."

"That'll be all," Hektor said, dismissing him.

Dayana was the last to be called in, and after her practical session was over, the group was left alone. But as the minutes went on and there was no sign of Lukas or Hektor, they began to grow antsy.

"I wonder what's taking so long," Dayana mused to Kaleb when there was still no verdict after an hour and a half. "I'm going to find out."

"Wait—" Kaleb said, unsure if it was a good idea, but she was already out of her seat, making her way toward the door to the adjoining room.

The whispers around the room abated as she raised her fist, poised to knock. But then she froze, frowning. She carefully pressed an ear to the door, her eyes growing wide, before she returned to her seat without interrupting them.

"What happened to not being afraid of the royal family," Alexander taunted.

But this time Dayana ignored him. "They're arguing," she whispered to Kaleb. She hesitated for a moment and then revealed, "I couldn't make out much through the door, but I heard them mention your name."

Kaleb's brows rose. "Really?" He didn't know what that meant—or how long it would take for them to come to a decision.

Finally, after another half an hour, the door opened, and Hektor returned with Lukas. Hektor's lips were pursed in annoyance, which seemed to suggest that he'd lost this fight.

Hektor turned to address them. "The three new scholars will be Alexander, Dayana, and Kol," he announced.

Kaleb stared at him in shock, not entirely believing what he'd heard.

"See!" Dayana said, flinging her arms around him with an excited squeal even as the pronouncement elicited frustrated grumbles from the rest who hadn't been selected. "I told you it would work out. And now we're going to be scholars! We'll be working together!"

"I can't wait," Kaleb said honestly, relief filling him. He'd actually done it. He'd have access to the emperor's research.

But then an uncomfortable realization struck him. If Hektor had argued against Kaleb joining the artificers, it meant that Lukas had argued *for* it. Maybe it didn't mean anything. Maybe Lukas just didn't share Hektor's snobbishness for university degrees. But when Kaleb glanced back over his shoulder, Lukas was still watching him with that quiet intensity.

And Kaleb couldn't shake the feeling that getting what he wanted was going to cost him more than he was willing to give up.

CHAPTER FIVE

— RONAK —

SPIT STREET WAS just as Ronak remembered it: dimly lit, overcrowded, and reeking of paan. It was early enough in the night that he didn't think he was in any significant danger, but it was difficult to know for certain that a fight wouldn't break out at any moment. The crowds that gathered here were volatile, unpredictable, and tended to believe dead bodies were easier to search.

Ronak had managed to change into a simple kurta after his encounter with Vira, but he could still feel eyes trailing him as he walked, as if they knew he didn't belong here. He was used to being watched in the palace, but this felt different—like they were judging *him* and not the rajkumaara.

Pay attention, Ronak reminded himself. He didn't have Jay—or anyone else—beside him to stay vigilant and make up for him being too much in his own head.

He forced himself to take in his surroundings—to feel the crunch of red-stained dirt beneath his shoes, to smell the smoke that spilled out of taverns every time the doors opened, to carefully and quickly navigate his way past clusters of armed people gathered around the food stalls that lined the street. Ronak found himself doing a double take as he walked past someone ladling dosa batter onto a flat metal pan. It sizzled as the cook drizzled oil along the edges, helping it crisp up, and Ronak's stomach rumbled in sudden hunger as he remembered that he hadn't eaten since he'd picked at his lunch hours earlier.

He exhaled as the tavern's door came into view. He pushed his way inside and then to the back, where stairs led down to the private parlor that Ekta frequented. It was less crowded than the last time he'd been there, but it was just as opulent as any room in the palace, decorated with low wooden tables, plush silk cushions, and lacy curtains, all designed to cater to the wealthy clientele drinking Lyrian wine and gambling at the card tables. Soft music played from somewhere Ronak couldn't see, but he barely registered the notes over the thumping of his own heart.

Ekta was sitting alone at the booth she always used, tucked away in a quiet corner and separated from the rest of the tavern by a wooden screen. Ronak paused to take a deep breath and square his shoulders, wiping his sweaty palms on his kurta before stepping toward her.

"I really don't like having to summon people twice," she said by way of greeting. Her voice was rich and sultry, and she wore a bottle-green velvet sari studded with glittering diamonds, like she'd scraped the stars from the night sky. But instead of her usual dark smile, there was something sinister and serious lurking in her demeanor. Her cold eyes lacked any emotion as she met his gaze. It had been easier to ignore her note from the comfort of his own room, to pretend there would be no consequences for crossing someone who wore deadly artifacts as everyday jewelry, but now that he was here, he could feel fear creeping into his veins.

His heart skipped a beat as he slid into the divan opposite her. "I'm sorry. I've been busy."

"Don't forget, *Rajkumaara*," Ekta said, twisting a ring around her finger, "I know what you care about. *Who* you care about."

"I'm well aware," Ronak said, his tone clipped. But his eyes stayed on the ring: a gold band with an emerald. He'd seen it before. It was full of cobra venom; all she'd have to do was snap the gemstone off and press it into his skin and he'd be dead in a matter of hours. Ronak kept his hands firmly on his lap.

"Then why weren't you here?" Ekta asked.

"Giving up a Council seat takes time. I'm working on it," he said.

"I see. Perhaps you'll be glad to learn that I've changed my mind."

"What?"

"Upon further reflection, I realized that I don't actually want to sit in meetings all day, discussing dreadfully dull things." She reached for her goblet of wine. "I think I'd rather have you do that, my little pawn."

"That wasn't the deal," Ronak said, panicking. He'd offered to give up his Council seat so he could leave. This would tether him even tighter to the palace.

Ekta sipped her wine. "I have a new opportunity. One that benefits us both."

Ronak eyed her suspiciously. "An opportunity?"

"I can help you get what you want most in the world."

"And what is it that you think I want?" Ronak asked.

"To clear your brother's name."

Ronak felt his breath catch as Ekta watched him with a knowing smirk. The rational part of his brain was telling him that it was another trap somehow, that he couldn't trust her. But she was right. This was the one thing she could dangle in front of him that he wouldn't turn down.

"How?"

"Someone in the palace hired mercenaries to assassinate the old maharani and frame your brother for it."

"I'm aware." He'd spent hours making notes about each councilor, trying to draw connections and discover motivations for who would possibly benefit from his mother's death, from framing Kaleb. But his investigation had turned up nothing. Whoever was responsible had gotten away with it.

Ekta reached for something on the seat beside her and slid it across the table. It was a letter. Ronak picked it up hesitantly. It was one of the ones Kaleb had received from his aunt in Lyria—or someone he'd believed to be his aunt. It was laden with pinpricks beneath certain letters that, when strung together, formed hidden messages orchestrating their mother's assassination.

"Why do you have this?" Ronak asked.

She pointed to the postal seal on the letter. "See the golden harp? That stamp is only used when the letters are sent from the emperor's palace." Ekta tossed another letter on top. It was the first letter Kaleb had ever received from Lyria. The stamp was of an olive branch. "Letters that come from outside of the palace use a different seal. If your brother truly was writing to his aunt, all the letters should have the same olive branch stamp, shouldn't they?"

Ronak stared in surprise. He had no idea how she'd managed to get her hands on the original letters when even he had struggled to find where the Council had stored the evidence. And he had no idea how he'd missed this detail. "The letters are several months apart," he pointed out. "Maybe they changed the stamp."

Ekta rolled her eyes and then produced a third letter. It was dated recently, a personal correspondence addressed to her. She didn't allow him to read more than two lines before yanking it back. But the stamp was of an olive branch.

"So my brother was writing to someone inside the Lyrian palace," Ronak said slowly. "Someone working for the emperor." Someone who certainly wasn't Kaleb's aunt.

He'd assumed that the letters were merely a ruse to implicate Kaleb—that they'd never actually mattered. But maybe Lyria was more involved in his mother's death than he'd originally suspected.

Ekta swirled her wine again. "According to my intel, your sister's Council is planning to send emissaries to the emperor's palace to negotiate peace. I want you to be on that trip and bring back something."

Ronak tried to keep his surprise and disappointment from showing. Of *course* Vira had caved to the Council's demands even though she'd spent months insisting that she had no desire to negotiate with Lyria.

"What's this item?" he asked.

Ekta's eyes gleamed in the lamplight, much as they had the day she'd asked him to go on another trip and bring back a mythical object. His stomach twisted as he remembered that he'd lied to Ekta about that. They *had* found the Ivory Key and it was in Vira's possession.

"A compass," she said.

Ronak blinked, sure he'd misheard. "Excuse me?"

"The emperor has a compass he keeps with him at all times, but it isn't used for navigation. It's a powerful magical device where the emperor stores his detailed plans and secrets. It would have the evidence you need to present to your Council in order to clear your brother's name."

Ronak couldn't stop his heart from soaring with hope. Definitive proof of Kaleb's innocence. He'd nearly given up on ever getting it.

A hazy memory stirred in the depths of his mind. He had met the emperor once, years ago when Kallias visited Ashoka. There had been a compass that he'd worn on a chain around his neck—something Ronak remembered only because Vira had complained that it clashed with the rest of his clothes. It made sense now why he'd kept it close, if it did indeed contain all his secrets.

"If I do this, no more deals," he said carefully. "No more threats. I bring you this compass and we walk away from one another forever."

Ekta smiled—her first genuine smile of the night, but it made Ronak feel more on edge. "Is that what you truly wish for?" she asked.

"Yes."

"Hmm." She swirled the wine again and lifted the glass to her lips. "You've had multiple chances to walk away, to leave *all this* behind." She gestured at him in a way that indicated that she meant his life as a rajku-maara. "And yet here you are. I just wondered if perhaps you were actually searching for something else."

Ronak felt a flash of irritation. She was acting as though she knew him better than he knew himself. "I'm sure," he said resolutely.

"Very well. One more thing," Ekta said as Ronak rose. "Don't even think about clearing his name without first bringing the compass to me. I have connections in all corners of the world, and I *will* find you and your brother. You won't like the very slow and painful death I have planned if you double-cross me again."

Ronak felt a shudder pass through him. "Understood."

CHAPTER SIX

— VIRA —

VIRA SAT IN her room, hunched over a small table, carefully translating the letters of the Ivory Key into groups of numbers according to the book Sharadha had given her. She squinted at the last number, verifying that she'd written it down correctly, before moving on to the last line. It was slow, tedious work, but after weeks of making no progress, Vira couldn't complain now.

As she flipped back through the pages of the book, she absently reached up to the pendant that hung around her throat. Her fingers closed on air.

The necklace, gifted to her by Papa, had been a gold coin stamped with the crest of the Kamala Society: twin swords crossed over a lotus. She'd never taken it off—until she returned from Ritsar.

She wondered what Papa would think now—if he'd still have given it to her if he'd known that the Kamala Society didn't represent what they'd believed their entire lives. Savitri, the founder, hadn't simply sealed the quarries to protect her citizens. She'd lied about what magic could truly do, and she manipulated history so no one would remember the past—a choice that now left Ashoka defenseless and weak.

Vira rolled her shoulders back, trying to shift into a more comfortable position. She twisted her neck to one side, trying to work out a crick, when her eyes landed on the dark sky outside the open balcony door. She blinked in surprise. She couldn't remember when the sun had set—or even getting up to light the lanterns. She had a vague memory of servants walking in with her dinner, but she wasn't entirely sure if that had happened several hours or several days earlier.

Vira twisted to the other side and saw that there was indeed a platter of food left on a side table for her, no doubt cold by now, since she'd asked for the kitchens to stop using mayaka-forged serving dishes to keep the food warm. It was one of the many decrees she'd issued to try to conserve magic.

She sighed, turning back to the table, which was covered in hundreds of sheets of paper filled with her failed attempts from the last two weeks at deciphering the key.

A maharani's space is an extension of her rule, Amma's voice sounded in her head. *It's imperative to keep it tidy and organized.*

She'd followed that rule for years, obsessively picking up after herself, never allowing even one thing to be out of place. She'd never understood how her father or Ronak could live in virtual chaos, their ideas never contained on one piece of paper but in dozens of journals and books scattered all around their work area. But she was discovering now how freeing it was to allow herself to take up as much space as she wished, to leave traces of her presence for people to find instead of erasing all evidence of it.

Vira carefully finished copying out the last few letters, translating them into numbers, and double-checking that she'd done it correctly.

And then she was done.

It was a momentous occasion. She was the first person ever to find and decipher the Ivory Key—something scholars and treasure hunters had long sought. She waited for the elation to set in, the joy she'd expected to feel at achieving a lifelong dream. She did feel a sense of accomplishment, she supposed, but even that was overshadowed by other feelings. Worry. Fear. Stress.

For the first time in years, Vira wished she had someone to talk to. A friend she could call on to distract her. She didn't even have her siblings.

After they'd returned from Ritsar, Riya had moved in to make it easier for them to work together, but the maharani's suite was large. Their paths didn't need to cross often, and besides, Vira was fairly certain her sister had gone to Indra and Neha's engagement ceremony. Kaleb was off in Lyria alone, spying on the emperor and learning what he could about magic. And Ronak was . . . well. Ronak.

And what about a good sister?

His words from earlier that day were still plaguing her. Every insecurity, every bit of guilt she'd ever felt—about Riya, about Ronak, about Kaleb—had flooded her mind. Unlike the stories she'd heard of family competition in other countries, Vira had never had to fight for a claim to the throne. She hadn't asked for this—and she didn't think any of them wanted that kind of power either—but still they blamed her.

Things will be different soon, Vira promised herself.

According to the palace librarian she'd visited earlier, an original copy of Rasika's epics was on display at the Fire Temple in Paliya, located a two-day journey away in the Harya province. It was the last piece of the puzzle, one last thing to get her hands on magic.

And yet, all Vira could think about was how she'd need to invent some new lie to convince the Council to let her go. She felt a flash of irritation that she needed the Council's approval to travel through her own country, but she wasn't going to let them stop her—not when Amrit was also after the same thing.

Her stomach knotted uncomfortably. It made her anxious that she didn't know what he was doing—if he'd already deciphered the key, if he'd already gotten his hands on Rasika's songs.

Don't think about him, she could hear Riya's voice say in her head. *Focus on what we're doing. He doesn't matter.*

She knew she should push these thoughts away, think about anything else. But alone in her room, she allowed herself a wildly indulgent moment, pressing her eyes closed and recalling his face, his smile, the way he saw *her.* Not the maharani, but Vira.

And then the image faded, leaving her with nothing but deep, aching sorrow. It was one thing to use her, but there was a special kind of cruelty in manipulating her emotions. In making her *feel,* just to rip it all away.

And even now, weeks later, no matter how many times she reminded herself that none of it had been real, there was a tiny, shameful part of her that was waiting for him to come back into her room and tell her that it had all been a misunderstanding.

But he wasn't coming back.

He'd betrayed her, in more ways than she could count. He'd been a distraction, nothing more, and her life was better off without him in it.

And maybe, if she told that to herself enough times, she'd actually believe it.

It was late, and Vira knew she should eat something. She could feel the way her eyes were burning, the stiffness in her spine. She needed a bath and, more importantly, a good night's rest.

She rose to close the balcony door when a knock at the front entrance startled her. She made her way out to the receiving room, surprised to find Neha—the new captain of her guard who'd replaced Amrit—on the other side.

"Neha?" Vira's brows furrowed in confusion. "What are you doing here?"

She was dressed in a heavy deep purple lehenga instead of her formal guard attire, her hair swept into an elaborate updo studded with pearls and jasmine. She'd requested the night off for her engagement party, and Vira had happily granted it to her.

The expression on her face was grim. "Something's happening with the Council, Maharani. I think you should come with me right now."

✳

The Council meeting was already in session.

"What's the meaning of this?" Vira strode toward the front of the room, trying to hide her shock that the Council had convened late at night without her knowledge. She froze when she found that her seat was already occupied. "Councilor Meena?"

The older woman sitting at the head of the table was the leader of the Military Affairs Ministry and had once been her mother's closest friend. There was always an air of severity to her, from the scars littering her arms to the graying hair scraped back into a tight knot at the nape of her neck.

"Welcome, Maharani," Meena said, making no move to rise. "We were just discussing the future of our country."

"I wasn't aware that there needed to be a discussion about it," Vira said. "And certainly not one without me present."

Meena's sharp eyes pierced Vira's. There was a ferocity to her gaze that made Vira want to back down, but she refused to give Meena the satisfaction.

"We don't know if we believe in the direction of your leadership."

"Excuse me?" Vira said, trying to hold on to her composure. There had always been snide comments whispered about her, but no one had ever outright questioned her leadership. She looked around the room. The discomfort was palpable. It was quiet enough that Vira could hear the rustle of papers being shuffled, the scratch of silk as the councilors fidgeted in their seats, but none of them met Vira's gaze.

Cowards.

"We've tried to offer you counsel," Meena said, as though she spoke for all of them. "But time and again, you have refused to heed our advice."

Fury filled Vira as she whipped her head back toward Meena. "I don't need to do only what I'm told," she said coldly, drawing herself up to her full height. "In case you've forgotten, the Council is supposed to aid the maharani, not rule in her stead."

"Can you blame us when you've largely left the ruling to us, Maharani?" Meena's tone was mild, but there was an undercurrent of venom that worried Vira. "Not to mention, you've been lying to us for weeks."

"Lying to you?"

"Did you really think we wouldn't find out that you never went to Gauri Mahal to honor your father, as you claimed?" Meena asked. "Or that your brother Kaleb isn't there despite what you and your siblings said about him staying behind? And did you think we wouldn't notice all the times you snuck out of the palace doing goddess knows what?"

This was the moment Vira had feared. She'd hoped she'd have the magic by the time the Council discovered her lies, so she could explain where she'd been, where Kaleb was currently. But this was happening sooner than she'd expected, and she was unprepared.

What would Amma do?

But her mother would have handled the Council long before now. She would never have let it get this far—and the Council had believed enough in her leadership that they wouldn't have challenged her so overtly.

"I don't need to justify my actions to you," Vira said, trying to muster every ounce of regal confidence her mother had instilled in her. "Not when I'm out there trying to protect our country."

"No." Meena slammed her first on the table—her first outward sign of emotion. "*We're* protecting Ashoka. What you're doing is chasing fairy tales," she growled.

Vira lifted her chin defiantly. "We need magic." There was no longer any point in denying it. "I found the Ivory Key. And I am one step away from decoding it."

"You have to face the reality that magic is gone," Meena spat back. "We need to renegotiate with Lyria."

Vira's nails dug into the flesh of her palms as she clenched her fists. "Why would Lyria negotiate with us exactly," Vira asked, "when we have nothing that they would want other than magic, which we can't even give them? They have a stronger army than we do. A larger population. If we go to war, they will decimate us."

"There is always a deal to be made," Meena said stubbornly. There were several folded sheets of paper on the table, and when Meena moved her hands, Vira could make out exactly what they were: letters bearing the golden harp seal of Lyria.

"You went behind my back?" Vira was shocked. She didn't think they would ignore a direct order from her.

"The Emperor of Lyria has agreed to a meeting at Shantha Mahal in three weeks time," Meena announced.

"No," Vira said, shaking her head. "That's a waste of time. As the maharani, I dictate the course we're following."

"Then perhaps we've reached the end of your reign."

The room was excruciatingly silent.

"What did you just say?" Vira rarely allowed herself to get angry when she was inhabiting the role of the maharani, but for the first time, she could feel the rage that she'd kept at bay threatening to break out. She'd weathered their insolence for months, but she wouldn't let them act as though this was all solely her fault. These people had served her mother—several had even served her grandmother. They'd had every chance to stop problems before they ever came to Vira, but they'd let her inherit a failing country and laid the blame at her feet.

"We invoke rule two hundred and forty-three as set forth by Savitri, the first maharani of Ashoka," Meena recited flatly. "The Maharani's Council is authorized to act as a collective leadership force if we feel the maharani is not of sound mind."

"Not of sound mind?" Vira turned to the rest of the Council. "And you all agree with this?"

None of them met her gaze.

"The vote was unanimous," Meena said. "Guards."

"What are you doing?" Vira asked as guards began to encircle her. One of them was Neha. "This is absurd!" Vira jerked away, but there were too many of them—far more than she'd seen stationed at the entrance to the hall just minutes earlier. She was surrounded, and there was nowhere for her to go.

"It's best if you go quietly," Meena said, looking her straight in the eyes.

Panic began to rise up within Vira. "You can't do this." She turned to face the councilors and demand answers, but one of the guards grabbed her wrists and held them in place. She struggled, trying to pull free, but she wasn't strong enough.

Neha approached, holding the mayaka-forged manacles worn by the prisoners in the dungeons. Horror set in as Vira realized what was happening.

"I'm sorry, Maharani," Neha said, her eyes full of regret.

The iron bands fit snugly around her wrist, closing with a tight *snick*. She looked down at her hands. It was too late.

The Council had won.

CHAPTER SEVEN

— RONAK —

RONAK PACED THE corridor outside of Councilor Meena's office. It was late, but he could see a glimmer of light shining through the crack beneath the door.

When he'd returned to the palace, the first thing he did was read all the missives he'd ignored from the Council. Ekta had been right: the Council *did* intend to negotiate with Lyria, and the delegation was departing in the morning. He'd rushed out the door, sprinting through the palace composing arguments in his head for why he should be among the emissaries when he'd shown no interest in what the Council was doing before.

But now that he was standing there, he was nervous. He *needed* to be on this trip.

Squaring his shoulders, he finally raised his fist and knocked.

Meena's voice sounded from inside. "Come in."

He pushed open the door. If Meena was surprised to see him, she didn't show it. She merely glanced up briefly from whatever she was reading. "Rajkumaara."

Ronak wasn't sure if he'd ever been inside any of the councilor's private offices despite their proximity to the large chamber where Council meetings were held. He knew there was one assigned to him as well, but seeing as he'd never stepped foot in his, it wouldn't surprise him to learn that it had been taken over by another councilor or repurposed into a storage space.

Meena's office was decorated sparsely and efficiently, with nothing except a large wooden desk, bright lanterns crackling with balls of magic, and cabinets crammed with books and files. Three half-dead potted plants sat in one corner, the leaves that added the smallest bit of color to the room wilting from neglect. Ronak was willing to bet that acquiring them hadn't been her idea.

"I was hoping we could talk," Ronak said, dropping into the chair opposite her.

"About?" She turned to the next page of the document.

"The trip to Lyria." He inhaled deeply. "I'd like to be on it."

Meena's fingers stilled, and she finally looked up at him. "You've picked an interesting time to care about your political duty."

"It makes sense to send me," Ronak said. "You need someone with clout and status who doesn't have much to do with the actual ruling of Ashoka. I'm the perfect candidate. Lyria would be foolish to harm a rajkumaara."

"Perhaps, but the emissaries for the voyage have already been selected."

"I speak Lyrian better than anyone else on the Council," Ronak insisted. "I've studied the culture. I can be an asset."

Meena stared at him for a moment, her gaze as stern and emotionless as always. "Why do you want to go so badly?"

He'd expected the question. "This is my future, and I've decided to take it seriously," he said. "My sister told me my wedding has been moved up. I thought this would be a good opportunity for Preethi and me to work together and prove that we can be of use to the Council."

This time, the surprise was clearly readable on Meena's face, even if she schooled her features into indifference quickly. Ronak had crafted the answer knowing it would appeal to her, but it was different seeing it actually work. He hadn't asked Preethi—or even spoken to her before volunteering her for the mission—but he'd worry about that if Meena even agreed to let them go.

"And this has nothing to do with your brother?" Meena spoke precisely, folding her arms on the table as she leaned forward.

Ronak's jaw tightened. This, too, he'd expected. "My brother is at Gauri Mahal."

Meena snorted in disbelief. "Of course." But she didn't press further as she studied him. "Very well," she said finally. "I'll notify the other councilors and have the guards and servants prepare for your departure."

It took Ronak a moment to fully comprehend that his plan had actually worked. His eyes widened. "Really?"

"However," she said, "unlike your sister, I will not coddle you. The carriage will leave with or without you first thing in the morning."

And she dismissed him wordlessly with a wave of her hand.

✳

The door to Ronak's room was ajar when he returned. He knew for certain that he'd closed it before leaving, so he cautiously approached the entrance, peering through the gap at a dark figure standing beside his bed. He watched nervously for a few moments, heart pounding as he tried to decide how dangerous it would be to interrupt the intruder. It would take far too long to fetch one of the guards, and he wanted to know just who was rifling through his things. Hoping he wasn't making a terrible mistake, Ronak gently pushed the door open, simultaneously reaching for the magical lantern that hung beside the entryway.

The person turned just as the lamp flared to life.

"Vaishali's bones," Ronak breathed as he saw Riya's familiar face, a hand pressed against his chest. "You terrified me. What are you doing skulking about in the dark?"

"It's not my fault you insist on living like a wild mongoose," she said glibly. "It wouldn't kill you to open the drapes you know. Get some sunlight."

His heart was still racing but he exhaled in relief as he closed the door behind him. "Did you actually need something, or are you just here to insult me?"

She was dressed far more formally than usual, wearing a green silk lehenga paired with silver jhumkas and a heavy statement necklace. She cradled a teetering stack of books in her arms.

"I'm returning the books I borrowed," she said, as though it should have been obvious.

Ronak frowned as she dropped them all on his freshly made bed. He'd never been as fastidious as Vira, but he'd always found that a clean space made it easier to think. He'd spent more time tidying his room that afternoon than he had in days, and he didn't like that Riya was introducing clutter he'd just cleared away.

Ronak's brows rose. "When exactly did you take them?"

"Last week," Riya said. "You said I could come by to look at Papa's books. So I did."

The room had once been their father's private office, tucked away in one of the towers far from the residential wings of the palace. When Ronak moved in, he'd cleared out Papa's many cabinets of ephemera, but he hadn't removed the shelves that lined the circular room, which were filled with Papa's own collection of books, maps, and artifacts.

The room was never meant to be a permanent residence, but there were memories here, pressed into the knickknacks tucked between the books, into the thirty-year-old faded rug that covered the stone floor, into the cracked windowsills and broken sconces Papa had never cared about enough to have fixed. Ronak had spent so many of his early years here, quietly reading or painting while his father studied old maps at his desk, scratched out theories in his journals, or pored over ancient texts for any sign of the mysterious treasures he was certain existed just out of sight.

"I meant a time when I was here," Ronak said incredulously. "That was not an invitation for you to break into my room and steal my things."

"Borrow," Riya corrected. "And you left the door unlocked. I didn't even have to pick the lock, Ronak. I'd hardly call that breaking in."

He glared at her, but he wasn't angry, not really. "You're a bit over-dressed for reading," he commented.

"I'm on my way to Indra's engagement party," Riya said. "I'm sure you received an invitation."

"I'm sure," Ronak agreed. He vaguely recalled seeing something from Indra—and he also vaguely recalled trashing it without reading.

Ronak eyed the titles of the books she'd dropped on his bed. *Origins of the Mayaka. Quieting The Mind: A Practical Guide to Mayaka Practice. A Brief History and Timeline of Magic.* Ronak glanced up. Riya stood in front of a shelf, chewing on her lower lip as she scanned more titles. When she'd come to ask about Papa's books, he assumed it had something to do with the Ivory Key. He realized now that she'd had a more personal reason. They hadn't talked about her magic since that day when she'd used it to heal him.

"Is it . . . Are you having trouble? With the magic?" Ronak asked carefully. They didn't exactly have the closest of relationships, and part of him felt like he was prying. This wasn't the first time she'd stopped by in the last few weeks, nor was it the first time they'd talked, but this easy way of conversing still felt so fragile and he was afraid of disturbing it. They'd been close once, Ronak supposed. When they were kids, it had usually been the two of them running around and getting into trouble, but their relationship had never really progressed beyond that; whenever they needed to talk to someone, they'd both turned to Kaleb.

Riya whirled around. "What?" When she saw Ronak looking at the books, her shoulders slumped. "I don't know. I'm trying to figure out how—if I even can—control it." She looked more tired than Ronak had first realized, despite the kaajal lining her eyes.

"Did the books help?"

Riya shrugged. "A little. The one on meditation wasn't half bad, but it's not like there are a lot of guides on what to do if the magic is in *you*." There was a harshness to her voice.

Ronak didn't know how to respond. He wasn't that much better with magic than she was—that had always been Kaleb's area of expertise.

"What does Vira think?"

It was the wrong thing to say. Riya tensed. "Vira doesn't want to talk about it. Vira doesn't want to talk about *anything*," she added bitterly.

He knew that she'd moved into Vira's rooms and that they were working together. He'd assumed it was going well, but maybe Riya hadn't been entirely truthful with him. After all, Vira was still the same as she'd always been—keeping her secrets close and her family an arm's length away.

"I could help," he offered. "If you'd like." He didn't know what he was offering exactly—or why.

Riya seemed a bit surprised, but she nodded. He joined her, scanning the books on a shelf that was too high for Riya to see comfortably, when he noticed her tugging something out of the space between two bookcases.

"Is this your investigation?" she asked.

Almost reflexively, his heart skipped a beat in panic—which was ridiculous. It didn't even matter anymore, given that Vira and the Council knew about it. He'd just gotten so used to hiding everything that had to do with Kaleb's imprisonment.

"This is . . . thorough," she said.

It was Ronak's turn to shrug noncommittally. "I thought I could clear his name," he admitted. "It doesn't matter now, I guess. He's not even here."

Riya looked down. "He's in Lyria because of me."

"He's in Lyria because of himself," Ronak said. "He could have helped you in another way. Helped you actually control the power, maybe. But he chose to walk away from us."

Riya didn't say anything.

Ronak plucked a thin book from the shelf. It was bound in red cloth, the pages faded yellow and the binding fraying at the edges. "Try this one."

It was a simple treatise on meditation that Papa had tried to get Ronak to read when he was younger. It had nothing to do with magic, but some of the more practical lessons had helped him focus his attention better. Maybe it would help her.

Riya nodded gratefully as she took it. "Thanks." But she lingered there, biting her lip as she looked up at the shelf again.

"Did you need something else?" Ronak asked.

For a moment he didn't think she was going to answer, but when she finally spoke, he heard a note of hesitation in her voice. "Have you heard of the Order of the Mayura?"

Ronak shook his head slowly. "No." He couldn't remember seeing that name, but Papa's notes were vast, and there was an entire section of the room dedicated to books on various groups and secret societies. "Was that a lead you got from the scholar?"

He'd been the one to find Sharadha's name in a stack of letters Papa had left in one of the dust-laden drawers. As far as he knew, Riya hadn't told Vira where she'd gotten the letters—not after Vira made it clear that she didn't want Ronak anywhere near the key. He was perfectly happy with that arrangement, but having more magic would solve a lot of his problems too, and he wanted to hasten the process if he could.

Riya scowled. "Sharadha wasn't a scholar. She was a smuggler and a thief, and we were lucky we got out alive."

A smuggler? Ronak wanted to ask more, but it didn't escape his notice that she hadn't answered his question either.

"I can search through Papa's things later," he offered. "I'll let you know if I find anything."

But Riya shook her head. "It's nothing. Just something silly." She gave him a small smile. "Thanks again for this," she said, waving the book at him.

As she left, Ronak shoved the canvas of his investigation back into its hiding space even though he didn't need it anymore. He'd convinced the Council to send him to Lyria. All he had to do now was find the emperor's compass and get it to Ekta, and he'd have the evidence he needed to clear Kaleb's name.

And then finally, *finally*, he and Kaleb would be free to leave the palace and this world behind.

CHAPTER EIGHT

— RIYA —

INDRA'S ENGAGEMENT PARTY was in full swing by the time Riya slipped through the unlocked door to one of the suites in the eastern wing of the palace.

She hadn't meant to be nearly an hour late, but she also hadn't expected to spend so much time in Ronak's room. The book he'd given her was small enough that she'd tucked it into the pocket of her lehenga. She could feel the sharp edges pressing against her thigh when she walked.

Riya knew she should be focusing all her time and efforts on helping Vira with the quest for the quarries or finding some way to control or get rid of her magic, but she was tired of being cooped up in Vira's rooms. She hadn't seen her friends in days, and she just wanted a break.

I'll work for an hour when I get back, she promised herself, to assuage her guilt. Ronak seemed confident that the book would help her, and that counted for something. But still, Riya couldn't deny that part of her was terrified that she would *never* be able to control it—that no matter how much time she spent practicing, the magic would do what it wanted, as if it had a mind of its own.

She hadn't let herself think about the argument she'd had with Vira in Adhura—or the painfully raw feelings that had triggered it. She'd been lucky that it was only the cave that had crumbled, and that no one was inside when it had. But Riya couldn't rely on luck again. She couldn't keep putting everyone around her in danger.

As she made her way through the suite, she could see Indra's touch in all the decor. Gossamer and satin fabric in delicate pink and silver coated everything: lining the tables piled with sweets and savory snacks, framing the open windows letting in the cool night air, wrapping around the sconces that held dim, flickering lights.

"Riya!"

Riya barely turned around before Archana threw her arms around her shoulders. Riya could smell the palm wine on her breath.

"You're finally here!" Archana screamed in her ear. "Come on! Everyone is over there."

Riya winced but let Archana drag her to the adjoining room, where divans and cushions were artfully arranged around low tables. Preethi was sitting with two other girls Riya didn't recognize. Archana all but shoved Riya into one of the seats, furiously waving at her to slide over and then dropping down next to her.

"Vaishali's bones, Arch," Riya muttered, rubbing the side of her elbow where she'd knocked it against the table in her haste. It was still tender from when she'd scratched it while fleeing the collapsing cave.

"I think that's enough tadi for you," Preethi said, reaching for the tumbler in front of Archana.

Archana just rolled her eyes in good humor and let her take it. "Riya, you know Indra's cousins, Padma and Lalita."

Riya didn't, but she smiled politely anyway. "Where's Indra?"

"You know, I haven't seen her in a while," Preethi said, looking over her shoulder thoughtfully. "Or Neha for that matter."

"Help yourself," Padma or Lalita said, pushing a platter of food on the table toward Riya.

As the smell of ghee-roasted herbs and spices wafted over her, Riya remembered that she'd skipped both lunch and dinner. It hadn't seemed important at the time, but now she realized just how hungry she was. She slid nearly half of what was left over onto the small plate that Preethi passed her, spooning coconut and mint chutneys over deep-fried vada, aloo bonda, and slices of battered paneer.

She was barely paying attention to the petty gossip the conversation had slid into, and she was startled when the topic abruptly shifted toward her.

"Ri," Archana said suddenly. "Whatever happened to that scholar?"

Riya jerked up. "What?"

"The scholar. From the library," Preethi clarified. "We were there the other day, and the librarian said he was gone."

"Oh." She inelegantly wiped her mouth with the back of her hand despite Preethi's disapproving look.

Riya had hoped they wouldn't notice Varun's departure, but of course that was silly. Gossip was currency in the palace, and she was certain they'd been alerted to his absence the moment he left. That they waited two weeks to bring it up meant either that they'd been too busy with Indra's engagement preparations or they'd waited for Riya to broach the topic, which of course she never had.

"He, uh, had to return to his family," Riya said. It wasn't a lie, but Riya felt a tightness in her chest anyway. It had been nearly three weeks since she'd been kicked out of the Ravens—since Varun had discovered there was no magic left in the quarry and demanded answers that Riya couldn't give him. The Ravens were her family, her best friends, and the thought that she might never see them again—never have a home with them again—was too painful to even consider.

She'd had a copy of the Ivory Key. She could have taken it to Varun, to the Ravens, and cemented her place within them again. But she'd chosen to give it to Vira—to trust her sister to ensure that the magic they unearthed truly would benefit all the people, not just the wealthy nobles. Riya didn't regret that choice exactly, but she couldn't deny the spark of doubt in her heart flickering to life every time she and Vira argued.

"Kausalya help me. Pree, look! She actually came." Archana leaned over Riya to nudge Preethi's shoulder.

Riya turned to where she was pointing, confused. "Who?"

"Tanu," Preethi said, leaning close and whispering conspiratorially. "This was after you left."

"What happened?" Riya asked, staring at the girl sitting alone on one of the divans nearby, adjusting the pleated pallu of her sari. She looked nice enough, with soft features and wide eyes.

"We used to be friends with her," Preethi said darkly. "She was staying with her aunt, who was trying to get her married off to someone in the court. But then we found out she was lying to us the whole time."

Archana nodded in agreement. "She would tell us she was busy with her aunt, and then we found out she was actually sneaking out to meet these lower-level guards."

Riya frowned. "Maybe she thought you wouldn't approve."

These girls were less elitist than most, but it wasn't exactly an uncommon sentiment. Many members of the nobility considered it acceptable to socialize with guards who worked in the palace like Neha, but not those who worked on the lower levels of the fort.

"It's not about that, Ri," Preethi said emphatically. "We wouldn't have cared if she hadn't lied for *weeks*."

"And when we found out," Archana added, "she had the gall to act like we'd forced her to lie by being snobbish." She rolled her eyes. "Real friends don't lie to one another."

That was exactly what Riya was doing—lying to them about why she'd come back, about how she'd spent two years with the Ravens, about the magical power that was coursing through her veins. She felt a little like she was going to throw up. She was supposed to be making a home here with these girls, a new life. She wasn't a Raven anymore, but a rajkumaari.

She stood abruptly.

"Riya?" Preethi looked at her with concern. "Are you all right?"

"I just need some fresh air," she said, clambering over Archana. "No, no, don't get up. I'll be back in a minute."

Riya had said the first thing that came to mind, but the balcony seemed as good a place as any, so she made her way there, grateful that it was empty.

It was a cool, dark night, the stars hidden behind hazy swirls of gray clouds. A gentle ocean breeze washed over her as she rested her elbows on the railing, looking down at the lights cascading over the Dvar Fort. She didn't know why Preethi's words affected her so much. It wasn't as if she'd ever intended to stay in the palace, so it shouldn't matter that she was lying to them. But . . . somewhere along the way, these girls had actually become her friends. They'd listened to her complain about Vira and dragged her out so she didn't sulk alone in her room.

It was getting harder to justify keeping secrets from them when they were her only friends. She was lying to everyone, and it left her hollow to think that none of them really knew her. Maybe she didn't even know herself.

She wasn't a Raven anymore, and if she wasn't really a rajkumaari either, then who was she?

She took a deep breath and turned to go back inside when she noticed a figure sitting on a divan in the very corner, shrouded in darkness.

"Indra?"

Indra gave a small, resigned sigh. "I was hoping you wouldn't see me."

"What are you doing here?" Riya asked, taking a step closer. Indra was dressed as beautifully as always, in a pale pink brocade lehenga. Dark brown mehendi twirled up her hands, all the way to her elbows, the design accented by the silver and diamond-studded bangles stacked along her wrists. But she was slumped down in the seat, her sullen gaze fixed at some point on the ground, her dupatta crumpled in her lap.

Indra sighed again and shifted over. Riya dusted off a few jasmine petals that had fallen from the garland that adorned Indra's hair, sitting beside her.

"What's wrong?" Riya asked, her concern growing. It wasn't like Indra to miss a party—especially her own.

"Nothing," Indra said. And then shrugged. "Everything."

"Is Neha—"

"Goddess no," Indra said at once. "Neha's perfect. It's my mother."

Riya hesitated. "Do you want to talk about it?"

"There's nothing to talk about," Indra said, toying with a silver tassel that hung off the end of her dupatta. "She called me into her office an hour ago—because of *course* she's still there and not here with her only daughter—and showed me all the wedding plans she's already made. Apparently she's decided everything about the wedding and my marriage and my entire life, and I have no say in any of it."

"Oh."

"She keeps telling me I'm too young to know what's best for my future, that I'll understand when I'm older," Indra said bitterly. "It's like ... it's like she's trying to live her own dream through me."

The words touched a wound deep inside Riya that had never fully healed, a jagged scar left behind by her own mother. It was what they'd fought about most often: Riya's youth. It was what her mother used to dismiss her, to dismantle her arguments. Nothing Riya said was ever worth listening to because it was coming from a child. And in her mother's eyes, children never knew better than adults.

Well, in her mother's eyes, no one at all knew better than she did.

"My mother was like that too," Riya admitted. "It was never a conversation. She would tell me what to do. We'd have a giant screaming match. And then she would still get her way because she was the maharani before she was my mother."

As she spoke, Riya realized it wasn't just her mother she was thinking about in that moment. It was Vira, too.

"How did you deal with it?"

"I didn't," Riya said. "I ran away." She'd sometimes wondered if there had been any way to fix her relationship with her mother—if things would be any different if she had stayed and her mother were still alive. She supposed she'd never know, and that made her ache in a strange way too.

Indra exhaled. "Sometimes I wish I could do that. I could go back to Kalavat, live with my father, and escape my mother altogether. But Neha's life is here. I can't do that to her."

Riya squeezed Indra's hand. "Want me to sneak into your mother's office and misplace some of these plans?"

Indra laughed. "She would be so angry."

"I'll do it," Riya said. "I can pick a lock, you know." It was the truth, but Indra only laughed, dismissing it as a joke.

"Thanks, Ri." She sighed and then stood, shaking out her skirt. "I suppose I can't avoid my party forever."

Riya rose too and linked their arms together as they walked inside. Indra was surrounded by well-wishers at once, so Riya let her go with a reassuring smile. The other girls were still at the table she'd left, but her conversation with Indra had put her in an introspective mood. She didn't want to stay there any longer, speaking more half-truths and lies.

Riya was almost at the door when a tall, stocky guard with a beard stepped into her path. "Rajkumaari," he said, as though he'd been waiting for her. "My apologies for interrupting your evening, but I've been asked to escort you back to your chambers."

Riya's brows furrowed. "By who?"

"The Council," he said. "It's for your safety."

"Did something happen?" Riya asked, alarmed. "Is my sister all right?"

"Your sister is fine," the guard said, his voice calm as he took a step toward her. "This way. Please."

Riya hesitated. Something felt off. Following a man she didn't know felt like the start of a very bad decision. She didn't even have any weapons on her. Riya looked over her shoulder, trying to spot anyone she knew who could accompany her as well, but the room had grown empty as guests flocked toward the food being served in the adjoining suite.

"It's just a precaution," he said, sensing her apprehension. "I'm here to ensure that no harm will come to you."

Realizing that there was little she could do, she unhappily stepped out in front of him. He trailed her like a shadow—always a few paces behind, walking so softly he could have been a thief. They'd nearly reached the end of the hallway when Riya heard hurried footsteps behind her. She turned to see Neha rushing toward her, heavy skirts clutched in one hand, wisps of hair falling out of her updo.

"Rajkumaari. Mohan." She greeted the two of them. "You left these behind," she said to Riya, a too-wide smile on her lips as she handed Riya a set of bangles that didn't belong to her. Embedded among the delicate colored glass was a golden bracelet that was slightly larger, the metal stamped with patterns. Riya recognized it at once, even before she felt the magic.

The girls passed secret notes using jewelry. Neha was trying to get a message to her.

"Oh, thank you so much," Riya said, matching her smile. "How silly of me." She slid them onto her wrist, thanking the goddesses that she'd decided to forego bangles of her own that night.

"It means the world to both me and Indra that you were able to attend the festivities," Neha said, and then nodded imperceptibly.

Riya couldn't tell what she was trying to communicate, but chose to trust her. She continued down the hallway, her mind racing with questions. When they finally reached the maharani's rooms, Mohan graciously opened the door for her.

"Where's Vi—" Riya started to ask, but the door shut in her face. And then she heard the distinct sound of the door locking from the outside.

Riya lunched for the door handle—but it didn't move. "Hey!" She banged on the door with her fists. "What's going on? Let me out!"

But there was no response from the other side.

She was locked inside the maharani's suite, and she had no idea why.

CHAPTER NINE

— KALEB —

WHEN KALEB LEFT Ritsar, he'd taken any valuables he'd been able to carry, with the intention of selling them in the capital to acquire Lyrian money. The merchant in the pawnshop had eyed the jewelry—crafted in a decidedly Ashokan style—with bemusement, but she'd accepted it, offering Kaleb enough to afford lodgings at a comfortable inn and several pairs of well-fitting Lyrian clothes.

Still, he didn't have too many belongings, so it took him all of twenty minutes to pack up his tiny room. He sighed as he looked around at the space that had been his for the past two weeks. It was impersonal, but not lacking character. The walls were painted a pale, cheerful yellow, and every three days the innkeeper replaced the flowers in the vase on his bedside table. The bright red shutters on the window of his third-floor room faced the main street, and when Kaleb opened them in the mornings, he'd heard the bustle of the city—laborers hurrying to work, shopkeepers gossiping as they opened their stores for the day, couriers delivering the day's newspaper.

This was the first place he could call home that belonged entirely to him. There were no ghosts here, no memories of his family or his past. He'd miss it when he moved to the palace.

He glanced up when there was a knock at the door, and when he opened it, he was surprised to find the innkeeper there, looking at him over the edge of her spectacles. "Someone left a note for you at the front," she said, holding out a folded slip of paper.

It was a request to meet at a tavern a few streets over. He blinked in confusion. "Are you sure this is for me?"

The innkeeper nodded. "Yes, definitely. He asked for you by name and everything."

"*He?*" Kaleb asked warily. "What did he look like?"

"He was a young man about your height. Spoke very politely." She thought for a moment. "He had kind eyes."

It wasn't a useful description, and Kaleb had no idea who could possibly be looking for him. Unnerved, he debated about going. But this person already knew where to find him and could easily return. Kaleb snapped his suitcase shut and reached for his woolen coat.

It was crisp outside, and he tucked his hands into his pockets to keep them warm as he walked out of the inn. Despite the inn's proximity to a local market, Kaleb had been there only once, to purchase his Lyrian clothes. The street was bathed in the gold of the setting sun, and patrons were milling around leisurely, arms laden with paper-wrapped parcels and heavy cloth bags as they perused the stalls and shops that lined a large courtyard.

Stores were grouped by the type of wares they sold, and Kaleb walked past signs advertising everything from gold-plated jewelry and painted vases to musical instruments and chiffon dresses. He still hadn't grown accustomed to the absence of magical objects—a staple in every Ashokan market—which was why he noticed the sudden, familiar prickle of magic along his skin.

For a moment he thought he'd imagined it, but then he spotted a tiny stall tucked into the corner of the plaza. Curious, he walked closer, but one look at the items on display was enough to reveal that they were identical, mass-produced trinkets. Disappointed, he flashed a regretful smile at the shopkeeper before hurrying away.

The tavern had a ram's head mounted above the entrance. When he pushed the door open, warmth from a fire blazing in a hearth and the smell of liquor and smoke greeted him. It was different from the few taverns he'd been to in Ashoka, which were filled with low tables and colorful cushions on the floor. Here, patrons huddled together in private booths with plush leather seats, separated by dark wood panels. The kind-eyed stranger had left a booth number along with the name of the tavern, so Kaleb's eyes tracked the numbers etched into a metal plate on each panel until he found number seven.

The man sitting there was neither kind-eyed nor strange. It was Prince Lukas. Kaleb's heart skipped a beat, and panic set in, freezing Kaleb to the spot.

Lukas pierced him with his intense stare. "Have a seat, Kol," he said coldly. "Or should I call you Kaleb?"

Kaleb wondered how bad it would be if he simply ran. He glanced at the door. It was a straight shot, and he could make it before Lukas could stop him. Probably.

"I wouldn't do that if I were you," Lukas said, tracking his gaze. "If you flee, I'll get you arrested. I don't think a scholar like you would like jail very much."

Kaleb nearly laughed. Lukas had no idea. But the threat worked anyway—and now that the initial shock had worn off, Kaleb found himself immensely curious as to why the Lyrian prince had tracked him down and asked to meet here of all places. He carefully slid into the empty seat across from Lukas.

The prince had changed out of his formal wear. Dressed in a casual, loose-fitting gray tunic he looked so . . . approachable—indistinguishable from any other young man meeting a friend for a drink. Maybe not indistinguishable. His delicate features and long lashes would attract second glances no matter where he went, but Kaleb noted that Lukas seemed quite comfortable in this noisy, crowded tavern, sitting back and waving at the barkeep for a drink with a familiarity suggesting that this wasn't his first time here. As a server approached their table with a decanter of red wine and two glasses, Kaleb wondered how many unsuspecting scholars the prince had threatened with imprisonment from this very booth.

"How did you find me?" Kaleb asked when they were alone again.

Lukas poured them each a glass and slid one over to Kaleb. "Your application."

"Oh." Kaleb felt silly. Of course.

Kaleb wasn't much of a drinker, but he sipped the wine. It was surprisingly cold, a little bitter, and it made his mouth dry. He'd had Lyrian grape wine only once, and he remembered it being sweeter and easier to drink. But he still took another sip.

"You lied to me," Lukas said directly. "I remember you from Ritsar, but I checked the documents. There was no record of a Kaleb. Or a Kol."

Kaleb's heart raced as he carefully set down the wineglass. "You mistake me for someone else. I don't—"

"There are very few things I trust more than my own memory," Lukas cut in, his voice as sharp as his gaze. "So let's try this again. What were you doing in Ritsar?"

"I—" Kaleb tried to think of a feasible reason that would explain why he'd been in Ritsar. According to Riya, the best lies held some truth to them. "I heard from a friend that the emperor had discovered an Ashokan boy with magical powers," he admitted. "And I was curious."

"Curious enough to journey all the way to Ritsar, infiltrate someone else's troops, and then lie your way out, all to meet one Ashokan boy."

When Lukas said it like that, it sounded a bit absurd. Kaleb felt his face heat.

"Magic is my passion," he said, trying to change tactics. He leaned forward, trying to communicate his joy of working with magic. It should be easy. After all, that was the only thing he'd allowed himself to care about for over ten years. "If it was true, if there was magic that could work with people—it would change everything. I had to see for myself."

"And what did you find there?"

"Nothing." Everything the emperor's troops had found had been sent back to the capital—which was why Kaleb was *here* and not still in Ritsar.

Lukas studied him for a moment. "How much are they paying you?"

"What?"

"My father's advisors. How much did they pay you to spy on me?"

"Advisors?" Kaleb echoed, bewildered. "Nothing. I mean I've never spoken with them. I told you, magic is—"

"Your passion," Lukas finished dryly. He paused for a beat. "Were you truly trained by your father?"

"Yes," Kaleb said, and then he lifted his chin defiantly. "I've been working in this field for far longer than many people who've been to prestigious universities, and I'm just as capable of any of them." He didn't add that it had been his own dream for years to attend one of those universities, until his life had changed course abruptly.

If Lukas thought his lack of education was an issue, he didn't comment. "How is raw magic processed?" he asked.

It took Kaleb a moment to recalibrate. The abrupt shifts in the conversation were throwing him off. "It's cooled down until it's mostly inert and then ground into powder." There was a bit more to it than that, but it was the simplest way to explain it.

"What happens if you heat it instead of cooling it down?"

Kaleb frowned. "No one's ever tried it." He paused as he considered that. It couldn't possibly be true. Surely *someone* had thought to experiment with other temperatures at some point. "I don't know," he amended. "If it wasn't taught to artificers, it's probably because the reaction wasn't notable enough to be worth mentioning."

"Or because it was dangerous." Lukas swirled the wine in his glass, staring at it rather than at Kaleb. "That's what my father's scholars have been working on. Heating raw magic. Trying to melt it down into a liquid. And I want to know why and what exactly he intends to do with this."

A liquid. It sent a shiver down Kaleb's spine. Riya had touched a pool of liquid and walked away with magical power. Was that what they'd inadvertently found at the temple just outside of Ritsar—raw magic that had been heated instead of cooled?

Maybe it was because the alcohol had dulled his senses, but it took Kaleb far too long to realize the implication of the pointed look Lukas was giving him. "Wait . . . You want *me* to find out?"

"Yes."

Kaleb wanted to laugh again. He was already here as a spy—a job that he was only partially confident he could do. And to spy for another person—for the Lyrian prince, no less—was yet another chance for him to get caught.

"Why?" Kaleb wasn't sure what he was asking exactly. *Why spy on your own father when you're the favorite to inherit the throne? Why do you think your father's advisors are paying me to trail you?* Or perhaps more simply, *Why me?*

"Because my father never does things without a reason," Lukas said. "And he never keeps things from me."

"So this is a bid for the throne," Kaleb said after studying him for a moment.

Kaleb seemed to have struck a nerve, because Lukas's jaw tightened. "The throne is irrelevant to me."

"I have a hard time believing that," Kaleb said.

Lukas's gaze pierced him like shards of ice. "Just because you've read about me in the newssheets doesn't mean you actually know anything about me."

Kaleb looked away, admonished. He'd done the same thing to Lukas that he'd resented others for doing to him: making judgments based on rumors rather than forming their own opinion. "You're right," Kaleb admitted. "That was unfair of me."

Lukas blinked in surprise. He hadn't expected that response. "I'm not my father," he said after a beat of hesitation. "And it might not seem like it, but I have the best interests of the Lyrian people at heart. If you choose to help me, I truly believe we'll be doing a lot of good."

He sounded sincere, but Kaleb didn't know whether he could trust that either. "And if I refuse?"

"I tell my father you were snooping around a military base, impersonating a soldier. You're clever enough to guess how that would turn out."

"So it's not really a choice, is it."

Lukas lifted a shoulder. "It would be foolish of me to not have assurances."

Kaleb exhaled, considering his options. For all that he couldn't trust Lukas, Lukas couldn't trust *him* either. And true, Lukas could have Kaleb jailed or killed, but that he'd approached him at all was an indication of something more fundamental: desperation.

Desperate people make mistakes.

Amma had said that often, instructing all of them—but especially Vira—to always have full control over their desires and actions. This could work to his advantage. After all, Lukas was offering him exactly what Kaleb wanted: access to the emperor's magical experiments. All Kaleb needed to do was fool the prince long enough to get the information back to Vira.

Kaleb's heartbeat quickened and his stomach knotted, but he nodded. "All right. I'll be your spy."

CHAPTER TEN

— VIRA —

THE GUARD WHO escorted Vira into the dungeons wasn't gentle. As he shoved her into the cell, she tripped on the metal bar that lay across the entrance. She gasped in pain as her knees hit the hard stone floor, sending pain shooting through her legs. Before she could even pick herself up, a wall of magic crashed over her as the guard inserted a key into the metal rod and activated the magic in it. The mayaka-forged shackles they'd put on her wrists began to hum, too, and she knew there was absolutely nothing she could do now. There were no doors, but there didn't need to be. If she took even a single step out of the cell, her body would be hit with enough pain to subdue an elephant.

"Please," Vira whispered, knowing that she was begging and hating herself for it. "Don't do this."

A maharani doesn't ask, and she certainly doesn't stoop so low as to beg, her mother's voice sounded in her brain. *She simply takes what she is owed.*

A cruel smile curved over the guard's lips. "Enjoy your night," he said, not bothering to hide the obvious glee in his voice as he walked away.

There was a small part of her that had hoped that it was all a terrible dream, that she'd wake up any moment back in her own room, curled up on the divan after working too late. But it wasn't. This was all painfully, horribly real. And as the seconds passed, Vira deliberately snuffed out any shred of hope that remained in her heart. She was all alone.

She shouldn't be that surprised, she thought bitterly, because wasn't that how it had always been? Vira against the weight of her mother's expectations. Vira against her siblings. Vira against the judgment and disapproval of the Council, the citizens.

She sank to the floor. The world blurred before her as tears pooled in her eyes. She wiped them away furiously. Maharanis didn't cry. But her body had never listened to her, and for once, in the cold, pitiful dark of the cell, Vira released the leash she had on her emotions. A sob tore from her as she doubled over, tugging her knees to her chest as though it would somehow dull the anguish.

She'd been foolish. The Council had made it clear that they disapproved of her, but it had never occurred to her that they would go this far. She should have seen it coming. Her mother certainly would have—and she would have been charming and agreeable and used her pretty words to fix everything long before it got to this point.

Her mother had been hard to love, but she was easy to like. Vira had never been very good at either. And now she was paying the price for it.

I'm not the maharani anymore.

The words made her feel empty.

She had shaped her entire life around that crown. She'd bled for it, she'd broken her own heart for it. She'd sacrificed everything she'd ever loved, every bit of joy or hope or pleasure. But it wasn't enough. It had never been enough. And only now that it was gone did she realize that the crown wasn't actually synonymous with her name. It was just a piece of jewelry that could be easily removed and put on anyone's head. The crown didn't need her.

But without it, Vira was nothing.

She used the bottom edge of her kurta to wipe away her tears—and jumped as something tumbled out of her pocket. It was a folded-up piece of scrap paper. Vira unfolded it.

There wasn't much light, but she could read the hastily scrawled words in Neha's efficient handwriting: *I'm sorry. Key hidden in cell. Wait until midnight to escape.*

Vira read it three times in rapid succession before she finally processed the words. She wasn't trapped here. There was a way out.

The Council had no idea what they were doing. They couldn't trust Lyria to honor any deal, not when the emperor was experimenting with magic that the Council knew nothing about.

I can still fix it. I can save Ashoka.

She just had to find the key before the bells chimed midnight. She had no idea how much time she had, so she crumpled the note and stuffed it back into her pocket, surveying the cell more closely. There weren't a lot of places where a key could be hidden.

Vira began by dismantling her pallet, pulling the straw mat away from the wall, shaking out the single flimsy blanket they'd left her.

"Well, well," a familiar voice said from the dark.

Vira jerked up. She'd been so focused on herself that she hadn't paid any attention to where the guard had taken her. Or who else might be locked away in the neighboring cells.

Surya stood in the cell opposite her. The mercenary who had killed Vira's betrothed. He looked just as she remembered him: long hair, crooked nose, a thin scar slicing through one eyebrow. And even in the darkness she could practically see the arrogance radiating from him.

"I have to say, Rani, you're the last person I expected to see in here."

"You," she snarled, anger overpowering all her common sense as she tossed the blanket back on the ground. "You knew."

"I know a lot of things," Surya said, sounding bored. "You'll have to be more specific."

"Amrit," she rasped, because it was all she could manage.

"Ah." He was too far away for Vira to make out much of his facial expressions, but she could see his shoulders tense as he stepped even closer to the edge of the magic wall. "I take it things didn't go according to plan."

"My plan? No," Vira said. "But it turns out Amrit had a different one that didn't involve me."

"I guess we have that in common," Surya said with a dry laugh. "We were supposed to leave you out of this. We were supposed to take the map pieces and go. But he chose to involve you. And he left me rotting in here, so it seems that my brother betrayed the both of us."

The word *brother* sent a jolt through her. They weren't related by blood—none of the mercenaries were as far as Vira knew—but they'd been taken in and raised by the same man who killed her mother. She hadn't allowed herself to think of Amrit as one of *them*. Surya looked every bit the part of the remorseless killer that he was, but she couldn't picture Amrit like that, couldn't reconcile the soft-spoken guard who'd protected her and brought her sweets.

"You're lying," Vira spat.

"You can believe what you wish," Surya said, shrugging carelessly.

His voice was so infuriatingly calm, and something snapped inside of her. Rage, raw and powerful, coursed through her veins, and for a moment all she could think was how desperately she wanted to rip free of her magical shackles, grab him by the neck, and slam him against the wall until she dragged some real emotion out of him. But just as quickly as it had come, the anger vanished, and Vira suddenly felt exhausted.

"Why?" she asked, her voice barely a whisper. "Why did he involve me?" She was revealing something primal of herself to Surya, and it would be wiser not to, but she could no more stop herself from asking than she could stop her heart from beating.

"I don't know."

He was lying. He had to be.

"I'm getting out of here," she swore, turning back to her search. "And when I do, I *will* save my country."

"Is that so?" he asked mildly.

"I know you have no loyalty to us, so I don't expect you to understand," Vira said coldly. "Our borders are failing, we're out of magic, and my Council would rather let another country invade us than put any faith in me or the Ivory Key, because they're convinced that it's a tale for children." Surya had told her that once, too, dismissed her like everyone else. "I don't care if you believe me or not, but if Amrit or anyone else gets in my way, I will take them down."

She crouched in front of the small clay pot of water they'd left her. There was nothing around or underneath it, but on a whim, she turned it over and emptied it. Water sloshed around her feet along with a small metal rod. She exhaled in relief.

The clocks still hadn't struck midnight, but she used it to unlock the shackles that bound her wrists, letting them clatter to the floor. They weren't attached to anything—it was the magic laced in them that had kept her confined within the barrier.

Surya studied her silently. "You're wrong."

Vira lifted her chin. "You wouldn't be the first to underestimate me."

"About where my loyalty lies," he clarified.

Vira's brows furrowed in confusion. "What?"

He hesitated for a moment, as if he were selecting his words carefully. "I can help you. Get the magic you need, I mean."

Nothing could have prepared her for that. "What?" she said again.

"Believe it or not, we're on the same side, Rani."

Vira's eyes flashed. "And what side is that?"

"The side that wants the key put to use," he said cryptically. "Amrit wants to destroy it."

"Destroy it?" It had never occurred to her that Amrit might have different plans. She'd only ever thought he wanted the magic for himself.

The bells began to strike then. It was midnight. Vira easily stepped over the magical barrier of her cell. She knew it would be fine, but she still let out a small sigh of relief when no alarms were triggered and no pain wracked her body. She turned toward the exit, but Surya's voice called her back.

"I can help you find him before he does." His eyes lingered on the key in her hand. "I know how he thinks and what he's planning. If you want to outsmart him, I'm your best bet."

It was tempting. "I don't need to find him."

"You could get answers." The corner of Surya's mouth lifted. "Or revenge."

I don't want revenge, she wanted to say, but the words died on her lips because it wasn't true. Amrit had betrayed her, and the part of her that wanted to go after him, to make him pay, roared inside of her. She thought about how she'd felt just minutes earlier, the fury that had threatened to consume her. It hadn't been Surya she'd wanted to hurt. It was Amrit. She wanted to hurt him the same way he'd hurt her—just to know that she *could*.

"There's nothing wrong in wanting retribution," Surya said, his voice quiet. "And you look like you need all the allies you can get."

"You know what he's planning to do?" Vira asked, ignoring his comment.

"I do." But he didn't say any more. That was his bargaining chip: freedom in exchange for information.

Surya had never pretended to be her friend or confidant, or even a good person. She didn't trust him. But their interests were aligned—at least for the time being—and Vira was too pragmatic to turn down help when she so desperately needed it.

"We do things my way," she said.

Surya nodded. "Your way."

Vira took a deep breath, hoping she wouldn't regret this choice as she tossed the key into his cell.

CHAPTER ELEVEN

— RIYA —

RIYA WAS PRETTY sure Vira wasn't in the maharani's suite, but she tore through it anyway. "Vira? Vira!"

There was no answer. The lights were still on in Vira's office, papers scattered all over the room. The balcony doors had been left open, and a gust of wind had caused everything unweighted to fly off the table. There was a platter of cold food, untouched. Vira hadn't intended to be gone for very long.

Riya crouched down, ripping the bangles off her wrist. She rummaged for a piece of scrap paper and reached for the half-closed pot of ink. She picked out the bangle that had magic laced in the metal and slathered it in ink. When she rolled it across the paper, she could make out a string of words.

Vira's in trouble. Have plan. Climb down. Midnight.

Riya glanced at the clock. She had twenty minutes. She ignored her rising anger and confusion and panic and forced herself into action.

She fished out the bag of belongings she'd hidden under the bed with her old kurtas and a dagger gifted to her by Papa. She dumped the contents out and quickly changed. She didn't have anything of sentimental value here in the palace, but she grabbed a fistful of jewelry—earrings and necklaces that wouldn't make too much noise but would be easy to pawn—and the book of meditation Ronak had given her, shoving them into the bag. She hesitated and then grabbed the necklace with the ruby pendant as well—the one Sharadha had said belonged to members of the Order of the Mayura.

Then she went back to Vira's office, sifting through the papers until she found the ones she needed: the original copy of the Ivory Key that she'd made in Ritsar and the one where Vira had translated it into numbers. She pulled open the almirah door and grabbed three of Papa's journals. She didn't have time to look through them, but they'd been set to one side, and the first one was clearly about the Kamala Society, so she hoped for the best.

Riya looked at the clock again and then looked around the room one last time. She wouldn't be back here. She slung her small pack over her shoulder and stepped out onto the balcony, letting the cool night air wash over her.

She was dressed the same as when she'd come to the palace: a thread-bare red kurta, black dupatta tied around her waist. The familiar weight of the dagger pressed against the side of her hip reminded her of who she'd once been. A Raven.

Riya peered over the edge of the balcony. There were no guards on the grounds below that Riya could see, which was odd, because this part of the palace, right below the maharani's suite, was always teeming with them. Coincidence, perhaps, or a part of Neha's plan. Either way, Riya had precious few moments. She began to climb down the trellis beside the balcony, moving as quickly as she dared, trying not to put too much weight on the wooden rungs, trying not to crush the jasmine vines beneath her feet.

This was how she'd left last time too, she thought, disoriented. Then she'd been fleeing from her mother. From a world that she'd believed didn't want her. Apparently that hadn't changed.

Riya dropped silently onto the ground and cast her eyes around. She was alone—and then she heard footsteps and hushed voices. She pressed herself flat against the wall, a hand on her dagger. When the figures came into view, Riya's shoulders sagged in relief. It was Indra and Archana, still dressed in their extravagant outfits.. Riya stepped out of the shadows.

Archana spotted her first. "Oh, thank the goddesses."

The girls threw their arms around her, and Riya hugged them back tightly. "What's going on?" she asked.

Indra bit her lip, guilt in her eyes. "I'm sorry. I'm *so* sorry. I swear I didn't know anything or—"

"I don't understand," Riya cut in. "What happened?"

"There's been a coup," Archana said, sounding strangely detached. "The Council took over."

Riya felt all the blood drain from her face. "*What?* Where's Vira now?"

"The dungeons." Archana responded again in that same flat tone while Indra pressed her hands to her mouth as if to stifle a sob. "Neha has a plan to get you all out of here."

Riya could feel the magic hum insistently in her veins, desperate to be unleashed. She tamped it down and took another calming breath. "What's the plan?"

"Neha went to get Ronak," Indra said, her voice shaky. "They'll meet you outside the dungeons. Neha cleared the path through the servants' quarters so you shouldn't run into any guards on your way. She'll guide you from there."

"It's not your fault," Riya said, squeezing Indra's fingers. This was her engagement night. It was meant to be a joyful celebration, and instead she was helping sneak Riya and her siblings out of the palace. If she was caught, she too could be branded a traitor, Meena's daughter or not.

"Will you be all right?" Archana asked, looking worried. "Where will you go?"

Riya hadn't thought that far ahead. She needed to get her siblings out of the fort first. "We'll figure something out."

"Be careful," Indra said, giving her a sad smile.

"Thank you for doing this," Riya said, her voice heavy with emotion. There was friendship, but this was something else. There was no reason for Indra or Archana to side against the Council, against their parents. Riya looked at the two of them, trying to commit their faces to memory. She'd never meant to stay here, nor had she ever wanted her old life back, but even though they didn't know her past, her secrets, they'd become true friends in the short time since she'd been back. She wished they had time for a proper goodbye, where she could tell them how much they meant to her, how much she'd miss them, how much she hoped their paths would cross again in the future. But they didn't, so Riya kept her sentimentality to herself.

They hugged one more time, and then Riya pulled away, slipping into the darkness. She didn't look back.

✻

The servants' quarters stretched nearly the full length of the palace, with many different entries and exits, and would be the fastest way to get to the dungeons unnoticed. Riya kept her head down and walked quickly from room to room. Despite the late hour, it was busy, and she could see servants polishing lanterns and sorting clothing to be washed and cutting vegetables for the next day's meals. No one paid her any attention.

She walked until she emerged on the other side of the palace and then approached a side door that led as close to the dungeons as she could manage. She cracked it open, verified that the coast was clear before opening it wider. The stone path leading to the dungeons was uneven with overgrown foliage, making it even more difficult to navigate in the dark. Riya had to pick her steps carefully, not wanting to twist her ankle or trip. She knew she wasn't being nearly as quiet as she ought to be, but she had to hurry.

Usually there were guards stationed outside the dungeons, but when Riya approached, she could see only two tense figures standing together. The taller one she immediately recognized as her brother's lanky frame, his hands awkwardly tucked into his pockets. The second was Neha, now changed back into her formal guard uniform, though her hair was still in the elaborate updo from her engagement party.

Neha turned, relief evident on her face. "I wasn't sure if you'd get my message. I'm *so* sorry. If I'd known th—"

"It's not your fault," Riya interrupted. "Where's Vira?"

"The maharani has a key in her cell. She'll be out any minute." Neha pointed to the path that curved around the back of the dungeons. "Go that way, past the rose gardens and down to the lowest level of the fort. There'll be an unmarked carriage waiting for you with a driver named Kishore. He'll take you wherever you need to go. I tampered with the guard schedules to buy you as much time as I could, but move quickly. They'll be here soon."

"We'll hurry," Riya promised. "Thank you for everything. I don't know how we can ever repay you. I'm sorry your night was ruined."

Neha shook her head. "It's the least I could do. And besides, it's Amrit who deserves the gratitude."

Ronak frowned, speaking for the first time. "Amrit?"

"This was his plan," Neha explained. "He told me that if something happened to him, I was to be the next captain. And he said that if the maharani was ever overthrown, I had to make sure your family got out of here alive."

Riya exchanged a glance with Ronak, who looked just as surprised. She didn't know what to make of the fact that Amrit had guessed this might happen, and he'd planned for it—ensured that it would be carried out even if he wasn't here. If he'd intended to betray them the entire time, why did he care about their safety?

"I've got to go before someone notices I'm missing," Neha said regretfully, looking back at the palace. "Be careful."

"You too," Riya said. When she vanished into the dark, Riya turned to her brother. "Are you all right? Did they lock you in your room too?"

"I suppose they didn't need to," Ronak said dryly. "It's not like I have any claim to the throne. I'm insignificant no matter who rules Ashoka."

Riya stared at him blankly. It hadn't occurred to her that if anything happened to Vira, *she* would be next in the line of succession. Riya had never wanted to rule, and Amma had made it clear that she never would. She was still reeling from the vision of a parallel life, where she was the maharani, when the door to the dungeon opened and Vira emerged.

She wasn't alone. There was another prisoner behind her. Riya had never seen him before, but she could guess who he was. "No," Riya said at once. "This is a bad idea."

"He can help." Vira's voice was stern, but as she drew closer, Riya could see that her sister's eyes were bloodshot and puffy, like she'd been crying. Only Vira didn't cry.

"You want to trust another mercenary after what Amrit did to us?" Riya asked, glaring at Surya. He didn't shy away from her gaze or try to defend himself.

Vira flinched at the mention of Amrit's name. "It's my decision."

"And it's *our* lives you're endangering," Riya returned.

Vira didn't respond.

After a painfully long pause, Ronak cleared his throat. "You have to go," he said. "It's not smart to linger."

"Fine," Riya said. "Come on." She started to turn when Vira's voice stopped her.

"*You?*" Vira said to Ronak, her eyes narrowing. And then she seemed to realize something. "You're not coming."

"What?" Riya asked incredulously. "You cannot be serious, Ronak."

Ronak didn't look at them when he spoke. "I convinced the Council to send me to Lyria."

Vira looked as though she'd been slapped. "You—you're siding with the Council?"

"Don't be ridiculous," Ronak said. "You think I care about them? Kaleb's in Lyria."

"We'll find a way to get a message to him," Riya said. "He can come meet us wherever we are."

"No, I can't just abandon him," Ronak said. But there was something about his demeanor that made Riya feel like he wasn't telling them the whole truth.

"You made another deal with her, didn't you?" Riya guessed, disappointed. Even after everything she'd told him in Ritsar, even after he'd sworn he wouldn't give Ekta the Ivory Key, he was still working with her.

Ronak's eyes flashed with annoyance, but he didn't deny it.

"Made a deal with who?" Vira asked slowly, looking between the two of them. "What aren't you telling me?"

Neither of them answered her.

"Is she threatening you?" Riya asked.

"Who?" Vira demanded.

"Drop it, Riya," Ronak snapped.

"Then what did she promise you this time?" Riya asked, still ignoring Vira. "Because she's lying." She'd never met Ekta, but she'd heard enough rumors during her time with the Ravens to know that making a deal with her never ended well.

"It doesn't matter," Ronak insisted stubbornly. "I'm staying."

Irritation filled Riya. She was tired of being the rational one, the one who was trying to do the right thing and keep everyone safe while Vira and Ronak were apparently in a competition to see who could behave more recklessly.

"Fine, if this is what you want to do," Riya spat, "you're on your own. For the record, I think you're being irresponsible—both of you," she added, pointing at Vira. "All of this will invariably blow up, and I'll be the one who has to pick up the pieces."

Feeling herself getting worked up, Riya tried to calm down. Adrenaline and frustration were a potent combination when it came to fueling the magic that lived under her skin, and she already had too much of both coursing through her from the events of the night.

Vira was still staring at Ronak. "Come with us," she said. It wasn't a request, but it was the closest thing to one that he'd get from Vira.

"I can't," Ronak said, refusing again. "Look, the Council is meeting the Lyrian emperor at Shantha Mahal in two weeks. If you find the quarries before then, you can still stop them and get your throne back. Now you have to go before the guar—"

"Rani," Surya cut in, jerking his chin in the direction of the palace.

A guard was walking directly toward them. They'd stayed there arguing for too long, eating into the time Neha had bought them.

The guard's eyes widened as he spotted them, his hand jumping to his talwar. "Don't move," he ordered.

"We have to go." Riya shoved her siblings and Surya toward the path. "Now!"

But Riya didn't move quickly enough. The guard caught her, grabbing her bag and tugging her backward. She hissed in pain as the strap dug into her shoulder. She struggled to tear free, but his other hand wrapped tight around her upper arm, holding her in place.

"Let me *go*," she said forcefully, trying to shove him off her.

It was sudden. All the magic she'd been holding back erupted from her like a gust of wind. The guard went flying back, hitting the outside wall of the dungeon with a sickening thud. And then he crumpled to the floor.

Riya pressed her hands against her mouth in horror. She felt sick to her stomach as she waited a moment, and then another for him to move. But he didn't stand up. Riya took a step forward, wanting to make sure he was still alive, but her knees buckled. Ronak grabbed Riya's shoulders to keep her steady.

"Is he breathing?" Vira asked as Surya rushed over, pressing his fingers to the man's throat.

Surya nodded, and Riya squeezed her eyes closed in gratitude.

"I'm sorry," Riya said, emotions overwhelming her. Someone was hurt because of her. "I . . . I lost control."

But that was a lie. She'd never had any control in the first place. The power inside of her hungered to escape, and every time Riya used the magic, it only seemed to grow stronger while Riya grew weaker. She could feel it now, humming contentedly inside of her.

"You were just protecting us," Vira said. But Riya could see the fear in her sister's eyes as her gaze lingered on the unmoving guard. Vira was scared of her—of her power. And Riya couldn't even blame her, because it scared her too.

"We can't leave him here, Rani," Surya said. But though he was addressing Vira, he was watching Riya with a mix of curiosity and apprehension.

"I'll take care of it," Ronak said. "Go quickly before more guards come."

"Two weeks," Vira said to Ronak.

"Here," Riya said, shoving a fistful of mayaka-forged paper into his hands, the magic in them brushing her fingers. Anything he wrote on it would appear on the matching sheets she had. "Just in case you need to reach us."

Ronak tucked it into his pocket, then grabbed the guard under his arms and began to drag him into the dungeons.

Riya allowed herself to be pulled away, but she was barely paying attention to where they were going. Her mind was still on the guard, at the look of shock on his face when her magic struck him, at his vacant gaze as he dropped to the ground. Papa's words kept running through her head. *Some acts, like taking a life—those leave a mark on your soul. And they never disappear.*

She'd gotten lucky this time—every time, if she was being honest. But she couldn't guarantee that it would be the same next time, that she wouldn't hurt someone for real.

Because the thing that terrified Riya the most wasn't that she'd lost control. It was how good it felt when she had.

They were hurrying down the stairs that led to the lower levels when the alarm began to blare. It was a clanging sound of bells that echoed throughout the fort, and slowly, tier by tier, lanterns began to be lit. Riya looked at Vira, panicked. The guard she'd attacked had no doubt been discovered—and they'd know by now that Vira and Surya weren't in their cells.

The carriage was *right* there, at the end of the staircase with the shadowy figure of the driver lingering anxiously beside it. But before they could even debate whether it was worth the risk, there was a loud grating sound of metal scraping against stone. Guards were manually closing the massive metal doors of the fort.

"We can't take the carriage," Vira said, pained. "They won't allow anyone in or out."

"Is there another way out?" Surya asked.

Vira looked at Riya. "How did you escape last time?"

Riya had never intended to reveal her secret exit to anyone just in case she needed it one day. But guards were emerging all throughout the fort and they were officially out of all other options.

"This way," Riya said, leading them back up the stairs toward the rose gardens that overlooked the ocean. They sprinted the whole way, not caring about being seen anymore, just trying to outrun the guards as they cut across the training arena and sprinted through a fully lit courtyard.

The hole in the wall wasn't very wide, hidden by scraggly rosebushes with branches and thorns that tore at Riya's skin and clothes as she shoved her way through.

"Quickly," Riya said, holding the branches away as first Vira then Surya crawled through the gap and dropped down onto a ledge they could use to sneak around the outside of the fort.

The fort hadn't felt like home for a long time, but Riya felt bittersweet as she took one last look behind her, unsure if she'd ever be back there again. She took a deep breath and then she, too, slipped out, the only trace of her presence the subtle fragrance of roses that wafted through the air as the branches of the bush sprang back into place.

CHAPTER TWELVE

— KALEB —

IT WAS NEARLY dusk when Kaleb arrived at the Lyrian palace. Twilight painted shadows across the grounds as he walked to the side entrance, where two servants were waiting to escort him to his new lodgings. They deposited his suitcase in the bedroom and, before leaving him alone, pointed out the semiprivate baths at the end of the hall that he'd share with the other scholars in residence.

Kaleb knew what the scholar accommodations looked like in Ashoka, and they were single rooms—sometimes shared with others—with nothing more than a small cot and a desk. To his surprise, his new living quarters were spacious, made up of a receiving room with comfortable sofas and a sleeping area with a large bed and a wooden armoire. Everything was decorated in neutral shades of tan and gray, but given the silk sheets and plush rugs, it was much more lavish than he'd expected.

Kaleb didn't have many things, but he dutifully unpacked the handful of new tunics he'd purchased. He tugged open the wardrobe door, pausing when he noticed odd scratches on the inside of the door. There were four rows of small, crude cuts made into the wood, as though scratched out by a blunt knife. There were five in the first row, eight in the second, two in the third, and five again in the last. He stared at them for a moment, more than anything confused that they'd left something marred in an otherwise pristine room.

He rinsed the day's grime off in the baths, and when he returned, he found that Dayana had slipped a note under his door, informing him that she was just a few doors down the same hallway and he should stop by when he was settled in. When he knocked, she opened the door holding a gray and white kitten in her arms. Her hair was twisted into a messy braid and sweat glistened over her forehead as she greeted him with a wide grin.

"Kol! Come in!"

"Who's this?" Kaleb asked, delightedly holding his hand out for the cat to sniff.

"Ephyra," Dayana said fondly. "She's a tiny little terror."

Ephyra cautiously allowed Kaleb to scratch her behind the ears. "She's adorable," Kaleb said. Amma had never allowed them a pet growing up, though it certainly hadn't stopped Riya from trying to adopt every single stray animal that had snuck into the fort.

As Kaleb closed the door, Dayana crouched down and let Ephyra go, and she disappeared under a table with a swish of her tail.

"How are you settling in?" Dayana asked.

"Not as well as you, clearly." Kaleb surveyed the room. It was identical to his down to the furnishings, but Dayana had been in the middle of rearranging all the furniture to suit her own tastes. There were two open trunks pushed up against one of the walls, both overflowing with clothes and jewelry. A third was already unpacked.

"They said they'd bring me another wardrobe tomorrow," she said as she tracked his gaze.

"Another wardrobe?" Kaleb asked, a little amused. Even as the rajku-maara of Ashoka, Kaleb wasn't sure he'd ever owned this many clothes.

"I *might* have overpacked," she admitted, but she didn't sound partic-ularly contrite. "Help me with this, will you?" She gestured toward the sofa in the middle of the room.

"I didn't think we'd actually be staying in the palace," Kaleb admitted as he grabbed one end of the sofa.

"The scholar annex was definitely not this nice," Dayana agreed. She tilted her head, surveying the space as if trying to decide if she liked the new decor. "Oh," she said, turning to him. "Did you hear about what hap-pened to it?"

Kaleb shook his head. He'd seen it again on his way in, curiously eye-ing the silhouette of the half-ruined building, but he hadn't dared ask the servants any questions.

"There was an *explosion*," Dayana said, lowering her voice, like she was sharing a bit of salacious gossip. "Apparently the scholars were doing some kind of experiment with raw magic that went wrong."

Kaleb's eyes widened. He wondered if this was what Lukas had been talking about—his father trying to heat magic to create the liquid form. "Was anyone hurt?"

"Two scholars who had raw magic poisoning had to be rushed to heal-ers," Dayana said. "A few suffered bruises and burns. But apparently it took artificers *weeks* to clear the magic out and make it safe for people to even start rebuilding it."

"That's why everyone was moved into the palace."

Dayana nodded. "And why they were hiring more scholars."

Interesting. Kaleb filed that information away.

"Actually, I don't like where this is," Dayana declared, looking at the sofa. "Help me move it again?" She posed the question in a soft voice, pairing it with a small pout and pleading eyes.

Kaleb sighed. "If I'd known we'd be moving furniture, I would have waited to take a shower." He groaned, but he grinned at her to make it clear that he was only teasing.

This was nice, he thought as he lifted the settee again. Having friends. He'd missed it.

✱

Lukas was waiting outside his door.

Kaleb had spent over two hours helping Dayana set up her space, and now it was late enough that most of the lanterns that lined the hallways had been snuffed out for the night. But even in the dark, Kaleb could recognize him.

"Making friends already, I see," Lukas commented. He was dressed casually once again, resting a shoulder against the doorjamb. He'd evidently just bathed. His hair was still wet and dipping into his eyes, the scent of bergamot and orange blossom clinging to his skin.

"What are you doing here?" Kaleb asked as he fished his room key out of his pocket. Belatedly, he realized he was being quite familiar—and possibly rude. At the very least, he should be addressing Lukas by one of his titles.

But Lukas didn't seem to notice or care. "I thought we should talk."

He didn't step back, and Kaleb was acutely aware of how close Lukas was to him as he unlocked the door.

"Sure, come in," Kaleb muttered as Lukas followed him inside.

"Do you want me to go?" Lukas asked. He lingered by the door hesitantly—as if he would actually leave if Kaleb wished.

"No," Kaleb said after a beat, closing the door behind him. "So what do you want to talk about?"

Lukas made himself comfortable on the sofa, tucking his bare feet under his legs and pushing his hair back from his forehead. Kaleb was abruptly struck by how young he looked. His research had revealed that Lukas was just a year older than he was, but it was almost difficult to believe that this boy was the same intimidating lieutenant who'd interrogated and blackmailed him into being a spy.

Dayana's impression of him hadn't been particularly kind after their interview. *Ruthless, aloof, secretive*, she'd said, rolling her eyes. That hadn't shocked him—from their handful of interactions it had become pretty clear that Dayana seemed to dislike and distrust most men. But what did surprise Kaleb was that the newssheets he'd gotten his hands on after their encounter at the tavern hadn't been any more flattering.

There were articles about Lukas almost daily, ranging from gossip magazines romantically linking him to numerous socialites and military leaders of all genders to more legitimate sources detailing his political prowess and quick wit. The labels attached to him seemed to be endless: cold, spoiled, talented, flirt, clever. It was all contradictory—and some of it clearly had to be untrue.

Kaleb knew what it was like to have people assume the worst, and part of him felt that he owed it to Lukas to decide what he believed, rather than trusting the opinion of strangers. But he also wasn't foolish enough to discount them. After all, rumors originated somewhere.

"I have something for you," Lukas said, reaching into his pocket and withdrawing a ring.

"What's this?" Kaleb took it, turning it over. It was made of silver, with a wolf on top that had two onyx eyes.

"It'll be our way of communicating. Put it on."

Kaleb hesitated. The last piece of metal jewelry he'd worn had shackled him to the dungeons. He didn't intend to be anyone's prisoner again.

Sensing his wariness, Lukas lifted his right hand, revealing a matching ring on his smallest finger—a tiger instead of a wolf, but with the same glittering black eyes. "It's safe, I promise."

Kaleb slid it on. It was surprisingly heavy. "How does it work?"

Lukas used the edge of a fingernail to pry out one of the eyes. Kaleb felt a prickle of magic around his finger as his wolf too lost one eye. It was a simple mirroring magic, similar to what mayaka used in forged paper, but it was clever and easy to conceal.

"Did you make this?" Kaleb asked.

"I did," Lukas said. "Now try walking away."

Kaleb took a few steps back, and as soon as he did, a surge of magic flickered over his skin, insistent like a warning—as though telling him he was going in the wrong direction. He stepped back toward Lukas. The ring was quiet. Lukas slid the gemstone back in place. The eye reappeared on Kaleb's ring as well, the magic subsiding.

"It's not safe for us to be seen together too often, and I don't want any written records that can be traced or intercepted. When you find anything—or you're in trouble—remove one of the eyes and I'll find you at once. And I'll do the same if I have any information to share with you."

Kaleb's brows rose. "This is impressive," he said. Forging something like this required true skill and creativity—not to mention a sizable amount of magic.

Lukas lifted a shoulder, not fully acknowledging the compliment. "I wanted to make sure I had safeguards in place this time."

"This time?" Kaleb asked, confused.

"You aren't the first scholar I—"

"Blackmailed?" Kaleb couldn't resist cutting in.

Lukas gave him a look. "That I worked with," he finished. "There was another one before. Theo. This was his room actually."

Kaleb's mind drifted to the scratches in the wardrobe. "What happened to him?"

Lukas looked off into the middle distance. "The official story is that he quit unexpectedly."

Official story. "But you don't believe that," Kaleb said slowly.

Lukas shook his head. "I think he found something that got him caught in my father's crosshairs."

Kaleb felt a shiver crawl down his spine. "What was he looking into?"

"I don't know exactly," Lukas said. "In the days before he disappeared, he was paranoid, sure that someone was following him. I had one of my personal guards trail him for a few days to assure him that he was safe. She never saw anyone, but it didn't matter." Lukas ran a hand over his face, looking a bit tired, a bit haunted. "He stopped trusting me, and by the time I realized that he was in danger, it was already too late."

Kaleb had known this would be a dangerous assignment, but thinking about it in the abstract was very different from learning that another scholar investigating the exact same thing had gone missing. He didn't know what to say.

"He kept extensive notes," Lukas said, finally looking at Kaleb. "He had a journal he was always writing in—small, leather bound, stamped with a feather in the lower right corner. But when I searched his things, I couldn't find it. And I know my father doesn't have it, because I overheard Hektor asking the other scholars about it as well. If you find that, there will be answers there, I'm certain of it."

"I'll try," Kaleb promised. "What can I expect from the other scholars?" He hoped the question didn't betray his nerves. Given the way the interview had gone, he'd been fairly certain that the response from the others wouldn't be that much better.

"Focus on the work," Lukas said. "People can say what they want, but it's hard to argue with results."

Kaleb smiled a little. "That's good advice. I see why you're considered the favorite to be named heir."

Lukas smiled dryly. "You've done your research."

"A little." Kaleb hedged, not wanting to admit just how much research he'd done. "It seems people are . . . opinionated about you."

"Opinionated. How very diplomatic."

Kaleb pressed his lips together. It sounded like an insult. "I just wanted to know what I'd gotten myself into."

"And what did you learn?" Lukas asked, a glint in his eye as he leaned forward.

"You quit your position as a scholar," Kaleb said.

"That was the most interesting thing? Not my parade of lovers or how I'm supposedly trying to murder my brother?" He looked amused, but there was an undercurrent of bitterness in his tone.

"Having met you, I figured if you wanted your brother dead, you would have succeeded."

Lukas laughed. It caught Kaleb off guard, but as Lukas watched him with seemingly genuine delight, Kaleb found himself smiling as well. "You're not what I expected," Lukas observed.

Neither are you, Kaleb wanted to say, but he held himself back. This conversation was getting out of hand, turning into something too familiar. Had they met under different circumstances, they would be on equal footing. But Kaleb couldn't forget that he was posing as a powerless commoner talking to the future emperor of a country trying to start a war with his homeland. Lukas was in his room because he needed Kaleb for his own gain.

"It's late," Kaleb said, rising. "If that's all . . ."

Lukas's forehead furrowed, confused about the abrupt change of tone—but it was gone in an instant, the mask of aloofness back in place. "Be careful," he said as he stood. "In these halls, fear keeps you alive."

And with that ominous warning, Lukas was gone.

CHAPTER THIRTEEN

— RIYA —

THE SWAPNA FOREST was just as Riya had left it. She breathed in the scent of the neem and mango trees, savoring the crunch of leaves and twigs under her feet. She was guided by instinct, the paths just as familiar to her now as when she'd called the forest home.

Going to the Swapna Forest wasn't Riya's decision, but Vira insisted that it was the best chance they had of evading the palace guards searching for them, so she'd caved. Again.

Logically, Riya knew that Vira's argument was valid. Even before they'd fully left the fort, guards had been dispatched through the city to search for the three of them. They couldn't stay in Dvar, and carriages traveling through the main roads at this hour would be stopped and searched. The forest was one place where they wouldn't be followed, especially in the middle of the night—not to mention that it was the most direct path to the Harya province, where they needed to go to get Rasika's book of poetry.

Emotionally, however, it was a different matter.

This wasn't how Riya had pictured returning. She was supposed to be a savior bringing magic to the people and cementing her place among the Ravens. Except she wasn't a Raven anymore. She was a fugitive fleeing the palace with a murderer and a deposed ruler, relying on myths and stories for solutions. She was far from the hero of this story.

She wasn't sure she ever had been.

Riya buried her anxiety and prayed to whatever goddesses were listening that they would be able to avoid the Ravens on their way. She felt a crackle of power inside her. Unleashing her magic twice in as many days had broken down any defenses she'd built up. The magic had spread throughout her body, and she could feel it humming under her skin, turning her hot and almost feverish. It *yearned* to be used, to be free, to—

"Riya, you have to slow down."

Vira's labored voice came from much farther away than Riya expected, and when she turned, she found that her sister and Surya were lagging so far behind she could barely see them in the faint light of the moon. She'd charged ahead of them, so compelled by her restlessness that she hadn't even noticed that they were struggling to navigate the uneven maze of fallen logs and moss-covered stones.

Keep it together, Riya.

She had to figure out how to control this magic—and fast. She inhaled deeply again, fanning herself despite the cool night, as she waited for Vira and Surya to catch up.

"We have to keep moving," Riya reminded them sternly. "The forest isn't safe at night."

Vira just gave her a dark look as she leaned against a tree to catch her breath. "I'm moving as fast as I can."

"We need to rest," Surya said, though he didn't look the least bit winded, and Riya realized that he'd purposefully walked slower to keep pace with Vira.

Riya pursed her lips. "Just a little farther," she said. They were too close to the Ravens' campsite here, but there was a clearing on the other side where they could rest for a few hours in relative safety.

But they'd taken no more than a handful of steps when Riya heard the familiar whistle of a mynah bird. She froze, putting her hand out to stop Vira and Surya. "Quiet," she whispered, her stomach in knots as she surveyed the tree line. She couldn't see them, but they were there. The Ravens.

She heard the rustle of leaves first, then the snap of a twig—a purposeful indicator of their presence. And then a figure silently materialized in front of her.

"I thought we told you to stay out of the forest, *Maharani*." Kavita's familiar voice. It tugged at something in Riya's heart. She'd missed her best friend so much more than she wanted to admit.

Former best friend, she reminded herself as she raised her arms to show that she was unarmed. "Hi, Kavs."

"Riya?" Kavita's surprise was clear even in the dark. A moment later she tugged down the dupatta tied around her mouth and nose. "What are you doing here?"

Silently, three more armed Ravens dropped down from the trees. The first was Tarini, tucking a small glass orb filled with thick gray smoke into a satchel at her waist. Then Yash, straightening as he slid his talwar back into its sheath and uncovered his face as well.

And then there was Varun. He wasn't much more than a shadowy blur, but Riya would recognize him anywhere: tensed shoulders, messy hair, the quiver of arrows slung across his back slightly askew as he lowered the bow in his hand. After days of seeing him in the rich silks the palace scholars wore, it was strange to see him in the plain kurta of the Ravens. She wondered if he was thinking the same about her.

"We're just passing through," Riya said.

"Passing through," Yash repeated, frowning as his gaze slid toward Vira, then back.

"So its's true," Kavita said, shaking her head. "You're going to stay at the palace with *her*." She spat out the word with a glance at Vira. Riya could feel Vira stiffen behind her, but she stayed silent.

"Is that what he told you?" Riya pointed at Varun. "Because *he* was the one who told me I didn't belong here anymore. That—"

"I told you to make a choice," Varun interrupted, stepping forward. "Raven or rajkumaari. And you chose."

"I chose the people," Riya snapped. She could feel the fury simmering inside of her, tangling with the magic, fueling it. She clenched her fists, fingernails digging painfully into the flesh of her palms as she tried to keep her emotions in check. "I'm trying to help everyone. I'm trying to fix everything."

"Fix what?" Kavita asked, staring at her in confusion.

Yash and Tarini too were looking at her with blank expressions, and all at once, the uncomfortable truth hit Riya: Varun hadn't told them that there was no magic left. Instead he'd made her out to be a spoiled rajkumaari playing at being a bandit for attention before returning to the comforts of the palace.

"I—" Riya's gaze flew to Varun, but he was purposefully not looking at her. "It doesn't matter," she said. An awkward silence lingered between them, punctured only by the hoot of an owl in the distance. "We should keep going," she said finally. The wind was picking up and the air smelled of rain. "We have to find a place to make camp for the night."

"Stay with us," Yash said easily.

Riya gaped at him. "Really?" She hadn't expected that to be an option.

He rolled his eyes like he thought she was being a little ridiculous. "Of course, Riya. This is your home too. You're always welcome here."

She was glad that it was dark and he couldn't see the look of longing on her face when he said it was her home. She still wanted that—to follow them back to the glades, for it to be like it had been before.

"Thank you," she said, tucking loose strands of her hair behind her ears.

The Ravens began to walk back in the direction of the camp, but before Riya could follow, Vira grabbed her arm, eyeing the Ravens distrustfully. "Are you still . . . on good terms with them?"

"Good enough," Riya said, trying to convince herself as much as Vira. "They'll have supplies . . . Food. Water. Weapons."

Vira bit her lip, and Riya could practically see the unasked questions she was holding back. But all she said when she let Riya go was, "Fine, but we leave in the morning."

"The morning," Riya agreed.

Riya had thought about the Ravens' camp almost every day since she'd left, but it still took her breath away when she walked in. It was nothing more than a clearing sectioned off by colorful cloth strung up between trees. In the center, a group of Ravens were laughing around a firepit. It had probably been hours since the last meal of the night, but the warm smell of spices lingered in the air. To one side Riya could see the sleeping forms of a handful of Ravens. They'd be woken up in a few hours, when the first watch returned from their patrols at dawn.

It wasn't fancy or beautiful, but it was home. And, Vaishali's bones, she'd really missed this.

Riya lingered beside Vira and Surya while Kavita disappeared into one of the tents to fetch mats woven out of palm fibers as well as light blankets. She wanted to follow Kavita, to pretend that everything was just as it had been, but she was acutely aware that it wasn't. She could see it in the way the Ravens still awake were watching her with a kind of distant wariness.

Things had been strained when she left. The secret she'd kept from them—her identity as the rajkumaari of Ashoka—had driven an invisible wedge between her and the Ravens. And she wasn't sure she could ever fully repair it.

"Don't tell them," Vira said abruptly.

Riya twisted toward her, brows furrowed. "What?"

"About the . . . *coup*." Vira had to force the word out, almost as if saying it aloud would mean having to accept it as the truth.

Vira hadn't said much about it since they'd left the fort, but her discomfort was clear. If Riya was being honest, she couldn't wrap her mind around it either. She'd always known that Vira would someday be the maharani of Ashoka. She couldn't even consciously recall learning that; it had been a simple fact of life for as long as she could remember. And now she felt like she suddenly had to accept that there were actually two suns in the sky or that gravity didn't exist. It was incomprehensible.

"I won't," Riya promised. She paused for a moment and then asked Vira, "Are you all right?" It was a silly question—of course she wasn't, but Riya didn't know what else to say. She couldn't even pretend to understand what Vira was feeling, being exiled from the life she'd been born into, that she'd been promised.

Vira looked at her wide-eyed as she licked her lips. "I'm just—" She stopped suddenly and forcefully swallowed back whatever bit of vulnerability she'd been about to reveal. "I'm fine," she said instead, lifting her chin ever so slightly as though daring Riya to challenge her declaration.

As Riya waited for Kavita to return, she unwound the dupatta around her waist, balling it up and stuffing it into her pack. Her fingers brushed the edges of the book Ronak had given her. She tugged it out—groaning as half the jewelry she'd taken from the palace also spilled to the ground.

"Did you steal from the palace?" Vira asked incredulously. "Is that *mine*?"

"We need money to get around," Riya said, trying her best to dust all the dirt off the necklaces and rings.

"Where did you get that?" Surya asked suddenly. He hadn't said much as they'd fled the palace, sticking close to Vira the whole time. Riya didn't like it. It was one thing to confide in a mercenary you didn't know was one, but it was beyond foolish to trust someone who told you full well that they were a killer.

Riya followed his gaze down to the ruby pendant. "Oh. It's a family heirloom," she said, giving him the same answer she'd given Sharadha as she shoved all the jewelry back inside and closed her bag.

"It belongs to a cult," Surya said, his eyes narrowing.

"The Order of the Mayura?" Vira asked, looking at him in confusion. "It's a cult?"

Surya pinned his gaze on Vira. "What do you know of the Order?"

"Nothing," Vira said immediately. "Just the name."

"Stay away from them," Surya warned. "They do strange experiments with magic."

"Experiments?" Riya looked up sharply. She glanced over her shoulder and lowered her voice to a hushed whisper. "With *people*?"

"Never mind," Surya said, looking like he regretted bringing it up at all.

"No, you have to tell me," Riya insisted. "What kind of experiments?"

He glanced at Vira, who was also looking at him expectantly, and then sighed. "With plants," he said reluctantly. "Supposedly they have secret greenhouses throughout Ashoka where they grow and sell strange plants with magical properties. But that's all I know about it."

"Plants with magic?" Vira frowned. "That's—"

"Impossible?" Riya finished wryly. She could feel Vira's eyes snap toward her, to the magic entwined inextricably within her. But she didn't say anything else—and even if Vira wanted to talk about it, Riya didn't want to discuss that in front of Surya.

"Some ancient feuds are best left buried in legends and folktales," Surya said cryptically.

"What does that mean?" Riya asked, frustrated by his nonanswers.

"It's a piece of advice, Rajkumaari," Surya said, his dark eyes cutting into hers. "You can disregard it if you wish, but I wouldn't be caught wearing that if I were you."

✻

The inn behind the campsite was in ruins. It was probably no more than twenty or thirty years old, but it looked as if a century had passed since its prime. The crumbling walls crawled with tangled vines. Plants sprouted from cracks in a floor already caked with a carpet of moss. Roots snaked over the foundations, possessive claws reclaiming the stones for the earth.

The Ravens rarely came here, with the exception of two people: Tarini and Varun. Tarini had hoped to grow vegetables in the plot of empty land behind the inn. She hadn't been very successful, but she'd gotten medicinal herbs to thrive. It was where Varun procured his endless supply of tulsi.

Riya had rarely sought out the inn voluntarily, but she found herself slipping away from the camp in the middle of the night toward the one place where she might get the answers Surya refused to give her. She'd replayed his words over and over, and the thing she kept returning to was his claim that this secretive order grew magical plants. Vira had been right to call it impossible, because until a few weeks earlier, Riya, too, would have staked her life on the claim that magic was incompatible with living organisms.

But the energy inside her was proof that it wasn't.

And Riya had a sudden suspicion that one of those plants had been growing under her very nose for years.

The earth here was soft, masking her footsteps, but Riya walked cautiously through the garden toward the bluish-green fern she knew grew in one corner. If it had an actual name, Riya didn't know it. The Ravens had always called it the smoke plant. When it was crushed and lit on fire, it released a thick, viscous smoke that had the power to render anyone exposed to it unconscious for several minutes. It was why they wore dupattas around their faces—the cloth was mayaka-forged, laced with magic to protect them from exposure when they shattered the small glass orbs in which they collected the smoke.

Riya crouched in front of the fern. She didn't know what she was looking for exactly. It didn't *look* magical, and when she ran a finger over the edge of a thick, waxy leaf, it didn't feel magical either. A part of her had expected that the magic in her veins would somehow recognize it, but after several minutes of staring at it, she began to feel foolish.

"What are you doing here?"

Riya nearly toppled over, putting a hand on the ground to steady her as she looked up at Tarini's heart-shaped face peering down at her in surprise. "Oh. Um. Nothing." She felt her face flush as she stood. "I just couldn't sleep."

Tarini looked at her with empathy. "I understand." She gestured behind her to the garden. "I can give you something for that if you'd like."

"Oh, no, it's fine," Riya said. "Actually . . . can I ask you something?"

"Of course," Tarini said brightly, sweeping her long hair over one shoulder. She'd taken it out of its usual braid, and it hung down nearly to her thighs in loose waves.

"Where did you find the smoke plant that we use?" Riya asked. "Does it grow wild in the forest?"

It was only because Riya had been watching so closely that she noticed Tarini momentarily tensing. But when she spoke, her voice sounded as lighthearted as usual. "No. I got the seeds at a special greenhouse."

"A greenhouse?" Riya's eyes lit up. "Do you remember where?"

This time, Riya definitely didn't imagine the shift in Tarini's demeanor. Her smile faded. "Why are you asking?"

"It's a useful plant to have on hand," Riya answered, not quite truthfully. "I was just wondering if I'd maybe find it on my travels."

Tarini hesitated, but her shoulders seemed to relax a bit. "No," she said. "But feel free to take a few leaves with you if you think it would be helpful on your journey." Without waiting for a response, Tarini leaned over and plucked several leaves near the base of the plant.

Riya stood and accepted the offering, carefully tucking the leaves into the pocket of her kurta. "Thank you for this," she said with a small smile, because it *would* be helpful to have.

"Of course."

"Anyway, sorry for interrupting your night," Riya said. "I should probably head back to camp."

Tarini didn't stop her or say anything else, but Riya felt her eyes following her until she rounded the corner around the inn—and slammed right into a solid chest. Riya gasped as two hands wrapped around her shoulders to steady her. Even before she looked up, she knew it was Varun, glaring down at her.

"What are you doing skulking around in the middle of the night?" she asked. She didn't mean to sound so irritated, but it was the primary emotion he evoked in her. As he let go, she could feel her skin tingling where he'd touched her, and she took a step back from him.

His jaw tightened. "I should be asking you that, considering you don't even live here anymore."

"Only because you lied to them," she said, gesturing back toward the Ravens.

"What would you have me say? That there's no magic? That Ashoka is *doomed*?"

"That I'm fixing it," Riya snapped. "You threw me out for lying to the Ravens. And yet *you* did the same thing."

Varun looked furious for a moment, but he seemed to deflate as his shoulders slumped. "You're right."

Riya opened her mouth. And then closed it. It was so unlike him to back down from a fight—from her—that she felt unmoored. "Why?" she asked, and she found that she genuinely wanted an answer. This wasn't the first time he'd kept a secret on her behalf—a secret that would have changed *every*thing. And she had no idea what to make of that.

He didn't answer, his gaze fixed on some point behind her. But he didn't walk away from her either.

"Say something," she blurted out when she couldn't bear the silence anymore.

"What do you want me to say, Riya?" he asked. There was the usual edge to his words, but he sounded more tired than anything.

"Why?" she asked again. "Why didn't you tell them?"

He looked at her then, and Riya could see the smear of stars above reflected in his eyes. "I don't know." There was rawness to his words, an honesty, but it wasn't enough. She needed more.

"You told me I was done because I was dishonest," Riya insisted. "You said you wouldn't give me time."

"Vaishali's bones, Riya. You asked me to trust you. I did. Will you let it go?"

It struck Riya just how uncomfortable he was. Varun had always been so sure of himself, but looking at him now, he seemed out of his depth.

"Do you?" she asked. "Trust me," she clarified.

He looked conflicted, and then he shook his head. "I don't know," he said again, shrugging helplessly.

She'd known what his answer would be, but hearing it stung anyway. She'd always felt as if he were evaluating her, like every one of their interactions was a test somehow and she never passed. And she was done trying.

Riya stepped around him, but his voice made her freeze.

"You can come back."

All air left her lungs as she turned around, not sure if she'd heard him correctly. "What?" she breathed.

"I can talk to Yash," he said, not quite meeting her gaze. "If you want."

Her heart thudded painfully. She wanted to so badly.

"But Riya." Varun's voice was as sharp as a shard of glass. "You can't keep secrets from me again." He cleared his throat. "Us. Keep secrets from *us*. The Ravens."

Riya swallowed as the latent magic inside her buzzed insistently, a power she couldn't wield or be rid of. But for the first time since Vira had walked into the forest all those weeks ago and upended her life, Riya had a sliver of hope that things could go back to the way they'd been.

"No more secrets," she lied.

CHAPTER FOURTEEN

— VIRA —

VIRA COULDN'T SLEEP. She wished she could blame it on the hard surface of the forest floor, or on the fact that she had to sleep among strangers, or even on the relentless whisper of the wind hissing through the trees. But it was just that she hadn't been able to quiet her mind long enough to relax.

When the first fragments of sunlight dusted the sky a pale blue, Vira left a still sleeping Riya on the mat they'd shared and went to sit by the empty firepit. Morning chill had chased away the humid warmth of the night, so she wrapped her dupatta around her shoulders and sat watching the campsite come to life around her.

It looked even more barren than she'd remembered. It was haphazardly thrown together, clearly built from scraps stolen and stitched together into a patchwork home. But Vira couldn't deny that there was a warmth to it.

She had expected to feel many emotions being here. Anger, irritation, maybe even sadness. But as she watched the Ravens, the feeling that rose to the surface caught her off guard. Jealousy. These bandits, who didn't even have a roof over their heads, had something that all the wealth and privilege and power in the world couldn't give her: a sense of community, not created out of blood or obligation, but from a love for a family that each of them—including Riya—had chosen and pledged themselves to.

As the Ravens began to wake, she could feel their gazes flicking toward her. She felt like she was on display. She was used to stares and gossip, but within the palace, she could use her clothes and her title as armor. They were speaking about the *maharani*, not her. But she didn't have that protection anymore. Now she was just Vira.

And whatever was said felt acutely more personal.

"Relax, Rani," Surya said. "You'll get splinters."

Vira blinked, realizing that she'd been clutching the side of the log too tightly. She let go. "Don't call me that."

She turned to find him sitting cross-legged, facing her, his back perfectly straight despite not having any support. Her mother had trained Vira out of fidgeting years ago, but there was a stillness to the way he held himself that felt a bit unnatural in its unattainability. The kind of stillness one had to develop as a killer hunting prey.

His shoulder-length hair hung around his face in wet waves. He'd evidently bathed in the stream that cut through the glades and shaved off the beard he'd grown during his time in the dungeons. He looked so different. Were it not for the scar that sliced through one eyebrow—and the superiority that laced his voice every time he spoke—Vira might not even have recognized him.

"What do I call you, then?" A corner of his mouth lifted. "Vira?"

She inhaled sharply. So few people had called her by name over the last few years. In fact it had only been her family and . . . Amrit. It was strange hearing her name said in an unfamiliar voice. But it was better than the pain of being called a title she no longer possessed. "That's fine," she forced herself to say.

"You continue to surprise me," he said. "I didn't take you for the sort to associate with rebels, given your *principles*."

Vira's jaw tightened. "I'm not exactly in a position to turn down a safe haven, no matter where it comes from."

"A pragmatist." Surya sounded delighted. "I like that."

Vira didn't need him to like her. She needed him to do what he'd promised: help her find the magic before Amrit found it. "You never told me how you know so much about the Kamala Society," she said.

Surya gave her a measured look. "How much did Amrit tell you?"

"About what?"

"So nothing," Surya said. "Typical." He looked away. "I know about the Kamala Society because we *are* the Kamala Society."

"The *mercenaries*?" Vira stared at him uncomprehendingly, feeling as though all the air was being squeezed out of her lungs. "I don't understand."

"Once, there were three branches," Surya said, as though he were reciting a story from memory. "A lotus for the magic wielders. A scroll of the secret keepers. A sword for the protectors. We were the protectors." He paused. "Are," he amended. "Our existence, our purpose, is for one thing: to protect the Ivory Key at all costs. It was all we ever trained for. All we were ever taught."

A hundred thoughts were racing through Vira's mind, but the only thing she could think to say was, "A scroll? I thought it was two swords." She reached up to her throat only to come up with air. She'd never put the necklace back on. It was still in the palace with the rest of her things.

"Strange, isn't it, how symbols can morph over time?" Surya said. There was a mix of sorrow and pity in his gaze as he finally turned back toward her. "I told you once that the members of the Kamala Society were the original mercenaries." He laughed bitterly. "You know now how true that is."

Vira didn't know what to make of the venom in his tone. It was more emotion than he'd ever shown.

"So Amrit—" She couldn't finish that question. She couldn't speak over the tightness in her throat. How could Amrit not tell her? How could Amrit listen to her talk about the Kamala Society for years and never once show the slightest hint of recognition?

But Surya seemed to know what she was asking. "He was sent to the palace to spy on your father."

"My father?" Vira asked, surprised. But a moment later the answer came to her. "Because he was looking for the key."

"We needed to make sure your father wasn't getting close. And Amrit would have left after he died—"

"Except I took over his investigation," Vira finished.

So Amrit had to stay. He had to get close to her, to find a way to get her to trust and confide in him. It wasn't as though it was a hard task; she'd made it exceedingly easy for him. She'd been so desperate for attention—for someone to *see* her—that all he had to do was pretend to notice the girl beneath the title and she'd voluntarily spilled every one of her secrets.

She felt like she was going to be sick.

"He betrayed me too," Surya said.

It's not the same, Vira wanted to say, but she was afraid she would start to cry if she opened her mouth. Amrit had been her best, most trusted friend. But all she'd ever been to him was an assignment. The entire time she'd been reading meaning into his glances and his smiles and his fleeting touches, he'd been plotting to betray her.

"You said he wants to destroy the key." Vira had to force the words out.

Surya nodded. "That was always his plan. He's convinced that the only way to truly protect the magic and ensure that no one will find the quarries is to destroy every clue left behind."

"He could have already destroyed it." It made her stomach twist to think that she was chasing something that was already gone.

"That's not how he thinks," Surya said. "He would have alerted the elders, because he'd want to do it right, and it'll take time for the society to convene and issue a decision. And—" He held up a hand as she opened her mouth to interrupt him. "You said he doesn't know that Riya made a copy. He has no reason to rush, because he doesn't know that he has to outrun you."

He was right. Amrit, for all that he'd advised her on how to navigate the Council, had made the same mistake that everyone else did: he'd underestimated her. He didn't see her as a threat to his plans. He didn't expect her to find the magic.

Vira watched Surya for a beat. "Why are you helping me?" she asked. It couldn't just be that he didn't want the key destroyed—there had to be something more.

"Because in my experience, buried secrets always come out," he said. It was a nonresponse, just like he'd given her in the dungeons. "And because, like you, I believe that Ashoka needs magic to survive."

It wasn't enough, but she could see Yash, the leader of the Ravens, walking toward them, and she had a feeling that pressing Surya wouldn't yield any more answers—at least not today.

"Riya mentioned that you needed weapons," Yash said. "One of the girls picked up some magical artifacts last night, and you're welcome to look through them and take anything you like."

Picked up. As in, stole. But she didn't comment on that.

Vira eyed Surya, debating whether to arm him or not. But she knew that it made no difference. If he wanted to kill her, he could do it with his bare hands. The two of them followed Yash back toward one of the tents, where another Raven—Varun, she thought his name was—stood guard over a wooden chest.

The weapons were of higher quality than Vira expected, and when she squinted, she could see initials and a family crest carved into the inside corner of the lid. It belonged to one of the noble families then. Surya rummaged through it, taking three small knives and a sword.

"Do you have a spare bow?" Surya asked.

"In the other tent," Yash said, and escorted him out.

Vira crouched down in front of the box, sifting through the weapons until she found a silk pouch with two thin silver bracelets. According to the note of instructions inside, they worked somewhat similarly to the magical shackles that were used in the dungeons. The two bangles couldn't be separated more than several feet—useful for tethering someone to a specific location if needed. Vira pocketed it.

When she rose, she found that Yash was back, watching her carefully.

"Thank you for your hospitality," she said stiffly.

"*Hospitality.*" Yash smiled. "That's such a fancy word for all this." He gestured around him.

Vira took the time to study him. He looked like a leader: handsome, charming, carrying himself with the confidence of someone who knew he was admired. He looked like the kind of person Amma would have liked. He'd always have pretty words—and prettier smiles—to offer. And she didn't think he was lingering there to make small talk.

"If there's something you'd like to say, I'd rather you just say it directly," she told him.

"Our hospitality, as you put it, comes at a cost," he said. "We need some guarantees that the people will be taken care of."

"Guarantees," she echoed, smiling blandly. "It's easy to make demands—to identify flaws and lead a rebellion against a system created by someone else. It's far harder to be on the other side, to be the one actually responsible for addressing those complaints."

The smile dropped from Yash's face. He looked so much older, so much more tired in the stark light of day, when the shadows couldn't hide the circles under his eyes or the way the skin clung to his bones a little too tightly. For a split second, Vira felt a kinship with him. She recognized that soul-deep exhaustion within him.

But it was Varun who responded. "Then perhaps we need a new system."

Of course, a bandit who operated outside the law thought it was that easy. Vira twisted toward him, irritated. The two were brothers, she realized, but the resemblance stopped at their shared traits: their broad shoulders and dark eyes, sharp jawlines and unruly hair. Where Yash's features were softened by frequent laughter, Varun looked like a sculpture come to life, all hard lines and stoic intensity. Yash was exactly what one expected a ruler to be, but as Vira felt the full force of Varun's gaze on her, she had the oddest sensation that Varun was *actually* in charge.

"People aren't asking for a lot," Varun said quietly. "Just for their basic needs to be met. A roof over their heads. Stable jobs so they can care for their families. They don't need protection from invaders—if they felt like the maharani genuinely cared about them and took care of them, they'd happily take up arms and lay down their lives to defend the borders."

He made it sound so simple, so logical, that Vira almost believed him. *Almost*, because the first lesson Amma had instilled in her was that humans were never altruistic—and councilors even less so. Maybe, if she were the kind of ruler that people were devoted to, she could persuade detractors that there was value in what Varun was proposing.

But she'd never been good at inspiring loyalty. After all, that was why she was there, alone in the middle of a forest with nothing to her name and only criminals for allies.

"Look," she said, frustrated, "it's not that I disagree with you."

"It's just that you aren't going to do anything," Yash said, resigned.

"It's more complicated than issuing decrees," Vira said, trying to get them to understand even though she knew they never would. "There are alliances to consider. Politics that will affect trade."

"I suppose we aren't all lucky enough to consider our morals only when it's convenient to do so," Varun said, frustration blazing in his eyes.

"And some of us aren't lucky enough to operate on principles alone," Vira snapped.

The brothers exchanged glances, but they didn't say anything else as they ducked out of the tent. When Vira followed, she found Surya waiting outside with a bow and holding two talwars. He flipped one of the swords, gripping it by the blade and extending it toward Vira. "You look like you could work off some energy." Surya grinned. "And I'm curious to see what my brother taught you."

She didn't move. The last time she'd held a talwar with any intent of using it was when she'd drawn it against Amrit. "We have to leave soon," she said.

He knew it was a flimsy excuse. His smile turned feral. "How will you get your revenge if you won't even pick up a sword?" he said.

"That won't work on me."

Surya stared at her for a moment. "You know he told me about you. He didn't write often, but he did owe the Kamala Society updates. He called you cold. Distant. Unapproachable."

Vira's breath hitched, wishing that his words didn't sting. Amrit was the one person she'd thought had seen beneath the icy veneer she'd been forced to adopt.

"Of course I found that particularly funny," Surya continued, "because that's how most people characterize Amrit."

Every part of Vira told her to ignore his taunts, but she found herself reaching for the talwar anyway and following him toward the far side of the clearing where there were no Ravens. She rolled her shoulders back and tested the weight of the talwar in her hand. It was lighter than she expected—similar to the one she'd trained with, not like the cumbersome one that had once belonged to her mother and that the Council had saddled her with. Across from her, Surya kicked off his shoes, ridding himself of all the other weapons, and tugged up the slightly too long hem of the kurta pants he'd borrowed from the Ravens.

At first they traded easy blows, moving back and forth as Vira's muscles settled into movements and she tried to get a handle on his fighting style. Amrit had always moved with grace, smoothly transitioning between various stances and martial arts styles almost like dancing. Surya on the other hand was efficient and precise, like a cobra moving with almost lazy disinterest—until it was time to deliver the killing blow.

It was disorienting, and all at once Vira remembered just how dangerous Surya was. Mercenaries, Kamala Society—it didn't matter what they called themselves. It didn't change what they were. What they'd been trained to do.

But Vira had let her thoughts distract her, so when Surya drove forward, she didn't move quickly enough. He struck her hand at just the right angle, and the talwar clattered to the ground.

"It seems my brother went easy on you," Surya observed. "On the battlefield, if you lose your weapon, you die."

Vira's eyes blazed as she picked up her talwar again. She attacked first this time—but he grabbed her wrist easily and knocked the weapon out of it again.

And again.

And again.

Amrit had matched his movements to meet Vira where she was, changing his training regimen to suit her skills and needs. Surya gave her no such concessions. He fought the way he wanted, and if she couldn't keep up, she took the hit. And each time he disarmed her, Surya would critique something—her stance, her grip, her balance, her focus—and Vira was growing increasingly irritated.

"Come now, Rani. Surely you can do better than that," Surya taunted. "Change up your patterns."

It was just what Amrit had said, and it upset her irrationally. She swung her talwar forward with a ferocious force, all power and no precision. Surya neatly sidestepped the arc of the blade, but he looked absurdly pleased. "Hit a nerve, did I?" He smirked.

He had, but he'd also unleashed something wild in her. She'd never been particularly good at combat, even before she'd failed the Ashokan army at Ritsar. She'd never been good at strategy either, or pretty words, or inspiring loyalty. In fact, Vira was fairly certain she wasn't good at *anything* except being determined. No matter how many people doubted her—no matter how many times she failed or disappointed those around her—she didn't know how to stop wanting.

"I told you not to call me that," Vira said, and that was all the warning he got before she charged forward. His eyes widened ever so slightly as he brought his weapon up just in time to block her blade. The clash of steel echoed through the air as Vira spun, forcing him to yield ground until he was up against a tree with nowhere to go. She held her talwar to his throat, victory dancing in her eyes. "Drop it."

"Well done," he said, letting his sword fall out of his hand. And then he reached up to Vira's face. "May I?"

Vira stilled as he brushed an errant strand of hair out of her eyes and tucked it behind her ear, his fingers lingering on her skin. "What are you doing?" she said.

Surya used her moment of distraction to grab her hand with the weapon, spinning them around so she was the one pinned against the tree, Surya holding the sword to her neck. He laughed as he lowered the weapon. "If there's one thing you take away from today, it's this: if you want to win, you have to be willing to use whatever tools you have at your disposal."

"Where's the honor in that?" Vira asked, furious at herself for letting him get under her skin. She pushed him away and stalked back toward the camp.

"There's no honor on a battlefield," Surya said, following her. "And I don't mean a literal one either. When my brothers and I would spar, there was nothing that was off-limits. A fight didn't start when we drew our weapons, but long before then. In scraps of information we gathered, studying one another's weaknesses and strengths, in crafting the exact right insult to hurl at an opportune moment." He paused. "You think Amrit didn't use everything in his arsenal to get what he wanted?"

She had nothing to say to that. Surya had picked his words carefully to elicit the exact emotion he wanted in her, and once again, it had worked.

"Just because you don't want to hear it doesn't mean I'm not right," he called after her. "You said you wanted revenge."

"I didn't, actually," she corrected, but they both knew that was a lie. She wanted to plunge her talwar into Amrit's heart just to make sure he had one. She wanted to hurt him just to know that she could.

"Then the fight has already begun," Surya said. "Are you willing to do whatever it takes? Are you prepared for him to try to manipulate your emotions?"

Her heart knocked against her rib cage uncomfortably, but she straightened her spine and steeled her gaze. "Yes."

CHAPTER FIFTEEN

— KALEB —

WHEN KALEB ARRIVED at the library, he expected to be meeting the other scholars. But it was empty save for the librarian at the front and a few early risers hoping to snag the best table for their research.

"Add your name here," the librarian instructed, heaving a giant tome from under the counter when Kaleb introduced himself. Dust motes fluttered through the air as he slammed the book on the table, making Kaleb sneeze. It was a ledger with the name of every scholar who had ever worked there, spanning centuries.

Kaleb waited until the librarian was distracted with another scholar before he carefully flipped through the pages, searching for Papa and Alena's names. He found them both just a few pages apart. It was strange to think they'd touched this very book, flipped through these same pages. As he traced his fingers fondly over the ink, he noticed that both of them had cramped, messy handwriting. Papa had always rushed to get his words out quickly enough, his hand struggling to keep up with his racing thoughts. He wondered if Alena had been the same way.

As the librarian reemerged, Kaleb hastily flipped to the last page and added his name at the very end. He stared at the ink, a twinge of sadness pinching his chest, wishing he could have written his real name instead of Kol.

The librarian directed him toward the back, past rows of sleek tables outfitted with non-magical magnifiers, where a portion of the library had been converted into a makeshift research center until the old building was restored. Kaleb looked around as he walked, marveling at the painted ceilings and ornately carved bookshelves that held the emperor's vast collection. Kaleb had hoped to have a moment alone to explore the space, but he wasn't lucky enough. Hektor was already walking in. He scowled when he saw Kaleb. "You're early."

Kaleb wanted to point out that it was better than being late, but he thought better of it. "I was eager to start."

"Hmm." Hektor didn't look impressed. He led Kaleb toward one of the desks, which was littered with scraps of paper. "This is where you'll be working," he said.

"I don't understand," Kaleb said. He picked up one of the scraps. It held the title of a book. Another contained a topic of interest: how magic could be used in glass objects.

"Your job," Hektor said with a huff of irritation that Kaleb hadn't simply read his mind, "is to assist the other scholars with the research they need to conduct their experiments. Those are their requests. And once you've found the books they need, you can start going through those." Hektor gestured. The librarian was pushing a cart toward them that was piled high with ancient-looking books. "You're to read them cover to cover for any mentions of varying temperatures while processing raw magic."

"Varying temperatures?" Kaleb echoed, but Hektor had evidently decided he was done with the conversation and was already turning away.

"And clean up that mess," Hektor called over his shoulder, waving his hand at the desk.

Kaleb's heart sank. He was nothing more than a glorified assistant, not allowed to do any kind of actual work with magic, but to fetch books and read about experiments others had conducted.

"You can leave the ones that aren't useful on the cart," the librarian added before he too left.

Kaleb sighed and stared at the two other desks there. He'd hoped there would be more scholars joining him to split up the work, but as the minutes wore on, he realized that he was there all alone.

Hektor had ordered him to start with the papers, but Kaleb reached for one of the books on the cart at random. He carefully opened it and read the title. *The Craft of Processing Raw Magic.*

It was easily several decades old, water damaged enough that some of the pages were stuck together. If he'd been back in the mayaka lab in Ashoka, he would have simply gotten some processed magic and woven it into the book to repair it and expel the excess water. But he was in Lyria, where access to magic was limited, so he'd have to painstakingly peel them apart by hand.

He set it aside and scanned the titles of some of the others. *The Origins of Magic Vol. 3. Beyond the Quarries: A Comprehensive Guide to Raw Magic. Unearthing Magic.*

So Lukas was right. The emperor *was* investigating melting raw magic, finding a different way of processing it so it turned to liquid instead of powder. But judging by the number of books, the scholars hadn't made much progress.

Focus on the work, Lukas had said to him.

So that's what he'd do. Rolling up his sleeves, Kaleb sat down and began to read.

✳

Magic fluttered over the skin of Kaleb's right hand, jolting him away from the book he'd been poring over. It took him a moment to notice what had interrupted him: the onyx eye of the wolf ring was missing. Lukas was summoning him.

Kaleb blinked tiredness out of his eyes, trying to get them to focus as he realized he'd lost track of time. Bright sunlight was streaming in through the large windows, and nearly every seat in the library was now taken by the scholars who'd trickled in while he'd been absorbed in a particularly interesting book that outlined the evolution of the tools that were used to excavate magic from the quarries.

The librarian had informed him that the scholars were allowed to set their own schedules, to come and go as they pleased so long as they got their work done, so Kaleb closed the book and rose.

Cold wind raked through his hair the moment he stepped outside, and Kaleb, still not used to the cooler climate, drew his coat tighter around his shoulders. The ring was tugging him toward a large courtyard lined with oak trees and marble benches. It was empty now, save for a lone pigeon pecking at the remnants of an abandoned meal, but the tour guide had said that it was a popular place for scholars to take their breaks.

He crossed the length of the square toward the colonnaded building on the other side. Sunlight filtered through the space between the pillars, striping the broad stone steps of the sanctuary in gold and gray.

The building had caught his attention earlier while he'd been exploring the grounds with Dayana. At first he hadn't thought anything of it—it looked the same as any other sanctuary he'd seen around the capital. But as they walked past the steps, he'd been hit with a sudden flash of memory, Papa's voice echoing in his head so clearly he couldn't believe he'd ever forgotten it.

My favorite place in the palace was the sanctuary. It was strange how peaceful I felt, surrounded by unfamiliar idols and rituals so different from our own. I'd often spend my free time there, just sitting quietly, absorbing the energy.

Beyond answering any questions that Kaleb asked, Papa hadn't spoken often of his time in the Lyrian palace. It was rare for him to divulge anything of his own volition, but this had been one such detail—something important enough that he'd wanted Kaleb to know about it.

As a child, Kaleb had carefully preserved every scrap of information his father had ever shared about Lyria, treasuring and hoarding details for the day when he and Papa could finally visit the country together. But Papa was gone. He'd never gotten the chance to show Kaleb around his former home. And the thought that the memories Kaleb had once held close—memories that were all he had left of his father—were fading was too much for him to bear.

The ring was telling him to go inside, so he slowly climbed the steps. The wooden doors opened into an antechamber where other visitors had left their sandals. Kaleb toed off his own shoes, adding them to the small collection. It was surprising that there were only a handful, considering the sanctuary was open to the entire palace, nobles and servants alike. But then again, it *was* still early in the day, and most devout people tended to pray in the evening hours before twilight.

The interior of the temple was not so different from places of worship in Ashoka. There was only a single main hall, flanked by more smooth columns that led toward the far end of the room, which housed altars to the four primary goddesses the Lyrians worshipped. The slabs of marble that made up the floor had been polished until they shone, gleaming in the light streaming in through large windows near the vaulted ceiling.

Two ornate metal lamps stood beside the base of each column, fitted with candles that would be lit after sunset.

But unlike Ashokan temples, where the walls and pillars were full of extravagant carvings depicting stories from legend, there wasn't much to see here beyond the sculptures of the goddesses themselves.

Yet Kaleb could understand why Papa had liked this place so much. There *was* a serenity, a stillness, and Kaleb could picture Papa sitting with his back against one of the walls, meditating. Kaleb exhaled. It had been a long time since he'd meditated—or had a clear mind. It felt like his thoughts were so muddled these days, torn between his family in Ashoka and his family in Lyria and the challenges that came with being a spy.

He scanned the area for any sign of Lukas, finally spotting him near one of the altars. Except he wasn't alone. Kaleb hesitated, not wanting to interrupt. But when the figure turned, Kaleb recognized him at once from the statue: Elias, the other prince.

Unable to help himself, Kaleb crept a little closer, grateful for the wide columns that kept him out of sight as he took a moment to observe the two princes.

Up close, he could see that they did bear a family resemblance. Despite being elder, Elias was shorter than Lukas, a little stockier, with longer hair that curled around his ears. He was dressed in his formal military wear, and though Kaleb couldn't make out the details, he could see a round patch attached to the sleeve of his dark blue tunic that, as Dayana had pointed out, signified his rank as general.

"—going to get suspicious if you're not cautious," Elias was saying. He stood with his arms crossed over his broad chest, clearly irritated.

Lukas, on the other hand, carried himself with a quiet confidence, an easy aloofness as he stood with his back against one of the pillars.

"Aren't I always?" he asked carelessly. But Kaleb could see the way his shoulders tensed ever so slightly, as though his casual demeanor were nothing more than an act.

Kaleb strained to hear Elias's low voice. "Father's not the type to—"

"I can handle Father," Lukas said. "He doesn't suspect me."

"I suppose this is where it helps to be the favorite child," Elias said. It was meant to be a sharp retort, but there was an obvious undercurrent of envy beneath those words. And given the beat of silence that lingered in the air, Lukas heard it, too.

"Elias, *please*," Lukas said. "I just need this one thing from you."

"And in exchange?" Elias prompted.

"What do you want?"

Elias mulled it over. "The house in the south. The one attached to the winery that Father gifted you for your birthday last year."

Lukas smiled dryly, looking down at his feet. "Ah." He bit the inside of his cheek. "Is that all that matters to you? Properties and promotions?"

"Can you do it or not?" Elias demanded impatiently. "I've got places to be."

"It's yours," Lukas said.

"Excellent. I'll make some inquiries." Elias turned to leave, and Kaleb hastily realized he was in the prince's path.

Kaleb took a step back—right into one of the candleholders. It tumbled to the ground, metal crashing into the marble floor with a loud clang. Both princes whirled toward him in sudden shock. Kaleb felt his face flush a deep red as he hurried to right the lamp.

Elias's eyes narrowed as Kaleb mumbled an apology and then hurried toward the altar, his heart racing. He took a deep breath, willing his embarrassment to fade as he stared up at one of the sculptures without actually processing anything he was seeing.

Seconds later, Kaleb heard footsteps approaching. He knew even before he turned that it was Lukas.

"Well," Lukas said, looking at him with a mix of annoyance and interest. "That was certainly some entrance."

"I really didn't mean to—"

"Eavesdrop?" Lukas raised an eyebrow.

Kaleb didn't deny it. "I'm sorry," he said again, hoping he sounded sincere. "I didn't want to interrupt, but I should have walked away."

Lukas shrugged. "It doesn't matter. It's not like it's a secret." But it was clear it *did* matter to him.

The wise thing would be to avoid the subject entirely, to ask Lukas why he'd been summoned, and here of all places. But Kaleb had never been good at doing the smart thing. "Has he . . . was it always like this between you?"

"Transactional?" Lukas asked, smiling, though there was little humor in it. "Believe it or not, we were close once. But as you pointed out, I *am* to be named heir and Elias has not forgiven me for our father's decision." He laughed a little. "You must think I'm nothing more than a privileged prince, complaining about being the emperor."

"No . . . I—" *I understand*, Kaleb had almost said. He knew all too well what one had to give up for power and status. "It's unfair that the throne comes at the cost of losing your brother."

"Unfair," Lukas echoed. "It wasn't as though I asked for it. I had my life mapped out."

This, too, Kaleb understood. "Then why not abdicate? You must have considered it."

"Because I'd be the better ruler." Lukas said it simply, as though it were a fact, and the raw honesty of the confession surprised Kaleb. "It's why Elias never contested it. He doesn't actually want the responsibilities of running a country. He's only upset that he lost face being passed over."

Succession in Ashoka was so different—so much more straightforward. There had never been any doubt that Vira would be the maharani. Kaleb and Ronak had never had any claim at all, and Riya, who'd be the next in line until Vira had any children of her own, had never wanted it. But for the first time Kaleb found himself wondering if Vira felt the same as Lukas, falling into the role simply because of circumstances rather than an actual desire. But perhaps that was what made for the best rulers, the ones who treated it as a job to excel at rather than being intoxicated by power.

"Can I ask you something?" Kaleb asked after a beat.

Lukas looked at him. "Why am I spying on my father?" he guessed. "Would you believe it's out of the goodness of my heart?"

"Is it?" Kaleb asked.

"Something like that." He ran a hand through his hair. "Elias calls it a misguided hero complex, but I can't help but think that whatever my father is doing will result in bad consequences for innocent citizens. Elias is happy to ignore our father's actions as long as they serve his interests. I can't."

Kaleb tried to judge the sincerity of the pronouncement. Lukas *sounded* like he was being truthful, but perhaps he was just a good actor. But Kaleb couldn't deny that this conversation—and witnessing the private interaction between the brothers—had shed new light on the situation.

A bell rang in the distance, signaling the time. It brought Kaleb to the present as he realized they'd been standing there talking for far too long. Lukas seemed to realize that at the same time because he suddenly turned toward Kaleb and cleared his throat.

"I found out that my father is organizing a trip in two weeks," Lukas said. "To Ashoka."

"Ashoka?" Kaleb echoed, shocked.

"The maharani of Ashoka is sending emissaries to meet with my father," Lukas said, his voice oddly distant. "They're set to arrive tomorrow to formally initiate peace negotiations."

Kaleb's mind was still trying to process the fact that Vira had sent Ashokan dignitaries—that after all the trouble they'd gone through, she'd simply caved and done what the Council wanted.

But perhaps that wasn't too surprising. Maybe Ronak was right. Maybe she did want their approval more than she claimed.

"I'm having Elias look into the details," Lukas continued. "But I know he's taking several members of his army as well as artificers working on some special project. There's no diplomatic reason for him to take them, and I have a bad feeling that whatever my father is doing with magic is connected to this trip. You need to find out what that is and ensure that you're selected to join them."

"What? How am I supposed to do that?" Kaleb asked. Hektor wasn't exactly his biggest fan. He didn't think he could simply walk into the room and ask.

"I don't know," Lukas said. "I can't help you directly because Hektor or my father can't find out that we know one another. It's not safe for you."

Kaleb stared at him for a moment. He'd assumed that Lukas wanted to rule and that spying on his father was in service of ensuring that he would. The idea that he might simply want to do the right thing—that he might genuinely care about the fate of his country and its citizens— seemed almost impossible.

And yet, wasn't that why Kaleb was in Lyria?

"All right," Kaleb said. "I'll find a way."

CHAPTER SIXTEEN

— RONAK —

As the carriage hurtled along the sand-dusted roads of the Inara Desert on the way to Lyria, Ronak leaned his head back against the seat cushion and feigned sleep. They'd been traveling for the better part of two days, and he *was* tired from being trapped in a cramped space for most of that time, but the real reason for the pretense was that he didn't want to make uncomfortable conversation with Jay and Preethi—the two people he'd specifically been evading for days.

He'd been the one to suggest that Preethi accompany him, and he'd accepted that he'd have to play the role of the happily engaged couple that the Council expected them to present. But what had been shocking was discovering that Jay was *also* here.

Unbeknownst to Ronak, Jay had evidently decided days earlier that he would accompany his brother Kunaal—the original representative the Council had intended to send to Lyria.

"I thought I'd give you some space," Jay had murmured in explanation when the two of them showed up at the same time to board the carriages, stunned to see the other.

The tension had only gotten worse when Preethi also arrived. Preethi had looked between the two of them carefully, accurately determining that

Jay had in fact told Ronak that she and Jay had been romantically involved before Preethi's untimely engagement to Ronak. The three of them had clambered in after Kunaal, and after thirty minutes of painful small talk, Ronak had very maturely decided the best way to deal with the situation was to ignore it altogether.

You're here for Kaleb, he reminded himself. Preethi and Jay and the rest of the Council were irrelevant. All he had to do was get through the two weeks, and once he had the emperor's compass, he could use it to barter for Kaleb's freedom. His stomach lurched at the thought that it would be the Council he'd be negotiating with, not Vira. Despite all that had happened between them, Ronak knew with absolute certainty that as long as there was definitive proof that Kaleb had been framed, Vira would have exonerated him without hesitation.

He still hadn't wrapped his mind around the fact that Vira was no longer the maharani—that she hadn't been the one to organize this trip to Lyria like he'd initially believed. There hadn't been a successful coup in centuries, but it wasn't only that. Ronak simply couldn't fathom a world in which Vira wasn't the ruler. And every time he thought about it, there was a knot in the pit of his stomach, threads of complex, conflicting emotions too painful and raw for him to want to untangle.

Councilor Meena had been waiting for him beside the carriages, raising a brow as though surprised to see him.

"You're still here," she'd proclaimed unceremoniously.

"I like my life, and I'd like to keep living it," Ronak had said, seeing no use in pretending that he didn't know what she was talking about. "I don't know where they disappeared to," he'd added pointedly.

"I didn't ask," Meena responded, but he hadn't missed the slight scowl hinting that perhaps she was lying. "If Vira wants to run off and live her life in exile, that's no concern of mine."

"You're not worried?" he asked, genuinely taken aback by her cavalier attitude.

"Why should I be?" Meena said. "She has no public support with the people, and your sister is smart enough not to reveal that she is no longer in power."

She was underestimating Vira. If there was one thing Ronak knew about his sister, it was how much she valued her title—her role of maharani—over everything else in her life. He didn't know how they couldn't sense her hunger. It was all he'd ever been able to see.

"One more thing," Meena said. "It would be best if the emperor remains unaware of the fact that your sister is no longer in charge here. We don't want to project an air of instability in the middle of negotiations that are so crucial to the future of Ashoka."

Perhaps you should have thought about that before you ousted Vira, Ronak thought. It was probably why they'd opted to keep her in the dungeons instead of simply killing her—so they could trot her out as a puppet when needed.

"The emperor won't find out from me," Ronak promised before climbing into the carriage.

As the carriage began to slow down, a hand shook Ronak's shoulder. He blinked his eyes open just as they stopped in front of the inn where they'd be spending the night. Warm desert air blew through the vehicle as Kunaal pushed the door open. As Ronak disembarked, he instinctively lifted a hand to shield his eyes from the sand.

The sun had nearly set, and swatches of orange and purple bruised the twilight sky behind the large sandstone manor. They were far from civilization, and sand dunes stretched endlessly as far as the eye could see. Palm trees lined the walkway that led to an arched entrance that opened out into a large courtyard where servants awaited them with platters holding spiced buttermilk.

As the innkeeper greeted them with a deep bow, Ronak gratefully accepted one of the chilled tumblers to quench his thirst. They weren't traveling with formal royal banners or a full retinue of guards, but every inn they'd stopped at along the way had quickly identified them as, at the very least, extremely wealthy patrons.

As the innkeeper led them to their rooms, he prattled on about the owner—a wealthy perfumer whose family had spent generations honing the craft of creating the oil-based attars that were famous in the neighboring province of Vrindh. Ronak was only half listening, his gaze instead sweeping through the beautiful parlors that they passed, each filled with framed paintings and elaborate designs inlaid in the mosaic tiles that made up the walls. He wanted to explore them thoroughly, but they weren't staying here very long; it was merely a place to sleep before they'd cross the border into Lyria in the morning.

Ronak had every intention of spending the night sequestered in his room, requesting that his dinner be brought there as well, but when he emerged from his bath dressed in clean clothes free of sweat and sand, there was a note that a special dinner for the four of them had been arranged in one of the private parlors. It was in Jay's familiar handwriting, which meant that this was a personal request rather than a political one. Still, Ronak hesitated, torn between wanting to maintain his distance from Jay and Preethi and being tired of his own company.

In the end, he allowed himself to be escorted downstairs by servants. He was the last to arrive, so he took the empty seat left for him between Jay and Kunaal. Moments later, steaming platters were set in front of them: rice flavored with dried fruit, cinnamon bark, and slivered almonds; onion kachori drizzled with mint and date chutneys; thick bread doused in ghee and steaming hot daal; oven-roasted eggplant simmered in a tomato and onion sauce.

"This is the last Ashokan meal we'll have for a while," Kunaal reminded them, ladling heaping portions of everything onto his plate. "Eat well, because we don't know how things might be in the palace."

It was so like Kunaal to be worried about disliking the food they'd be served in Lyria that almost instinctively Ronak turned toward Jay, a smile shared between them. But then they both simultaneously remembered that it wasn't like that between them anymore. They quietly returned to their meals, and Ronak pretended he didn't miss the way things used to be.

"Did you sleep well?" Preethi asked. "You must have been tired."

It took Ronak a moment to realize she was addressing him. "Oh. Um. Yes," he said.

He knew he should ask her something in return, especially since she'd been the only one to ask Ronak how he was doing after the coup, but he didn't know what to say. She looked a little disappointed that he wasn't going to continue the conversation, especially when neither Jay nor Kunaal made any attempt to speak.

The meal was spent in uncomfortable silence. Preethi excused herself first, saying that she was tired from the day and wished to sleep. Kunaal left after that to find the innkeeper and settle their bill, leaving Ronak and Jay alone.

"Well," Ronak said dryly. "That was a fun dinner."

Jay didn't meet his gaze. "You decided how things would be between us, Ro. I didn't want this."

"I didn't either." He missed his friend, and he wanted to call a truce.

"You said you didn't intend to marry her," Jay said. "Is that still true?"

"It is."

"Does she know that?"

"I'll tell her," Ronak said slowly. "I'm not just going to leave without a word."

Jay shook his head. "Just . . . keep her out of whatever you're doing with Ekta."

Ronak frowned. He'd never intended to involve her, so promising Jay would be easy, but this wasn't how he'd expected the conversation to go. A part of him wanted to point out that Preethi wasn't entirely innocent here—that she was using Ronak just as much as he was using her. She was here because she wanted the title, not because she cared about Ronak.

But for once, Ronak didn't respond impulsively. "I'll keep her out of it," he said, and then exhaled deeply. *Swallow your pride*, he told himself. "Can we just put this behind us and try to . . . I don't know? Go back to how things used to be?"

Ronak bit his lip, nervous as he waited for Jay's response.

Jay nodded. "All right," he agreed.

✳

Lyria was different from what Ronak had imagined. Based on Papa's stories and the way it was depicted in the historical texts he'd been forced to study as a child, he'd expected it to be a drab place, full of militaristic regulations and serious people. But the capital city was as vibrant as Dvar, bursting with just as much color and energy. Flowering vines crawled up the sides of buildings with brightly painted windowsills and shutters, and people in colorful tunics and gowns spilled out of the stores that lined the wide streets.

"I didn't think it would be so busy," Preethi said, peering out the window on her side as they slowed to allow pedestrians to cross the street. Two young boys rushed past, carrying rolled-up rugs on their shoulders, while a vendor pushed a cart advertising steaming hot coffee and pastries.

"I didn't think the palace was so close to the city center," Jay added, looking over her shoulder at the towers in the distance piercing the blue sky.

Ronak, Preethi, Jay, and Kunaal were in the first of four carriages the Council had sent on their journey. The second two held their clothes and supplies as well as expensive gifts for the emperor and his family. The last one contained several chests of raw magic—the very last of what had been mined from the now completely empty quarries. It was intended to be a gift from the Council to prove that they were willing to negotiate in good faith. Ronak thought it was a terrible idea to give the emperor the very thing he'd attempted to invade Ashoka for, but he'd kept his mouth shut when Meena had informed them what was inside each vehicle.

Ronak, tired of being cooped up in a carriage for nearly three days, was looking forward to arriving at the palace. His stomach was in knots, nervous energy coiling through him as he thought about Kaleb. He hoped his brother was safe. And he hoped even more that he'd be able to find this mysterious device full of the emperor's memories and leave with Kaleb.

The carriage turned onto a quieter street leading toward the spires of the palace, and Ronak finally indulged his curiosity and lifted the curtain over the window closest to him. He could see lush green gardens and elaborate fountains that lined the cobblestone path leading to the entrance. The carriage stopped, and two armed guards rapped on the side of the door, waiting for Kunaal to present their formal invitation from the emperor. The guards searched all the carriages and then let them pass through several sets of wrought iron gates, following a road flanked by date palms.

As they disembarked, they were greeted by a retinue of servants and guards waiting to escort them to the throne room, where the emperor waited. Ronak, as the rajkumaara, didn't need to bow, but he did anyway, his palms pressed in front of his chest in the Ashokan style.

"Oh, come now," the emperor said, speaking in heavily accented Ashokan. "There's no need for all that formality."

He looked younger than the fifty years that Ronak knew him to be—his hair barely graying, his face still mostly devoid of wrinkles. His light brown eyes twinkled as he rose from his throne and walked down the stairs toward Ronak, a wide smile on his face. He was as tall as Ronak, but he was considerably more muscular, his tunic stretching across his defined shoulders. And just like the time that he'd visited Ashoka, the emperor was wearing a small and sleek silver compass on a chain around his neck.

"Thank you for receiving us as your guests," Ronak said, switching to Lyrian as was considered polite. He held out the formal document from the Council of Ashoka inviting the emperor to Shantha Mahal.

The emperor accepted it but spared it nothing more than a cursory glance before handing it off to an attendant. "We'll have plenty of time for politics," he said dismissively, continuing the conversation in Lyrian. "Let me look at you." He gripped Ronak by both shoulders, studying him like a father examining his son after time away. "My dear boy, you look the spitting image of your father."

He pulled Ronak into a tight embrace—like they were family or old friends—and it caught Ronak off guard. His mother would never have acted this informally. He could barely remember a time when she'd embraced *him*, let alone a visitor from another country.

"I didn't know you knew my father so well," Ronak admitted. Papa had rarely spoken of his time in Lyria, and when he had, it was about the mundane elements of his life with Alena, his first wife and Kaleb's mother. He hadn't mentioned the palace much. Or the emperor.

"Oh yes," the emperor said. "He was a brilliant scholar, and we were lucky to have him here. I was sorry to hear about his passing." He glanced over at Preethi, Jay, and Kunaal, standing behind Ronak. "Come," he said, waving them to follow as he put an arm around Ronak's shoulder to guide him. "Let me escort you to your rooms."

It seemed beneath the emperor's station, but Ronak didn't protest. He didn't know what he'd expected, but it certainly wasn't this kind of warm greeting. They walked through vast colonnaded halls and statue-laden courtyards, the walls and vaulted ceilings full of artwork depicting stories of Lyrian mythology.

"I'd be happy to offer you a tour," the emperor said, watching him take in the space.

Ronak didn't want to pass up the chance to see the grounds and the scholar quarters where Kaleb would be, but he didn't want to sound too eager. "I don't want to impose," he said politely.

"I insist," the emperor said. "We've got a truly impressive collection of art and books and artifacts, and I so rarely get to show it all off." He laughed, and the sound echoed around them.

"Thank you," Ronak said. "I look forward to it."

As they approached what looked to be the residential wing of the palace, the emperor finally stopped, gesturing that they should follow the servants. "Please rest and recover from your travels," he said. "We've organized a gathering to welcome our Ashokan friends into our home after so long. I hope you'll do me the honor of joining me and my court tonight."

"Of course." Ronak responded automatically, though it was the very last thing he *wanted* to do. He didn't like public functions full of court politics and boring discussions of local affairs. But this was what he'd come here to do: get close enough to the emperor to steal his compass.

"The honor is ours," Preethi added.

When Ronak opened the door to his room, he discovered that his belongings had been brought inside and unpacked. The four of them had been given separate rooms—Jay and Kunaal's at the end of the corridor, and Preethi's right next to his.

They were nice rooms, decorated in silk and marble, simpler than anything in Ashoka but no less rich. A set of double doors opened out onto a balcony overlooking the grounds. From his vantage point Ronak could see artfully carved hedges and shaded walkways surrounding a pristine lake with a gazebo in the center.

He turned away as he heard a knock at his door. He opened the door, surprised to find Preethi there.

"Can I come in?" she asked.

"What's wrong?" They hadn't really talked beyond communicating necessities.

"Did something happen between you and Jay?" she asked directly. "You weren't speaking much during the trip."

"Did something happen between *you* and Jay?" Ronak returned. He didn't want to keep pretending that he didn't know that his best friend was in love with his fiancée.

Preethi looked down, fiddling with a bangle on her wrist. "He told you."

"Not in so many words, but it's pretty clear that I'm in the middle of something I have no desire being involved in." When she didn't immediately respond, he added, "You're free to run off with him. We are in another country after all. No one would notice."

It would certainly make things a lot easier for Ronak.

"If I wanted to run away with him, I wouldn't have needed to go to another country to do it," Preethi said sharply. "I made my choice."

"Power over love," Ronak said, unable to keep the bitterness out of his voice. Just like his mother. Just like Vira. And look where that had landed them—dead and exiled.

Preethi lifted her chin defiantly. "You don't know anything about me," she said. "You don't get to judge my choices, not when you have power and choose to squander it."

"You think *I* have power? You know nothing about this title you want so badly—of the conditions and shackles attached to it. And let's not pretend that you're a commoner." He knew her background—her family's considerable wealth and political power.

"And let's not pretend that you understand what it's like to be the most skilled person in a room and constantly overlooked." Preethi's eyes flashed with anger. "Your prison is better than most, *rajkumaara*. The rest of us have even tighter shackles."

Ronak opened his mouth and then closed it. Because he did know what that was like. Maybe not about being skilled, but being overlooked. Being underestimated.

He'd been so sure that they had nothing in common. But maybe they did. And perhaps they could have become friends—if one of them getting what they wanted didn't mean that the other would lose everything.

"We should get ready," he said quietly. "We don't want to keep the emperor waiting."

Preethi looked at him for a long while before walking out without another word.

CHAPTER SEVENTEEN

— RIYA —

WHEN RIYA WOKE, she felt feverish. Her eyelids were heavy, and when she sat up, her head was spinning. Yet she knew it wasn't an illness. It was her magic. The power seemed to be telling her it needed to be unleashed.

But she wouldn't. She *couldn't*—not when the Ravens could get hurt.

It was still early in the morning, and the camp was deserted. The Ravens were either sleeping or out on various assignments. Just a few weeks ago she'd have known exactly where everyone was and what they were doing, but that was information she wasn't privileged to have anymore.

Riya rolled up the woven straw mat and blankets she'd shared with Vira, tossing them inside one of the tents. When she returned to gather her belongings, she noticed black ink on one of the mayaka-forged sheets of paper. It was in Ronak's handwriting, messily scrawled like he'd been in a hurry, and she had to squint to make out some of the words.

I found some information on the Order of the Mayura that you might find interesting. According to one of Papa's books, they were (are?) people who worshipped a goddess that they believe would one day return from the dead and grant her loyal acolytes great power. They were originally connected to some place known as the

Crimson Fortress, but I couldn't find a record of any fort with that name. The Order used to have bases throughout Ashoka where they would conduct ritual sacrifices and recruit new members, but it seems like most of those were destroyed centuries ago. The last confirmed location I could find was a greenhouse in Tasgarh. However, the book I found was written eighty-five years ago. I have no idea if it's still in use, but it might be worth looking into. I also found a description of their crest: a peacock with ferns instead of feathers fanned out behind it. I hope some of this is helpful. Stay safe.

A greenhouse in Tasgarh. Tarini had already been living in Dvar when she joined the Ravens, but Riya knew she'd grown up in the Harya province, in a town close to Tasgarh. Maybe it was a coincidence. Or maybe this was the same greenhouse where Tarini had gotten the seeds for the plants in her garden.

Riya glanced up at where Vira and Surya were talking on the far side of the camp. But instead of approaching them, Riya stuffed Ronak's note deeper into her bag and walked out of the clearing. She didn't make her way to the nearby stream the Ravens usually used but the larger Dhaya River that cut through the forest. It was farther away but it would be empty at this hour, and Riya wanted some time to herself.

She took a deep breath and looked at her reflection in the water. She looked . . . different. Her eyes were too wide, her skin too flushed, her hair wild around her shoulders as it fell out of the loose braid she'd put it in. She'd taken off all the jewelry and the expensive clothes she'd worn to Indra's engagement party, but she hadn't washed her face, so the kaajal the maidservants had used to line her eyes was smeared, lending her an air of ferocity.

A bird flitted down from the trees, skimming the surface of the water. Ripples shattered the image.

As she submerged herself in the cold water, the searing haze of the magic retreated a bit and slowly rational thought returned to her.

You can come back.

Varun's words had been exactly what she wanted to hear. It was a second chance to prove herself to the Ravens.

But her mind kept drifting back to the guard at the palace—to the vacant look in his eyes as he'd crumpled to the ground. She'd only meant to push him away, and the fact that he'd gotten hurt made her gut twist with guilt and regret. She'd seen the way that Vira and Ronak had looked at her with such horror and fear, and the notion that the Ravens might look at her the same way made Riya's stomach churn. Maybe the book on meditation Ronak had given her would help her learn how to control this power, but she didn't know how long that would take or how many people she'd harm in the process.

By the time she'd pulled herself out of the water, gotten dressed, and settled on the grass, she knew one thing for sure: she couldn't stay here. She tugged her still-wet hair over one shoulder, combing through it with her fingers as she considered Ronak's note and her conversation with Tarini.

Finding one specific greenhouse in Tasgarh was a long shot, but she had to try something. If it was true that this order had actually been successful in fusing magic with living things, maybe they'd know how to remove it. She didn't want to get her hopes up, but the thought of being rid of this power once and for all was too tempting.

When Riya went back to the campsite, Vira was waiting near one of the tents. She'd also bathed judging by the damp curls that hung loose around her shoulders. She was fully dressed and packed. Surya was nearby, sharpening the weapons that Riya assumed he'd taken from the Ravens.

"Where have you been?" Vira demanded as soon as she saw Riya.

Riya pulled her sister away from the tents, glancing over her shoulder and then up at the trees to make sure no one was close enough to overhear them. "I need to talk to you."

Vira was immediately on guard. "About what?"

"You'll have to go to Paliya on your own," Riya said. "I'll meet you there, but there's something I have to do first."

"Which is?"

Riya hesitated, wondering how much to say. Vira wasn't the one with magic. She didn't understand. But Vira wouldn't let her leave without an explanation. "I want to find the Order of the Mayura."

"The *cult*?" Vira asked, far too loudly.

"Shh!" Riya looked around again, but they were still alone. "Keep your voice down."

"Surya said they were dangerous," Vira said.

"I know what he said, but forgive me if I don't take the word of a murderer. They might be able to help me."

Vira shook her head. "No. You can't go."

"*Can't?*" Riya's eyes narrowed. "That's not your decision to make."

"It is when it concerns the safety of our country," Vira said, scowling. "You can't just go around telling strangers that—"

"Is that truly all you care about?" Riya cut in, furious. "That people will find out?"

"It's not safe for you either, Riya. How do you know you can trust them?"

"How do I know I can't?" Riya countered. "We trusted the Kamala Society and look how that turned out."

Vira glared at her, but she couldn't argue with that. "Fine, if you really want to do this then I want to come with you. Once we find the quarries—"

It was Riya's turn to shake her head. "I'm not asking for permission, Vira. You saw what happened back at the palace. I can't control this. And maybe you don't care if more people get hurt, but it's *my* hands that will be covered in blood. *My* soul that will be marred."

Guilt flickered over Vira's face, as though she was only just realizing how much this was affecting Riya. "You were the one who wanted to do this together," Vira said quietly.

"Don't," Riya said harshly. "Don't act like I'm the one keeping *you* at arm's length when you've spent weeks neglecting my advice and pretending that nothing happened at Ritsar. Unlike you, I can't just ignore this until it goes away."

For a moment Vira looked so vulnerable that Riya's resolve wavered. But she held firm. She needed to do this now whether or not Vira approved.

"I'll meet you at the temple by noon in two days' time," Riya said. Paliya was farther away from the Swapna Forest than Tasgarh. It would take Vira a day and half to get there—which gave Riya plenty of time to find this greenhouse, get answers, and journey north to meet her sister.

"Fine," Vira agreed unhappily.

Riya split the remaining mayaka-forged paper and stolen jewelry between the two of them. Vira huffed at the sight of the gold that had once sat on her vanity table, but she wordlessly accepted the half Riya handed her.

"It's a straight path out of the forest," Riya said. "You'll be safe with Surya." She didn't know what his end goal was, but she believed he wanted to keep Vira alive—at least for the time being. "Stick to the main roads," she added as she slung her bag over her shoulder. "You should reach the edge of the forest well before nightfall. There's a town just outside, and you'll be able to hire a carriage there."

"Wait, you're not going to say anything to the Ravens?" Vira asked as Riya turned away from the camp.

Riya shrugged. She didn't know what to tell them. They would ask questions she didn't want to answer. "It'll be easier this way," she said, hating how much like Amma—like Vira—she sounded.

The look on Vira's face was unreadable. "Be careful."

"You too."

As Riya took one last look around the campsite, she caught a blur of movement out of the corner of her eye. Kavita's familiar features peered out from between the trees, looking at her first with confusion, and then disappointment as her gaze slid to Riya's bag.

"Kavs, wait," Riya said, but Kavita disappeared before Riya could try to muddle her way through an explanation.

Riya hesitated. She owed Kavita a real conversation. But she also knew that having it now would only lead to another fight.

When I come back, Riya told herself. Once she'd gotten rid of her magic and unlocked the quarries, she'd come back to the Ravens and finally tell Kavita everything.

Despite what she'd told Vira, Riya knew the fastest way to Tasgarh would be veering off the larger paths. It made Riya a little nervous—she wasn't as familiar with the forest closer to the Harya border, and while she could navigate using the sun and stars, it had been a long time since she'd done anything on her own. She'd always paired up with someone. Usually Kavita.

Riya sighed and tried not to think about the Ravens.

It was still early enough that the forest was quiet, except for the drone of insects and the chirping of birds—which was why, when she heard the rustle of leaves, Riya was immediately on high alert, one hand on the dagger at her waist as she twisted around.

"Varun?" She lowered her arm, confused. "What are you doing here? Is Vira all right?"

"You were just going to *leave*?" He looked furious as he stalked toward her.

"Wait . . . you *followed* me?" Riya scanned the forest behind him, half expecting more Ravens to appear.

"Where are you going?" he demanded.

"It's none of your business."

"You left your sister behind."

Riya's eyes narrowed. "Vira's leaving any minute. And she can take care of herself."

But Varun didn't let it go. "You said no more secrets," he reminded her.

She'd lied to him again, and they both knew it. "It's personal," she said evasively.

"Personal?" His brows furrowed, as if he couldn't fathom what that even meant. Maybe he couldn't. The Ravens didn't exactly have a life outside of the forest. A few had families in other provinces but most of them had joined because they had nothing else—no one else.

Riya stood up to her full height—still nearly a head shorter than he was—determined to look him in the eyes. "You're not entitled to know everything about me just because you decided to involve yourself in my life."

He looked taken aback, and then a little guilty. "I didn't mean—" His eyes grew wide and he abruptly grabbed her elbow and tugged her toward him.

Caught off guard, she stumbled forward, crashing into his chest just as searing pain erupted through her left shoulder. She gasped, feeling like her skin was on fire. Varun swore as he wrapped an arm around her waist and spun them.

A distant part of her registered just how close they were standing, pressed up against each other behind a tree that was barely wide enough to hide both of them. She could feel the pads of his fingers digging into her side, feel the hammering of his heart beneath her palm.

She used her free hand to reach over her shoulder blade, where an arrow had pierced her; her fingers came away sticky with blood. "Someone shot me," she said, a little dazed.

All the color had drained from Varun's face as he looked at her with a mixture of shock and fear. "We have to get out of here." He carefully peered around the tree trunk—then jerked back as another arrow whistled through the air and embedded itself in the earth. Riya hissed in pain at the sudden movement. "Sorry," he whispered. "Are you all right?"

"Of course not," Riya said through gritted teeth. *"There's an arrow in my shoulder."* The pain radiating down her arm was muddling her thoughts, flooding her brain with fury. She could feel her magic start to wake.

Not now, she begged, squeezing her eyes closed.

"What's wrong?" Varun asked. "Riya?"

"Nothing." Riya forced her eyes open and immediately regretted it when she saw the concern creasing Varun's forehead. She didn't need his help and she certainly didn't need his pity. "I'm going to make a run for it," she announced, trying to tug herself free of his grip.

"What?" Varun asked, alarmed. "You can't just run off."

Riya was tired of people telling her what she couldn't do. "Yes, I can. I was doing just fine on my own before you showed up," she snapped.

Varun flinched, and Riya pretended not to notice the hurt flickering across his face. She wouldn't feel guilty, not when he was the reason she'd gotten hurt in the first place. He'd distracted her, gotten under her skin, and she'd stopped paying attention to everything around her.

"You're hurt," he said.

"I'm *fine*."

"We don't even know who's attacking us or what they want," Varun said. "Just—just give me a second to think."

There were other bandits who used the forest as a hideout, but it had been a long time since any of them had attacked the Ravens. This felt purposeful, like someone was following—

"Vira," she said suddenly. "I have to go back."

"No," Varun said sharply. "Riya. We can't go back there. They could follow us."

Riya looked at him, wide-eyed, her panic growing. "I can't just leave her. She might be in trouble."

"Then she'll be safer staying with the Ravens," Varun insisted.

"So what am I supposed to do?" Riya asked helplessly.

Fight back, the magic seemed to say. She could. She could decimate whoever was on the other side of the clearing, wipe out the threat all together.

Varun chanced another glance around the tree. It was quiet—but it didn't mean that their attacker was gone. "I have an idea," he said. "I think it's just one person. We can outrun them." He pointed straight ahead. "There's a stream nearby—if we can get across to the other side, we'll be able to lose them."

"We?" Riya echoed shrilly, too horrified to remember to whisper. "You can't come with me."

Varun gave her an irritated look. "Believe me, it wasn't my intention," he said. "But I can't go back to the Ravens either. And you're injured. We shouldn't split up."

"I don't have enough supplies," she argued weakly. He didn't have anything with him—not even a weapon—but the real reason she didn't want him to come along was that she couldn't have him finding out about her magic. Her hold on it was already fraying.

But she knew there was no use fighting him when his mind was made up. She inhaled deeply, gripped the part of the arrow closest to her shoulder, and then leaned back against the tree, twisting hard so that the end snapped off. The arrowhead was still lodged in her skin. She'd have to deal with that later. A new wave of pain tore through her body.

"I'd have helped you with that," Varun said with a small frown.

"Ready?" Riya asked, ignoring him.

She waited just long enough for Varun to nod. She took off through the forest, Varun on her heels. More arrows rained down on them.

"Look out!" Varun yelled in warning.

Riya leapt to the side, narrowly avoiding an arrow to the back of her head. But as she tried to keep running, she tripped on a root hidden beneath a layer of dead leaves. She crashed to the floor, slamming her knee against a rock.

Her shoulder stung to the point where she couldn't even think properly, but she had to keep moving. She tried to push herself up, but it had rained a few days earlier, and the earth was too soft; her hands just sunk in deeper.

A twig snapped. Riya jerked up, twisting just in time to see a hooded figure drop down from the trees.

Come on, she thought, frustrated, hurriedly wiping her mud-covered hands on her kurta. She used a nearby tree for leverage, clambering to her feet just as the hooded figure lifted a bow with three arrows nocked simultaneously. Riya stopped breathing.

"Riya!" Varun's horrified voice sounded from somewhere to her right. He'd doubled back for her.

The assailant let the arrows fly.

There was a blur of movement, and then Riya was falling once again as Varun shoved her out of the way, throwing himself between her and the arrows.

"No!" Riya shouted.

She threw up her hands and let her hold on the magic go. It erupted from her in a flash of blue light.

Stop, she commanded desperately.

The arrows froze midair. And then they fell to the ground, broken and useless.

For a brief second there was just stunned silence, pierced only by the distant cry of a mynah. Varun's eyes darted back and forth between Riya and the arrows, surprise and incomprehension lining his gaze. Riya's heart was pounding as everything disappeared except for the delicious hum of magic that numbed her pain and dulled her senses.

The hooded figure moved first, reaching for another arrow. Their quiver was empty.

Varun grabbed Riya by the arm on her uninjured side and hoisted her up to her feet. And then they ran.

*

"Are you going to tell me where exactly we're going?" Varun asked as they finally slowed down on a half-hidden path.

They'd run to the stream, not stopping until they'd waded through the shallow waters and reached the other side. But Varun had insisted on keeping up their relentless pace even though the forest behind them was still, showing no signs that they were being followed. In fact, Riya might have thought she'd imagined the whole thing if it weren't for her injured shoulder.

Or the fact that she was stuck with Varun.

"*I'm* going to Tasgarh," Riya said, glad for the chance to catch her breath. "You're free to go wherever you wish."

"Where in Tasgarh?"

"I . . . don't actually know," Riya admitted.

"What?" Varun glared at her. "How can you not know? If you don't want to tell me—"

"It's a greenhouse, all right?" Riya interrupted, irritated. "I don't know exactly where it is. Tarini wouldn't tell me."

Varun gave her an odd look. "I went to a greenhouse with Tarini once."

"Really? Do you remember where it is?" Riya tried not to get her hopes up, but this was the only real lead she had.

He lifted a shoulder. "I could probably find it again." He looked at her out of the corner of his eye as he lifted up a drooping branch, holding it so she could duck beneath. "I didn't think you were particularly interested in plants."

Riya scowled. "What's that supposed to mean?"

"It was just an observation, Riya," Varun said with a tired sigh as he let the branch go. "Not everything is an insult."

He walked ahead, and because Riya didn't know how to continue the conversation, they fell into an uncomfortable silence. She didn't know why he always made her feel so combative. Everything felt like a game, a competition between them—one she didn't know how to win but desperately wanted to.

For a long while, the only sounds were the crunch of leaves and twigs beneath their feet, but Riya could feel Varun's gaze flick toward her every few minutes. He hadn't said anything yet but he'd seen her use the magic. It would only be a matter of time before he started asking questions. She could practically feel the heavy weight of unsaid things in the space between them.

They didn't speak again until midday. They'd veered away from the original shorter route Riya had intended to take, but they were moving in the right direction—southeast toward the Harya border. The terrain wasn't difficult to navigate, and yet the distance between her and Varun had grown. Her shoulder was burning, she could feel sweat beading along her temples, and she was struggling to breathe.

"I think it was poisoned," Riya called out. "The arrow."

When Varun turned, he looked surprised to realize how far behind she'd fallen. He walked back toward her, his expression concerned. "Does it hurt?"

"A little." The pain had grown steadily worse, developing from something sharp and acute to a dull throb that she could no longer ignore.

Varun looked at her for permission and then pressed a hand to her forehead. His palm felt cool against her skin. She bit back a sigh and resisted the urge to lean into his touch. Maybe she was more ill than she'd thought.

"You have a fever," he murmured. "This isn't good."

"You have to take the arrowhead out," Riya said.

Varun knew it too but he shook his head. "The arrow's barbed. You could bleed out if I try."

She probably needed a proper healer, but they were in the middle of the forest, hours away from anyone else who could help. "You have to do it," Riya insisted. "It'll only get worse if we leave it in."

Varun looked uncomfortable, but he reluctantly nodded. "All right. But we need to find fresh water first."

He reached for her bag, tugging it away from her shoulder and slinging it over his own. And then he threaded their fingers together as they resumed walking. Riya wanted to protest. She could carry her own things, and she didn't need him to literally hold her hand. But for some reason the objections died on her lips. She decided it was the fever that was making her act so irrationally.

They had to move slowly, so it took nearly an hour before they heard running water. Riya exhaled in relief as Varun directed them toward the source: the Dhaya River. Her entire body felt like it was on fire, and she was parched despite having emptied her waterskin. She all but collapsed onto the bank, falling to her knees as Varun washed his hands in the water and then crouched behind her.

"Here." Riya unsheathed her dagger and unwound the dupatta from her waist, pushing them both into his hands.

He cut the kurta around her shoulder, gently peeling it away from her skin. She couldn't see him, or the wound, but she heard his sharp inhalation.

"How bad is it?" Riya asked.

"Not too bad."

"You're lying."

"I'll try to be quick," he promised.

He rummaged through his pockets and pulled out things he'd gathered on their way: a handful of leaves from medicinal plants, some fallen eagle feathers, and a packet of paper-wrapped turmeric powder left as an offering outside a small shrine.

"I'm going to clean the wound first," Varun said. He ripped the dupatta into three pieces and soaked one of them in river water.

Despite the warning, Riya jumped as she felt the brush of cold, wet fabric on her bare skin. She squeezed her eyes closed and braced herself for pain, but Varun was surprisingly gentle with her.

He dropped the cloth when he was done and reached for the feathers. "Ready?" he asked when he'd thoroughly cleaned them as well.

Riya nodded.

Varun took a deep breath and then slowly slid the quills into the wound. Riya hissed. Tears prickled at the corner of her eyes, and she clenched her fists tightly on her lap.

Varun froze. "Are you sure you want me to do this?"

"I'm sure," Riya said, gritting her teeth. She forced herself to take a deep breath and relax her muscles.

He pushed the feathers deeper into the cut, trying to slide the hollow end of the quills over the barbed edges of the arrow. Riya thought she might pass out from the agony, but after several excruciatingly painful minutes, Varun exhaled in relief.

"I got it," he said. He carefully tugged the arrow out of her flesh. The metal clattered to the ground beside them, covered in her blood and a sticky black poison.

Varun took a fresh scrap of cloth and cleaned the whole area one more time. He pressed turmeric powder into the injury site and then crushed the plants he'd collected between his palms, releasing the oils within them before pushing them against her skin as well.

"How did you learn to do all of this?" Riya couldn't help but ask as he took the last part of her torn dupatta and began to wrap it around her shoulder.

His fingers momentarily tensed. "My father," he said after a beat as he continued to bandage her. "He was a healer."

"Oh."

Varun had never spoken about his father before. Questions burned on the tip of her tongue wanting to know where his father was, if he was still alive, when Varun had last seen him, what else he'd taught him. But they didn't have the type of relationship where she could ask those things, so she said nothing.

When he was done, he turned away while she changed into a spare kurta. She pulled it over her head, wincing as the movement tugged at the bandage.

"How do you feel?" he asked when she was dressed.

"Better," Riya said. The poison was still in her blood, but it hurt less. "Thank you," she said after a beat. He gave her a small smile in acknowledgment.

He'd helped her even though she'd lied to him—even though she was still keeping a huge secret from him. And she realized that despite everything, she'd never truly doubted that he would take care of her. She trusted him implicitly.

And she didn't know what to do with that.

CHAPTER EIGHTEEN

— RONAK —

RONAK WAS USED to lavish parties in Ashoka, with delicious food, lively music, and expensive silks, all dusted with the prickle of magic that perpetually hung in the air. The fact that the emperor had managed to accomplish the same level of extravagance without any magic at all was impressive.

Square tiles painted with white and black geometric designs lined the floor of the massive ballroom. Round tables topped by smooth marble surfaces and wooden chairs with elaborately carved legs were set up around one half of the hall, leaving the rest open for socializing. Glittering chandeliers with lamps nestled in crystal orbs hung down from the high ceiling.

Rectangular tables had been laid out toward one side of the room, filled with decadent dishes that smelled heavenly as Ronak walked past: roasted squash glazed with a date and red wine sauce, a hearty soup of lentils and vegetables cooked with herbs, thick slices of warm bread served with fresh coriander and olive oil, sliced figs and walnuts drizzled with pepper-infused honey.

Members of the emperor's court and their families were milling around, half-finished glasses of wine in their hands. Jay and Kunaal were among them, laughing with a group of the emperor's advisors. Two musicians sat on a raised platform, plucking gentle melodies on their gold-plated lyres that wafted over the hum of conversation.

Out of habit—or perhaps hope—Ronak cast his eyes around for any sign of Kaleb's familiar features. He didn't find his brother, and belatedly he realized that this was foolish. Even if Kaleb had successfully managed to arrive at the palace, it would have been as a scholar. He wouldn't be among the nobility invited to the emperor's private party.

Ronak accepted the glass of wine that one of the servants handed him. It was bloodred. When he swirled it, it smelled sweet and fruity, and though he was hundreds of miles away from Ekta, he could have sworn he got a whiff of her perfume. His stomach roiled.

Preethi watched him carefully as he set the glass down on the nearest surface, untouched. "Do you not like the taste of wine?"

"Not really," Ronak said.

"Oh." She sipped her glass and looked somewhere off into the distance.

They hadn't spoken since their conversation in his room earlier, but Preethi was dutifully staying by his side, insistent on presenting the facade of a happy betrothed couple. A part of him felt guilty because she believed that this was real, that he intended to actually go through with the wedding.

He glanced at her out of the corner of his eye. They'd both dressed in Lyrian-style clothes sent over by the emperor, Ronak in an embroidered emerald tunic similar to a sherwani and Preethi in a gown made of the same fabric as his outfit. Her long hair hung in cascading waves down to her waist, clipped back on one side with a golden peacock. She was taller than either of his sisters, but the proud lift of her chin and the defiance in her eyes reminded him of Vira.

Ronak sighed internally, debating whether it would be worse if he engaged in conversation. They *were* going to be stuck together for days. Perhaps it wouldn't be terrible to talk to her.

But he was saved the trouble of making the decision when the entire room fell silent. Ronak turned to see heralds at the entrance to the room, announcing the arrival of the royal family: Prince Elias, Prince Lukas, and Emperor Kallias. The empress was away for the week, according to the information Preethi had gathered.

The emperor was as jovial as ever, raising a glass of wine to the crowd and encouraging them to continue mingling. It seemed as though he hadn't been lying when he said that he didn't care much for formality. The others in the room didn't need any further encouragement to keep conversing as they had been before.

Ronak, however, kept his gaze trained on the emperor. He wasn't wearing the compass tonight. And as he greeted his guests and laughed heartily with them, his eyes sparked with genuine warmth. This was . . . unexpected. Not just because it was so far removed from the way Amma or Vira would have ever behaved, but because it was making it far too easy to forget that this man was responsible for invading his home country, murdering his mother, and framing his brother for it.

"Come on," Preethi said, tugging on his elbow. "We should go say hello."

Ronak allowed her to pull him toward the emperor, who turned around and greeted the two of them with exuberance.

"The guests of honor," he said in a loud, booming voice. "Let's have a toast." He looked at Ronak's empty hand in surprise. "Where is your drink?" He snapped his fingers, and a servant immediately appeared with fresh glasses of wine.

Feeling that it was rude to refuse, Ronak reluctantly took a glass.

"To old friends and new alliances," the emperor said with a wink, raising his glass in the air. Those around him did the same, and Ronak followed suit before taking a small sip. It was colder than he expected it to be, and dryer, given the initial sweet smell.

As Preethi made small talk with the emperor, inquiring about the large gardens they could see from their rooms, Ronak's gaze drifted toward the two princes. Elias seemed to be more like his father, with a stocky build, sandy brown hair, and a cheerful presence. His smile was dazzling the crowd around him as he told a story that captivated his audience. Beside him, Lukas, the younger brother, stood quiet and serious, an untouched glass of wine in his hand. He wasn't trying to charm anyone—he didn't need to. He was clearly respected by his father's court even if he didn't appear to be quite as beloved as his brother.

When the emperor noticed what had caught Ronak's attention, he waved the boys over. Elias detached himself from his admirers with all the grace of a politician trained from birth, following Lukas toward their father.

"My sons," the emperor said, clapping each of them on the back. "This is Rajkumaara Ronak and his betrothed, Preethi." But before he could say anything else, one of the other guests—dressed in a midnight blue dress studded with diamonds that glittered like stars—approached the emperor, saying something in a low voice. "Excuse me," the emperor said before he followed her, disappearing out of sight.

"Rajkumaara," Elias greeted Ronak, the Ashokan word clumsy in his foreign tongue. "Rajkumaari."

"Just kumaari," Preethi corrected as Ronak stiffened. "We're not married yet," she said with a light laugh. "It's a pleasure to meet you."

"The pleasure is all mine," Elias said, smiling. He reached for Preethi's hand, bending down to brush a kiss against the back of her fingers. She blushed.

Up close, Ronak could see that Elias's smile didn't quite reach his eyes, as if the pleasant demeanor were nothing more than a mask.

"We should find our seats," Lukas said, as attendants began escorting guests to their tables. "It looks like the demonstration is about to start."

Ronak was seated between Lukas on one side and the emperor's empty chair on the other. Preethi was on the emperor's other side, next to Elias, who was regaling her with stories in Lyrian that were making her laugh a little too loud. Ronak could see Jay's gaze lingering on the two of them from the adjacent table.

Lukas, on the other hand, didn't say much. He looked just as uncomfortable as Ronak felt as he glanced around the room, and for a brief moment Ronak felt a kinship with this prince. Unlike Vira, who'd been trained into it—or Riya and Kaleb, who actually liked it—Ronak neither enjoyed nor was skilled at playing the role of rajkumaara. His mother had taught him only enough to ensure that he wouldn't embarrass her, but beyond that, she'd left him to his own devices. In her eyes, he'd only ever been a tool—a pawn to marry off for political growth—rather than a son.

Suddenly the lights of the chandeliers began to flicker and fade. Ronak glanced up in surprise, but as a hush fell over the room, he realized that it was a part of the demonstration.

"What kind of demonstration is this?" Ronak asked Lukas.

"My father likes a bit of theater," Lukas said vaguely, sipping his water. Elias was clearly uncomfortable speaking Ashokan and had limited vocabulary, but the only sign that Lukas wasn't a native speaker was the Lyrian accent that laced his words.

Ronak felt the magic first—a soft whisper that washed over his skin like a breath of fresh air after days of absence. The emperor walked out first, shrouded in darkness.

"Welcome everyone," he said. His voice was naturally loud, but it reverberated throughout the room as though magically amplified. "I hope you're all enjoying the night with our esteemed guests from Ashoka."

He gestured toward Ronak and Preethi, and the room broke into polite applause.

"I have an especially wonderful treat for you all today. We've been working on bringing about a new era of magic and innovation, and it only seems fitting to unveil it here tonight. After all, it's thanks to the generosity of our Ashokan neighbors and their incredible quarries that we're even lucky enough to have this magic."

He stepped away, revealing a young Ashokan boy standing on a raised platform. The boy closed his eyes, took a deep breath, and then looked up toward the chandelier that hung directly above the half of the room where the guests were seated. He held his hands up, and blue light shot out of them, shattering the glass chandelier into a million pieces. There were gasps—and even a scream—as shards began to rain down on them.

Yet the shards all stopped a hair's breadth away from hitting anyone. Every piece stood suspended in air, almost like time was frozen.

Ronak stopped breathing. He had seen images of something similar in Ritsar, but to see it in real life, without the aid of mayaka-forged objects, felt too strange, too incongruous with everything he'd known magic to be. Even Riya couldn't control her power this way.

He reached out, touching one of the pieces. A sharp edge pierced his skin, and he drew his hand back quickly, wiping away the blood that welled on the surface of his finger.

The boy moved his hands again, and slowly, the pieces began to coalesce, fitting back together to re-form the chandelier.

There was only silence. And then the crowd broke into thunderous applause. Ronak glanced around the room. Lukas and Elias were staring at their father, slack-jawed and apparently unaware of what the emperor had been doing. Preethi had a hand pressed against her mouth, while Kunaal and Jay were wide-eyed and confused.

"This"—the emperor's voice boomed over the din as light flared to life all around them—"is the future of magic. And I have wonderful plans to bring this power to all of Lyria."

Ronak stared at the chandelier in shock. It looked exactly like it had been minutes earlier, as if he'd imagined the whole thing. But the stinging pain of his finger was proof that it had been terrifyingly real.

CHAPTER NINETEEN

— KALEB —

WHEN DAYANA INVITED him to the emperor's ball, Kaleb had accepted without question. It had only been two days since he'd moved to the palace, but he was already exhausted by the mind-numbing tedium of working in the library, pulling books off shelves for other scholars, and spending the rest of his time reading dull, repetitive books on excavating and processing raw magic.

He'd thought it might be a good distraction—a chance to finally see the emperor, to learn more about the Lyrian court, maybe glimpse the Ashokan delegation so he could know exactly who he needed to avoid.

He hadn't expected . . . *that.*

Kaleb's eyes were still trained on the podium where the Ashokan boy had been standing. He'd broken apart a chandelier and put it back together like it was nothing, with just a few flicks of his wrist. This was power unlike anything Kaleb had seen.

Questions raced through his mind. How many months of practice had it taken the boy to gain this amount of control? What else could he do? Could Riya do this too?

"That was incredible," Dayana gasped, grabbing Kaleb's arm.

"Incredible," Kaleb echoed. The room was abuzz, identical whispered conversations sweeping through the crowd.

Dayana was awestruck. "This changes *every*thing we ever knew about magic," she gushed.

"We should find our seats," Kaleb said. The two of them had arrived well after everyone else, slipping into the back just before the emperor's speech. Ephyra had slipped out the door just as Dayana had opened it, so they'd spent nearly thirty minutes chasing the kitten until they'd managed to corner her behind a statue.

Dayana led the way to one of the tables, still talking about the magic. "I knew some of the soldiers have this kind of power, but it's one thing hearing about it from the other scholars and another to witness it like this, you know?"

He did, but Kaleb couldn't share in her excitement. It *was* a miraculous feat, but the emperor had just announced to the entire world the existence of this power. People would covet this kind of magic, and Kaleb could already see all the ways in which it would lead to catastrophic outcomes, especially for Ashoka.

A moment later Dayana's words actually hit him, and Kaleb turned to her. "Wait . . . what soldiers?"

"Oh," Dayana said, frowning. "Didn't you hear?" When he shook his head, she lowered her voice and explained. "The emperor found barrels of liquid magic in Ashoka. It was enough to give a handful of soldiers powers just like this."

The same liquid magic that Riya had touched in the temple. And the emperor was running out of that magic now—or had already—which was why he was so desperate to figure out how to make more of it.

"How many soldiers?" Kaleb asked.

"I think four or five. Oh . . . I think that might be—" Dayana abruptly stopped walking. "Them," she finished quietly.

Kaleb followed her gaze toward a table where six soldiers still dressed in their military clothes were seated along with the Ashokan boy and Hektor. At first he thought it was the sight of Hektor that made Dayana stop, but he realized that her eyes were actually on a different soldier.

"Dayana?" Kaleb prompted when she didn't move. "Who is that?"

That finally got her attention. "Oh. No one," she said immediately. But then she bit her lower lip. "Her name is Thalia," she said quietly. "She—well, we were together for a while."

She continued walking, but Kaleb let his gaze linger on Thalia for a moment, taking in her dark red braid and light eyes. She was having a quiet, seemingly serious conversation with one of the other soldiers, but her eyes flicked momentarily toward him.

"Is she why you came to the palace?" Kaleb asked when he joined Dayana. She'd told him once that she hadn't always intended to join the emperor's scholars—that she hadn't even been sure she wanted to be an artificer until recently.

Dayana nodded. "But I didn't know she was one of *those* soldiers." She exhaled. "I liked her a lot. But a few months ago she just . . . stopped talking to me. Stopped writing. She was planning to leave the military at the end of this year, but then she got some opportunity to join a special team the emperor was putting together and . . . it was like her personality completely shifted." She laughed a little bitterly. "At least now I know why."

"I'm sorry," Kaleb said. "Have you talked to her?"

"She refused to see me. I thought that by coming here, I'd be able to finally get some answers. But she told me to leave her alone."

Dayana fell silent after that—but Kaleb didn't miss the way she craned her head over her shoulder to look back at the soldiers when she thought Kaleb wasn't paying attention.

He scanned the large room, trying to find the Ashokan visitors, but he couldn't see them anywhere. The promise he'd made to Lukas about finding a way to join the scholars on the trip to Ashoka was weighing on his mind, but Kaleb still had no idea how to do that.

"Does the emperor throw parties like this very often?" Kaleb asked.

Dayana jumped, her knee knocking into the table and rattling the silverware as she whipped her head away from staring at Thalia. Her cheeks were a little red as she mumbled an apology to the others seated beside them.

"Sometimes," she said when he repeated the question. "Though not usually as lavish as this. He must be trying to impress the prince."

"The prince?" Kaleb asked, confused.

"The Ashokan prince," Dayana clarified. "The younger one, I believe. I wonder what he's like," she mused. "My aunt used to be married to his father, you know."

Kaleb jerked up. *"What?"*

She gave him an odd look. "It's not scandalous. It was long before he was maharaja of Ashoka, and he left when Aunt Alena passed away."

"No, no. I meant—" Kaleb cut himself off before he said Ronak's name. "The prince is truly here?"

"That's what I heard." She twisted in her seat and then pointed toward a table near the front. "I think that's him over there next to Lukas. It's too bad his brother isn't also here—my cousin. I'd always hoped to meet Kaleb someday, but I guess he didn't feel the same way. He never even responded to the letter my mother wrote him."

Kaleb had to look away to keep himself from blurting out something he shouldn't then and there. *I did write back,* he wanted desperately to admit to her. *I did want to meet you and your entire family.*

He'd believed for months that he was corresponding with his aunt, with his cousins. But the letters had never reached his family. They'd been manufactured by someone specifically to frame him for Amma's death, and now they believed that he didn't want anything to do with them.

"I'm sure if he was able to respond, he would have," Kaleb said, his voice heavy.

"Perhaps," Dayana said. She was still looking at him strangely. "Are you sure you're all right?"

"I'm fine," Kaleb managed, forcing a smile.

But his brain went entirely blank as someone seated in front of him shifted and Ronak's face came into view.

Ronak was here. Ronak was in Lyria, and all Kaleb could feel was a deep sense of betrayal. He'd asked for one thing, the chance to get to know his family, the chance to get to know Lyria on his own terms. And his brother couldn't even afford him that. Ronak would only ever see him as a sad, broken boy trapped in the dungeons.

Still, maybe Ronak wasn't wrong. It had been days, and all Kaleb had managed to do was lie to his cousin and get himself tethered to a prince who was blackmailing him.

※

Getting a message to Ronak proved far more difficult than Kaleb expected. Ronak was never alone, and worse, the others with him—Jay, Preethi, and Kunaal—would easily recognize Kaleb. In the end he took a chance, following Ronak when he stepped outside the ballroom to get some air, brushing past him and whispering a message he hoped that his brother heard.

He'd lied to Dayana—yet again—feigning a headache as an excuse to slip out early. But instead of returning to his room, he walked to the library. It wasn't far from the ballroom, and it would be empty at this hour. He let himself in and paced around the shelves until he heard footsteps outside.

Kaleb held his breath, hoping this meant that Ronak *had* heard him.

The door opened, and his brother stepped inside. It had been weeks since Kaleb had last seen him, and despite his irritation, for a moment he was grateful to see him.

Kaleb tugged him toward one corner, partially behind a bookcase just in case anyone else happened to walk in.

"What are you doing here?" Kaleb hissed, keeping his voice low and speaking in Ashokan. It felt a bit strange on his tongue after so long trying to train himself out of using it instinctively.

"I can't help where the Council chooses to send me," Ronak said, stuffing his hands into his pockets.

"And since when do you care what the Council tells you to do?"

"Since they're the ones ruling Ashoka now."

Kaleb frowned. "What are you talking about?"

"Didn't you hear?" Ronak asked, his voice strangely tight. "Our sister is no longer the maharani."

"*What?*" Kaleb searched Ronak's face for any sign that it was a lie. Ronak would be honest about this, wouldn't he?

"She went looking for the magic," Ronak said. "Riya too."

Kaleb ran a hand over his face. Things were far worse than he'd expected, and now their family was scattered. He had no idea where his sisters were or how to contact them. He'd been under the impression that everything he'd been doing here was helping Vira. But if she was no longer in charge, he had no idea what to do.

"Why did the Council send you here?" Kaleb asked.

"To formally invite the emperor to Shantha Mahal."

So that was the trip the emperor was taking. Weapons weren't allowed inside Shantha Mahal. It was technically on Ashokan soil, but it was a neutral meeting site.

"And that's the only reason you're here?" Kaleb asked skeptically. "It has nothing to do with me?"

"There's been a coup, Kaleb." Ronak snapped angrily. "Forgive me for wanting to check on my brother."

Kaleb exhaled. "I didn't mean it like that." He didn't want to fight.

"What have you learned?" Ronak asked. "About the magic."

"He has more soldiers with power," Kaleb said. "Not a lot, but I'm sure he intends to create more. His plans seem to have stalled."

"Let me help you," Ronak said.

"No," Kaleb answered instinctively.

"I have access to the emperor. It'll be better if we work together."

Kaleb wanted to disagree, but Ronak had a point. As much as they had their differences and conflicts, in this Kaleb knew they were unquestionably on the same side.

"Fine," Kaleb said. "But we do it my way."

Ronak nodded. "All right."

"I'll be in touch," Kaleb promised. He gestured toward the door, letting Ronak leave first.

While he waited, Kaleb could see there were more scraps of paper placed on his desk after he'd left—no doubt more books for him to find for other scholars. He sighed as he collected them all into a pile to deal with in the morning. At least one person had helpfully written the four numbers that made up the library's catalog system. It would make his life a lot eas—

Kaleb stopped as a sudden thought entered his mind.

There had been four scratches on his wardrobe door: 5, 8, 2, 5. Could it really have been that simple?

He made his way to the fifth section, found the eighth shelf, the second row, then counted over to the fifth book.

It was thin and leather-bound, and when Kaleb pulled it out, he saw a feather stamped on the lower right corner of the front cover. He flipped through it. Tiny, cramped handwriting covered each page from edge to edge, with very little white space.

He'd found Theo's missing journal.

CHAPTER TWENTY

— VIRA —

IT WAS EARLY morning when Vira and Surya reached Paliya.

The jostling of the hired carriage had made Vira feel a little nauseated, but she'd summoned all the grace her mother had instilled in her and silently bore the discomfort. It had been an exhausting day and a half of travel, first walking through the forest and then traveling in cramped coaches. Unsurprisingly, no one had been willing to drive them all the way to the other side of the province, so they'd stopped and changed vehicles three times in roadside villages. She'd gotten very little rest, and her legs and back ached, but while Surya had promptly closed his eyes and fallen asleep, Vira couldn't do the same.

She rested her head against the window and stared out—not that there was much to see, especially in the dark of night. Harya was primarily flat farmland, and the view Vira managed to catch in the moonlight was of endless fields and an occasional grazing cow or goat.

There was nothing to occupy her mind except her conversation with Riya. For all of Riya's insistence that she was on Vira's side, that she would see this through to the end, she'd abandoned Vira at the first chance. It was Vira's own fault—she didn't know why she'd expected Riya to behave any differently from anyone else in her life. In the end, Vira only ever had herself to rely on.

Surya stirred as the carriage began to slow, blinking his eyes open and stifling a yawn as he peered outside. At some point in the middle of the night he'd pushed up the sleeves of his baggy borrowed kurta, revealing the dark lines of the three jagged mountain peaks tattooed on his forearm. It was the only thing that identified him as a mercenary.

Vira's breath hitched as a sudden memory hit her: a burn mark on Amrit's forearm in the exact same spot. She'd seen him absently trace it so often, watched his face close off every time she asked about it. The truth had been right in front of her face the entire time and she'd been too foolish—too caught up in his pretty lies—to see it.

"Did you manage to sleep?" Surya asked, jolting Vira back to the present.

"A little," Vira lied, dragging her gaze away from the tattoo. Her eyes were burning with sleeplessness, but her body and brain were too wired to rest. "I think we're almost there."

Even though they'd paid him to take them all the way to the temple, the carriage driver dropped them off near the center of the city. "The streets up there aren't wide enough," he insisted as he pocketed the two gold rings Vira handed him. "It's just a twenty-minute walk from here."

Vira glowered at him as the carriage peeled away. She wondered if he'd have treated her the same knowing that she was the maharani.

You're not the maharani anymore, she reminded herself.

Paliya was a vibrant city, already bustling with activity though the sun hadn't even risen. It was more urban than Dvar, and the buildings were taller than what Vira was accustomed to, towering over her like wiry spindles piercing the pale morning sky.

"The temple's this way," Surya said, but Vira was only half listening. She was too busy craning her head, trying to peer into the stores that lined the narrow, intersecting streets.

To Vira's shock, quite a few of them were already open, the mayaka-forged signs hanging above the doors glowing as bright as lanterns as they advertised goods and services.

There was an apothecary with large cabinets full of tinctures and salves for ailments ranging from stiff joints to insomnia. Vira was eyeing a vial of turmeric- and saffron-infused oil in the storefront when a gentle breeze caused the aromas of ghee and cardamom to waft over her. Her stomach tightened in hunger, and she remembered that she hadn't eaten anything in hours. She turned and looked around until she found the neighboring sweetshop.

Peering inside, she was awestruck to realize that two people were making soan papdi before her very eyes, using their elbows to repeatedly stretch a thick cord of besan-coated caramel until it disintegrated into wisps of papery spun sugar. As they began to spool the strands of soan papdi into paper cones, Vira couldn't help but eye the other desserts in the store: kesar milk pedas dusted with gold leaves, cubes of halwa topped with slivers of almond, rasgulla soaked in rose-flavored syrup, cups of creamy basundi and tart mango shrikhand and sweet pongal made with jaggery and camphor.

Unable to resist the temptation—and despite the incredulous look Surya gave her—she forked over a dozen seyrs for an assortment of desserts.

"You continue to surprise me, Rani," Surya said. "Sweets for breakfast?"

Vira shrugged. It had been an impulsive decision and she was fairly certain that all this sugar would give her a stomachache, but she'd earned a little indulgence, hadn't she? She held the box out to Surya. He declined with a small grimace. More for her then.

She picked at the sweets as she and Surya walked down the winding streets toward the temple that would soon open its gates. She couldn't help but keep looking around at the stores flanking their path, selling everything from handloom textiles to garlands of flowers meant to serve as offerings to the goddesses. She'd traveled extensively through Ashoka as was expected of the maharani, but she'd seen it all from behind gilded screens, sequestered in lavish residences inside forts while her Council told her about life in each province and took her to visit hand-selected landmarks. She'd never had this kind of freedom before, and she liked it.

But as they crossed a courtyard, Vira caught sight of a statue in the center that had been defaced, slathered in paint and smashed fruit, and papered with flyers for protests against the maharani. Her breath caught and her mood deflated—but a moment later she realized that it wasn't a statue of her, but of her mother.

Vira couldn't look away from it. "Why would they bother to vandalize a statue of a dead ruler?" she asked.

"Most people don't really care who's in power, not when they're treated the same under every ruler."

She turned toward Surya. "Do you really believe that?"

He only shrugged. "My existence is devoted to serving a dead maharani. The Kamala Society, for all its flaws, has been nothing more than a pawn in an ancient battle between two long-gone rulers. We've always borne the brunt of the cost and gained none of the benefits."

Vira didn't know how to respond, but she mulled over his words as they resumed their walk. Was this how the rest of Ashoka felt? That they were pawns, used and discarded at the whims of capricious leaders? And if that were true . . . then perhaps everything she'd ever assumed about the world was wrong.

Her Council had never passed up any opportunity to remind her she was nothing like Amma, that her mother had been adored everywhere she went—that she had loyal followers and supporters in every corner of Ashoka. But perhaps her mother had been no more beloved than Vira was, and the Council had simply woven a narrative that they could use to control her—comparing Vira to her mother and pointing out all the ways in which she didn't measure up until Vira convinced herself that she was a failure.

They'd brought forth citizens for her to meet, those with an endless string of complaints, to make it clear that they didn't like her or how she led Ashoka—to make it clear that she had to play the game just the way the Council wanted if she wanted to change this.

But perhaps those visitors hadn't been random. Perhaps they'd been carefully selected by the Council with an ulterior motive in mind: to convince her to care about the opinions of a vocal few that suited the councilors' personal agendas and not the desires of the general populace.

✳

The Fire Temple of Paliya was a huge walled complex with buildings stretching out in all directions. A large open mandap with intricately carved pillars was just to the left of the entrance—empty at this hour but usually reserved for weddings or concerts. The path to the right led to several smaller pavilions that held idols of minor deities and beyond that, the temple pond.

They'd walked in through a side entrance rather than the main gates, so the building directly in front of them was the actual temple that housed altars to the three goddesses. Vira raised a hand to shield her eyes from the rising sun as she tilted her head back to look up at the massive gopuram tower, each tier of the pyramidical structure crowded with sculptures depicting scenes from Ashokan mythology.

The temple had been built to honor the goddess Devyani. She was known as the goddess of beginnings and endings, depicted carrying a ball of blue flame in the palm of one hand that she used to usher souls into the afterlife and, in the other hand, a scepter topped with a golden snake. However, the main appeal of the temple was the blue flame—supposedly lit by Devyani herself—carefully tended to and kept burning for centuries.

Surya led the way, and she followed him inside. The temple was popular with both local devotees and pilgrims journeying from far off locales, and it was already busy as worshippers hurried by with garlands of flowers and platters of fruit. Vira and Surya trailed behind a group of laughing young women dressed in colorful silk saris and silver anklets that had tiny bells that jangled with every step.

Behind the temple proper was a smaller, secondary shrine, but this building didn't house another deity. It held the Infinite Flame. Vira had read about this in Papa's journals, but she was unprepared for the brilliant blue hues of fire dancing in the center of the stone firepit.

The shrine was roped off, and a woman in a plain white sari and graying hair was seated at the entrance. She had a large basket of jasmine buds she was weaving into a garland. "Two tolahs to see the flame," she said, not looking up. "Each."

Vira handed her five, and because the woman didn't have change, she reached for one of the finished garlands coiled inside a second basket. She held one end in her palm and wrapped it around her elbow twice to measure the length before shearing it off and handing it to Vira. The flowers were fragrant, so Vira tucked it between several strands of hair at the top of her braid, letting the garland drape over her shoulders.

Despite the size of the flame—nearly as tall as Vira—the room wasn't stiflingly hot. Magic in the stones kept the space cool and ventilated. Two guards flanked the firepit, arms crossed over their chests, menacingly glaring at anyone who dared come too close. Only trained mayaka priestesses could tend to the flames and replenish the magical coals that gave the flame its striking color. People came from all over Ashoka—and even other countries—to see it.

"Now what?" Surya prompted as Vira came to a stop in front of it.

"Now we find the book of Rasika's songs," she said, pulling away from the flame and facing the rest of the room. It wasn't exactly a true museum, but there were several dozen podiums spread through the space, each holding ancient, historically important stone slabs, scrolls, and books for visitors to peruse.

"I guess we'd better split up," Surya said, making his way to the far side of the room.

Vira approached the row of objects closest to the firepit. Unlike the artifacts reserved for serious scholars, those here were magically preserved and of interest to the general population—as long as they had the money to pay the entrance fee. The first held a vase painted with lesser-known myths about the goddess Vaishali. Another held a heavy tome full of carefully painted designs chronicling fashions and textiles through the decades. A third had a broken pillar, etched with lines from a poem by an unknown bard.

Someone was looking at the book on the next stand, copying something from it onto a piece of paper, so Vira politely lingered to the side as she waited her turn. The person looked up—and all the blood drained from Vira's face.

"Amrit?" she whispered. She forced herself to look elsewhere, to blink several times and clear her head, sure he was a figment of her imagination. But when she turned back, it was unmistakably him. He was dressed in a plain cotton kurta, far simpler than Vira was accustomed to seeing him as the captain of her guard. He'd foregone cutting his hair or beard in several weeks, and both were longer, framing his angular features differently.

But she'd recognize him anywhere, anytime.

As he saw her, his eyes filled with what Vira could have sworn was pain, but it disappeared so quickly it might have been a glint of light. They both realized at the same time why she was here: Rasika's book.

Vira dove for it, but Amrit was quicker. He slammed it closed and snatched it off the pedestal. A horrible clanging noise of bells reverberated through the air. An alarm, Vira realized, to prevent people from stealing the artifacts.

But Amrit didn't care. He elbowed his way through the guards converging on them. Vira ran after him. But instead of making his way to the exit, he paused in front of the flame.

Vira could see the faded gold lettering on the spine glowing blue in the light half a second before he flung it into the fire.

"NO!" For a moment the entire room was suspended in time—in horrified shock, as slowly, the pages of the book began to burn.

More guards began to rush inside, jostling past stunned, frozen bystanders. Amrit took advantage of the commotion to run for the exit. Vira stared at the burning book for a heartbroken beat. And then she turned and took off after Amrit.

She caught up to him at the edge of the compound. "Stop!"

For a second she didn't think he would, but he slowed down until he froze at the end of the empty courtyard, right beside the square pond. She could see the tense line of his shoulders as he warred with himself. The back gates were just several feet away; he could easily make a run for it. But then he finally turned around.

Vira's heart was pounding. It was because she'd chased after him, she told herself, and not because the very sight of him overwhelmed her senses. She'd thought about this moment constantly, practiced her words and her movements in her mind, but that hadn't prepared her for what it would be like to actually stand in front of him.

What it would be like to look at his familiar face and see a stranger staring back at her.

He stood very still as she approached. "What are you doing?" he asked. There was a warning in his eyes, but he didn't stop her as she stepped into his personal space.

"Making sure you're real." It wasn't entirely a lie. Drenched in daylight, he looked like a vision she'd conjured.

His hand shot out to wrap around her wrist. She wondered if he felt her racing pulse beneath his fingers. He was angry, but there was a yearning in his gaze that she wasn't imagining—a sign that he wasn't nearly as unaffected as he pretended to be. Time between them slowed as he warily released her hand. "You shouldn't be here."

"Then maybe you shouldn't have lied," Vira said. Her voice was hoarse with pain. She'd meant to keep a hold on her emotions, on her anger, but one look at him and her resolve had crumbled.

"There are things you don't understand," he said.

"I think I'm smart enough to keep up."

Amrit's eyes narrowed. "It's not a question of cleverness."

"Then?" she prompted.

He didn't answer other than to take a step back, as if he needed to put distance between them. But Vira wasn't going to let him escape that easily. She moved too. They were close to the edge of the pond now. The water rippled in the wind, making the hazy reflection of a nearby pillared pavilion tremble. Somewhere in the distance, the alarm was still blaring, and temple workers were ushering visitors out. Vira half expected someone to interrupt them, but this area was off-limits, and they were partially hidden from view. They were alone. For now.

"You want me to fail *that* badly?" she couldn't resist asking. "That you would rather burn the book than let me have it?"

He looked away, fixing his gaze on something over her shoulder. "You should leave, Vira."

Vira. It sent an involuntary shiver down her spine. He was giving her nothing, refusing to talk to her, refusing to even look at her anymore. *He doesn't care*, she reminded herself. *He doesn't regret it.*

The fight has already begun, Surya had told her. Amrit had picked the battlefield, and he'd set the rules. She was just playing by them. Her heart clenched painfully as she slid her hand into the pocket of her kurta, reaching for the metal band she'd taken from the Ravens' campsite. It was cold against her clammy palm. "I know about the Kamala Society," Vira said, trying to keep her voice steady. "I know who you are."

That was the wrong thing to say. His eyes turned cold. "You have no idea who I am."

She inhaled sharply, the words slashing at a wound that was still too fresh, and all the courage she'd summoned to follow him out there left her all at once. Her shoulders slumped as she looked up at his emotionless face, searching for answers he was determined to keep from her. There was only one thought running through her mind—a question she knew she shouldn't ask, but could no more stop herself than a moth could resist the allure of the flame that would obliterate it.

He moved again slightly, realizing too late that she'd cornered him. His back was against the metal railing that ran around the perimeter of the pond. "Vira."

"Was it real?" Her voice was barely louder than a whisper, as though saying it quietly would hide her desperation, her vulnerability. "Was any of it real?"

A flicker of emotion passed over his face, gone before she could read it. "Does it matter?"

"Of course it matters," Vira said. "It—" *It was real to me.* She couldn't say the words, but they hung between them nonetheless, as if she had said them aloud.

"Don't make this harder than it has to be." His voice was just as raw as hers.

She searched his gaze, and then lifted a trembling hand to his face. Her thumb brushed over the edge of his bottom lip. His breath hitched, but he didn't pull away from her. "Why won't you just talk to me?" She stood up on her tiptoes and pressed a barely-there kiss to the corner of his mouth. "Amrit. *Please.*"

His eyes closed, as though it was too painful for him to look at her. "Leave, Vira." He sounded like he was pleading. "We can't do this."

"I can't." Vira felt her heart break all over again as she wrapped the bangle concealed in the palm of her other hand around his wrist.

It wasn't until the clasp closed with a loud snick that Amrit realized what she'd done. He looked down just as Vira snapped the second bangle around the metal railing. She pressed her hands to her mouth as she saw the horror and betrayal growing on his face.

"What did you do?" He tried to jerk away, but he was stuck.

"I can't have you following me," Vira said hoarsely. She reached into his pocket and withdrew the paper on which he'd copied the letters from Rasika's book as well as the original Ivory Key he'd taken from her.

"Vira. This isn't the time." He was furious.

This was what she'd wanted, wasn't it? To feel like she had the power between them for once. But all she felt watching him trying to rip free of the magical trap was a visceral pain. She could take her knife out and run it through his heart, but that wouldn't make her ache any less.

"Well done, Rani," Surya said from somewhere behind her. "I didn't think you had it in you."

Amrit's anger grew as his eyes flicked toward Surya. "What are you doing here?"

"Did you think I'd stay locked up forever, brother?" Surya asked almost lazily.

"Vira," Amrit said urgently, trying to muscle his way out of the shackles. "You don't know what you're doing. You can't trust him. I'm only trying to protect you."

Vira's eyes blazed as she stepped away from him. "I don't need your protection."

"Vira, listen to me. The Ivory Key doesn't lead to—"

"I think you've told enough lies," Surya said coolly.

"Vira, please. The key is dangerous. I swear I'll explain everything."

Amrit was begging, offering her exactly what she wanted, and it tugged at the part of her that had seen him as her trusted advisor—who'd had sat on the banks of a lake in Ritsar and kissed him because she'd been so sure that they wanted the same thing. But that girl was gone now—he'd seen to that.

"It's too late." She steeled herself. "You were the one who decided the rules of the game."

The look on Amrit's face mirrored the anguish she felt in her soul. "This isn't a game," he said.

"Nevertheless, this was the path *you* chose," she said. "Goodbye, Amrit." And then she turned and walked away.

CHAPTER TWENTY-ONE

— RONAK —

WHEN RONAK AWOKE in his Lyrian accommodations the day after the emperor's welcome ball, the first thought he had was that in order to get close to the emperor and find the compass, he would need help.

After he'd gotten ready for the day—in his own Ashokan clothes rather than the wardrobe of Lyrian tunics the emperor had provided—he nervously paced in the hallway before working up the nerve to knock on Preethi's door. She opened it almost immediately, surprise evident on her face.

"Ronak? What are you doing here?" She too was dressed, but unlike him, she'd selected a Lyrian-style gray silk gown that swished around her ankles as she moved.

"Can I come in?" he asked, rubbing the back of his neck awkwardly.

"Of course." She opened the door wider, allowing him in.

He recalled the promise he'd made to Jay, that he'd keep her out of his deal with Ekta, but he stifled the guilt he felt as he stepped inside. The layout of the room was identical to his, but it was decorated so differently with warm-toned furniture and patterned wallpaper that it looked almost like an entirely new space.

"Did you have a good evening?" he asked as he sat on the edge of the chair she offered him.

"I did. Did you?" She sat across from him.

Ronak lifted a shoulder. "Big gatherings aren't really my thing."

"I'd never have guessed," she said dryly.

"You're good at this, though," he said. "Talking to people," he clarified.

She eyed him carefully. "Are you here to make sure I don't tell anyone about your brother?"

Ronak thought that he'd been subtle when he'd gone to find Kaleb, but Preethi was sharper than he'd given her credit for.

"No," he said. "I'm actually . . . I wanted to apologize." He exhaled, looking out to where she'd opened the terrace doors, allowing the brisk morning air in. He'd practiced his words and considered carefully what he intended to say, but he'd never been particularly good at being vulnerable. At asking for help. "It's hard for me to trust anyone when people rarely see me for *me*. I'm a tool first and foremost, for my family or for the Council to use and discard as necessary."

Preethi relaxed in her seat for the first time since he'd walked in. "I know the feeling," she said. "People only seem to see me as a manipulative social climber or a vapid girl obsessed with boys. Whatever suits their needs on that day, I suppose." She smiled wryly at his surprised look. "You think I don't know what's said about me?"

"I didn't think you'd address it so directly," he admitted.

She smiled. "I don't believe in wasting people's time. I learned a long time ago that if I want something, the best way to get it is to own up to it." She lifted a shoulder. "What's the point of lying about your desires? The truth always comes out anyway."

This was the first time the two of them were actually conversing honestly, away from the emperor or her friends or Jay, and Ronak had the feeling that he was finally seeing the real Preethi—not the girl who knew how to make easy conversation or always had a smile for everyone. He'd thought her naive, wanting the luxury that the life of a rajkumaari promised, but seeing her ambition laid bare like this was informative; Ronak found himself reconfiguring his opinion of her.

He'd thought to appeal to her sentiments in asking for her help, to suggest that they spend time getting to know one another before the wedding, but that wouldn't work on her. She cared about him even less than he cared about her. She would play the part of the dutiful rajkumaari, but he knew the offer she'd made him before their engagement still stood.

We're different people with different lives, she'd said. *That doesn't need to change.*

And if there was one thing she desperately wanted, it was to be the rajkumaari of Ashoka. Which would be irrelevant if there wasn't even an Ashoka to be the rajkumaari of.

"Did you mean what you said back in Ashoka?" Ronak asked finally as he tried to gather his thoughts. "About . . . about making the most of our situation?"

She arched an eyebrow. "Are you asking me to be your friend?"

"Something like that." Ronak bit his lip, trying to decide how much to divulge. In the end he decided it was better for her to feel like he trusted her. "You asked me about Kaleb earlier. A few weeks ago, my family and I were supposed to go to Gauri Mahal. But that's not where we went. We went to Ritsar, looking for a new source of magic."

"The Ivory Key," Preethi said. She didn't sound surprised, which meant she'd already suspected.

He nodded. "While we were there, we discovered that the emperor of Lyria was doing some experiments with magic—as you saw last night. And so Kaleb came here to investigate what happened."

"That's why you volunteered to go on this trip," Preethi guessed.

"Because your brother was here."

"One of the reasons," he amended. "My brother didn't kill anyone," he said flatly, watching her carefully for any shred of doubt.

"I didn't think he did."

Ronak exhaled, a little relieved. "After Vira was ousted, I wanted to make sure he was safe. But another reason is because"—he considered his words—"I know we're here to negotiate peace, but I think there's something else going on. Whatever the emperor is doing with magic, it has to be more than parlor tricks."

Preethi's brows knit together. "I don't understand."

"I don't believe the emperor intends to negotiate peace," he said plainly. "I don't trust him, and you shouldn't either."

She gave him a measured look and then nodded resolutely. "All right. So what do we do and how can I help?"

Ronak felt a heaviness inside him disappear. He hadn't been entirely certain that she would agree to help—that they could even trust one another. But knowing that he wouldn't be doing this alone eased a burden, and he was grateful for it.

"The emperor has a compass where he stores important information. Memories. Plans."

"The one he wears around his neck," Preethi said. "I noticed that."

Ronak nodded. "I have reason to believe that whatever he intends to do will be on it."

"So you want to get that compass," Preethi said.

Ronak nodded. "And then we can finally get answers about how to protect Ashoka."

✻

As promised, the emperor sent word for Ronak and Preethi to meet him for a tour of the palace. To their surprise, it wasn't the emperor alone, but his eldest son, Elias, who met them at the foot of the stairs.

"I hope you don't mind if my son joins us," the emperor said, patting Elias on the back.

"It would be our pleasure," Preethi said, giving him a polite smile.

Elias didn't smile back, but he graciously offered Preethi an arm, allowing Ronak to keep pace with the emperor as he led them through the halls.

Ronak wasn't surprised that the emperor was a thoughtful guide, excitedly sharing the history of the various rooms and wings they passed, stopping to highlight select paintings and sculptures, explaining various stories from Lyrian mythology they might not be familiar with. For the first time since he'd met the emperor, Ronak understood just why Kallias and Papa had been friends. His father too had had the same eager glint in his eyes as he detailed stories of the past.

"I heard that you're a bit of a painter yourself," the emperor said as he led them through an art gallery.

Ronak was surprised that the emperor had looked into him at all. "Just a hobbyist," he admitted. "Mostly an admirer."

"Don't be modest," Preethi said. "You're excellent." She'd fully committed to the role of the besotted fiancée. Ronak found it annoying, but the emperor seemed to like her—and seemed to like Ronak more as a result—so he'd decided to go along with it.

"You're welcome to paint anywhere in the palace," the emperor offered. "Just say the word and someone will bring you supplies."

"Thank you," Ronak said. He'd hesitated bringing up Papa, but he couldn't deny that he was genuinely curious. "What was my father like when he was here?"

The emperor glanced at him. "I was waiting for you to ask," he said, laughing as he clapped Ronak on the shoulder. "We were not that much older than you are now when we met, but he was really bright. There are some people you just like being around—people with the kind of energy that makes you feel light. He was like that. He lived here for a while before he married Alena."

"He spoke fondly about his time here," Ronak said. In reality Papa had barely spoken about Lyria at all, but Ronak saw no reason to admit that to the emperor.

"He had a lot of interesting notions about magic," the emperor said, directing them to turn down a hallway—and then changing his mind and continuing straight ahead.

"Interesting?" Preethi asked curiously. Next to her, Elias seemed a little irritated that her attention kept drifting away from the animated story he was telling her.

"About secret organizations and buried treasure and lost history. I was genuinely sad to hear about his passing." He sounded like he meant that. "I'll show you where he used to spend most of his time."

It wasn't until the emperor pushed open a set of heavy wooden doors that Ronak realized they were in the library—where he'd met Kaleb the night before. He took in the musty scent of old books and cast his eyes over the scholars hunched over the tables, using lenses to magnify old manuscripts. He scanned the room for any signs of his brother, but Kaleb wasn't there.

"Papa did always like libraries," Ronak said as they walked through the various reading rooms toward the back shelves. He could easily picture him in this space, engrossed in some large tome, scribbling notes for hours without a break.

"Ah, Hektor," the emperor said, greeting a scholar who was walking toward them with a stack of books. "Rajkumaara, Preethi, meet Hektor. He is one of my head artificers."

"I suppose you're the one responsible for that truly impressive magic demonstration," Preethi said easily, giving him one of her dazzling smiles.

"I worked with a team," Hektor said modestly.

"Nonsense," the emperor said, laughing. "Hektor truly deserves the credit."

"I didn't know magic could work in this way," Ronak said.

"We didn't either," Elias said. "Not until quite recently."

"There's a lot we don't know about magic," Hektor answered diplomatically, shooting Elias an unreadable look.

"And we're just scratching the surface," the emperor added. "The raw magic you so generously gifted us will go a long way toward letting us discover just what is possible. Actually, let me show you both something." The emperor gestured toward the back wall of the library.

"Emperor—" Hektor started to say, frowning a little as though cautioning him against showing Ronak and Preethi whatever he was about to show them.

But the emperor simply waved him away and led them toward another room in the back, this one accessible only through a locked door. The emperor lifted a chain from under his tunic. Ronak had seen it before— the one with the compass. But instead he reached for a small key the chain also held.

Inside the room were a few books laid open on pedestals. The emperor led them toward one, which was open to a page about magic.

"Please," the emperor said, gesturing for Ronak to peruse the text. He stayed back, but he was watching Ronak closely.

Ronak leaned closer, realizing the text was in Ashokan. He skimmed a few passages, but the language was so dense, filled with formal terms that only mayaka would know, that he wasn't sure he understood anything. However, one thing was clear. This book—just like the notes they'd found at Ritsar—spoke about people with magical powers.

His heart rate quickened. This was how the emperor had learned about magic working with people. This was what Riya needed in order to understand how her power worked.

Ronak flipped through a few pages. There were more formulas and large blocks of dense explanations. But there were also drawings, beautifully rendered in color. One in particular stood out to him: a sketch of a human form, with various focal points marked throughout the body, each of them corresponding to different powers.

His breath caught, and he traced a red circle placed at the heart to a list of powers: *healing, including of the self; destruction of matter; elemental manipulation.* These were the powers that Riya had.

Noticing the emperor's eyes still on him, Ronak reluctantly continued flipping the pages—only to discover that the entire next section was gone, roughly ripped out, judging by the jagged edges, as though the person didn't care about leaving the stolen pages readable but wanted only to destroy knowledge.

"A former scholar," the emperor explained as Ronak stepped back. "I've learned to keep an eye on my prized possessions."

Ronak's gaze unwillingly drifted to the compass the emperor hadn't tucked back under his tunic. "This seems like an impressive book," he said. "I've never seen anything like it."

"You know, I actually have your father to thank for leading me to it," the emperor said.

"Really?" Ronak didn't know why he was surprised. Papa talked about magic to anyone who was willing to listen, and it was clear that the emperor had listened.

"Did you know that Lyria and Ashoka were one country once?" the emperor asked. "What we delineate as Lyria and Ashoka were modern inventions. But magic really existed throughout all these lands. And after looking through your father's research, I discovered that there was in fact a tomb on the eastern edge of Lyria. And four years ago, on an excursion, I found this ancient book created by the people who lived there. They had such interesting ideas about how magic could function with living things, and we're finally able to put them into practice all these years later."

The words tugged at something in the depths of Ronak's memory. Kaleb would know far more than he did, but Ronak was fairly certain that Papa had spent many years searching for a book exactly like this one. Four years ago Papa had been alive. And yet the emperor had not told him.

"I wish I was more of a scholar so I could appreciate the nuances," Ronak said. "I'm sure Papa would have loved to see this. Or even my brother. He's a mayaka." He watched for any reaction from the emperor at the mention of Kaleb, but he only raised an eyebrow as though mildly curious.

"I suppose that's why you and I have scholars in our employ," the emperor said, turning away.

As they moved on, Ronak couldn't help but glance back at the book one more time. The emperor's interest in magic had existed for a lot longer than anyone had expected, and Ronak had a feeling they were underestimating him.

But in order to find out just what Kallias was planning, he'd need to get his hands on that compass.

CHAPTER TWENTY-TWO

— KALEB —

WHEN KALEB WAS a child, he'd been a voracious reader. He'd stayed up for hours, well past the time his parents had insisted he go to sleep, sneaking a flameless lantern under his covers so he could know what happened next. But as he'd gotten older, he'd lost the time—and then the inclination—for reading. It was Ronak who was now the reader in their family, spending any and all leisure time with a book in his hand, living far more often in imaginary worlds than in their own.

Staying up through most of the night for several days to read through Theo's journal reminded Kaleb of his childhood in some ways, though instead of getting lost in an engrossing tale, he was huddled over the table, trying to parse out tiny, cramped handwriting detailing magical theories.

He stared blearily out the window at the lightening sky, rubbing the tiredness out of his eyes as he realized that it was already dawn. He reached for the cup of tea beside him, grimacing at just how cold it had gotten.

He'd flipped through a few pages as soon as he found it, but it had become quickly apparent that this journal would require a more thorough review to even begin to understand it. Theo had written down nearly every thought he'd had, oftentimes crossing things out or jotting addendums in the margins—sometimes scratched at odd angles and orientations that required Kaleb to turn the book entirely in order to read it. It was difficult to know where one thought ended and where the next picked up, especially because, as the pages went on, they were turning from the somewhat odd musings of an eccentric scholar to paranoid rants. Theo was convinced that he was being followed, that someone was watching his every move, and he feared that the journal would fall into the wrong hands.

Yet the journal *was* useful in helping Kaleb discover two things. The first was that the research the scholars were now conducting—trying to figure out how to create more liquid magic—was a waste of time. The emperor *already knew* how to create it. Theo had written out the exact steps to follow, the correct formula that he'd derived. Why then was the emperor having them research it again?

The second was that Theo had been involved in the explosion that led to the collapse of the old scholars building. It wasn't entirely clear just *how* he'd caused it, but Kaleb was almost certain it hadn't been a simple accident. Theo had wanted to destroy something.

But after that, the journal was virtually unreadable, filled with fragments and phrases that made very little sense to Kaleb. There were ramblings about some book—a book the emperor had in his possession that he believed was too dangerous. There were scratched-out musings about the correct wording of intentions of a magical item he was trying to forge. And oddly enough, there was a lot of theorizing about how magic faded out of objects.

On the last page, there were just a few words.

Magic fades. Magic fades with use.

With use was underlined three times. Below it was the question: *Amplify use?*

And that was the end. The pages after that were entirely empty.

He closed the journal and stared at it, left with more questions and mysteries than answers. But one thing was clear: he had to go look at the annex.

✳

Kaleb had fully intended to keep Dayana from learning about his complicated reasons for being in Lyria, but he needed access to the lab. He didn't know any other scholars he could ask for help—and even if he did, he wasn't sure he could trust them.

He waited, lingering in the library during the hour that most people took their lunch break, and when he saw Hektor leave as well, he slipped into the artificers' lab. He hadn't spent too much time there, given that his duties mainly left him confined in the library, but he was familiar enough with it to quickly spot Dayana in her usual spot in the back near a window.

The lab more or less looked the same as those found in Ashoka, with long tables and benches where mayaka could work on imbuing magic into objects. However, this one was different in that it was connected to a training facility, which was a rectangular room built in one corner. It was made of clear glass, forged to be unbreakable but able to offer visibility into the room. The young Ashokan boy was sitting on a mat in the center of it, conjuring color-changing flames in his palms while two artificers stood outside, one calling out instructions in accented Ashokan of which color to change the fire to next, while another took diligent notes.

The boy's name was Shiv, Kaleb had learned from Dayana. He'd been the first one to manifest magical power as far as anyone knew. The soldiers who'd invaded Ritsar had found him, and he'd been brought to the capital several weeks earlier. That was all the information Dayana had, but Kaleb knew one other fact about the boy: he had a sister that the Lyrians were holding captive. Kaleb had seen her briefly, watched Vira vow to free her one day. He hoped they could honor that promise.

Kaleb averted his eyes despite his curiosity about the progression of Shiv's power. It felt wrong somehow to watch him treated like an odd creature to study. The artificers were supposedly treating him well, ensuring that he was fed and given rest and never pushed past his limits, but that wasn't the point. Kaleb couldn't even imagine what it felt like for the boy, having strange magical powers and then being brought to another country and forced to be part of an experiment.

Dayana looked up when she heard footsteps, smiling confusedly when she saw Kaleb. "Kol? What are you doing here?"

"I wanted to talk to you about something," he said, lowering his voice even though they were alone.

She frowned a little. "That sounds serious."

Kaleb held up Theo's journal, which he'd brought with him, but he didn't hand it to her yet. "You know the emperor is taking artificers with him to Ashoka? How badly do you want to be on that trip?"

Her eyes widened. Thalia would be there, and the more Dayana worked with magic and saw what Shiv could do, the more concerned she'd grown about Thalia and the other soldiers. "Very," she said. "But there's no way Hektor would pick us."

That was the problem. Kaleb hadn't been emotionally prepared for the politics, for the favoritism or the assumptions that were thrown his way. He'd heard it was like this in some parts of Ashoka too, but he'd never experienced it. He'd only ever worked with Papa—who was revered within the Dvar Palace—and in Papa's absence, Kaleb's status as the rajkumaara assured that he would be respected by the other scholars in the mayaka lab as well.

"I think I have a solution," Kaleb said, finally flipping to the page of the journal he'd marked, handing it to her. "I found this in the library."

She glanced down at it—and then did a double take. "Is that a formula for liquid magic?" She pressed a hand to her mouth. "Do you think it works?"

Kaleb shrugged. "There's one way to find out."

Dayana bit her lip, and then she nodded. "All right. Meet me back here at midnight, and we'll try it out."

✳

Kaleb met his brother outside on the grounds as planned. He'd hesitated about reaching out to Ronak, but in the end had decided that it would be better if he knew what Ronak was doing. They were dressed in nearly matching tunics, dark colored and made of simple cotton. He had an hour before he was due to meet Dayana, and the grounds were deserted.

"What exactly are we doing here?" Ronak asked, looking up at the ruined building.

"I'm not sure," Kaleb said. "Let's circle around first."

It was what Riya had done at the fort in Ritsar, surveying it for any guards and weak entry points before coming up with a plan. Kaleb was hoping they would seem like two people taking a leisurely stroll through the gardens while he surreptitiously examined the area around the building.

"It looks as though no one has been here in months," Ronak argued, tugging his coat tighter around himself, still unused to the cooler climate of Lyria.

Kaleb secretly agreed, but he was hesitant to simply walk in without verifying that they were indeed alone. Ronak reluctantly followed. But after they circled around once without running into anyone, Kaleb finally conceded that it was unlikely that too many others would be skulking around a construction site at this hour.

He used a small amount of processed magic he'd stolen from the lab to turn a smooth stone into a source of illumination. He pulled it out of his pocket as they stepped over some wooden beams that were laid on the floor. "This building used to be where the scholars worked," Kaleb explained. "Until there was an explosion."

Ronak looked at him sideways. "You think someone did that with magic? Like—" *Riya.*

"I don't know," Kaleb admitted. He wasn't sure exactly what he was even looking for. The structure was larger than he'd expected, and the construction equipment left behind cast eerie shadows in the dim light he held in his hand. "I do think it was purposeful."

As they walked through the building, he told Ronak about Theo and the journal—carefully leaving out all details about Lukas or the deal he'd made with the prince. In return, Ronak told him about a book he'd found in the emperor's personal library—an ancient tome that Ronak suspected to be the source of the emperor's knowledge about magic working with people.

"Do you think you could get that book?" Kaleb asked. It sounded like the same one Theo had written about in his journal.

"It won't be easy," Ronak said, kicking a small rock that went skittering over the stone floors. "He's keeping a close eye on it. But I'll try."

Kaleb nodded, and as he breathed out he allowed himself to relax. It had been so long since they'd spoken without fighting that Kaleb realized he'd been unconsciously tensing his shoulders, bracing for another inevitable argument. But he'd forgotten how freeing it was to be around someone without hiding any part of himself. For all that Ronak infuriated him, he was still someone Kaleb could trust and rely on.

The rooms that were most intact were the sleeping quarters and other residential areas. There was one room that seemed to be the library, full of shelves charred as though by fire damage. However, all of them were devoid of furniture or any other personal artifacts, leaving them all eerily empty. But the closer they got to the actual artificers' lab, the more in ruin things were, forcing them to climb over fallen beams and collapsed walls.

"Something feels off," Ronak said as they got closer to the destroyed lab. "Like . . . raw magic."

Ronak had become sensitive to it after a mild case of raw magic poisoning, but Dayana had told Kaleb the magic had been cleared out weeks earlier. There was no way it was still present in high enough quanitites to affect Ronak.

But when Kaleb glanced over, he saw that Ronak had started shivering.

"Maybe you should stay out here," Kaleb said.

"No," Ronak said stubbornly. "I'll be fine."

With a resigned sigh, Kaleb carefully crossed the threshold into the lab. It was well illuminated, thanks to the bright moonlight streaming in through the holes in the scaffolding, so Kaleb put the stone away. Accident or not, it was clear that there had been a huge amount of damage, leaving the foundations exposed.

Ronak's breathing was shallow as he carefully trailed behind Kaleb, trying not to touch anything that could still contain raw magic as Kaleb pulled out the second item he'd brought with him: a hand mirror. It was one of the items he'd taken from the vault beneath the fort at Ritsar. He'd taken as many of Savitri's items as he could carry, intending to sell them, but when he'd actually studied the mirror and realized just how powerful it was, he'd known he couldn't get rid of it. It was forged to reflect the past, showing events that had previously occurred in a space—something he'd accidentally discovered while staying in the inn and seeing reflections of former occupants.

He angled it back and forth, trying to find the best position from which to view the past. Flashes of memory flickered over the surface. He'd discovered that the mirror was most likely to show the most memorable event, so it wasn't long before it settled on the explosion.

"Hold this," Kaleb instructed Ronak and then had him slowly turn while scanning the room.

Ronak looked ill, his eyes half closed, but he did as ordered while Kaleb studied the space through the mirror. Most of it was covered in exploding debris and stone—and then he found it. The source of the explosion—a crystalline ball dropped by a hooded figure into the middle of a large slab of raw magic. Almost instantaneously, purple and pink light had radiated out from the point of impact, incinerating half the room. Kaleb lifted a hand to shield his eyes from the sudden brightness. He tried to squint through the pain but almost as soon as it appeared, the image was gone—and where the raw magic had been, there was nothing but empty space.

Kaleb was staring at it, trying to make sense of what he'd seen, when with a groan, Ronak fell. The mirror slipped out of his hands and crashed to the floor, shattering. Kaleb lunged for his brother, but he was too far away to get there before Ronak collapsed.

"Ronak!"

It was the raw magic. They'd been there for too long. He lifted Ronak up and slipped one of his arms over his shoulder as he dragged Ronak out into the fresh air. As soon as they were away from the building, Ronak's breathing returned to normal. He slowly blinked his eyes open.

"What happened?"

"I told you to wait outside," Kaleb said, irritated.

"I'm fine," Ronak said, pulling himself free from Kaleb. "So? What did you learn?"

"I don't know," Kaleb said. He wasn't entirely sure what he'd witnessed. Raw magic was poisonous, but it was mostly inert. He couldn't think of anything that would make it simply explode outward like that. The mirror had been his only way of learning what had truly happened, but it was gone now.

But the explosion *had* been purposeful. Someone—maybe Theo—had wanted to destroy all the raw magic the emperor had before he could use it to power an army.

"When did Vira get the first letter from the emperor?" Kaleb asked as a sudden thought struck him.

Ronak frowned. "I'm not sure. Two months ago, I think? Why?"

"Right after the explosion." The emperor had lost all the magic in his possession, and he needed more. "I don't think he ever intended to negotiate with Ashoka," Kaleb said quietly. At least not in good faith.

"The Council doesn't know that," Ronak pointed out. "We have to warn them. Has the emperor agreed to let you join the trip yet? We leave in a week."

"I'm working on it," Kaleb said, not elaborating. He didn't like keeping secrets, but for the first time, he didn't want to divulge the details of his plans to Ronak, not when it involved Dayana. He and Ronak hadn't spoken about Alena or her family yet, and Kaleb could feel it hanging over them like storm cloud on the verge of breaking.

"Kaleb. You *have* to be there. It's our chance to ensure that the Council hears us out and clears your name."

"Clear my name?" Kaleb blinked in surprise. "I don't care about that."

"What are you talking about?" Ronak demanded. "That's all you've ever wanted. For the Council and Vira to exonerate you so you could go back to your life."

"I—" Kaleb looked away uneasily. He *had* wanted that—more than anything. But the prospect of returning to the life he'd left behind was not as appealing as it had once been. The life of a scholar was not all adventure and clever discovery like Papa had made it seem. It was dreary and monotonous, and doing the same thing day after day was more challenging than Kaleb had anticipated.

But of course his brother knew him too well. "You do want to come back, right?" Ronak asked sharply, his stare piercing Kaleb.

"Yes, of course," Kaleb said hurriedly. "We should get back before someone sees us."

He turned and walked quickly toward the palace, but the entire time he could feel Ronak's gaze on his back.

CHAPTER TWENTY-THREE

— RIYA —

IT WAS MORNING by the time Riya and Varun reached Tasgarh, the capital of the Harya province. It was situated right on the banks of the Rayu River and was a bustling trade hub—an oasis of commerce in the midst of farmland.

Her injury had put them way behind schedule, and she didn't have a lot of time before she had to meet Vira. Varun was familiar with the region, and he'd been to the greenhouse before, so Riya let him take the lead on instructing their carriage driver through the cobbled streets at the base of the Tasgarh Fort. If it were anyone else, Riya might have doubted that he remembered a location he'd visited once years earlier, but Varun had always had a strangely good memory for things like this.

He ordered the carriage to stop beside one of the gates of the fort, near an area that he thought looked familiar. Varun disembarked first, but to Riya's surprise, he turned and held out his hand.

"Thanks," she murmured as she placed her palm in his. He let go quickly, but Riya could feel her skin tingle from the brush of his warm hand against hers.

Something had shifted between them, and Riya wasn't entirely sure what or how it had happened. Maybe it was when he'd insisted on carrying her bag for the rest of their trek through the forest. Or when they'd stopped to make camp for the night, and despite promising to wake her to take the second watch, he'd let her sleep so her fever would break. Or maybe it was when she'd caught him staring at her hands as she split what little food she had with him, questions plainly evident on his face—but instead of pushing her about the magic, he'd simply stretched out on the ground beneath the starlit sky and pointed out his favorite constellations.

"How's your shoulder?" Varun asked. Instead of walking inside the compound, he directed them down the street that bordered the fort's outer wall.

Riya moved her arm a little. It still hurt. "Fine," she lied.

Varun huffed. "It's all right to admit you're in pain."

Riya scowled. It wasn't that she was pretending to be strong. It was just that he'd already done so much to take care of her, and she didn't want to seem ungrateful.

"Thank you again," she said awkwardly. "For helping me."

"I'd always help you. I hope you know that." He sounded so serious that Riya looked up at him in surprise, but his attention was focused on a fork in the road. "I think it's this way," he said, speaking more to himself than her, setting off down a dirt road that led away from the fort.

They walked for twenty minutes before they approached a large glass greenhouse attached to a smaller stone building. Butterflies and bees fluttered between the rows of potted ferns and bushes with brightly colored flowers that lined the exterior. There was a small white image painted on the door. A peacock with ferns instead of feathers behind it. If there was any doubt that she was in the wrong place, it was gone now.

Varun hesitated at the entrance, his hands tucked into the pockets of his kurta. "Do you want me to wait out here?"

Riya found herself shaking her head even before her brain processed the question. She didn't want to admit it, but it was comforting to have him with her. "No, it's fine. But just . . . let me talk to them?"

Her palms felt clammy with nerves as she reached for the door handle. She wasn't sure if she'd be able to get any of the answers she needed so badly, but she was here to try.

Inside, it was warm and bright. Large windows let in copious sunlight, illuminating plants that covered every available surface—crowded on staggered shelves, hanging down from the rafters, crawling over the trellis that spanned one entire wall. A man dressed in black stood with his back to them, sweeping up dirt, leaves, and pieces of a pot that had shattered on the floor.

He turned to greet them. He had deep-set eyes, and hair that hung down to his shoulders. "Welcome," he said. His skin looked like it was stretched too thin over the bones of his face, lending him a sinister quality even as he smiled. "How can I help you?"

Riya had insisted on being the one to talk, but now that she was here, she didn't know exactly what to say. "I was . . . I heard you had some special plants in your possession, and I was hoping to speak to someone about them," she said finally, hoping it wasn't too cryptic.

"We cultivate many unusual and rare species," the man said. "You're welcome to take a look around."

"That's not—" Riya bit her lower lip. She didn't want to draw too much attention to herself, but there was no point in coming all the way if she couldn't get answers. "I meant magical plants," she said directly.

"Ah," the man said, gaze flitting between her and Varun. "I see." He set the broom aside and gestured for them to follow him into the adjoining room, which held a low wooden table and several threadbare divans. The room smelled faintly of smoke, and there was a bored-looking girl sitting on the floor beside an open ledger and a metal crate of coins. "Please," the man said, gesturing to the divan. "May I offer you some chai?"

They hadn't eaten anything in hours, so neither Riya nor Varun declined. The man—who introduced himself as Prem—vanished through the door and returned a few minutes later with two tumblers and a platter of snacks. Riya gratefully selected a murukku and snapped it in half, offering one piece to Varun. He took it wordlessly.

"How did you hear about this greenhouse?" Prem asked, taking a seat opposite them.

"A friend," she said vaguely. Riya knew that she had to be honest if she wanted him to help, but Vira's warning was still ringing her ears. "But she didn't tell me much, so I was hoping to learn more about how these plants came to exist and what sort of powers they possess."

Prem smiled ruefully. "You can understand why I'd be hesitant to divulge that information to strangers."

"I understand, and I assure you that we mean you no harm," Riya said. "I just . . ." She took a sip of chai to buy time while she searched for the right words. It was a bit odd, prepared with some unfamiliar herbs that gave it an earthier taste than she was used to. She took another sip to avoid being rude and then set it down. "I just want to know, hypothetically, how magic can work with living things. And how one might . . . remove it."

Prem's face was carefully blank. "Remove it?"

Riya felt Varun staring at her. "Hypothetically," she repeated.

Prem studied her for a long moment and then leaned forward. "Where did you get that necklace?" he asked.

"I found it in a vault under the Simha Fort in Ritsar," Riya said. And then she froze. She hadn't intended to reveal that. She looked at Prem in confusion. "What did you do to me?"

"Nothing that won't wear off," a familiar voice said behind her.

Riya whirled around. "Tarini?"

"What are you doing here?" Varun asked.

"I knew I should have never brought you here," she said to Varun, shaking her head as she strode forward. "How's your shoulder?" she asked Riya, dropping into the seat beside Prem. "Glad to see you survived the forest."

"It was you," Riya said numbly, realization dawning on her. "You attacked me. Why?" Tarini had been a part of the Ravens for even longer than her, and Riya couldn't wrap her mind around the fact that she had betrayed them.

"To slow you down," Tarini said, as though it should have been obvious. She'd always been soft-spoken with a kind smile for everyone, and Riya couldn't reconcile the Tarini she'd known with the cold, detached girl in front of her.

"I don't understand," Varun said slowly, looking between Riya and Tarini. "What is this place exactly?"

"I'm the one asking questions," Tarini said. "Why don't you start by telling me what you and your sister are up to."

"We're following the Ivory Key to get more magic for Ashoka," Riya said before she could stop herself.

Tarini and Prem exchanged a glance. "You found the Ivory Key?" Prem asked eagerly. "Where?"

"In Ritsar." Riya gaped at Prem. "What did you do to me?" she demanded again.

"You wanted to know about the magical properties of our plants,"

Prem said with a dark smile. "One of them compels those who consume it to speak the truth." He pointedly eyed the tumblers of chai.

Riya felt more than heard Varun's sharp gasp. Her stomach twisted in horror and regret. "We're leaving," she snarled. She put a hand on Varun's forearm, intending to pull him up with her, but Tarini's voice stopped her before she could move.

"Where is your sister now?"

"She went to the Fire Temple of Paliya," Riya blurted. She clamped a hand over her mouth, but Tarini only laughed.

"That won't work," Tarini said. She reached over the table. Riya flinched, but Tarini only tugged at the chain around Riya's neck, lifting the ruby pendant out from under the collar of her kurta. "You have no idea what this is, do you?"

"A necklace," Riya said. "Give it back." Riya grabbed for it as the clasp snapped and Tarini pulled it away.

"It belongs to the Order of the Mayura," Tarini said, holding up a matching one that hung around her neck.

"Order of the *what*?" Varun asked. "What are you talking about?"

"And it's not *just* a necklace," Tarini continued as if Varun hadn't spoken. "It was crafted by the goddess Niveda herself."

"Niveda wasn't a goddess," Riya said.

Prem scoffed. "You have no idea who she is."

"She was Savitri's sister," Riya said. But she couldn't help but think about what Ronak had written—that the Order worshipped a goddess that they believed would rise again and grant them power. Suddenly she understood why Surya had called them a cult.

"She was the rightful maharani," Tarini snapped. "Savitri stole the throne from her."

"What do you want with the Ivory Key?" Riya asked, changing the topic.

Riya didn't think she would get a response, but Tarini surprised her. "The Ivory Key belongs to *us*," she said. "Not the Kamala Society, and certainly not your sister. And when we finally have it, the goddess will reward us—her most loyal servants—greatly."

"You want to control the quarries," Riya guessed.

"Control?" Prem scoffed. "Magic shouldn't be restricted. It belongs to the people, not the rich and powerful who dictate how and why it should be used."

Riya actually agreed with that, but somehow she didn't think they were talking about the same kind of restrictions. "So you want to create more magical plants, is that it?" she asked.

Tarini's eyes slid down to Riya's hand. She'd seen her use her power. She knew what Riya could do. "I liked you," she said instead of answering. "I liked you both. It's a shame it had to end like this."

"Then how can you betray us?" Varun asked. Riya had seen him angry before, frustrated, even disappointed, but she'd never seen him hurt. He and Tarini had been friends—the only two who'd taken care of the plants in the garden behind the campsite.

"The Ravens were my home," Tarini acknowledged, standing up. "And I am grateful for that. But the Order is my calling. I don't expect you to understand." She nodded to someone behind Riya, and before she or Varun could move, they were grabbed by the shoulders and dragged.

"What are you doing?" Riya demanded, trying to twist away from the grip of her captor. Varun was also trying to break free, but they were overpowered and thrown into the greenhouse.

Riya desperately lunged for the door, trying to wrench it open, but it was locked. Tarini's face stared back at her from the other side of the glass.

"Thank you for your help." Tarini smiled cruelly. "We'll let you out in the morning after I've had a chance to find your sister."

And all Riya could do was watch in horror as Tarini walked away.

✳

Riya had made a huge mistake. Vira was right—she should never have come here. She'd accused her sister of being too naive and trusting, but she was no better. Riya had let her own desires cloud her judgment, and she'd made a mess of everything. Vira was in danger because of her.

Ashoka was in danger because of her.

"Riya?" Varun was right in front of her, and Riya realized he'd been trying to get her attention.

She blinked up at him. "I'm sorry, what?"

Varun's gaze softened as he searched her face. "I asked if you were all right."

"I—" Riya had no idea how to answer that. "We have to get out of here," she said instead.

He nodded. "We'll find a way."

They spread out. It was already hot and humid inside, and the sun—now directly overhead—wasn't helping. Riya felt like her skin was on fire again, overheating with panic and the remnants of poison.

The greenhouse consisted of just one rectangular building, but it was hard to move through it quickly. Wooden tables spanned the length of the room in neat, parallel lines, but they were covered completely in plants with leaves hanging over the sides that kept blocking her path or catching on her clothes. She shoved them aside angrily as she tore through the space, searching for anything that could help them escape. There were no other exits, but Riya found bags of dirt, gardening tools, and empty pots stacked in one corner.

Riya reached for a shovel and swung it at one of the glass panes that made up the walls. It was all fury and no precision—but the glass didn't shatter with the force of her strike. The shovel bounced back with a dull thud that reverberated all around her, the momentum jerking her shoulder back. A strangled gasp escaped Riya as the sudden movement ripped at the bandage around her shoulder.

But she didn't care. She swung again. And again. And again. She didn't care that the glass was heavily fortified and didn't have a single dent in it. She didn't care that she could barely think straight through the pain. She *had* to get out of there.

"Riya. Riya. Stop." Varun's voice sliced through her haze, and Riya stilled. "You're bleeding." His voice sounded strangely far away, laced with horror and fear.

Riya reached over to touch her injured shoulder, barely registering the slide of blood under her fingers. "Oh."

"Do you trust me?" he asked.

Whatever Prem had put in their drinks was still coursing through her body, so the answer came easily. "Yes."

She didn't fight him as he tugged the shovel out of her hand and tossed it on the ground. Or when he led her back the way they'd come. She was feeling lightheaded, her skin flushed and feverish like in the forest, but she followed his silent instructions, sitting on a stool as he peeled back the blood-soaked bandage and kurta to look at the wound.

Varun snapped off a few leaves from a nearby succulent. He used his nails to carefully pry the leaves apart, revealing a gold liquid inside that shimmered like melted sunlight. He pressed one of them against her shoulder, and Riya sighed. It was cool but not uncomfortable, and as the minutes passed the fog of fever dissipated.

"Incredible," Varun breathed, his breath fanning over her neck.

When Riya touched the back of her shoulder, she found that it was completely healed—except for a small scar where the arrow had pierced her skin. "How did you know that would work?" she asked, amazed, shrugging the kurta back on.

"I found this." Varun stepped side, revealing a table of colorful plants. *Magical* plants, it was immediately obvious, now that Riya was alert and paying attention.

There weren't as many varieties as Riya had expected to find—only seven or eight different species. There was the blue-green fern that Tarini grew in the forest that created smoke to render people unconscious. The red succulent that Varun had used to heal her. An oily black vine with sharp thorns. She'd seen that one before too—in the Koranos Mountains. Kaleb had cut his palms on its thorns and nearly died. Riya wondered if Tarini had used the same thing to poison her.

"This is what they put in our chai," Varun said. He was holding a slip of paper with handwritten notes about the properties of each plant and how to care for it.

It looked like any other fruit-bearing tree—albeit a small one that wasn't even as tall as Riya yet—with clusters of small brown pods hanging from the branches. It looked like tamarind except for the fact that the pods were glowing with bright white light.

She wondered if plants like this had once been commonplace all throughout Ashoka—if Papa had ever suspected that they'd existed. She wished he could have seen this bit of ancient history, illicitly preserved.

When she turned back, she found Varun sitting on the floor, watching her with an unreadable expression.

"You keep helping me," she said, a little shyly as she sat next to him. "Thanks. Again."

He nodded in acknowledgment but he remained quiet, looking uncharacteristically nervous as he chewed on his bottom lip. Riya felt her own apprehension grow the longer he stayed silent until she couldn't bear it anymore.

"What is it?" she asked.

"How did you destroy those arrows that Tarini fired?" he asked finally.

She'd expected him to broach the topic hours earlier, but she still found herself caught off guard. "I don't know." She looked down at her hands. She could feel the hum of magic under her skin, but it was faint—like it had receded after she'd used it in the forest. "Well, I do know, I suppose, in that I can tell you literally what happened, but I can't control it."

"Control the magic," he said slowly, as though he needed to say the words aloud to believe them.

She smiled a little wryly. "I was waiting for you to bring it up."

"I was hoping you'd just tell me on your own," he admitted.

She'd been so afraid of this conversation, avoided it at all costs—and maybe it was because she knew that he couldn't lie either—but the thought of telling him the truth wasn't as terrifying as it had been in the Ravens' campsite. So she did. She told him about everything that had happened when they'd gone looking for the Ivory Key, about the magic she'd unexpectedly touched, about the days back in the palace trying and failing to get the power under control.

"You wanted to get rid of it?" Varun asked when she'd finished. He sounded surprised.

She shrugged. "It seemed easier that way."

He looked out at the empty road outside the greenhouse. "You could break the glass."

Riya shook her head. "I can't. I told you I can't control it."

"Try it," he urged. "I believe in you. I trust you."

The words touched Riya more than she wanted to admit. She wasn't sure anyone had said them to her. She put her hands out toward the glass. *Shatter*, she commanded it. *Break*.

Nothing happened. She didn't even feel the magic respond. She'd spent so long stuffing it down, refusing to even acknowledge it that now—when she needed it to work—she had no way to summon the power that she wanted.

She closed her eyes, took a deep breath, and tried to conjure everything she'd learned from Papa, everything she'd practiced with Ronak. She had to clear her mind and just focus on the magic within her. It should be easy. She'd done it before, after all. And though she'd never been great at it, she *had* studied theory with Papa and—

"I can practically hear you thinking," Varun said, and Riya's eyes flew open. "You're worrying about too many things."

"It's *not* working," Riya insisted, frustrated at her spiraling thoughts. "I don't know how to do this."

"You do," Varun said patiently. "Try again."

But suddenly, Riya couldn't focus on the magic, her thoughts too consumed by Varun and how nice he was being. "Why aren't you angry?" Riya blurted out.

"I—what?" Varun looked lost. "Um, do you want me to be?"

"No, of course not. But I lied to you. I got us trapped here. And you don't even like me. Why are you helping?"

"Because I want to," he answered simply, a strange look on his face. "Wait, is that what you've thought this whole time? That I don't like you?"

Riya looked away from him, suddenly unsure. "I didn't know what else to think. You followed me to the palace. You never trusted me. And you were always so cold to me. So distant—"

"Riya, I was intimidated by you," he interrupted.

It was Riya's turn to look at him with shock. "Intimidated?"

He didn't quite meet her gaze. "You're so confident, so sure of yourself. And once you decide to do something, you just do it. You throw yourself wholeheartedly into any situation no matter how dangerous . . . How could I not be?"

Riya licked her lips, trying to process his admission. "Intimidated," she repeated softly. That was . . . unexpected. She'd never seen herself the way he described her. She'd been called impulsive before, called stubborn and reckless and unyielding. But he was painting those traits in a different light, like they were qualities to cherish and cultivate instead of change.

"Then why did you follow me?" she asked.

"Because I didn't want you to go alone." He still wasn't looking at her, but his cheeks were tinged pink. "I guess I didn't do a good job of showing you, but I've only ever wanted to make sure you were safe."

The words hung in the air between them, taking up too much space, and Riya tore her gaze from him, not liking the weird way her heart stuttered, the way she felt herself heat from the inside out.

"You do," she said a moment later, feeling her own face flush. "Keep me safe."

There was more she wanted to say, words perched on the edge of her lips desperate to escape: *I'm sorry I misjudged you all this time* and *I wouldn't have made it this far without you* and *I'm glad you're here with me.* But it all felt too honest, too raw for this fragile moment, so she held her tongue.

"I have something that might help you control the magic," Varun said suddenly.

Riya turned quickly, startled by the abrupt change in topic. He was on his feet, reaching for a plant she couldn't see. When he sat back down, it was with a handful of tulsi leaves.

She looked at him in confusion as he pressed a few leaves into her hand. He'd always had an endless supply, but she didn't understand why he was giving it to her.

"Eat it," he said. He huffed a little when she didn't immediately move. "Trust me."

Riya put a leaf on her tongue. A burst of flavor erupted in her mouth with the first bite. Bitter and aromatic. Earthy.

"Focus on the taste. The smell. The way it makes your tongue tingle ever so slightly."

Riya chewed, letting the taste center her. Varun hesitantly reached out to touch Riya's hand and then threaded his fingers through hers. He brushed his thumb over her knuckles, and Riya felt her breath catch.

"Close your eyes and breathe," Varun said. "Just focus on my hand. On my voice. On the tulsi."

Riya took several deep breaths, rolled her shoulders back, and then focused on the things he told her to. But she couldn't resist asking him one more question. "Why the tulsi?"

"It reminds me of my home," Varun said. "We always had it around our house. It grew wild where we lived, so my mother would make garlands and take it to the temple as an offering to the goddesses. When Yash and I first moved to Dvar, I used to get these panic attacks whenever I felt overwhelmed. Dvar was so bright and colorful, so crowded and vibrant. Everything felt a little too intense. The tulsi is a bit of my home—of my childhood—and when I need it, it's my anchor. Something tangible to focus on."

"I . . . I didn't know," Riya said regretfully, thinking of every snide comment she'd ever made about him always smelling of tulsi. But of course he'd never told her—she'd never made him feel like he could talk to her.

But Varun seemed to understand. "It's all right," he said softly, his thumb once again fluttering over the back of her hand. "Just keep focusing. It's not about having a purpose, but about being in this moment."

Riya's hands shook as she called upon the magic within her. It didn't immediately respond, but Varun was right beside her, holding her hand, telling her to be patient. She didn't know how long she sat there, but eventually the world slipped away.

And all that was left was the tug of the magic. She didn't feel it in her hand, where she'd originally thought, but in the center of her chest—a warm feeling, familiar almost, like it was and always had been a part of her.

Shatter, Riya thought.

And this time she felt the magic obey. Her eyes flickered open, and she saw that once again, blue light was emerging from her hands, and right before her eyes, the glass shattered.

CHAPTER TWENTY-FOUR

— KALEB —

DAYANA'S PLAN WAS to approach the emperor at the palace sporting event with evidence of their success—a vial of liquid magic—to try to convince him to let them join the trip.

Kaleb was hesitant about giving the emperor something he so badly wanted and would use to invade Ashoka, but in the end, he decided it was just a small vial. The emperor would want to know how they did it, and Kaleb could stall by misrepresenting the steps. But it was getting perilously close to the day when the emperor would be departing, and he needed to be on the trip.

It had taken them several days of sneaking into the lab in the middle of the night to achieve success, but they had found a way to make it work. Though the instructions seemed straightforward at first, Theo had altered them cleverly to prevent those who weren't trained to actually work with magic from understanding them. Dayana had been the one to decode it in the end, and once they had the right instructions, processing the actual magic was easy.

The emperor had been on the right track. It did involve heating raw magic rather than cooling it down, but it mattered how it was heated—on a direct flame rather than in a pot, as in the other experiments.

Now all they had to do was present it to the emperor, but because they couldn't simply request an audience with him, Dayana had decided it would be best to wait and find him during the annual sporting competition, to be held two days before the emperor and the Ashokan visitors would be leaving.

"It's the emperor's most popular event," Dayana explained as she noticed Kaleb glancing around at the especially large crowd gathered in the gardens. "Everyone with even the slightest noble ties manages to secure an invitation—and no one turns it down."

"They all come here to play games?" he asked skeptically.

He knew that in Lyria, athleticism was encouraged, cultivated, and honored, but they had actual tournaments for that. He didn't understand why the emperor's informal games were such a big deal. But then again, in Ashoka, war wasn't a pastime.

"Well, not all of them," Dayana said. "Some, like us, are just here to watch."

"Technically we're not here for that either," Kaleb reminded her.

Dayana gave him a look. "The emperor won't be here for a few hours, so let's just try to enjoy ourselves and celebrate our victory."

As they stepped outside, a servant greeted them with glasses of wine. Kaleb wasn't intending to drink much, but he took the glass Dayana handed him just to have something to hold.

"The obstacle courses are that way." Dayana pointed to the far side of the garden. "That's always fun. But if you want to watch some of the more competitive events, there's archery and spear throwing over there."

"Whatever you'd prefer," Kaleb said distractedly, looking around for any sign of the Ashokan delegation—and realizing belatedly that they'd be with other members of the royal family, probably arriving late and sitting in specially designed booths to allow them the best views. They wouldn't be mingling.

"Obstacle course, then," Dayana said, navigating them in that direction. Picnic blankets had been laid out, and those who wished could retrieve baskets of dainty pastries and sandwiches to eat while they watched the various competitions.

The event had already started, but there wasn't a large crowd, so Dayana situated them on the grass near the front as several soldiers attempted the course. Dayana's eyes were fixed on them, but Kaleb plucked a blade of grass and toyed with it as he contemplated how to bring up the topic he'd been wanting to broach.

"Did you come here as a child with your family?" Kaleb asked carefully.

"Every year," Dayana said, looking around with a fond smile. "My mother's side of the family are all incredible archers. My aunt Alena held the record for the most consecutive bull's-eyes for many years." She laughed a little, oblivious to the way Kaleb's heart ached. "I can't describe the looks of disappointment I was met with when my family realized that I have the hand-eye coordination of a loaf of bread."

For a moment, Kaleb lost himself in a fantasy: one where Alena had survived, where Papa had remained in Lyria. This might have been his life, attending sporting events every year, drinking too much wine, and laughing with his cousin. Perhaps he would have become a skilled archer under Alena's tutelage—or maybe he would have stayed on the sidelines, cheering his mother on as she scored another victory.

"Oh, look," Dayana said, tugging Kaleb back to the present, the image in his head dissipating. "Lukas is participating."

Kaleb looked up, surprised. Lukas was indeed standing near the start, dressed in an ivory tunic with embroidered gold designs and a circlet of laurel leaves perched atop his curls. Kaleb suddenly noticed that the crowd around them had nearly doubled as people whispered and pointed toward Lukas.

"Of course he's going to win," Dayana said, rolling her eyes.

Lukas was stretching at the start line, smirking at the spectators and raising a hand to wave at his admirers. He looked carefree and relaxed as he winked at the audience—which invited cheers and hoots—but as soon as the horn sounded, his gaze turned serious and piercing as he began to make his way through the course.

"He seems well-liked," Kaleb commented.

Dayana laughed and sipped her wine. "I suppose that depends on your definition of *well*. Or *liked*, for that matter."

"I didn't realize those words had more than one meaning," Kaleb said.

Lukas was confident but clever. He assessed each portion of the course with an exacting eye, and when he moved, he didn't hesitate or make mistakes. The sun turned his hair to gold as he easily leapt into the air, untied a rope that had been tucked out of reach, and then swung across a small pond of water, landing in a soft crouch on the other side to loud cheers.

"Why don't you like him?" Kaleb asked. "He seems friendly enough."

"He's pretty and powerful," Dayana said, though it didn't sound like much of a compliment coming from her. "That amounts to a lot here."

That amounted to a lot everywhere, but Kaleb didn't say that aloud. He turned back to where Lukas was tackling the last obstacle. He had to use arrows to strike down a rope that held a wheel vertically attached to a wall. Once it was down, he had to use it propel himself to the landing on the other side.

Kaleb—who'd struggled to even pick up a bow long enough to aim it—knew that it was difficult, but Lukas moved fluidly, making it all look effortless as he easily finished the course to thunderous applause.

Dayana had positioned them close enough to the front that Kaleb could see the thin sheen of sweat clinging to Lukas's forehead, but otherwise there was no indication that he'd exerted himself at all.

One of the Lyrian officials approached to crown Lukas with a golden wreath, replacing the green leaves he already wore. The circlet glittered in the sunlight, stark against his dark locks. He *was* rather pretty, Kaleb conceded, as Lukas directed his dazzling smile toward the crowd.

And almost as though he could sense Kaleb's thoughts, Lukas looked right at him. Kaleb looked away, feeling his neck heat just a little as he took a sip of wine. He was being silly—Lukas was too far away, with the sun shining directly in his eyes, and there was no way he'd spotted Kaleb in the distance.

But unfortunately for Kaleb, Dayana *did* notice. "Kol. No. Listen to me. All his romantic entanglements end in heartbreak," she said.

"What? No, it's not like that," Kaleb said, flustered that she'd mistaken his curiosity for attraction.

"You can do better than him," Dayana said with a pointed look. "He's not worth it."

He wanted to protest again, but he swallowed the impulse. It was easier to simply agree than to explain why he was interested in Lukas. "All right," he promised. "I'll stay away."

But he couldn't help glancing back at Lukas. And this time, it was unmistakable that Lukas was watching him, a small smile playing on his lips as he raised his glass directly to Kaleb.

*

It was dusk when the sporting events were over and the atmosphere shifted to one of leisure. Lights had been strung up across an open pavilion where food and drinks awaited both spectators and those who'd participated in the activities.

"Now's the time," Dayana said, directing them toward the tented area reserved for the royal family and their personal guests. There weren't guards stationed outside, so she pushed open the tent without warning. And then she froze abruptly, causing Kaleb to stumble into her back.

It was empty save for the emperor, Hektor, and one of the soldiers. The soldier was standing in the center of the space, using magic to create a crystal sphere out of nothing.

The emperor too seemed entirely caught off guard, clearly not expecting to be interrupted. "Dayana?" he asked, surprised. He blinked and waved at the soldier to stop. The glow of light in the soldier's hands faded, leaving the sphere half formed as it dropped into his outstretched palm. It looked like a laddoo someone had taken a large bite of. The soldier set it on the table and then ducked out of the tent.

Kallias was younger than Kaleb had expected, with short-cropped hair that was just graying around his temples. He looked like an older version of Lukas with the same piercing eyes and striking jawline.

"Your Highness, I'm so sorry for interrupting," Dayana said, bowing low. Kaleb hastily followed suit, realizing that he was being rude staring.

Hektor glared at them. "This is a private area," he snarled, advancing on them, but the emperor put his arm out to stop him in his tracks.

"What are you doing here?" the emperor asked Dayana, his gaze flicking toward Kaleb momentarily. Unlike Hektor, he didn't sound upset but merely curious. "If you're looking for the boys, I'm afraid they just left. They're escorting our Ashokan visitors to dinner."

"I was actually hoping to talk to you about something," Dayana said finally, squaring her shoulders. "It's about the work the scholars are doing." But as she glanced at Hektor's scowling face, her bravado seemed to be withering.

Kaleb's gaze was fixed on the crystal orb still on the table. He could have sworn it was shrinking before his very eyes, as if some invisible creature were taking more bites out of it.

"Kol has done extensive work with magic," Dayana blurted out. "He's one of the top scholars from the north."

"Is he now?" The emperor reached for the orb and passed it to Kaleb. "What do you make of this?"

Kaleb turned it over, the crystalline material smooth in his hands. He could feel the telltale flutter of magic whisper across his skin, but it was less strong than a regularly forged object. He hadn't been wrong—it *was* shrinking, and all at once he realized what he was witnessing—a physical and visual manifestation of something he'd known about but had never actually been able to see.

"Magic fading out of existence," Kaleb said, his eyes widening. Theo's interest in magic fading out of objects suddenly made more sense.

"Fascinating, isn't it?" the emperor asked, his eyes fixed on Kaleb carefully.

"I've never seen anything like it," Kaleb admitted a little breathlessly. "I didn't even know this was possible."

That wasn't entirely the truth. He *had* seen this material before—twice in fact. The first time in Visala. There, too, it looked like animals had clawed out chunks of the crystal wall.

But the second time, he'd seen it in the mirror—an orb tossed onto the raw magic that made it explode outward.

"The realm of what is possible is changing," the emperor said.

"Is there a way to stabilize it?" Kaleb asked, still staring at the orb. "Or . . . imbue it with magic?"

The emperor's brows rose a little. "Now there's an interesting thought." He was looking at Kaleb with interest, and it reminded Kaleb so much of

Lukas that he found himself wishing he hadn't said anything at all.

Dayana rifled through her bag and produced the vial of liquid they'd made. "The two of us managed to create this," she said.

"And what is this?" the emperor asked.

"Liquid magic," Kaleb said.

The emperor's brows rose even higher as he stepped forward to take it from Dayana. "That's *very* interesting. And how did you accomplish this?"

Kaleb opened his mouth to make up a lie about how he'd pieced it together from several old books, but Dayana spoke first.

"Kol found some notes in the library left behind by a former scholar," Dayana said.

Kaleb didn't miss the glance Hektor and the emperor exchanged as the emperor pocketed the vial without opening it or questioning whether it would work.

"This is great work," the emperor said, offering them both a smile. "This is why I seek out the best scholars in the country."

"We're honored to be among them," Dayana said.

Lyrians believed in rewarding good work with more responsibility, but when the emperor remained silent, Kaleb's hope began to waver. But he finally glanced at Hektor. "You might have see the visiting dignitaries from Ashoka," the emperor said. "I'm accompanying them on a political matter, and I'm taking some scholars with me. I think you've earned a spot on that trip."

Hektor looked as though he'd bitten into a lime, but he nodded curtly. "Report to the lab tomorrow," Hektor ordered. "Both of you," he added reluctantly, looking at Kaleb.

Kaleb exhaled audibly as relief filled him. "It was an honor meeting you, Your Highness," he said, bowing again as Dayana ushered him out.

She squeezed his hand, grinning widely as soon as they were far enough away that the emperor or Hektor couldn't overhear. "See! That went great!"

Kaleb wasn't sure if he agreed, given the irritation on Hektor's face, but he was thankful they'd accomplished their goal, even if the thought of returning to Ashoka had him feeling far more complicated than he expected.

As they approached the dinner hall, Kaleb caught sight of Lukas leaning casually against a wall, a glass of wine held delicately between his fingers. The gold circlet he still wore gleamed in the candlelight.

"I'll be right back," Kaleb said.

Dayana frowned at him, confused, but he disappeared before she could protest, walking back outside. He walked in the opposite direction of the crowds, prying off one of the eyes of the wolf ring.

It was cold now that the sun had set, and the garden was virtually empty save for servants tidying the area. Kaleb glanced over his shoulder and walked in the direction of the pavilion.

At the sound of voices, he ducked behind one of the hedges, peering out carefully between the leaves. It was one of the generals and Elias.

"My brother is unreliable," Elias was saying. "He's barely been here, flitting from fort to fort on military orders."

The general looked at Elias strangely. "Your brother?" She frowned. "He hasn't been on an official military operation in three months."

Elias stopped and turned, his eyes narrowing. "Is that so? I guess I'm mistaken."

The conversation continued as the two of them walked through the gardens, but Kaleb had stopped listening. Lukas had been in the fort at Ritsar just a month earlier, when he'd found Kaleb. He'd been the commanding officer there, and he'd blackmailed him because Kaleb wasn't supposed to be there. But Lukas shouldn't have been there either.

If Lukas used this information against Kaleb, he'd have to reveal how he got it in the first place. Which meant that he'd been bluffing, and Kaleb had fallen for it. He squeezed his eyes closed and took a deep breath, trying to regain his composure, trying to make his way back to the party before Lukas found him.

But it was too late. When he emerged from behind the hedge, he crashed right into the prince. Lukas put his hands on Kaleb's shoulder to steady him.

"Meeting a lover?" Lukas asked, raising an eyebrow.

The question caught Kaleb so off guard, he found himself gaping at Lukas. "What?"

"Usually that's what people sneak out here to do," he said.

"Really? Wait—is that why you're here?" Kaleb asked, looking over Lukas's shoulder.

Lukas looked at him strangely, and Kaleb realized far too late that the prince had been teasing him. Lukas let his hands fall away. "I came here to meet you." He held up his ring. "What did you find?"

"I found—" Kaleb stopped himself. He'd called Lukas here to tell him about Theo's journal, about his success with the liquid magic, about the trip, but now all he could think about was that Lukas had lied to him.

It shouldn't have been so surprising. He'd known from the start he couldn't trust the prince. Lukas was the one with the power between them even though it was Kaleb who was risking himself to get the information they both needed. Kaleb had been a pawn for Vira in Ashoka, and now he was a pawn for Lukas here.

You haven't told him everything either, a voice in the back of his head reminded him, but all Kaleb could think about was that he'd been so foolish to let the prince get under his skin, to manipulate him.

"You lied to me," Kaleb blurted out.

Lukas's gaze became guarded. "Lied?"

"You weren't supposed to be at the fort in Ritsar," Kaleb said, forcing himself to meet Lukas's gaze.

Lukas went very still. "And how exactly did you learn this?"

"That's irrelevant. You're holding that over my head, but you can't use it, can you? Not without incriminating yourself."

The regret on Lukas's face was admission enough. "I can explain."

"You blackmailed me," Kaleb snapped. "You forced me to be your spy and let me believe that you were doing this for some noble cause."

"I am," Lukas insisted. "Please, just hear me out."

But Kaleb yanked the ring off and pushed it into Lukas's chest. "I think this arrangement is over."

"Kol, wait." Lukas's palm wrapped around Kaleb's wrist, holding him in place. Kaleb froze, startled by the abrupt contact. "I'm trying to stop a war."

"Oh." It was so far from what Kaleb expected him to say that he didn't realize that Lukas was still holding his hand. He tugged it away, and the wolf ring fell to the ground between them.

Lukas stepped closer. "I lied because I needed your help, and I didn't know if I could trust you." He exhaled and ran a hand through his hair. "I knew my father was up to something," he said. "I had to figure out what that was and how I could stop it. That's why I hired Theo. And that's why I went to Ritsar without anyone knowing."

"And what did you find there?" Kaleb asked skeptically, throwing back the same question Lukas had asked him in the tavern.

"The same thing you did. Whatever was there, my father had already brought back here." He glanced over his shoulder. "I'm sorry I lied. Truly. But this isn't a good place to talk about this." He picked up the ring and held it out to Kaleb. "Wait for me in your room at midnight. I'll tell you everything."

Kaleb hesitated. A part of him told him that he should cut ties with Lukas. He had everything he needed. He could do this on his own.

But he found himself accepting the ring and slipping it back on his finger. "All right," he agreed, hoping he wasn't going to regret this decision. "Midnight."

✳

It was just before midnight when Kaleb finally returned to his room. He'd stayed by Dayana's side for most of the evening, and he hadn't seen Lukas around after their conversation except for briefly at dinner. He'd half expected to find the prince already waiting for him, as he had on the first day he'd moved in, but the hallway was empty.

He unlocked his door. And froze.

It was ransacked. He looked around in shock at the mess that was his room. His belongings were strewn all over the floor, tables overturned, wardrobe thrown open.

Kaleb shut the door behind him. If someone had simply wanted to search his room, they could have covered their tracks easily. But this felt like they were trying to send a message. A threat. A warning.

What they were warning him about, he had no idea.

The emperor, he thought, despite the fact that he had no proof. He couldn't think of anyone else who would care—or anyone else with any kind of motivation to search his quarters.

Fear gripped him, but he pushed it down. *They didn't intend to hurt you*, he reminded himself. But it occurred to him that he *could* have gotten hurt. A part of him wanted desperately to ask for help. But . . . who could he ask?

Kaleb was, as always, alone.

He jumped as there was a knock at the door. Lukas. He opened the door carefully, just wide enough for Lukas to enter before locking it again.

"What happened?" Lukas asked, his face pale as he took in the state of the room.

"Someone broke in," Kaleb explained needlessly.

But the look on Lukas's face was fear, not shock. "What did you do?" he demanded. "What haven't you told me?"

Kaleb swallowed. There was a lot he hadn't shared with Lukas. He hadn't spoken to the prince in days. He hadn't even told him about finding Theo's—

Suddenly Kaleb ran to his wardrobe, yanking it open and digging through the clothes that were tossed everywhere. It was gone. The intruder had taken it.

When he returned to the living room, Lukas was standing in the same place. "What's missing?" he asked, accurately guessing what had happened.

"Theo's journal," Kaleb said shakily. "I found it. And now . . . I think your father has it."

Lukas pressed his eyes closed and exhaled deeply. "What were you thinking, leaving that here? Why didn't you tell me immediately?" There was anger in his tone, and under other circumstances Kaleb would have been afraid. But now he was just tired.

"Just as you said you didn't know if you could trust me, I couldn't know what you'd do with it," Kaleb said. "Not until I knew what was in it."

"And what was in it?" Lukas prompted.

"Information on how to make more liquid magic." Kaleb sank onto one of the sofas. He'd messed up. *Really* messed up. "All he needs now is to get more raw magic from Ashoka, and he can create an army."

Lukas stared at him for a long moment and then came to sit beside him. "He already has it," he said, pained. "Elias told me what he learned, and the Ashokan delegation brought raw magic with them as a part of their negotiations."

All the blood drained from Kaleb's face. "No, that's impossible. There's no—" He cut himself off just in time. *There's no more magic.* But the Council must have had some stashed away somewhere.

Lukas didn't seem to register what Kaleb had almost let slip. "I think he wants to use this trip to Ashoka as a way to invade the country." His voice was almost a whisper, as though he were afraid to say it.

Kaleb felt his stomach knot. It was one thing to suspect that, but another to hear Lukas say it so plainly. He looked over at Lukas. "How do we stop it?"

Lukas only breathed deeply. "I don't know if we can."

Despair curled in the pit of his stomach, and Kaleb found himself fighting back tears. Maybe Lukas would have been able to do something if Kaleb had gone to him instead of trying to do this on his own. But he'd made his choice and now it was too late.

He was a failed spy twice over. And innocent Ashokan citizens would pay the price for it.

CHAPTER TWENTY-FIVE

— VIRA —

VIRA WAITED FOR Riya on the steps outside the temple in Paliya for as long as she dared, but Riya didn't show up.

"We have to go, Rani," Surya said, glancing up at the darkening sky.

Riya was supposed to have arrived hours earlier, but now the sun was close to setting, and there was still no sign of her sister. Disappointment filled Vira. She'd thought it would be different this time—that Riya would truly keep her promise—but as always, Vira was alone.

"All right," Vira said, reluctantly rising and following Surya toward the main road.

"You all right, Rani?" Surya asked, looking over at her as they boarded a carriage he'd hired to take them to the Maravat Province. Amrit had already decoded everything before he'd thrown the book into the fire, so there had been nothing for them to do. The Ivory Key was leading them to the ruins of Banagha Stepwell. It was located over a day's journey away, and Vira didn't want to think about how much money the trip was going to cost.

"I'm fine," Vira said. Her knuckles were white from clutching the key and the cipher, and she forced herself to loosen her hold. "We got what we came for. That's all that matters."

"You took my advice," he noted. He'd mostly left her to her thoughts while they'd waited, but she hadn't missed the appraising looks he'd shot in her direction—or the way he'd kept a wary eye on the temple in case Amrit escaped. The priestesses had closed the temple after Amrit's stunt in the morning, but they had no idea how much magic was in the shackles that trapped him inside.

Vira looked at Surya out of the corner of her eye as the carriage began to move. "About?"

"Using whatever tools you have to get what you want," he said. "I doubt he saw *that* coming."

Vira felt her heart skip a beat at the memories she'd tried to repress— of his skin beneath her fingers, his mouth beneath her own. *It meant nothing*, she told herself. It was a means to an end, a way to beat him at his own game.

But she didn't feel like she'd won. She just felt empty.

In fact, if she were being honest with herself, for just a moment everything had disappeared from her mind except having him in front of her—close enough to touch, to kiss, to exchange whispered confessions. It had felt like before. And Vira had wanted that so badly, she'd been on the brink of dooming Ashoka for it.

"He said he was protecting me," Vira said, hating the way her voice broke. But that was a lie. It was *all* a lie.

"I'm sure my noble brother thinks that," Surya said dryly. "He always did see himself as a savior." Meaning that Surya didn't see him that way.

"Can I ask you something?" She waited for him to nod before continuing. "What happened between the two of you?"

Surya leaned back against the seat, arms folded behind his head. "I don't really know. I wish I could say it was one thing, but I suppose we've been growing apart for years. We were around the same age when we were taken in by the Kamala Society, so we did practically everything together.

And it was easier as children, you know? We were quick to fight, but quick to forgive. As we got older, it was harder to ignore the fundamental differences between us."

Vira wondered if the same thing was happening between her own siblings now—if, as Surya had put it, they were all fundamentally too different. There had been a part of her that had hoped things would change after Ritsar. But it hadn't—not really, not in the ways that counted. Maybe it was too late to fix what had broken between them.

"You wanted to use the key, and he wanted to destroy it," Vira said.

"That was a part of it, but we disagreed on a lot of things." Surya exhaled. "Amrit was always so . . . *good*. So righteous. It made it difficult to talk to him sometimes."

Vira didn't want to think about Amrit or his goodness. "You never did tell me why you changed your mind about the key."

"What's the point of having something and not using it?" It was a yet another non-answer, and she waited for him to elaborate, but he only turned his head and looked out the window at the blur of shadowed landscape sliding past them. "Tell me something," he said after a while. "Do you like being the rani?"

"What?" Vira stared at him in surprise.

"It's not a difficult question to answer."

Except that it was. No one had ever asked her that—and she'd never thought to consider it on her own. What was the point? Liking it was irrelevant. She'd never had a choice. She'd been born to rule, and she'd never had the option of wanting anything else.

"I just meant that you're determined to get your country back—to get this magic to protect it," Surya added, finally turning to her when she didn't answer. "I assume you must like it a great deal to go through all that trouble."

"I'm good at it," Vira said. But in the back of her mind she wasn't sure if that was true either.

"Hmm," Surya said, and Vira had the sense that he could read the doubt on her face. "I suppose that's as good a reason as any to do something."

He fell silent after that, and Vira let the conversation lapse. But the question lingered in her mind for a long while.

✳

It was dusk when they reached the Banagha Stepwell. Vira had seen the site on Papa's map, but as far as she knew, he'd never visited, nor had he noted any connection to the Kamala Society in any of his journals.

The well was built in the traditional style: an inverted pyramid descending belowground, three of its sloping sides inlaid with steps that villagers could walk down to fill their pots with the rainwater that collected there. The fourth side didn't have stairs but instead had hollow chambers carved into the stone. It looked like the front of a building with alcoves separated by ornately carved pillars. There was even an open terrace where musicians would have performed.

The well was dry now, and the stone steps crumbled beneath Vira's feet as she and Surya walked down to the bottom. Surya made his way to the alcoves, examining the carvings on the walls. Time had eroded and softened the stone, and a lot of the intricacies were lost now, but Vira could still make out the shapes of animals and flowers on the pillars.

She froze as she caught sight of a lotus—with two swords crossed over it. The Kamala Society's crest.

"Here," she called to Surya.

It didn't take them long to find more symbols. There were eight altogether, carved into small square stones that they could easily dislodge. And as soon as they pulled them all out, there was a rumbling noise. Vira held her breath as the wall at the back of the chamber began to shake and then lower.

This was the end. She hoped that she was worthy of what lay on the other side.

The wall stopped moving, revealing a dark tunnel that seemed to lead beneath the well.

"After you," Surya said.

As soon as she stepped inside, lanterns on the wall flared to life, filled with crackling balls of magic that seemed to stretch on forever. The tunnel was cold, and Vira unwound the dupatta from her waist and draped it around her shoulders for warmth.

"Stay close," Surya said. He was speaking quietly but it sounded too loud in the space around them.

"Do you know where this leads?" Vira asked.

Surya didn't answer for a moment. "I have a theory."

"What does that mean?" Vira asked, stopping in her tracks. He'd been forthcoming with information since they'd left the palace. That he didn't want to share something now was making her worry. "Is this a trap?"

Surya turned back toward her. "It's not a trap," he said. "At least it's not a trap for you. It was built for Niveda."

Vira frowned, and then realization hit her. "You mean this leads to her tomb." A shiver ran down her spine as he nodded. "But why?" There was no reason why information about the quarries would have been buried with her.

"Because Niveda grew too powerful, too bloodthirsty. No one could match her level of magical proficiency. Savitri wanted to stop her, and so, with the help of the Kamala Society, she orchestrated a coup against her own sister." His voice sounded strangely detached again, like when he'd first told her about the three branches of the Kamala Society—like he was reciting something he'd been forced to memorize rather than expressing his own thoughts.

"Why don't we know any of this?" Vira asked. It didn't make any sense why the Kamala Society had wanted to erase such a huge part of Ashoka's history.

"Because Savitri decided it was better to bury the truth than admit that she made a mistake in walking away."

"Does Amrit know?" Vira asked. "That this is where the key leads?"

Surya hesitated again. "I think so."

And he'd wanted to destroy it before Vira got here. She wished her heart didn't ache so much at that thought.

✳

The air grew even colder as the ground sloped down beneath Vira's feet, leading her and Surya deeper underground than she'd been expecting. The flickering light cast eerie shadows along the wall, their footsteps echoing in the quiet. Neither of them spoke, but Vira could feel Surya's presence right beside her.

After what seemed like hours of walking, the tunnel finally came to an end. Up ahead, she could make out a chasm with a series of rope bridges interconnected like a maze, and on the other side, a cavern.

"I think we're here," Surya said.

Vira couldn't stop the excitement making her fingers twitch. "There's—"

A noise from somewhere behind her made Vira start. She whirled around just in time to see something fly directly toward her.

"Look out!" Surya pushed Vira to the side just as an arrow whistled past and landed on the ground ahead of them.

Surya grabbed her hand and pulled her forward. She ran, ducking as more arrows flew toward them, but there was nowhere for them to take cover. They were almost to the bridge when an arrow grazed Vira's upper arm. She hissed in pain as she stumbled into Surya, knocking him off balance. She pressed a hand to the wound, trying to stifle the blood.

"Stop," a cold voice said from behind them. "Or the next arrow goes through your skull."

Her voice was too close for it to be a bluff. Vira slowly turned around.

"You." She recognized the girl. Tarini. She'd been at the Ravens' campsite. "What are you doing here?"

"The Ivory Key wasn't meant for you," Tarini said. "Give it to me, and I will spare you."

"It doesn't belong to you either," Vira said, drawing her talwar. It wavered in her wounded arm, but she held it tight.

"It belongs to the Order of the Mayura," Tarini said.

Vira's heart stopped. *Riya.* She'd gone looking for the Order and never returned. "What did you do to my sister?" she asked faintly.

Tarini smirked. "She's still alive. Barely. And if you want to see her again, I suggest you hand the key over."

"No." She couldn't give up the key. "Riya will get free," Vira spat— because her sister was a survivor and because she needed to believe that.

"Are you willing to take that risk?"

Vira glanced at Surya, but he wasn't looking her way. He was watching Tarini with an unreadable expression.

"What do you want with Niveda's tomb?" Vira asked Tarini, trying to buy some time.

Tarini lowered her bow uncertainly. "You know this is her tomb?"

Vira took advantage of Tarini being momentarily distracted and took a small step back. "I know a lot more than you think." She took yet another step.

"Then you know that it is our duty is to serve the goddess," Tarini said. "We've been preparing for her arrival for centuries, and she will reward us for our devotion."

A cult, Surya had called them. It was obvious now, seeing Tarini's wide-eyed reverence, the fanatical edge to her voice, as she spoke about Niveda like she was someone to worship.

She looked at Surya again. He was being uncharacteristically quiet. He turned, sensing her gaze on him. "Give me the key, Rani," he said under his breath. "We should split up."

Vira hesitated. He hadn't even drawn his weapon. Something felt off.

"We're on the same side, remember?" Surya prompted.

You can't trust him, Amrit had told her. She didn't know if she could trust Amrit either, but Vira wasn't going to make the same mistake twice.

"No one is on my side," Vira said. She took one last step, relieved when she felt the ground give beneath her. She'd reached the bridge.

Tarini finally noticed that Vira had moved. "What did I tell you?" She raised her bow again and fired.

Vira threw herself to one side of the bridge. It swayed beneath her feet, making her stomach twist—but it was enough for her to evade Tarini's arrow. She turned and ran.

The bridges were difficult to navigate. It wasn't a true maze—they weren't fully connected and Vira had to leap from one to another every time she had to make a turn. *Don't look down*, she told herself as she jumped out of the way, narrowly dodging another arrow.

She was almost to the other side, but Tarini and Surya were right behind her. So Vira did the only thing she could: she lifted the talwar in her hand and slashed at the rope behind her just as she dove for the landing.

Tarini screamed as the rope snapped beneath her feet. But she didn't plummet to her death. Surya caught her, holding on to her forearm as he slowly tugged her up.

"You're working with her," Vira said, looking at the two of them. "You're a part of the Order."

"And you're making a huge mistake," Surya said, dropping all pretense. "You need me."

"I don't." Vira would figure it out—she always did.

She walked deeper into the cavern until she came upon a massive wooden door with metal hinges. Instead of a keyhole there was a metal disk with a long, narrow indentation in the center. With shaking hands Vira took the Ivory Key out of her pocket. It fit perfectly.

The door unlocked with a click.

She felt her heartbeat quicken, trying to stifle her hope as she pushed open the door. Every time she believed she was at the end, the Kamala Society found a way to throw more obstacles in her way. She wanted this to be the final destination.

The room was large and dark—entirely devoid of objects save for a single casket in the center of the room. There were more magical lanterns here, illuminating empty walls.

She turned in a circle, looking around in confusion. There was nothing else here—no books or notes or even more puzzles. It was strangely anticlimactic. She'd come so far, crossed so many hurdles, fought so many people, and chased down so many clues only to reach an empty room that held a five-hundred-year-old corpse.

The answer had to be with Niveda.

Vira walked toward the coffin.

This room had been undisturbed for centuries, but there was nothing to indicate that. No dust. No cobwebs. Vira ran a hand over the latch that held the coffin closed.

She hesitated, some part of her cautioning her to think through her actions. But she unlatched it. The sound of the lock snapping reverberated around her. She gripped the edge and hoisted it open.

Niveda was inside the coffin, and she didn't look a day older than when she'd been buried. Her skin was pristine, her black hair neatly parted and hanging loose over her shoulders, her eyes closed. She was still dressed in the white sari she'd been buried in, an ethereal figure. But despite there being no magic in the coffin, there was no sign of the corpse rotting. If Vira didn't know better, she'd have believed that Niveda had just fallen asleep.

But the coffin held nothing else. Despair started to fill her.

She was missing something. A secret passage. Another puzzle. The Kamala Society wouldn't go through all this trouble just to hide a corpse.

But . . . what if they had?

She'd put her faith in the Kamala Society—in what they could offer her, in what they could do to save her country. Hadn't Amrit told her this wouldn't lead where she thought? Hadn't Sharadha ominously predicted that the key would only bring her strife?

Maybe it was a good thing that Papa had never made it this far. He wouldn't have to feel this disappointment, to live with the failure. This was the end. No magic. No way to get back her throne or fix Ashoka.

There was a gasp of breath.

Vira turned slowly, a chill snaking down her spine as she felt the presence of another person. Niveda was on her feet, standing in front of her.

Vira felt her entire body go numb. This wasn't possible. Niveda had died five hundred years ago. It didn't make any sense that she was here . . . or that she was still alive. The dead didn't rise again.

Vira opened her mouth to speak—or scream—but she froze when Niveda's hand came out and gripped her by the neck. She gasped as cold fingers dug into her skin, cutting off her circulation. She tried to speak, but there was nothing she could do except look into the cold, dark eyes of her distant ancestor as Niveda choked her to death.

And then Niveda flung her off to the side, where she landed on the ground, hard.

Vira gasped for breath, wincing as she tried to pull herself up to her knees. She looked up just as Niveda's hands rose in the air. The last thing she saw was a flash of light.

And then the world went dark.

CHAPTER TWENTY-SIX

— KALEB —

ON THE FIRST day of traveling with the emperor, Kaleb made his way to the artificers' tent located behind the training arena.

The days before they left Lyria had been a blur. Kaleb had wanted nothing more than to curl up in his bed and wallow about all the ways he'd failed, but he couldn't. The emperor was still planning to attack Ashoka, and without a way to stop him, the only thing Kaleb could hope to do was warn the Council first. It wasn't much of a plan, and he had no idea what the Council could even do against magical soldiers, but he had to at least try.

But that meant he still needed to keep his cover. So he'd reluctantly spent most of the time in the lab with the other scholars, turning all the raw magic that the Council had gifted the emperor into liquid. It ended up giving a dozen more soldiers magical power.

The training arena made up a large portion of the campsite, and though Kaleb was already a little late, he couldn't help but linger and watch the soldiers. They were learning how to rip things apart with their magic and put them back together, practicing with objects of various sizes and located at different distances. He didn't know any of them, but he saw a flash of bright red hair that belonged to Thalia.

It was still surprising to witness, but the oddest part of it was the way the artificers working with them were giving instructions entirely antithetical to everything Kaleb had been taught as a mayaka trained in Ashoka. The first thing Papa told him was that magic was only ever to be channeled from a place of peace and control. Emotions muddled magic, made it fickle and unpredictable. It was why mayaka were first and foremost taught how to meditate, to clear their minds and ensure that all their focus was on a singular intention.

Instead, here, the soldiers were told to reach into their anger, to channel their personal worries and fears and other negative feelings to fuel their power. And it was working. People who'd had very little control over their power when they left Lyria had all but mastered it in a matter of days, able to do precise feats that Kaleb had been sure would take weeks or months to master.

"Kol!" Hektor's voice barked out of one of the tents. "Stop dawdling."

Kaleb hastily tore himself away from the soldiers and hurried into the makeshift lab that was set up on the premises.

"Sorry I'm late," he said, but Hektor had turned away.

It was already busy as artificers rushed back and forth between a set of interconnected tents transporting slabs of raw magic in specially constructed metal crates that helped mitigate the symptoms of exposure. "We need to make more magic," one of them informed Kaleb with a small grimace. He held out the stack of folded aprons he was carrying in his arms. These were also forged to ward against raw magic poisoning.

"More?" Kaleb was confused, but he took one of the aprons. They'd brought five barrels of magic with them from Lyria. That was enough to power a small army. There was absolutely no reason they needed to be creating more already.

"The soldiers are burning through it," Dayana said, materializing beside him to reach for some equipment left on the table beside him. She looked stressed, her hair spilling out of her braid, and a moment later she disappeared into the adjoining tent.

Kaleb took off his coat and hung it up in the corner before making his way toward the other scholars. After seeing Riya plunge her hand into the pool at the temple in Ritsar, he'd suspected that people had to touch the liquid magic to acquire its power. But he'd learned that it was a bit more complicated than that. It was similar to the way the magic was imbued in objects—it still required a clear mind and a powerful intention, and it was obvious that some had more of a natural affinity for it.

Magic in people was also similar in that it had to be replenished as it was used up. But unlike objects that simply returned to their original state once the magic waned, they'd discovered that people had a negative response—as though their body were craving the magic.

Kaleb slipped the apron on over his clothes and was about to join Dayana in the lab when another artificer rushed in, snapping her fingers and pointing at him. "You, come here!"

He hesitantly followed—and then sped up when he realized that the Ashokan boy with magical powers had collapsed. Kaleb helped carry him into the medical tent, lowering him onto a pallet that had been set up in one corner.

The boy was distraught, fighting against the artificer, who struggled to hold him down on the bed. Kaleb stared wide-eyed.

"They're sometimes volatile after using too much power," the artificer explained. "Just hold him like this until one of the healers can come take a look," she instructed before rushing back out.

Kaleb did as he was told, wincing as the boy—Shiv—thrashed against the grip, sweat beading along his brow as he mumbled something unintelligible.

"You're all right," Kaleb said in what he hoped was a comforting tone.

"You promised," Shiv said.

Kaleb frowned, but then he realized that Shiv wasn't talking to him. His eyes were still closed. He was addressing an unknown person.

"You promised you'd get rid of it," the boy said more insistently. "I can't do this anymore. I hate the magic."

"It'll be all right," Kaleb repeated, switching to Ashokan. It was a risk, but they were alone and Kaleb hoped the familiar language would soothe him. "Just rest."

"You promised, Theo!"

Kaleb froze, carefully lifting his hands from Shiv's shoulder. He was still moving, but he looked to be a bit calmer now.

The tent was still empty, so Kaleb chanced a question. "How do you know Theo?"

Shiv's eyes flew open. He abruptly sat up and scrambled back. "Who are you?"

"I'm Kol," Kaleb said, continuing to speak in Ashokan. "I'm just trying to help you."

The boy glowered at him. "You're the one who gave them the magic. How is that helping me?" At Kaleb's surprised look, Shiv jerked his head toward the neighboring tent. "I heard one of the other scholars talking about how it was *your* discovery."

It must have been Dayana. No one else knew about his involvement in finding the journal.

"It's Shiv, right?" Kaleb asked. The boy flinched. "Did Theo tell you he could remove magic from you?"

"Theo's gone," Shiv said.

"I can help you," Kaleb said. Shiv looked at him with distrust, so Kaleb crouched down before him. "Theo and I are on the same side. I know he destroyed the old lab, so I'm trying to understand just why he did that and what he discovered."

"I helped him with the lab," he said after a beat. "Theo had me make something."

The crystal ball that had been dropped on the raw magic. Kaleb had assumed that it was something Theo had created himself, but it had been Shiv who had.

"How did you make it?" Kaleb shook his head as Shiv began to lift up his hands. "Don't use more magic. Just tell me."

"He told me to create an orb that would expel magic from an object. He said it would help him stop the emperor from giving more soldiers magical powers."

So Kaleb had guessed right—this kind of magical matter *could* be imbued with regular magic, just like other any other mayaka-forged object. And Theo had somehow known that if such an object came into contact with the raw magic, it would be expelled at a faster rate, causing the explosion.

But it was more interesting that Theo believed that a similar process could potentially work on people without causing them harm. As far as Kaleb knew, once magic was in something, it couldn't be removed. That was yet another thing Papa had told him. Magic was nature, and it had to be respected. It had to simply run its course naturally.

But if Theo was correct, then there *was* a way that Kaleb could still stop the emperor from attacking his home. The tiniest spark of hope flared to life within him.

"Did Theo tell you anything else?" Kaleb tried not to sound too eager.

Shiv hesitated again, then shook his head. But he didn't quite meet Kaleb's gaze, and Kaleb knew the boy was lying. Kaleb bit his lip as he heard voices outside the tent. He knew he shouldn't admit this, but he was running out of time. He might not get another chance alone with Shiv.

"I know you have no reason to believe me, but I'm on your side. I'm Ashokan," Kaleb said, lowering his voice even more. "My family and I are trying to stop whatever the emperor is doing. I know you have a sister in Ritsar and she's waiting for you. I promise I'll do everything I can to make sure you get back to her. But I need your help to do that."

Shiv's eyes were huge and round. "My sister's alive?"

"She was imprisoned, but she's still alive."

Shiv carefully lifted the hem of his tunic, and a few moments later, pages materialized from where he'd hidden them by using his magic. "Theo gave me these and told me to hide them."

The pages seemed to be from some old book—but to Kaleb's surprise, they were entirely in Ashokan. He flipped through them, skimming paragraphs about creating magical matter and their connection to life forces that Kaleb couldn't fully make sense of. The pages had been ripped down the middle, torn in such a way that without the original book, there was no way to understand what was written. Whatever it was, it was clear that Theo hadn't wanted the emperor to get his hands on this information.

"Thank you," Kaleb said gratefully.

Shiv swallowed and leaned back against the wall. "I didn't mean to cause all this." He sounded like he was fighting back tears. "I was just trying to protect my sister. We were hiding and I accidentally touched an old barrel. I didn't even know what had happened until this power just started to erupt from me."

"It's not your fault," Kaleb said. "It's the emperor's." He wasn't entirely sure if Shiv believed him.

As artificers began to enter the tent with another soldier in a similar state of distress as Shiv had been minutes earlier, Kaleb stuffed the pages under his own tunic. There was still more work he was expected to do in the lab, but when Kaleb walked away from the tent, no one stopped him.

He waited until he was closer to his own sleeping quarters before he pulled the wolf ring out of his pocket. With trembling fingers, he removed one of the onyx eyes. He hadn't spoken to Lukas in days—not since the night he'd found his room ransacked. He didn't know if Lukas was still wearing the ring, or if he would dare come and find him in the middle of the day.

But several minutes later the prince emerged from behind a tent. Lukas kept his voice low but his gaze was intense as always. "What is it? What's wrong?"

"I think I know what Theo was working on," Kaleb said quickly, relieved that he'd actually come. "And I might have a way of stopping your father." He pulled the ripped pages out from under his tunic and passed them to Lukas. "Have you seen this before?"

Lukas frowned as he flipped through them carefully just as Kaleb had done moments earlier. "No, but I think I know which book it's from. It would be in my father's tent."

"We need to get it," Kaleb said. "I think it might tell us how to get magic out of people."

CHAPTER TWENTY-SEVEN

— RIYA —

IT WAS DUSK by the time Riya and Varun reached the Fire Temple. It had taken them a long time to find a carriage driver in Tasgarh willing to drive them several hours to Paliya, and in the end Riya had to give up a necklace *and* a pair of earrings—which she thought was, frankly, obscene—to pay for the trip.

"The shopkeeper said the temple is closed today," Varun said, reemerging from one of the stores that lined the main street. He'd gone inside to ask for directions. "Apparently something was stolen. It's this way." He put a hand on Riya's back to guide her.

"Stolen?" Riya frowned, trying not the think about Varun's palm pressing against her. She could feel the imprint of his touch even over the kurta. She hoped it was just a coincidence and had nothing to do with Vira, Tarini, or the Ivory Key.

There's no such thing as coincidence, Amma's voice reminded her, so she just walked faster.

Riya could feel the magic in her awake and buzzing once again. Her hold on it was still tenuous, and every time she felt the edges of her control starting to fray, her gaze drifted to Varun and the power subsided. She had a bunch of tulsi leaves tucked into her own pocket now, but as reassuring as that was to have, she knew it was Varun's presence that was helping her stay calm. He'd helped her focus her power—control it in a way she hadn't believed possible.

"What is it?" Varun asked, giving her a small, confused smile when he caught her looking.

Riya shook her head and looked elsewhere, feeling her cheeks heat.

The area surrounding the temple was entirely deserted. Two scowling guards were posted outside, instructing them to turn back because the temple was closed.

"Renovations," one of them said with a glare when Riya pressed for a reason why.

Riya exchanged a glance with Varun. The guard was clearly lying, but they walked away as ordered. When they reached the corner, they wordlessly turned to the back entrance. The gate here was chained shut as well, but this one was thankfully left unguarded. Climbing it took no time, and Riya landed softly inside the compound. It reminded her of another day, breaking into a different temple with Kavita. It felt forever ago now.

"All right," Varun said, dropping down beside her. "Where do you think—"

But Riya stopped listening. Standing directly in front of her, leaning against a railing beside the pond, was Amrit. "You," she snarled, advancing on him. Almost unconsciously she drew her dagger.

Amrit's spine straightened as he eyed the weapon in her hand. "Good to see you too, Rajkumaari."

Riya pressed the edge of the blade to his neck. "I should slit your throat for what you did." But Amrit didn't move—not even to defend himself.

"Riya!" Varun said, shocked. "What are you doing?"

"Getting revenge," Riya said, eyes blazing with fury. "Give me one good reason I shouldn't."

"I know where your sister is," Amrit said.

The words had the desired effect. Riya lowered the knife. "What did you do with her?" she demanded.

"*I* didn't do anything," Amrit said. "I was just trying to protect her, but she left me chained here." He lifted his arm, revealing the magical shackles that tethered him there. "Free me, and I'll tell you where she went."

"Tell me, and then I'll free you," Riya countered.

Any trace of the Amrit she'd known in the palace was gone, leaving behind only cold ruthlessness. "Listen to me," he said carefully. "She's in real danger. We don't have time for this."

She didn't trust him, but he'd come up with a plan to protect her family—to protect Vira—in case he wasn't around during a coup. She owed him this one time, and then they were even. Riya reached down and unclasped the metal band, first from the railing and then from his wrist.

"Where is she?" Riya asked.

"Maravat," Amrit said, rubbing the back of his wrist. There were red welts pressed into the skin—no doubt from his attempts to forcibly break out. "That's where the Ivory Key leads. But it's not what she thinks it is. I have to stop her."

Amrit began to move, but Riya threw herself in front of him. Varun followed her lead, and the two of them stood blocking his path.

"What is it then?" Riya asked.

"There's no time," Amrit said, frustrated as he tried to step around them. "She's in—"

"We can always lock you up here again," Varun threatened, putting a hand on Amrit's shoulder so he couldn't escape.

Riya had told Varun briefly about Amrit, about the way he'd betrayed and abandoned them in the Koranos Mountains. Varun was skilled with a bow, but he was unarmed, and given that Amrit was a trained assassin, Riya had no doubt he could easily overpower the both of them. And yet,

Varun had put himself between her and Amrit. She hadn't expected Varun to back her up like this—to make it clear that he was on her side.

Amrit eyed Varun, sizing him up. A sense of recognition entered his gaze. "Do I know you?"

"No," Varun said.

"Answer the question," Riya cut in before he could fully identify Varun from when he'd posed as a scholar in the palace.

"The Ivory Key doesn't lead to more magic," Amrit said finally. "Not directly, anyway. I don't know where the rumor started, but it was safer for people to believe that than the truth."

"And what's the truth?" Riya asked, as a feeling of foreboding crept down her spine.

"It leads to Niveda." Amrit looked between the two of them. "And if we don't stop Vira before she gets there, she's going to unleash a terrible evil on Ashoka."

✳

The carriage ride to Maravat was long and tumultuous. Amrit had paid the driver extra to drive through the night, stopping only briefly to replenish the magic in the wheels that powered it. Riya had never been one to get ill on long drives, but even she was feeling fairly sick to her stomach as the carriage jerked along uneven roads.

Amrit was tense the whole time, vacillating between clenching his fists in his lap and staring out the window. Riya had demanded an explanation as soon as they started their journey, and though he'd obliged, Riya was still struggling to understand what he'd revealed.

The Ivory Key led not to a source of magic, but to Niveda—Savitri's sister and once ruler of Ashoka. It didn't make sense that there would even be a tomb. Ashokans didn't usually bury their dead, but according to Amrit, she hadn't been cremated because she'd never actually died. Niveda was still alive, simply trapped in some kind of suspended state until someone released her.

Immortal.

Riya couldn't even comprehend it. There was no such thing, and the very concept was making her head spin. No wonder the Order of the Mayura referred to her as a goddess.

No wonder the Kamala Society had destroyed all evidence that magic could do such a thing.

"Your father was right about the Kamala Society being founded by Savitri, but he was wrong about *why*," Amrit said. "Savitri did it not to keep magic from the people, but as a way to protect the people from her sister. Hiding the quarries was not her intention—not at first, anyway. But when she realized that Niveda was creating a magical army that was virtually unstoppable, Savitri knew that the only way to stop her sister was by making sure she and her acolytes wouldn't have access to more magic."

"So Niveda wants revenge?" Varun asked.

"She wants the country back that her sister took from her," Amrit said.

"She *was* the rightful heir then," Riya said. So Tarini had been right about that. "How could you not warn us? Warn *her*?" Amrit only lowered his gaze, not answering. Riya scoffed. "Of course. Why would we trust you to tell us the truth about things that concern our lives and the future of our country?"

"I thought I had it under control," Amrit said. "The Kamala Society was supposed to protect the people from this. I thought I'd be able to destroy everything that led to Niveda's tomb before Vira ever had to find out."

"That was uncharacteristically foolish of you," Riya said flatly.

Varun shot her a warning look, subtly reminding her that they needed Amrit's help. "But what does she have to do with magic?" Varun asked, trying to keep their conversation on topic. "How are they connected?"

"Because Niveda *is* the key to unlocking the quarries," Amrit said. "Savitri used Niveda to create the seal, so as long as she's still alive, there is no way to break it."

"So Niveda has to die," Riya said.

"Killing her isn't that easy," Amrit said. "The Kamala Society tried all those years ago, and they failed. She's far too powerful—and malicious. It's dangerous to even try."

"So what do you propose?" Riya snapped. "You're telling me there's nothing we can do? That we should just leave Vira at her mercy?"

"Let's hope we get there before anything happens" was all Amrit said.

It was unlikely that they would. Vira had too much of a head start, but they settled back into an uncomfortable silence as they drew closer to the stepwell.

Riya found her eyes drawn to Varun once more. At first it had just been because he'd helped her control her magic, but as time went on, she had to admit she was looking because she was curious about him. She'd never really taken the time to study him. Moonlight from the window washed over his skin, dusting him in a soft glow as he sat with his eyes closed. He'd spent half the carriage ride running his hands through his hair in frustration and confusion, and now it messily fell into his eyes. It made him look young and vulnerable and—*attractive*. That's what the girls in the palace had called him all those weeks ago, and for some reason thinking of that made her heart beat twice as fast.

"How is she?" Amrit asked, interrupting Riya's thoughts. His voice was so quiet that for a moment she wasn't entirely sure that he was speaking to her. But when she turned toward him, he was watching her expectantly.

"How do you think?"

A flicker of regret passed over his face. "I didn't mean to hurt her."

"Then maybe you shouldn't have betrayed us," Riya said sharply.

"I only did what I thought was right," Amrit said, holding her gaze. "And I won't apologize for that."

Riya shrugged. "It's not me who's owed the apology." She hadn't expected—nor wanted—it from Amrit. It was Vira who'd been a shell of herself for days afterward, spending sleepless nights ruminating on what had happened, on what she could have done differently.

"Is she—"

"If you want to say something to her, you can do it yourself," Riya cut in.

Amrit didn't look happy, but he nodded. "You're right. It's unfair of me to put you in the middle."

"For what it's worth," Riya said, perhaps a little too coldly, "I told her you weren't worth it. She trusted you, maybe more than she ever trusted anyone." *Certainly more than she ever trusted me.* "And you destroyed that."

"I *am* sorry about that," Amrit said.

He sounded genuinely remorseful, but for all she knew, it was still a charade, a way of manipulating her emotions—and by extension Vira's—for his own gain.

Riya's eyes flicked toward Varun once again. His eyes were still closed, arms folded over his chest. But he was too stationary, his breathing too quick for him to actually be asleep.

I trust you, he'd said. Those words had dislodged something in her chest, a tightness she'd held on to for so long she felt its absence within her. She hadn't known how badly she'd needed to hear those words from him. She'd thought she wanted to prove herself to Yash, but the truth was, Yash never needed proof of her loyalty, or her skills. It was Varun who'd questioned her at every turn, who'd pushed her and tested her, and whose approval she'd desperately—if unconsciously—sought.

A strange warmth filled her at the thought that she'd intimidated him. Stoic, stubborn, stable Varun who was unnerved by nothing—except apparently by her. She'd never felt particularly brave or seen herself in the way that he'd described her, but when he fixed that intensity on her, she felt like she could do anything.

Varun's eyes opened as the carriage began to slow. Riya quickly turned away to peer out the window, hoping the cover of darkness masked her flushed cheeks.

Amrit threw open the door even before the carriage rolled to a full stop. He took off at a run toward the stepwell.

"Wait," Riya called after him, but he had already disappeared into the night.

Riya hurriedly instructed the carriage driver to wait for them before she followed. The stepwell was ancient, and despite the full moon in a cloudless sky that offered them bright light, Riya found herself sliding as the stone steps crumbled beneath her feet. She hit her arm against the stone, wincing as the rough texture scratched the skin. She ignored the pain and pushed herself up—but the stone beneath her feet broke once again. She braced herself for another fall, but Varun caught her by the elbow and tugged her back against him.

"Careful," he said.

Riya's heart was racing as she caught her breath. Amrit's dark figure was almost near the bottom of the well, but Varun held on to her hand, threading their fingers together and forcing her to slow down. She didn't know when they'd gotten so comfortable being in each other's space, touching so easily like they'd been doing it for weeks instead of hours, but she liked it.

"Do you trust him?" Varun asked. Amrit was too far away to hear them, but he kept his voice pitched low.

"I think he has his own agenda, but . . . I don't think he would hurt Vira." Something in her gut told her that whatever he'd intended to do with the Ivory Key, Amrit wouldn't knowingly put her sister in danger.

One side of the well didn't contain stairs but instead had alcoves carved into the stone, and Riya and Varun reached the bottom just in time to watch Amrit disappear into one of them. They followed him down a passageway illuminated by magical lanterns that seemed to stretch on forever. The only sound was their footsteps echoing as they ran down the sloping tunnel until they abruptly came upon a chasm connected by a series of bridges fashioned out of rope.

Riya made to follow Amrit across it when Varun tugged her back, crouching to pick something up. It was an arrow, and as soon as she saw it, she recognized it—it was barbed, identical to the one Varun had pulled out of her shoulder.

"Tarini," she said, her eyes darkening.

"It's not poisoned," Varun said. But that didn't mean Vira was still alive.

When they made it to the other side they found Amrit standing in the middle of an empty room. Riya's heart was in her throat as she looked around. But there was nothing here except for a coffin, now open.

"They're not here," Amrit said unnecessarily. But there was no sign of a struggle either—nothing except for the arrow to indicate that anyone had been here at all in centuries.

She's still alive. Riya had to believe that.

"Where would your sister have gone?" Varun asked.

Riya forced herself to breathe. "The Council meeting," she said. "Vira wanted to use whatever she found here to stop the Council from making a deal with Lyria. She would take Niveda there."

Amrit noticed the arrow in Varun's hand. "What's this?"

"Order of the Mayura," Varun said, holding it out to him.

A flicker of fear crossed Amrit's face as he took the arrow. "We're too late then," he said, defeated.

"We have to go after her," Riya said. They had to find Vira.

"We can't go after Niveda without a plan," Amrit said. "She's too powerful."

"So what?" Riya asked, her eyes flashing in anger. "You want to abandon my sister? Again?" she added pointedly.

Amrit didn't rise to the bait. "I didn't say that. We just have to be smart about it." He eyed Riya. "How's your magic? Can you control it?"

Riya hesitated, looking to Varun. He'd helped her channel it once. "Maybe," she said. "Why?"

It was clearly not the confident assurance Amrit was looking for, but they didn't have a lot of options. "That'll have to do," he said. "You can practice on the way."

CHAPTER TWENTY-EIGHT

— VIRA —

VIRA OPENED HER eyes. She didn't know where she was. She sat up from where she was lying on a cold stone floor in a dimly lit room. The air around her felt . . . musty. Like she was underground somewhere.

As her eyes adjusted to the dark, she realized that the room was full of books. She blinked in confusion. It looked like a library with huge stacks of shelves that spanned entire walls, but she had no idea why she'd be there. She could see a door, however, so she rose and hesitantly made her way to it. She half expected to find it locked, but it opened easily, revealing a small hallway. At the end of that, there was another door, partially ajar, revealing a well-lit room.

She walked down the corridor, tugging her dupatta up as it slipped from her shoulders and trailed on the ground. She hissed as the cotton fabric scraped along the side of her arm. Tarini's arrow had only grazed her skin, but there was a visible cut caked with a thin layer of dried blood.

Vira froze when she heard low voices. She couldn't see anyone, but she heard them. She carefully pushed the door open, her heart racing. Surya. Tarini. They were talking too quietly for Vira to know what was being said, so she inched closer. She could almost make out the words if only— she winced as the hinges creaked and the voices stopped abruptly. Vira tried to back away, but Surya saw her.

"Rani," he greeted. "You're awake."

"And you're a member of the Order." Vira knew she ought to feel something—anger, hurt, a sense of betrayal—but all she could muster was confusion. "Why?"

"I was raised in the Order," he said. "We both were," he added, gesturing to Tarini. "Though I didn't know she was a follower of the goddess until we were both at the stepwell."

"We had to keep our identities a secret after the Kamala Society started killing us," Tarini added.

"You were a part of the Kamala Society," Vira pointed out.

"I was sent there to infiltrate them, to learn what they knew," Surya said. "My loyalty was never to them. And it worked perfectly until Amrit caught me."

"That's why he left you locked up," Vira said, realization dawning on her.

Surya smiled. "I really should thank you for freeing me, Rani."

"You're not supposed to be awake," a voice said behind her.

Vira jumped in shock, whirling around to see a figure clad in white right in front of her.

The girl from the tomb. Niveda.

Vira gasped as there was more bright light.

And then it was dark again.

✳

When Vira woke the second time, she was in a different room. She was lying on the floor again, but this room wasn't dark. There was a table with bright lanterns left lit.

Vira's heart leapt into her throat as something crashed to the floor beside her. She clutched her chest, only letting go when she realized it was just a book. She whipped around to see Niveda standing in front of one of the bookshelves that lined the wall. Niveda's back was to her, and Vira could make out something small and round embedded below her neck. It was hidden by the kurta, but black veins spidered out from it, curving up and around her shoulders.

Niveda held a book in her hand, flipping through it with idle disinterest. And then she snapped it shut and threw it over her shoulder with a frustrated huff. It landed right next to Vira, startling her again. The floor was covered in books. Niveda had clearly been doing this for a while.

Vira took a moment to study her. Her skin was dark, her black hair loose around her shoulders. She stood just as still as she'd been when lying in the coffin, but she didn't look nearly as gentle now.

"I know you're awake," Niveda said in a singsong voice. "I can hear your heartbeat."

Vira sat up, pulling her knees to her chest. "Where are we?" she asked, thinking that was the most innocuous of questions.

"The Eternal Library," Niveda said, as though it should mean something to Vira.

Vira sifted through her memories, trying to think of a time when Papa might have mentioned it to her. She couldn't recall.

"Where are Surya and Tarini?" she tried again.

Niveda smiled, and Vira found herself suppressing a shudder. "I sent them out to gather my loyal followers."

"Are you looking for something specific?" Vira asked as yet another book landed at her feet. She glanced at the title. It was a book on the maharanis of Ashoka.

"She erased me," Niveda said. "She rewrote history."

"Who?"

"My sister. *Savitri*."

She spun around and hurled the book in her hand directly at Vira. Vira barely had time to duck, throwing her hands up to shield her face before it hit the wall behind her with a heavy thud. She hastily scrambled to her feet.

Niveda's dark eyes scanned her. "You're short for a maharani."

"What?" Vira asked, startled by the sudden change of topic. She didn't know whether to be insulted or not, but she instinctively straightened a little. "I don't understand what we're doing here. I thought . . ." she trailed off, unsure what to say. "I was looking for magic," she explained even though Niveda didn't ask. "For the missing quarries."

"*Missing*?" Niveda said sharply.

"Sealed," Vira amended. "The quarries were all lost centuries ago, and the last one is running out of magic. I thought that whatever was in that tomb was the key to unlocking—"

"*I* am the key," Niveda said. She looked furious for a moment, and then her anger faded into amusement. "My sister did always love her jokes and puzzles, and her *irony*. I wanted the quarries, so she used me to seal them, to make sure I could never have them. But she always did underestimate me."

How many times had Vira thought that about herself? That her siblings, her Council, even Amrit had underestimated her? She hadn't expected to feel any sort of kinship with Niveda, but for a brief second she felt like she understood what drove her.

"You're the key?" Vira said. "I don't get it."

Niveda threw back her head and laughed. "Of course you don't, silly girl."

Vira bristled at that. "Then why don't you explain it to me."

Niveda scoffed. "I don't have to." She turned back to the shelf.

Vira waited a moment. This was where the Ivory Key had led her—to Niveda. And if Niveda could unseal the quarries, Vira couldn't let this chance pass by. "We need magic," she said. "Our neighbors to the west want to invade Ashoka. The border walls are running out of magic, but my Council thinks we can fix it through some peace negotiations."

"That's a temporary solution," Niveda said dismissively.

"I know," Vira said. "They're meeting a delegation from Lyria in just a few days' time. I need to stop the meeting, but I can't stop it without the magic." She knew she sounded desperate. If Riya were here, she would tell her to play her cards close to her chest. "Please help me find the quarries."

Niveda finally turned, studying her a long moment. "I see they let just about anyone wear that crown these days," she said. "That was a pathetic display."

Vira inhaled sharply, feeling like she'd been slapped. She'd well and truly failed now. If Niveda wouldn't help her, she had no way of protecting Ashoka.

"Why are you keeping me here?" Vira asked. "If I'm so pathetic, then—"

Niveda rolled her eyes. "Kausalya help me, you are *exhausting*." She looked at Vira with pity. "Is this how you spoke to your Council? No wonder they overthrew you."

Vira tried not to let the words get to her, but they were touching old wounds that had never healed. "You call me pathetic, but at least my citizens know who I am," she said before she could stop herself.

Niveda moved before Vira could even blink, slamming her against the wall. Vira gasped for breath as Niveda's elbow pressed into her neck. "The entire world will know who I am soon enough," she snarled.

And then she dropped her hold. Vira fell to the floor, coughing as air rushed back into her lungs. She clutched her neck. She knew there would be bruises there.

"My sister thought she was so clever," Niveda said. "She thought she could stop me, but she was not even half as powerful. Do you know how many people it took for her to trap me in that goddess-forsaken place? *Sixty*." She shook her head, almost like she was lost in a memory. But then she turned and smiled directly at Vira. "Of course, they all died."

"Why would your sister do that?" Vira asked to keep her talking.

It was clear that she was unstable, and Vira had to get out of there as soon as possible. Asking about the past upset her—but Niveda also seemed to want to talk about it. Talk about how she was better than Savitri. About how she was better than Vira.

Vira didn't have a plan exactly, but if she could get answers about the quarries, she still had a chance. And then she'd wait for a moment when Niveda was distracted and she'd escape.

"Because she was jealous of my power. They all were." Niveda exhaled, and this time Vira didn't even have to ask a question before she continued. "We were twins, you know."

"I have a twin too," Vira said. "A brother."

Niveda didn't seem to even register that Vira had spoken. "We grew up in Visala, and we did everything together. Our amma was the ruler of the city—not because she was born into it but because she earned it. She discovered that another city was going to invade our home, and she put a plan in place to stop it, leading us to victory. She was crowned the leader after that, and she decided it would be our family's legacy to carry on. She ensured that Savitri and I were trained together under the best tutors—but we both knew only one of us would be the next ruler."

"She chose Savitri," Vira guessed.

Niveda eyed her sharply. "Of course not. My sister was gifted with magic, skilled in a way that even the masters were sure she was destined for greatness. I had to work for everything I have, but she was just naturally talented." Niveda was seething with envy. "And yet she chose to give that all up for a *boy*. Amma was furious the day she found out that Savitri didn't want to continue her studies. No, she wanted to get married and raise a family and walk away from all that power."

The mural in Visala hadn't been a mistake then. It *was* Niveda who'd been crowned the maharani. "So you were your mother's successor."

"I was everything she wanted, and more," Niveda said. She was proud of that. "I was the enactor of her vision. My sister walked away, but *I* worked twice as hard. I became the best mayaka in Visala. I mastered using every kind of magic at the same time until I was the most powerful person. I took over as the leader of the army and expanded Visala's borders. One by one the cities fell. I was considered a goddess among mortals, and I gained loyal followers."

"The Order of the Mayura," Vira filled in.

"They were with me to the very end," Niveda said, her voice turning serious. "When my sister decided that she actually wanted the power she gave up, she created her own secret society, recruited spies from my court, all so she could keep me from having access to magic."

Vira furrowed her brows. "She sealed the quarries to keep them from you?" Surya had been vague about what Savitri exactly had done—how she'd sealed them exactly, how it was connected to Niveda.

"Yes. She knew I'd found a way to make myself live forever, so she created a seal and powered it with my life force. As long as I was alive, it couldn't be destroyed." Niveda stared off into the distance. "She didn't know that I have a weapon that can break the seal. A sword, more powerful than anything ever built before. All I have to do is find it again."

Vira's heart was racing. This was what she needed to know: there *was* a way to break the seal.

"What does it look like?" Vira asked. "Maybe I know where it is."

She wasn't sure if Niveda would actually answer, but she picked up one of the books on the floor and flipped through it before tossing it in front of Vira. There was a painting of the sword, the hilt studded with gemstones. It looked eerily similar to Chandrika's sword, except Chandrika's had only a single gem. "I think . . . I think I've seen it before," Vira said slowly. "But it only has one gemstone."

"She removed them," Niveda said, fury lining her face. "She removed the gemstones."

"Why?"

"Because they're not gems," Niveda said. "They're a condensed form of magic. That's what makes the sword powerful." Her eyes narrowed at Vira. "You said you saw it before. Where?"

Vira quickly shook her head. "Oh, I meant in paintings. A lot of old dangerous weapons either went missing or were confiscated by the Mayaka Association." It was a lie. She knew exactly where it was—assuming Sharadha hadn't sold it.

Vira wasn't sure if Niveda believed her, but she stopped talking, and Vira didn't ask for more information. She'd given Vira a lot to think about—about the past, about the future, about magic. And all Vira knew was that she had to get to Adhura and get Chandrika's sword back before Niveda got to it.

Vira waited until Niveda's attention returned to the books. She feigned sleep, waiting until Niveda wandered to a different part of the library. And when she was certain she was alone, Vira rose and quietly made her way out of the room and down several different corridors, trying to find the exit.

When she finally saw the door, she exhaled in relief. She was just about the reach for it when she was suddenly yanked back, magic slamming her into the wall.

She groaned from the force of the impact as Niveda stepped in front of her, eyes blazing.

"Where do you think you're going?" she demanded.

Vira didn't answer.

"You'll stay here," Niveda continued. "You're coming with me to this meeting your Council is holding, and you're going to help me take back this country. And if you do that again, I will snap your neck and leave you here to rot."

CHAPTER TWENTY-NINE

— RONAK —

THE EMPEROR HAD assured Ronak that they'd be traveling to Shantha Mahal with a small party. His idea of small turned out to be the royal Lyrian family, the visiting Ashokans, several dozen soldiers and scholars, and thirty servants, all packed into a fleet of fifteen carriages. And even with all the soldiers and servants working together, it was well past sunset when the tents were all set up for the night and a simple meal was served. After dinner, they were free to do what they wished, but Ronak stayed seated, lingering beside the firepit with the glass of wine he'd barely touched.

"So what's the plan?" Preethi said, leaning closer to him. They were far enough away from most others, but Ronak still glanced over his shoulder to make sure no one could hear.

"We need to find a way to get inside the emperor's tent," Ronak said. Kaleb had told him to wait—to let Kaleb handle the emperor's plans, until they could warn the Council about the magical powers the soldiers possessed—but this was Ronak's last chance to get the compass. The only time Ronak had seen the emperor take the compass off was when he was training with the other soldiers, so that was when they needed to search his space.

"We need to know when the emperor will be training," Preethi said. She bit her lip. "I could ask Elias."

Ronak looked at her sharply. "Elias?"

"Prince Elias," Preethi hastily corrected. "We've kept in touch," she finally admitted.

"We can't trust him," Ronak said immediately, alarmed.

"I can ask in a way where it won't draw suspicion," Preethi insisted.

Ronak didn't like it, but he couldn't deny that having Elias verify the details of the emperor's whereabouts would make his life a whole lot easier.

"All right," he agreed finally. "Tell me what you find out."

She looked eager to help—and confident that this would work. But Ronak hesitated. "Are you sure you want to be involved?" he asked.

"Of course," she said, smiling brightly at him.

This is the last time I'll ask for her help, he promised himself. He would tell her after this. "All right," he said, ignoring the twinge of guilt he felt.

And then she was gone too, leaving Ronak alone. But a few moments later he heard footsteps. He turned to see Jay approaching him. Ronak's shoulders tensed, but Jay didn't speak immediately as he sat down beside Ronak. They hadn't seen each other or spoken properly in days. Despite Ronak's intention to fix things, he'd been too busy. Their only interactions had been brief exchanges at formal dinners surrounded by the emperor's court.

"You still haven't told her." Jay was looking straight into the fire. "I know she's been helping you," he added before Ronak could speak.

"I will tell her," Ronak insisted.

"As soon as you get whatever you want, you mean," Jay said.

Ronak pursed his lips. "It's not like that." Except it *was* like that. They both knew it.

"You're putting her in danger," Jay said. "And she has no idea what she's getting into."

"She does," Ronak said. "She's fully capable of making her own decisions."

"No. She thinks she'll be the rajkumaari of Ashoka." Jay pierced him with a dark stare. "She's doing it for her future husband. Not for someone who intends to drop her the moment she ceases to be useful."

Ronak inhaled sharply. The words stung in a way he hadn't thought possible. "Is that truly how you see me?"

"It's how everyone sees you," Jay said flatly.

Selfish and unreliable. It was so unflattering. Ronak tried to convince himself that he didn't care what anyone thought, but his best friend thinking so poorly of him made his heart clench. "Then why were you my friend?" he asked.

The past tense hung between them, heavy in the silence as Jay once again looked away from him. "I can't stand by and watch you get her hurt," he said.

"I'll tell her," Ronak promised. "Tomorrow."

"If you don't, I will." Jay got up and walked away without another word.

Ronak *would* tell her. After he got the compass. He was so close to getting everything he wanted. He couldn't stop now, not when everything was already in motion.

❋

Preethi had discovered that the emperor would leave his tent at dawn and spend an hour meditating and training with the soldiers. And so Ronak waited outside the emperor's empty tent for Preethi's distraction.

He didn't know what she was doing, only that she was confident that the single guard left stationed outside the tent would leave his post, allowing Ronak to walk in.

It was early enough that most of the others were still asleep. Ronak could see a few servants milling about, but they were too far away to see him. As he waited, his mind kept returning to Jay's words—and the distance between them. Talking to him had felt like talking to a stranger. Someone who shared the face and mannerisms of his best friend but an entirely new person he'd never met. He'd believed Jay would be by his side, his best friend for eternity. That they'd grown so far apart was painful.

Ronak looked up as there was sudden movement. The guard was vacating his post as Preethi had promised. Ronak held his breath, waited to make sure he was truly alone, and then ducked inside. The tent was spacious and lavishly decorated with a plush rug and warm blankets, despite its being a temporary resting space. But in spite of the grandeur of the decor, the actual belongings were sparse. There was a trunk full of the emperor's clothes, a small writing table filled with boring letters and pots of ink, and several books stacked on the small table beside the bed. He rifled through everything as quickly and thoroughly as he dared, but it was clear that the emperor had the compass with him.

He was about to leave when the sound of hushed voices stopped him. There was nowhere to hide. He was about to make a run for it when he recognized one of the figures who'd entered the tent.

"Kaleb?"

His brother froze as well, his eyes wide in terror. Behind Kaleb stood the younger Lyrian prince, Lukas, equally startled.

"What are you doing here?" Lukas demanded, advancing toward Ronak. He was armed with a short sword, and it was in his hands in an instant.

"No!" Kaleb threw himself between Lukas and Ronak. "Wait."

Lukas stopped, looking at Kaleb incredulously. *"What?"*

"I can explain," Kaleb said.

Lukas's eyes narrowed. "Kaleb," he said. "He called you Kaleb." Lukas glanced at Ronak, the pieces sliding into place. "As in the rajkumaara of Ashoka."

"Ronak, leave," Kaleb said, glancing back at Ronak for half a second. "Now."

"No," Ronak said, glaring at Lukas, who still held the sword. "I'm not leaving you alone with him."

"Ronak, this isn't—"

But Ronak had no idea what Kaleb was about to say, because the emperor walked in, soldiers behind him.

"Seize them," the emperor ordered.

And there was nothing any of them could do to stop it.

CHAPTER THIRTY

— KALEB —

IT WAS ALL Kaleb's fault.

He knew it the moment he'd walked in and seen Ronak in the emperor's tent, and he was only more certain of it now as soldiers marched him through the camp toward an empty tent where he was deposited on the ground beside Lukas and Ronak, both of whom were already tied up. Lukas had tried to cover for them, to pretend that Kaleb and Ronak were there on his orders, but the emperor had instructed his soldiers to take him too.

Kaleb had handled it all poorly, and people were getting hurt because of him—as a result of his incompetence. If only he'd been a better spy. A better brother.

But he hadn't, and now his entire world was crashing down around him. All his efforts, all his pain had been for nothing. He'd lost everything he'd come here to do. His chance at knowing his family. His chance at proving that he was more than the helpless brother who got locked up.

The soldiers left them alone, and Kaleb chanced a glance at Lukas. Lukas wasn't even looking at him, but his fury was evident in the tense line of his body. He had every right to be upset with Kaleb for lying, when Kaleb had accused him of the same.

But Kaleb couldn't face Lukas yet, so he directed his frustration toward the other reason he was in this mess: his brother. "What were you think-ing, Ronak?" he demanded. "Breaking into the emperor's tent?"

Ronak's eyes narrowed. "I could ask you the same. What's your excuse, brother?"

Kaleb bit the inside of his cheek, trying to keep his temper in check. It wasn't actually Ronak he was upset with but himself. "I said we do this my way, but as always, you have your own agenda."

"I'm just trying to fix things so *you* can come home. You were the one who wanted your name cleared publicly, remember?"

Lukas's eyes darted toward Kaleb then—just for a second, but Kaleb caught it. They were speaking in Ashokan, but just as Kaleb had learned Lyrian, Lukas had no doubt been taught Ashokan by his tutors.

Kaleb gritted his teeth. "I told you I didn't need you to save me."

"And I told you that following Vira down this path would lead to nothing but pain," Ronak said bitterly.

"Well, I suppose you can feel vindicated when we're put to death," Kaleb said.

"My father won't kill us," Lukas said, speaking for the first time. His Ashokan was lilting, the sounds blurred by his Lyrian accent, but it was clear he was fluent. "You're of more use to him alive than dead. At least for the moment."

Kaleb's head snapped toward him.

Lukas's lip twitched a little. "A prince," he said, indecipherable emo-tions passing over his face. "I should have known. You're too pretty—and too confident—to be a mere scholar from the north."

Too pretty. Kaleb's brain tripped on the words. But before he could figure out just what Lukas meant by that or how to respond, there were footsteps outside. The emperor walked in.

He'd changed out of his military clothes and into formal royal attire. He looked at each of them with great interest, but when Kallias's eyes landed on his son, his gaze narrowed. "I didn't expect this," he said, crouching before Lukas and lifting his chin to look directly in his eyes. "I thought you'd let it go after the first scholar you sent to spy on me disappeared, but I see you're as determined as ever. An admirable quality under different circumstances."

Kaleb watched emotions flicker over Lukas's face—shock, anger, and then regret at the confirmation the emperor *had* actually been responsible for Theo's disappearance.

"It was my idea to spy on you," Kaleb blurted out without thinking. "I went to him and blackmailed him for access."

"What?" Ronak hissed.

The emperor turned to Kaleb with something like pity in his gaze. "I had a lot of respect for your father. Shame to see that he didn't pass on his integrity to his sons." He looked at Ronak and withdrew a necklace from around his neck. The gold chain had a clock pendant. No, not a clock—a compass. "I hear you're looking for this."

Lukas's eyes widened with recognition, but Kaleb had no idea what it was.

Ronak's expression was blank, but Kaleb knew his brother well enough to know that the emperor was right. Ronak wanted it for some reason.

"I don't know what you're talking about," Ronak said carefully.

The emperor just laughed. "That boy who came with you—Jay, was it? Well, he was very forthcoming. He seemed very concerned about your fiancée. Wanted to make sure she was all right."

Ronak's shoulders slumped knowing that he'd been caught. "I need it to free my brother," he said honestly.

Kaleb whipped his head toward Ronak in shock. "What?" he asked, incredulous.

The emperor seemed amused by that. "Ah, brotherly affection. Touching. You had hoped to discover, what? That I had him framed? I'm sorry to disappoint but it was in fact your mother's Council that had her murdered."

Sharp pain filled Kaleb. "The Council?" He'd suspected as much, but it stung hearing it confirmed. No wonder they hadn't wanted to offer Kaleb a fair trial. Without him to take the fall, there would have been a formal investigation which would have revealed the truth.

"I suppose I was the catalyst," the emperor mused.

"What does that mean?" Ronak asked.

"It means I gave your Council an offer. They could either surrender, and I would spare them. Or I would take Ashoka by force and bloodshed. They chose wisely." He tucked the compass back under his tunic. "You've both become quite meddlesome. It's a shame. I'd grown to like you." He gestured toward Ronak. He stood up. "Put them in the back of one of the carriages," the emperor told a soldier standing just outside the tent and then disappeared.

✳

Kaleb had no idea how much time passed while they were inside the carriage, so when they stopped moving abruptly, he had no idea why or how close they were to Ashoka. There were no windows to look out of, and though it had been hours, no one had bothered to bring them food or water. Kaleb tugged at the rope that bound their wrists and ankles. It didn't budge, just like it hadn't every other time he'd tried, and even if they were able to get free, the carriage door had been locked from the outside. So he sat in the heavy silence next to Ronak and Lukas, holding in the words he ought to say to them but didn't have the courage to.

Kaleb had caught both of them watching him at times, like they wanted to say something. But he'd also caught them eyeing each other warily, and so none of them said anything at all.

I'm just trying to fix things so you can come home.

Ronak still saw him as that broken boy—someone to save and protect—and maybe it was time for Kaleb to accept that. He'd wanted to prove to everyone, including himself, that he could survive alone, but all he'd done was underscore Ronak's point.

When there was a soft tap on the door, Kaleb jumped. His eyes darted toward Ronak and Lukas, who were also staring at the door apprehensively. The handle twisted and the door cracked open.

To his surprise, it was Dayana standing there. "Oh thank the goddesses," Kaleb said.

She looked relieved too as she climbed inside. "Do you know how many carriages I had to look through?" She used a knife to cut the ropes that bound them.

Kaleb rubbed the back of his wrists as she cut Ronak and Lukas free. There were red indents in his skin where the rope had bitten into it. "Where are we?" he asked.

"Ashoka. We don't have much time," she said, gesturing for them to follow her.

Outside, the camp that had been set up was mostly empty. But Kaleb knew immediately that they were back on Ashokan soil. There was magic all around them, the familiar sensation of it settling over his skin like a caress.

"Where's everyone?" Ronak asked.

"The meeting's happening now," Dayana said frantically. "They're already there." She looked at Kaleb. "And I'm *furious* that you lied to me for weeks. But we can talk about that later."

They began to run across the grounds toward Shantha Mahal looming in the distance, when Kaleb abruptly stopped. "Wait," he said. "The book."

"There's no time," Ronak insisted, but Kaleb shook his head.

They needed it to stop the emperor. "I'll get it," Kaleb said. "I'll meet you there. Go now." He shoved the three of them forward. "You have to warn the Council."

Lukas looked at him like there was something he wanted to say, but he just shook his head. "Be careful," he said.

Kaleb took off in the direction of the camp. As he ran toward the emperor's tent, he heard footsteps behind him. He knew even before turning that it was Ronak.

"What are you doing here?" Kaleb asked, irritated.

"I can't just leave you."

Kaleb pushed down his anger. "Fine. Stay close." He couldn't see any guards anywhere around or even servants milling about. It looked eerily deserted and that worried him.

He moved cautiously as they drew closer to the emperor's tent. It looked the same as it had before and they easily ducked in. It took them no time at all to find the heavy book left on the table. Ronak, who'd seen it before, identified the gilded cover. Kaleb grabbed it and pressed it close to his chest.

"Something feels off," Ronak mumbled as they exited the tent. "This was too easy."

Kaleb agreed. It felt like a trap. "Let's just get to the meeting," he said. He needed to go through the book and learn how to get magic out of the emperor's soldiers, but first they had to ensure the Council would survive. Kaleb rounded a corner and tripped over something heavy on the ground.

Ronak grabbed the back of his tunic to keep him upright. And that's when Kaleb saw what had caused him to nearly fall. A guard was splayed out on the ground, his throat slit.

Kaleb gasped, pressing a hand to his mouth.

"Vaishali's bones," Ronak whispered, pointing directly ahead, where there were dozens of bodies on the ground. Guards. Servants. Even soldiers who'd been left behind.

They were all dead. And standing over them was a familiar figure, a blade in each hand.

"Surya?" Kaleb asked. The assassin from the Ashokan dungeons. What was he doing here? Why was he killing Lyrians?

Surya looked up, a grin on his face. "Well, well. Fancy seeing you here, Rajkumaara," Surya said. He raised his weapons and began to advance on them. The swords were covered in blood. There was blood on his tunic too, Kaleb noted faintly.

"Run," Ronak said, tugging him backward, but Kaleb was frozen to the spot.

There was a flash of light, and Surya leapt out of the way as the ground beneath his feet was incinerated. Surya lay motionless on the ground. Kaleb whirled around and saw Shiv. He looked like he could barely stand as he stumbled forward.

"There's more of them," Shiv said, his legs shaking. "I tried to stop them, but—"

Kaleb grabbed the boy's arm. "Come on, we have to go," he said, tugging on him.

But Shiv was too overwhelmed, too weak. There was blood dripping from his nose. And then he collapsed in a heap, unmoving. Kaleb crouched down and slapped his cheeks. "Shiv? Shiv?"

He didn't wake up or respond.

"We have to go," Ronak said, panicked as he tried to grab Kaleb and yank him up. "Kaleb. Come on. There's more of them."

"I can't leave him here," Kaleb said, pushing Ronak's hands away. "I promised him—"

Ronak grabbed him by the shoulder and hoisted him up. "We'll come back for him," he said. "Kaleb, we have to go. The emperor—"

The emperor. They still had to find the Council. With one last look at the unconscious boy, Kaleb allowed Ronak to drag him away.

CHAPTER THIRTY-ONE

— VIRA —

SHANTHA MAHAL WAS a neutral site, established centuries earlier as a place where various communities could meet and discuss problems in a peaceful environment. Weapons weren't allowed inside, except those carried by the guards, who could use whatever means necessary to protect the peace. The site hadn't been used in over fifty years.

Judging by the carriages around the walled compound, the meeting had already begun. Vira's heart sank. She'd hoped there would be a chance for her to lie in wait and somehow find a way to stop the meeting before Niveda got there.

"It looks different than I remember it," Niveda commented as she marched Vira forward, a hand wrapped tightly around Vira's elbow to ensure that she couldn't leave.

Vira had only seen it in paintings, and the thought that Niveda had been around when it was constructed was still too strange for her to grasp. According to Papa, the original structure consisted of just a small domed pavilion. Over time, however, the maharanis had expanded it into a larger hall to hold meetings between larger groups.

"They won't let us in," Vira said.

This was supposed to be her only chance to prove to the Council that she could be trusted—that she would be a good leader. She had tracked the Ivory Key down to its conclusion and found the one person who could help her unlock the lost quarries and fix Ashoka the way she wanted to fix it. Niveda was proof that she knew what she was talking about—proof that the Ivory Key wasn't some mythological story for children, proof that the quarries existed and could be found and used to save Ashoka. And they'd finally see that Vira was a competent maharani and that her instincts and judgment were good. That they didn't need Lyria or anyone else to save them. Ashoka was quite capable of being its own savior.

"Let us?" Niveda asked, laughing. "I don't intend to ask for permission. A maharani doesn't have to ask for anything. We seize what is ours, and if something is in our way, we simply remove the obstacle."

"You mean by killing them," Vira said icily. "And you're not the maharani."

In response, Niveda shoved Vira forward again.

"Where are Surya and Tarini?" Vira asked, looking around. They'd returned to the library before Niveda wanted to leave, and she'd heard the voices of the other acolytes they'd brought back with them—people who worshipped Niveda. Vira hadn't seen them, and she had no idea how many there were, but she knew they were around somewhere.

"They're doing what I asked them to do," Niveda said with a smirk. "Surya told me why those Lyrians are here, and now they're going to learn what happens to people who try to take over *my* country."

Vira didn't miss the way she said *my*. The Lyrian emperor was trying to take away the thing Niveda wanted most: to be the ruler. Vira had wanted an easy solution to resolving things with Lyria, but this wasn't what she'd had in mind.

"And then what?" Vira asked. "After you convince the Council to reject the deal, what do we do?"

"I build the future that Ashoka was destined for." It was a cryptic answer, and Vira wanted to ask more questions, but they were nearing the guards who manned the doors.

The guards moved, drawing their talwars, but Niveda showed no sign of slowing down.

"You are not permitted to be here," one of the guards said.

"Then stop me," Niveda said, grinning at them.

"Wait—" Vira started to say, but it was too late.

The guards were already moving toward them—but Niveda simply swept her hand off to the side. There was a small flash of light, and the guards hit the wall, and then slid to the ground, dead. She neatly stepped over them, pulled open the door, and walked into the meeting already in session.

Benches lined the perimeter of the circular room. The Council sat on one side and the Lyrian delegation on the other—the emperor surrounded by a handful of soldiers. Meena, who was standing in the center, address-ing the group, saw them first. Her head jerked up, fury lining her face as she realized they'd been interrupted.

"What are you doing here?" Meena's eyes narrowed as she recognized Vira. "And who is this?" She glared at Niveda, but Niveda looked entirely unfazed.

"You seem to have misplaced your maharani," Niveda said, pushing Vira so she fell to her knees in the middle of the room.

Muffled whispers traveled throughout the room as Vira sat there, mortified.

Meena's face was flushed with anger, but Vira didn't miss the look she shot in the direction of the emperor. He was unaware about the coup. "Who are you?" Meena demanded again.

Niveda let her eyes travel up and down Meena. "And who are you to speak for Ashoka? You're all nothing more than cowards, so quick to give up *my* country to the first threat. You aren't fit to be rulers, and you certainly don't deserve the Ashoka that *I* built." She turned to the emperor. "You can leave now."

The emperor rose. "Excuse me?" he asked in heavily accented Ashokan. He looked younger than Vira had expected, and he stared Niveda down. "I don't understand what's happening. I'm here to renegotiate trade with the maharani." His gaze slid down to where Vira was still kneeling.

"That's no longer on the table," Niveda pronounced. "And I'm feeling benevolent, so I will allow you to disband this meeting and return to your respective homes."

Vira looked at her in surprise. This wasn't what she'd expected—and the moment she caught sight of the glee in Niveda's eyes, she realized that Niveda *didn't* intend to let them go peacefully. This was just an amusing game to her.

"Our negotiations are nearly complete," the emperor said. "So I'll have to respectfully decline." He waved at the soldiers around him, a look of triumph on his face.

Vira frowned. There were no weapons allowed into Shantha Mahal— and the soldiers looked unarmed, as did the rest of Council. But when the emperor gestured, the soldiers all moved in unison. As if it were practiced.

As if it were planned.

This had never been a negotiation—it had been an invasion.

But even more shocking, when the soldiers put their hands out, blasts of light erupted from their palms, directed toward every single Ashokan in the room, Niveda included.

A scream sounded as councilors began to drop to the ground. Niveda only smiled.

"Oh. This is going to be fun," she said, and then leapt toward the nearest soldier, easily swatting him away. She twisted and dodged out of the way of the magic that was hurled toward her, fighting back deftly and easily. Moments later, more guards from Shantha Mahal were storming in, talwars drawn.

Vira took the opportunity to scramble to her feet. "Run," she shouted at the remaining councilors, who stood frozen in the room.

But the exits were all blocked by Lyrian soldiers. There was no way out.

And then, with a ferocious roar, Niveda rushed toward the emperor. She moved too fast for him to do anything but try to block her. But it wasn't enough. Within seconds her hands were around his neck.

There was a sickening crack, and the emperor crumpled to the floor.

CHAPTER THIRTY-TWO

— RIYA —

Riya knew something was wrong as soon as they reached Shantha Mahal. There were dozens of carriages outside the compound, but no people.

"Where are the guards?" she asked, looking around at the emptiness of the exterior as she leapt out of the carriage. The meeting should have been in progress by now, and she'd expected that there would be more people milling about.

"It's too quiet," Varun agreed, reaching for the bow he'd bought from an innkeeper on the way.

"We need to hurry," Amrit said.

The three of them rushed toward the entrance—and then Riya froze. There were two crumpled figures on the ground beside the open doors, blood pooling around them from where their heads had cracked against the stone walls. She gasped, turning away from the glassy-eyed stares of two people who'd done nothing but be in the wrong place at the wrong time.

A scream pierced the air.

"This way," Amrit said. He broke out into a run. Riya forced herself to move.

They were too late. The meeting space was in chaos. There was a flash of magic, the clash of steel as Lyrian soldiers and Ashokan guards fought each other. There were more screams as councilors tried to clamber through a hole that had formed in the wall.

In the center was a girl dressed in white. Niveda, looking ethereal and bloodthirsty, and she was advancing on a crumpled figure on the ground.

Vira.

"No!" Riya screamed as she rushed forward, throwing herself in front of her sister.

Niveda didn't seem to care who she was attacking. She lifted her arms with a feral grin—and then staggered back as three arrows pierced her chest. Spots of bright red blood bloomed along her white kurta. It wouldn't stop her—this was just to buy them some time.

"Stick to the plan!" Varun yelled as he dove to the ground after unleashing the volley of arrows.

The plan. Right.

Riya dragged Vira to her feet. "Get her out of here," she said, shoving Vira toward Amrit. He looked conflicted for a moment, torn between wanting to fight and wanting to protect Vira. In the end, he chose Vira.

"No, Riya. Wait—" Vira started to say, but Amrit was already pulling her away.

As magic flew in her direction, Riya dove behind an overturned bench. A moment later Varun joined her. He was out of breath, but he moved quickly, readying more arrows to fire.

"You all right?" he asked, searching her face.

Riya nodded even though her heart was slamming into her rib cage. Varun had helped her practice summoning her magic on their way, but she wasn't sure she could go up against Niveda.

"Stick to the plan," he reminded her a second time. He was calm and confident, and it felt comfortingly familiar—like she was on a mission with the Ravens, doing something she'd done a thousand times.

Riya shakily withdrew the two bangles Vira had used to trap Amrit at the Fire Temple. It wasn't going to stop Niveda, but they hoped that it would buy them some time to get everyone out. She snapped one of the bangles around the metal armrest of the bench, and then she peered around the corner.

Niveda had ripped the arrows out of her chest and was fighting three soldiers from the Lyrian army. She hissed as one of the soldiers struck her with a sword, grabbing him by the throat and flinging him to the side as blood gushed down her arm. She dodged another attack, retreating around a pillar—and when she emerged on the other side several moments later, the cut on her arm had healed.

"Just breathe," Varun whispered, giving her a reassuring smile, like he knew that she could do it. Riya believed him. "I'll distract her again."

And then he stood and fired more arrows. Niveda let out a cry of anguish as she ripped the arrows out of her chest and dropped them on the floor. She was clearly in pain and furious and—

She's weak, Riya realized. Amrit had warned her about Niveda's immense power, and so Riya hadn't expected anyone to be able to get close enough to hit her. She was supposed to be stronger than anyone had ever been—and she had five hundred years of pent-up resentment and a thirst for vengeance. Perhaps she'd expended too much power, or her time in the tomb had affected her more than anyone realized. She was moving slower than she had been even minutes earlier. Hope flared to life within Riya. Maybe she had a chance.

She took a deep breath, summoning the power just as she'd practiced. When she felt magic coursing through her, she stood up and raised her hands. Niveda turned toward her seconds before Riya's power hit her full force in the chest, sending her flying back into a pillar.

Niveda was on her feet within seconds, walking directly toward Riya. "You think you can beat me, little girl?" she taunted.

"We'll find out," Riya responded, feigning bravado. She could feel her knees threatening to buckle even as the magic in her veins was humming.

Before either of them could move, another arrow flew through the air directly at Niveda's face. Niveda caught it midair. She rounded her gaze on the source.

Varun, Riya thought, her entire body going cold.

Riya lunged at Niveda, but she wasn't quick enough. Niveda moved with an almost inhuman speed, reaching for Varun. She grabbed him by the neck and pressed him up against the wall, her nails digging into his skin while his face turned blue.

Riya tried to summon her magic again, but she was too panicked to clear her mind. The power fizzled out almost immediately.

She reached for the dagger at her waist, tugging it free, and lunged at Niveda again. Niveda easily disarmed her, knocking the weapon out of her hand and sending Riya crashing to the floor.

"You think a *dagger* is going to stop me?" Niveda snarled, as if Riya were nothing more than an insect she'd like to squash under her foot.

"No," Riya said, and then leapt for Niveda's ankle.

When Niveda wrestled herself free, the bangle was attached to it. Riya used her moment of distraction to pick up the dagger and stab it into Niveda's thigh.

Niveda let out another frustrated yell—but it startled her enough that she dropped her hold on Varun. He was gasping for breath on the floor, but they didn't have any time to waste. Riya scrambled to her feet and yanked him up. He swayed on his feet as Riya grabbed his hand.

And then they fled.

CHAPTER THIRTY-THREE

— RONAK —

THE SMALL GROUP of survivors gathered at an underground shelter—a barely intact building inside the ruins of a fort. It wasn't an ideal place to gather. There was no running water nearby, no food or supplies to sustain them. The walls had cracks along the foundation, and the roof had partially caved in, exposing them to direct sunlight. But it was a secluded and quiet spot where they could tend to the wounded and make a new plan.

Ronak leaned against one of the walls, numbly looking around at the Lyrian soldiers and remaining Council members. Half the room had been turned into a makeshift infirmary. There were no real healers among them, but everyone who could was helping, communicating in a mixture of gestures and fragmented Ashokan and Lyrian.

It had been Kaleb's idea to have the Lyrians join them. There weren't too many of them: three soldiers, four scholars—including Dayana, Kaleb's cousin—and the two princes. The Ashokan boy that Kaleb had wanted to save was there too—unconscious, but still alive.

"They're victims here too," he'd argued until Vira had caved. That might have been the case, but Ronak didn't know if the decision was as logical as Kaleb was presenting it—if it didn't have something to do with the Lyrian prince Kaleb couldn't seem to stay away from.

Ronak could see Lukas flitting between various groups, checking in on patients, translating where he could. He appeared to be dedicated and hardworking, but Ronak hadn't decided yet if he liked him. More importantly, he hadn't decided if he liked him for Kaleb.

Ronak still hadn't processed what had happened at Shantha Mahal. When he and Kaleb had finally gotten to the meeting, they'd arrived to death and destruction. They were too late—the emperor was dead. The Council was in shambles.

And, in the middle of it all, was a five-hundred-year-old immortal being.

Riya had told him about Niveda, but *immortal* was something he read about in his favorite adventure stories, not something he witnessed in real life. It didn't feel possible.

He started at the sound of footsteps. "Jay," Ronak said, surprised.

Jay's arm was in a sling made from someone's dupatta. He'd broken his arm in two places trying to get his brother, Kunaal, to safety. Kunaal, who'd been attacked by a Lyrian soldier, had been unconscious when they'd left Shantha Mahal. Not that Jay had told Ronak any of this. He'd overheard some soldiers talking about it.

"Is Kunaal—" Ronak asked, his voice thick.

"He'll survive," Jay said.

"That's good," Ronak said. He and Jay hadn't spoken since they'd argued about Preethi at the Lyrian camp. Ronak wasn't sure when they'd last talked before that. "I'm glad you're all right as well," he said when the silence became unbearable. "I'll—"

"I'm leaving the palace," Jay interrupted. "For good."

Ronak gaped at him. "You were the one who wanted to stay," he accused, unable to keep the defensive edge out of his voice.

Jay shrugged with his good shoulder. "Things were different then."

"You mean Preethi. You'd only ever wanted to stay for her, not for me."

Ronak knew he sounded like a jealous child, but he was too angry to care. He felt like he didn't even know Jay.

Jay's lack of response was answer enough.

"That's why you told the emperor, isn't it?" Ronak asked.

Jay flinched but he didn't deny it. "I did what I had to."

"And you thought she'd—what? Want you back?"

"You were endangering her," Jay said, lifting his chin.

"Congratulations," Ronak said sarcastically. "You've heroically saved her from my evil clutches. And what was the result? Does she want to stay with you?"

The look of anguish on Jay's face revealed what Ronak already suspected: Preethi wanted the title more than she wanted love. She wouldn't have ever stayed with Jay.

"Are you happy now?" Jay asked, his voice harsh.

"No." Ronak had wanted to hurt Jay—and he had—but now he just felt hollow. Maybe Jay was right. Maybe he *was* a horrible person, because Ronak couldn't bring himself to regret his words. The silence that hung between them was awful. They'd been best friends for so long, the thought of not having Jay in his life hurt.

But . . . Ronak knew there was no way forward for them. It was the end of something that Ronak had taken for granted.

"For what it's worth," Ronak said quietly, "I'm sorry."

Jay looked at him, sadness mirrored in his gaze. "For what exactly, Ro?"

"All of it, I suppose."

Jay shook his head. "It's too late." He looked as though he wanted to say something else but thought better of it. He didn't look back when he walked away.

Ronak closed his eyes and leaned against the wall, trying not to crumble under the weight of his emotions. He wasn't in a private place, and Amma had instilled in him that a rajkumaara's true emotions were only to be felt in solitude.

When he opened his eyes, Kaleb was standing in front of him, a furious expression on his face. "Where is it?"

"Where is what, brother?" Ronak asked tiredly. He didn't want to do this now. Or ever.

"The compass." Kaleb glared at him. "It's missing."

"I didn't take it," Ronak said.

"I don't believe you. I know you wanted it." He stared Ronak down. "You have no idea what you're doing."

Ronak huffed in frustration. He was tired of Kaleb's endless accusations, of feeling like he was the family screwup. "Or maybe you just can't accept that I *do*."

"What's going on?" Riya asked, approaching them. She looked between them when neither of them answered. "People are watching," she reminded them. "Can you not do this right now?"

"I'm not doing anything," Ronak said.

Kaleb searched Ronak's face for a long moment and then took a step back. "You really have no idea where the compass went?"

"I don't," Ronak said.

"What compass?" Riya asked.

"It belonged to the emperor," Kaleb said.

"You asked me time and time again to trust you, to have faith in your choices," Ronak said. "Why can't you do the same for me? I'm telling you I didn't take it."

He didn't wait for a response from either of his siblings before he turned and stalked away, trying to keep his irritation in check.

"Where are you going?" Riya called after him, but he ignored her.

There was no where he *could* go, but he couldn't stay inside there with all those people and all those feelings. He needed fresh air.

He'd barely stepped outside when he heard footsteps following him. He turned to tell his siblings to leave him alone but he stopped when he saw it was Preethi.

"Oh." Ronak swallowed. He wasn't ready to have this conversation either. But he steeled his nerves and faced her.

Preethi looked at him with the utmost disappointment. "You used me. Jay told me everything—about how you never intended to marry me. That's true, isn't it?"

"Yes."

Ronak hadn't expected to feel any sadness or remorse. He'd been so sure that it was mutual, that it didn't matter, because she was using him too. After all, it wasn't as though she wanted to marry *him*. She would have married anyone with the title.

And yet, as he looked at her, Ronak was struck with regret. She was still a person, and he hadn't treated her particularly well.

"I'm sorry," he said, hoping she could hear the sincerity in his voice. "I . . . should have been honest with you from the start."

"You shouldn't have wasted my time."

Ronak couldn't look at her. He looked down at his feet as shame coursed through him. "I didn't handle this well."

"No," she agreed. "I helped you and trusted you. And instead you just lied to me for weeks." She exhaled. "I didn't believe Jay when he called you selfish, you know? I defended you."

Ronak looked up in surprise. "Why did you do that?"

"Because I'm a fool," she said. "He was right. I guess it's a good thing you have your brother, since you're determined to destroy every other relationship in your life for him."

Laid out plainly like that, the words stung. They painted a picture of him that was so unflattering, Ronak wanted to flinch. And after all that, he didn't even know where he stood with Kaleb anymore.

Preethi carefully reached into her pocket and withdrew a gold chain. It was the emperor's compass. Ronak's heartbeat quickened a little as she lowered it into his waiting palm. "This is the last favor I do for you," she said.

"Thank you," Ronak said, his fingers closing over the cold metal that he quickly slid into his own pocket. He hadn't lied to Kaleb—he hadn't been the one to take the compass off the dead emperor's body. It was Preethi.

It was strangely heartbreaking to think that the emperor, a man he'd resented, who had perplexed and vexed him, was just . . . gone. He'd intended to murder the Council, to take over Ashoka forcefully. And yet Ronak felt sorrowful. He'd been Papa's friend. And this was another part of Papa's life and history that was gone along with it.

"So this is it, I suppose," Ronak said.

"I suppose."

"You'll return to Dvar, then?" Ronak asked.

Preethi hesitated. "I think I'm going to stay in Lyria for a while," she admitted.

"Lyria?" He hadn't thought she'd liked it very much. But then it struck him. "Elias," he guessed, smiling dryly. He'd seen them talking inside. She truly did want the title.

Preethi met his gaze defiantly. "He asked me to stay."

"I wish you both all the best," Ronak said honestly.

She nodded, and with a small smile, she walked away from him as well. Ronak exhaled as he watched her disappear. He didn't know why it felt so bittersweet. He'd never intended to marry her, but losing her felt . . .

strange. He supposed rejection always stung.

But he forced himself to push those feelings away.

He'd lost everything, but he'd done what he'd come here to do. He would get out of his debt with Ekta. He would clear Kaleb's name.

And then he'd get his freedom.

CHAPTER THIRTY-FOUR

– VIRA –

IT'S MY FAULT.

The truth of that statement slammed into Vira as she looked around the room. Half the Council was dead. Lyrian soldiers were dead. The emperor was dead. Every time she closed her eyes, all she could see was the scene at Shantha Mahal—bodies flung everywhere, blood pooling beneath them. They'd all died because of her.

Because Vira had unleashed Niveda.

Ancient secrets stayed buried for a reason. She'd set this in motion, and now it was her duty to stop it. But she couldn't think of anything beyond the injured figures before her. Couldn't think beyond the fact that the councilors she'd grown up with—who'd first served as tutors and advisors, and then people she'd resented for refusing to take her orders—were just gone.

Part of her was all too aware that the country had no leaders anymore. Ashoka was defenseless—not against Lyria, but against Niveda.

Maybe her Council had been right. Maybe Ashoka didn't need magic. They needed a ruler who could actually protect the people.

All along she'd believed the Ivory Key would fix everything. She'd gotten what she wanted, but her problems hadn't disappeared—they'd just gotten worse. The bitter victory weighed on Vira's heart as she collapsed against the wall of the house that Amrit led them to. She sank to the ground, her heart pounding in her ears, her chest heaving and falling as the entirety of her face and fingers and body began to go numb.

"Breathe," a voice whispered.

She didn't know how. Her lungs didn't know how. She gasped more, trying to find something real to hold on to. Something to anchor her to the real world.

Warm fingers curled around hers, and slowly the world came swimming back into view.

Amrit was crouched in front of her, worry in his gaze. She was still angry, and there was so much they had to talk about, but for a moment she let herself pretend it was like before. He was by her side, protecting her, and even though she'd told him she didn't need it, she was grateful he was there—to have someone she could lean on, who could share her burdens and make her feel less alone.

"It's not your fault," he said, because he knew her.

"Then whose is it?" she asked harshly. "Yours?"

"Maybe." Something dark slid into his gaze as he eyed the bruises around her neck. "Vira, I—"

"Vira?" Riya's voice sounded from somewhere.

Amrit dropped Vira's hand. Her fingers suddenly felt cold, but she ignored that as she turned to see Riya—and then Kaleb and Ronak behind her.

"We need a plan," Riya said. "How are we going to stop her?"

Vira tried to gather herself and her emotions, using the support of the wall to pull herself to her feet. She had to be the one with the answers, with the plan.

"We don't even know what she wants," Kaleb said.

Vira had wanted a moment to herself, so she'd let Riya brief Ronak and Kaleb about Niveda.

"She's looking for Chandrika's sword," Vira said. "She wants to use it to break the seal that's hiding the quarries."

"Then why exactly are we stopping her?" Ronak asked. "I mean, why are we stopping her before she does that?"

"If she gets access to more magic, she'll have everything she needs to create an army," Amrit said.

"And why are you here?" Ronak stared at Amrit. "Are we all just forgetting the part where he betrayed us and abandoned us in the middle of nowhere?"

"Let him be," Riya muttered. "He's trying to help."

Both Vira and Ronak looked at her in surprise. Riya had been the one telling Vira to forget about him for days, telling her he wasn't worth it. They'd arrived at Shantha Mahal together, but Vira didn't know what Amrit had said to Riya—why she'd changed her mind about him.

"If she needs the sword to break the seal," Kaleb said, "we can just keep her from getting it."

"That might stall her," Amrit said, "but as long as she's alive, she's a threat."

"Then what do you suggest?" Riya asked. "Because she can't be killed."

"And we can't trap her again and leave her to become someone else's problem," Vira added. She wouldn't do that again. Delaying the havoc Niveda would wreak wouldn't make them noble. It would make them cowards.

"How does the seal work exactly?" Kaleb asked, addressing Amrit.

"I only know the basics," Amrit admitted. "When Savitri created the seal, she used Niveda's blood, which tethered her life force to it. Niveda isn't technically immortal. Her extended life is a result of magic, and magic always wanes. Without replenishment, she *will* run out some day, but that could take centuries."

Amrit had explained that what Vira had seen at the base of Niveda's neck was a source of magic she could call on to perpetually heal herself, and keep herself from aging. It was how she'd survived five hundred years locked in a tomb.

"They had no way to kill her," Amrit continued. "So the plan was to cut her off from the source by closing the quarries and preventing her from empowering more of her followers. Savitri thought this would be a solution to both problems. The seal would require a tremendous amount of magic to power it, so as long as Niveda remained alive, the quarries would remain hidden."

"So they doomed an entire country for one person," Riya said.

"They *saved* an entire country," Amrit corrected. "Niveda was a blight upon the land, and she had to be stopped through any means. There aren't many accounts of what life was like under her rule, but what exists is terrible enough that none of us should want to revisit that era."

"Where's the seal now?" Vira asked.

"The Crimson Fortress—or, more accurately, it's hidden in the labyrinth beneath it," Amrit said.

"The Crimson Fortress?" Riya blinked and then looked at Ronak.

"You've heard of it?" Amrit asked, surprised.

Ronak rubbed the back of his neck. "I found it mentioned in a book about the Order of the Mayura. There wasn't a lot of information, and I couldn't figure out which fort it was."

Vira wanted to ask why he'd been looking into the Order, but Amrit spoke first.

"It's not called that anymore," he explained. "The Crimson Fortress was Niveda's base of operations. And after she was defeated, the Kamala Society erased all evidence that she was ever connected to it. They renamed it after a nearby lake, Jhaner."

"I thought the Jhaner Fort has been empty for centuries," Vira said, frowning. It had been in one of Papa's journals, but there wasn't much about it. She didn't know if it was because he had never looked into it or because he'd never found any link to the Ivory Key.

"Savitri really wanted to make a point," Ronak muttered. Vira had to agree. Of all the places she could have hidden the seal, it felt distinctly personal that she'd hidden it beneath her sister's fort.

"I still don't fully understand how breaking the seal works," Riya said.

"The seal would have been crafted with a magical symbol on it," Kaleb answered. "Pieces of that seal were likely broken and woven into the doors of all the quarries, and as long as the original seal remains intact, there's no way to find or enter the quarries."

"Unless someone breaks it," Vira said.

"Or Niveda is killed," Ronak added.

Kaleb bit his lip. "I . . . might have an idea for how to kill her," he volunteered.

They all turned to him, waiting for him to elaborate. "Well?" Riya prompted when he didn't.

"I don't know if it'll work." Kaleb fiddled with the hem of his tunic nervously. "It's just a theory. I'll need some magic to test it out before I tell you."

"All right," Vira said. "We'll get the sword to stall her while you figure out how to stop her permanently."

"That's not so simple either," Amrit said. "She forged three gemstones out of magic and placed them on the sword, and it was so powerful the Kamala Society couldn't destroy it. Instead, they simply split the sword and the gemstones and tried to hide them. Niveda will go after them as well, to have enough power to break the seal."

"Do you know where these gemstones are?" Vira asked.

"One is still on the sword. The second was put into a ring that went missing—one that possesses the ability to store and inject cobra venom. That might take a while to track down. And last item is a lotus. That should be easy enough to get since it's in the possession of the Kamala Society at the monastery." Amrit's eyes flicked to Vira for a fraction of a second. He cleared his throat. "There's some magic there as well you can use," he told Kaleb.

"I'll go with Amrit, then," Kaleb agreed. "There might be more information there that could help us."

"I'll come too," Vira said quickly.

"I know where the ring is," Ronak said. "It's in Dvar."

"How do you know that?" Vira asked.

Ronak didn't quite meet her gaze as he mumbled a response she couldn't make out.

"I'll go with Ronak," Riya said. "And I'll get the sword from Sharadha."

Vira licked her lips as they all split up. Amrit been more forthcoming than she'd expected, but it was still difficult to trust him. Difficult to look at him and not feel her heart breaking in half.

Her stomach tightened at the thought of going back to the place where Amrit had betrayed her, but she had no choice. This was what they needed to protect Ashoka.

And all Vira could hope now was that they'd survive.

CHAPTER THIRTY-FIVE

— KALEB —

THE JOURNEY TO the monastery was quiet and uncomfortable.

Kaleb hadn't really known how to talk to Vira, and Vira hadn't known if she could trust anyone on the journey, so they'd all stayed silent, lost in their own thoughts.

He hadn't planned on inviting Lukas and Dayana along, but it had just slipped out. He'd justified it to both himself and to Vira by saying that he needed their help and expertise, but really, he'd just wanted a chance to talk to them away from everything, with the truth finally out between them.

The hours before they'd left were chaotic, spent tending to everyone that Niveda and her acolytes had injured. Thalia—the soldier Dayana had come to the palace to find—had survived with several broken ribs and a concussion. The rest of the Lyrians were worse off and in need of proper medical care. Lukas, who everyone knew would be crowned the next emperor, should have stayed to ensure they were cared for.

But he hadn't. He'd chosen to accompany Kaleb, leaving Elias in charge.

Though Amrit had called it a monastery, it was really a fort. Kaleb had seen it from afar, the compound nestled deep within the Koranos Mountains. But instead of forcing them back through the jungle, Amrit led the carriage straight through a series of tunnels.

The fort complex was empty as Amrit led their small group in—and not nearly as run-down as it seemed from the outside. The outer walls were covered in plants and vines, patrolled by mercenaries holding large weapons. Inside it was well lit by magical lanterns and torches tucked into sconces flickering with real flames. The compound was a lot smaller than Kaleb had expected, and a lot warmer.

Amrit led them through courtyards and hallways and up a flight of stairs, toward a series of rooms. He offered them four separate rooms near one another, but less than an hour later, Lukas and Dayana had wound up in Kaleb's.

It was painstakingly slow work piecing together the pages Theo had ripped out of the emperor's book. The book itself had a ton of useful information. There were drawings that Ronak had pointed out to Riya that indicated the different centers of magic and what they controlled. There were pages about channeling power through multiple centers of magic. There was even a section on how to tie a life force to a magical object, just like the seal.

Compared to all of that, the information that Theo had torn out seemed rather tame. It was how to create magical matter and infuse it with magic. It was what Theo had taught Shiv to do—how he'd caused the raw magic to explode.

"So this was how Theo did it," Kaleb mused as he read through the pages.

"It seems like intentions can be woven into the matter itself," Dayana said from where she was reading over his shoulder. "It's not like you have to create it and separately add more magic."

That was interesting. But they had no liquid magic—and with Riya having gone south with Ronak, they had no one who could test out that theory.

"I'm ready," Lukas said from where he'd been working on the bed, a handful of rocks next to him and a large pouch of processed magic Amrit had given them. He'd turned one of them into a glowing rock that emitted light.

Kaleb and Dayana turned to face him. Lukas pushed back his hair and then held up a smaller pebble.

"What's the intention you set?" Kaleb asked.

"To speed up the magic." Lukas touched it to one of the glowing rocks. Nothing happened. He frowned and picked up a smaller pebble. "This one is to expel magic contained within an object." But this too did nothing to stop the rock from glowing. He huffed in irritation as he reached for the pouch of magic again. "All right. Give me a minute."

"So tell me about this seal," Dayana said as they turned back to the book.

"It's like the trinkets you get in the Lyrian markets," Kaleb said. "The mass-produced ones."

Dayana made a face. Mass-produced objects were uncommon. Mayaka preferred making distinctive creations. After all, that was the artistry of magic, limited only by one's creativity and imagination. Objects manufactured in large volumes tended to focus on utility and efficiency.

Typically, mayaka started with raw material—a sheet of metal or a slab of stone or a block of wood. Then they would design and carve a specific, unique symbol or pattern before infusing it with magic and intention, such as turning light as a feather or becoming invisible. Pieces of that mayaka-forged material were then broken off and embedded into other objects, each of which would develop the same power.

The magic in those objects was only a fraction as powerful as the original, and there was no guarantee how long the magic would last. It was up to the mayaka who forged the original to replenish the magic in the raw material as it ran out. But these things were quick to make and cheap to produce, so they were popular in some places.

"The main seal is made of this magical matter and tied to Niveda's . . . life force, because she found a way to use magic to make herself immortal." Dayana rubbed her temples. "This is all really complicated."

Lukas let out a frustrated groan. Kaleb turned around to find him sitting with his head in his hands.

"Maybe you should take a break," Kaleb suggested. He could tell that Lukas hadn't been sleeping well, but it wasn't his place to mention that so he kept it to himself. "Fresh air could be good."

"Maybe," Lukas agreed. He got up from the bed, giving Kaleb a soft smile before he walked out the door.

"We should talk about that," Dayana said to Kaleb when they were alone.

Kaleb didn't particularly want to—not when he didn't even know what *that* was.

"We should focus on this," Kaleb said, gesturing back to the book.

They worked in silence for a while, but the longer they were alone, the more it was clear that the quiet between them wasn't that of two friends comfortable enough to simply be in each other's company.

Kaleb knew that Dayana was upset with him for lying. She'd made that pretty obvious from the start, but he was beginning to suspect that perhaps part of the reason she'd stayed behind was so they could finally talk about it.

Kaleb set the notes down and turned toward her. "All right. Maybe we *should* talk."

"You lied to me," she said at once. "You're my *cousin*. And you never told me." She shook her head. "I don't understand. How could you do that?"

"I had to keep my cover," Kaleb said. He'd played this conversation over and over in his head, but the longer he'd put it off, the harder it was to predict her response. And now he was afraid that it had gone on too long and she wouldn't ever forgive him.

"*You* involved me," she pointed out. "I mean I had my own reasons, but I didn't ask to be a part of this. You sought me out and asked me for help."

Kaleb lowered his gaze. "I only wanted to pay my respects to Alena," he said. "I never intended to actually meet you or befriend you."

"Is that supposed to make me feel better?"

Kaleb exhaled. "I'm sorry, Dayana. I truly am. I just did what I thought was best. I was trying to protect my family—"

"We're family, too," Dayana reminded him. "And I don't know what your Ashokan family made you believe about what it means to be a member, but using other people and lying to them all in the name of protection or love isn't healthy."

There was nothing Kaleb could say to that. He realized that perhaps there were more issues within his family than he knew or wanted to accept. All their problems, all of what they'd been taught, apparently stretched back generations.

"You could come back, you know," she said after a beat. "Actually meet everyone. We have some of your mother's things."

"Oh."

He swallowed. He wanted to, but he couldn't simply agree right then and there. He had his future to think about . . . his siblings. "Maybe," he said. "If we survive," he added, hoping the dry joke would lighten the situation.

"If we survive," Dayana echoed.

Moments later the door opened and Lukas returned. "I think I figured it out," he said with an excited gleam in his eyes, sitting down to weave magic into one of the pebbles again. This time, when he touched it to the glowing rock, there was a small flash of light—and then the rock was just a rock again.

Kaleb looked at him, surprised. "What was the intention this time?"

"It was what you said was in Theo's journal," Lukas said. "*Amplify use.* Magic wanes based on how it's used. So it's not about removing magic, but—"

"It's about getting the object to do what it was already doing, but *more*," Kaleb finished, understanding what Lukas was saying.

"So you just made the rock glow more," Dayana said, an excited gleam in her eyes.

"We know it's possible, then," Kaleb said. "We can remove magic from objects." But they needed to remove it from a person. And Kaleb had no idea if it would work.

✳

Later that night Kaleb found Lukas on a rooftop terrace, standing under the starlit sky, looking out at the forest. Everything was silent except for the occasional hoots of owls in the trees and the rustle of wind. He turned slightly when he heard Kaleb approach, moving over so Kaleb could stand next to him.

"Are you all right?" Kaleb asked.

Lukas took a deep breath. "I don't know," he said. "It's all just been . . . a lot."

It *was* a lot. They'd barely had time to process what had happened at Shantha Mahal. People had died there, including Lukas's father.

"Do you want to talk about it?"

"It hasn't hit me yet that I'm going to be the new emperor," Lukas said.

"This wasn't how you wanted things to go," Kaleb said.

"I wanted to stop him—"

"But not like this," Kaleb finished.

Lukas finally turned to look at him, searching his face. "Every time we talked, I kept wondering how you managed to understand me so well. It felt so often like you empathized—like you knew what it was like to be in my shoes. But even now, knowing who you are, it manages to catch me off guard."

"I don't know," Kaleb said, feeling strangely vulnerable under Lukas's gaze. "I was never in your position. It was always going to be my sister who would rule."

"Perhaps, but a life of choosing between desire and duty, that's the same."

Kaleb smiled a little. "I always chose duty."

"So did I," Lukas said. He shifted imperceptibly closer, and Kaleb could see the reflection of the stars in his eyes.

"I don't even know what I want," Kaleb admitted, looking back at the forest. He rested his elbows on the railing, clasping his hands together. "I had my life planned out, and I thought I would want to just go back to it. Become a scholar. Work in a lab. But I guess I don't know if I want those things anymore." It was the first time he'd admitted that aloud, and it was as freeing as it was terrifying.

"Or maybe you're no longer the person who wanted them," Lukas offered.

Kaleb mulled that over. He wasn't the same person he'd been two years earlier, when he was working with Papa in the lab. But he wasn't the same person he'd been in the dungeons either, waiting to return to a life he'd never really started to live.

"You went through a traumatic event," Lukas said, touching Kaleb's arm. "That changes people."

Kaleb turned to him in surprise. *Traumatic.* He'd never thought to apply that word to his own life. All things considered, it hadn't been *that* bad. He was alive. He was healthy. He still had his siblings.

And yet . . . there was no erasing the complicated feelings inside him, the remnants of which he'd carry with him for the rest of his life.

"I keep telling myself that there's no use in being angry about things that have already passed," Kaleb said.

"It's all right to be angry, you know," Lukas said. His fingers lingered on Kaleb's arm. "You don't need my permission—or anyone else's—for that. But if it helps you to have someone tell you it's all right to feel this way, I can be that person."

The words touched something in Kaleb's heart, and he felt himself warm under Lukas's gaze. "Thank you," he said, feeling almost shy.

"I keep thinking about the kind of emperor I want to be," Lukas confessed. "I want to do things differently. I want to fix things between our countries."

"You will," Kaleb said automatically, realizing belatedly that he truly believed it. "You'll be a good leader."

Lukas smiled, his hand sliding down to Kaleb's, tracing small circles along the back of his wrist. Kaleb shivered a little.

"Dayana said I should come back to Lyria," Kaleb blurted out.

Lukas's fingers stilled for a second. "Do you want to?"

"I want to go back as myself. As Kaleb."

They stood in comfortable silence for a few minutes. The wind was picking up, and Kaleb pushed his hair away from his eyes. When he turned back, Lukas was studying him.

"The palace is always open to you. If you want."

"You'd let me have my old room back?" Kaleb asked, a small smile tugging at his lips. "Blackmail me into being your spy again?"

Lukas smiled back, the corners of his eyes crinkling. "Technically, as you pointed out, I didn't have anything to hold over your head."

"That's still blackmailing," Kaleb said, keeping up the teasing tone.

But when Lukas responded, it was with sincerity. "You'd be there as my confidant. There was a lot of secret and probably terrible stuff my father was working on, and I'll need someone I trust to help me clean up that mess."

It was tempting.

He could go back as himself. Get to know Dayana. Get to properly explore Lyria. Help people with his knowledge, but not as a scholar trapped in a library or a lab. Maybe even see what this—the soft glances and lingering touches—was between him and Lukas.

And most important, if he went, it would be for himself. Not for his country or for Vira or even for Papa.

He hadn't actually lived his life in a long time.

And maybe it was time.

"All right," Kaleb said.

CHAPTER THIRTY-SIX

– RONAK –

THE COMPASS WAS tucked into Ronak's pocket, digging into the skin of his thigh every time the carriage jostled. He hadn't dared take it out while he was around Kaleb, but even now, he hesitated.

They were almost at Dvar. He didn't have much time before he'd have to meet Ekta and barter for the ring, but he had to know what was in it, if there was anything that could help Kaleb. It had taken him a while to figure out how it worked, but eventually he was able to cycle through the memories the emperor had stored. But there were a lot of memories and it was taking him longer than he preferred to sift through them all.

The Council was gone now, and worse they'd been the ones responsible for framing Kaleb. Even if he'd managed to approach them with the compass and its evidence, they were never going to clear Kaleb's name. It left a bitter taste in Ronak's mouth, as though everything he'd done was for nothing. This was the only way that Kaleb was ever going to come back home—a full and public exoneration and pardon so he could return to his life without needing to hide.

Riya and the Raven—Varun—had mostly stuck together, practicing with Riya's magic. She still had the book Ronak had given her, but it was Varun who was reading it, suggesting exercises for her to try. It seemed to be working. Riya had more control now, and more confidence. Ronak didn't know what to make of Varun. He was a Raven, and he kept shooting Ronak dark looks that made him feel like the boy was judging him simply for existing. But he was helping Riya, so he left them alone.

They weren't really paying much attention to Ronak either, but he waited until they stopped to replenish the magic in the carriage wheels to pull out the compass again. Riya and Varun had exited as well, wanting to stretch their legs, leaving Ronak alone inside.

Now that he knew how it worked, it was easy to access the compass. As he touched it, the memories played in his mind as though he were actually standing where the emperor had been.

It took him a while to find the right ones, going back far enough to learn about the emperor's conversations with Meena. But the emperor had been telling the truth. There was nothing about Kaleb there. Kallias had only wanted to make a deal with their mother—and when Meena said it would be impossible, he'd merely suggested that another maharani would be more malleable.

There was no actual evidence in the emperor's memories, but it was clear to Ronak that it was really Meena who'd orchestrated Amma's death. She'd been Amma's closest friend, and in the end, she'd betrayed her.

"What are you doing?"

Riya's voice startled Ronak, and he jumped, slamming his elbow against the side of the carriage. He hadn't heard her and Varun return. He tried to hide the compass, but it was too late. She'd seen it.

"So Kaleb was right." Riya crossed her arms over her chest. "You *did* take the compass."

"I need it to get the ring," Ronak said as an explanation. "It's the only way she'll give it to me."

Riya looked confused for a moment, and then horrified. "You're going to give it to Ekta?" She shook her head. "Ronak, no. You can't give this away." She reached for it, but Ronak angled away.

"Stop it, Riya," he said. "I listened to you about the Ivory Key, but she's not going to give me the ring without something in return."

"We can find another way," Riya said at once.

"What other way?" Ronak challenged. "Tell me a plan that we can enact in the next few hours."

Riya stayed silent. "It's a bad idea," she said. "We don't know what secrets are on there or what she's capable of doing with them."

"And there will be worse consequences if we can't stop Niveda," Ronak argued. "This is our best bet of succeeding and you know it."

"Do you want us to come with you?" Varun asked. Ronak could tell that he'd recognized Ekta's name, but he didn't say anything else.

Ronak shook his head. "I'll be fine." He'd seen how it had turned out with Jay. He didn't need to involve more people.

"And you're *sure* she has this ring?" Riya asked.

"I'm positive." He didn't add that he'd seen her use it. It was one of her more prized possessions, and he wasn't entirely sure she'd part with it. When Riya continued to look at him with an unreadable expression, he said, "I have it under control."

He hoped that was the truth.

✳

It was odd being back in Dvar, walking down Spit Street as if no time had passed. Ronak walked quickly to the crowded tavern, then to the underground parlor. Almost instinctively he felt his heart race with nerves.

Ekta looked up as he approached. "Well, well. If it isn't my favorite rajkumaara." A delighted smile crossed her face. "And what toy have you brought me to play with today?"

"I want to make another deal," Ronak said without preamble. He could see the ring sitting on her smallest finger, the emerald gem winking in the candlelight.

She raised an eyebrow. "You have the compass?"

"I do." Ronak produced it, flashing it in front of her eyes.

She was looking at it with overt longing. "I'm impressed, Rajkumaara. I wasn't entirely sure you'd be successful."

"I want two things," he said, ignoring her taunts. "I want assurances that this is the last deal that we make. And I want your ring."

Ekta glanced down at her hand, then back up at him. "I don't recall our deal being open for negotiation," she said.

"Then I'll destroy the compass," Ronak said. He held it up as though he intended to smash it down on the table. It was forged to hold memories, not to be infallible. It would shatter easily.

"Then how will you free your brother?" Ekta asked.

Ronak smiled. "There's nothing on here that will help him." He lifted his hand higher as realization dawned on Etka that she no longer had leverage over him.

"Wait," she said as his hand twitched. "I accept." She pried the ring off her finger and slid it across the table.

Ronak pocketed the ring and then tossed the compass to Ekta. "We're done," he said as he rose. "No more deals. No more threats. I walk away."

"No more deals," she agreed. "But I'm sure our paths will cross again someday, Rajkumaara."

"Don't count on it," he said, and walked away from her.

He thought about Riya's words—her insistence that there would be bad consequences if he gave Ekta the compass. But he didn't care. He was free of Ekta's clutches. He had the ring to stop Niveda.

In his eyes, he'd succeeded.

CHAPTER THIRTY-SEVEN

— VIRA —

THE MONASTERY WAS both familiar and unfamiliar all at once. The moment Vira had stepped inside, the emotions that had driven her to Ritsar—to look for the Ivory Key—had begun swirling around inside her again. It had been only a few weeks, but she felt like she was a totally different person now. Still, wasn't she doing the same thing? Seeking out mysteries and ancient truths and trusting people she shouldn't trust.

"This is yours to use for the duration of your stay," Amrit had said when he'd led them all to their rooms on the top floor of the fort. "You can ring for someone to draw you a bath and bring some food. And then we can meet to discuss the plan."

Vira had nodded, her gaze lingering on Kaleb and the two Lyrians he'd brought with him.

"I'll be in there," Amrit had added to Vira, pointing out his room. "I'll leave the door unlocked, so let yourself in when you're ready."

The room was simple, with a cot, a small table, and a wardrobe. She drew the curtains aside. The window faced the Koranos Mountains, and all she could see was the jungle. Once she'd bathed and eaten a simple meal of chapati and daal, Vira dressed. She hesitated and then reached for the small dagger Riya had given her before leaving. She didn't know why she felt that she needed to be armed, but it made her feel better to have it.

336

She knocked once on Amrit's door and then opened it. Amrit was sitting on the floor, his back against a wall, legs crossed, almost like he was meditating. He looked so resigned—so young—that for a moment all Vira could do was stare at him. It was so rare that she'd had the opportunity to see him unguarded like this. To take him in as he was and not as he presented himself to the world—a sharpened blade, honed for combat.

Vira realized belatedly that this was his space. Despite the fact that it was furnished exactly as her room, it was clearly lived in. His shoes were in one corner, a heavy cloak hung on the ajar almirah door, the bed covered with a warm woolen blanket.

"Come to stab me in the heart?" he asked, eyeing the dagger in her hand.

"I can't deny that I didn't consider it," Vira said. "But your heart's safe. For now."

He smiled a little. "I don't know that my heart was ever safe."

Vira turned away and tucked the weapon into the folds of the dupatta around her waist. She couldn't do this. Not with him. Not anymore. "We should get what we came here for," Vira said.

"I owe you an apology," he said, standing and walking toward her. He'd also bathed, his hair still wet where it curled around the nape of his neck. He'd rolled the sleeves of his kurta up to his elbows, and she could see the scars that littered his arms. She'd once hoped to learn the stories behind them some day.

Vira waited, and when he didn't say anything else, she crossed her arms over her chest. "Saying you owe me an apology isn't actually an apology."

Amrit's smile grew wider then. "You're right." He gestured at the door. "Let's talk outside."

She reluctantly allowed him to guide her up another set of stairs until they emerged at the top of the fort. She'd seen armed guards patrolling, but this stretch of the walkway was empty. The moon was lower in the sky now, and it was too dark to see much of the jungle stretched out in front of them.

"I'm sorry for lying to you," he said, resting his elbows on the crenelated wall. "And I'm sorry for leaving you. I truly was trying to protect you. I thought I was doing the right thing."

"You didn't ask me what I needed. Or what I wanted."

Amrit looked up at the night sky. His profile, lined with the moon's glow, looked just as she remembered it from another time, another conversation. It seemed strange that they were the same two people standing here now. Her heart clenched painfully. She felt a world away from Vira the maharani. And he felt a world away from Amrit the guard.

"I wanted to give you the magic," he said, still not looking at her. "I tried to find a way around it, I promise. But it was just too dangerous. We couldn't risk Niveda getting out. Or the knowledge that she came with. Knowledge about magic and the past and everything that the Lyrian emperor dug up. Our purpose was to protect Niveda and what her power represented—using magic in ways that aren't good for people."

"But that knowledge was already out there," Vira said. "The emperor. Riya. What were you going to do with my sister? Imprison her, too?"

"Never." Amrit turned to her. "She was never in any danger. Niveda was an exception."

"Right," Vira said bitterly. "I forgot you killed all the others."

"It wasn't like that," he said quietly.

"And what about my mother?" Vira asked, the words tearing out of her. "You killed her too." Her voice broke—and then she couldn't hold back her tears. She broke down, sobbing.

He let her cry, not speaking, not touching her or offering her any comfort, which she was glad for. It wasn't until she'd wiped her tears and looked up at him that he said anything.

"I didn't know about your mother," Amrit said. "I swear, Vira. I would have stopped it."

Vira looked at him, searching his eyes for any sign of a lie. "But your father killed her."

"He was misinformed," Amrit said. "We're not hired assassins—though there are some former members of the Kamala Society who choose to take on that kind of work, which is where those rumors started. We kill only those who are close to discovering information about the Ivory Key or Niveda."

"But my mother didn't care about the Ivory Key," Vira said.

"I know," Amrit said. "But your father did. When Meena wanted your mother killed, she contacted the mercenaries. And they contacted my father, and because he knew I was still in the palace—that I hadn't come back after your father died—he was led to believe that she was the source of danger, knowing too much about the Kamala Society."

Vira pressed a hand to her mouth. She'd thought having answers would make her feel better, but it didn't change anything—it didn't make it any less painful or terrible.

"Surya told me that you came to the palace to spy on my father," Vira said, recalling their conversation. "Or maybe that was a lie too."

"No, that was the truth. We knew he was looking into the Ivory Key. And we needed to make sure he didn't find anything." Amrit closed his eyes. "But then he died. I thought it was over. I'd planned to leave then."

"But then I told you I was picking up his research," Vira said, recalling the day. It was the first time they'd talked about anything other than their training. She'd been so overcome with grief that she missed their lesson. He'd found her looking through his old books. In a moment of vulnerability she'd told him about Papa's research. The first person she'd ever told.

She'd held that memory close, thinking it meant something. She knew now that it didn't.

"I had to stay. I wanted you to have the magic, but I didn't want you to find out the truth."

"You didn't think I could handle it," Vira accused.

"The opposite," Amrit said. "I didn't want you to have to make yet another difficult choice. I wanted the Kamala Society to die with me. With this knowledge."

The fact that he thought that he'd die at all sent a shiver snaking over Vira. "You wanted to disband the Kamala Society?"

"I don't want this secrecy anymore. I intended to destroy the key and the map and everything. I'd been doing research about what was in that tomb—and why they weren't able to kill her all those years ago." He drew in a ragged breath. "It was better for you to hate me and be alive."

Vira didn't know what to say.

She wanted to believe him, but there was a part of her that was still hurt. There had been one thing she'd believed she could take for granted, and that was Amrit—his presence by her side and her own gut in trusting him. And when he betrayed her, it wasn't just about what that meant for her future; it made her doubt whether or not she could trust herself.

✳

Vira knew they would get no help from the Kamala Society, but Amrit insisted on trying. Suyra had told her that Amrit would want to do things the right way, following protocol and alerting the Kamala Society as soon as he had the key. He'd done exactly that, and now, he wanted to meet with them again to discuss Niveda.

From what she'd gathered, the society members were upset, and Vira, who'd spent a lifetime disappointing her elders, could see that right away. She'd destroyed the one thing that had been their entire purpose. Amrit, for all he'd encouraged her to fight back and stand her ground, clearly had no experience being the one who had to justify his actions. Justify his mistakes.

He was supposed to stop Vira by any means necessary, but he'd failed. He could have killed her at any point, but he hadn't. He'd stood by her side. And even now, he was facing the wrath of his community for her.

"I don't know if I should be here," Vira said as they walked together toward the room where they'd be meeting the leaders of the three branches of the Kamala Society. "They hate me."

Amrit didn't disagree. "They might be able to help," he said.

Might. Not that they would, or even could.

"It'll be fine," Amrit added, giving her a reassuring smile as he opened the door to the meeting room. It reminded her of every other time he'd told her that, giving her the courage and strength to face the things she didn't want.

There were three people in the room: a historian, a mayaka, and a warrior. They were seated in a row behind a long wooden table, shrouded half in darkness, and they looked even more terrifying than the Council. Vira stood her ground, holding her chin high as she faced them head on. A maharani never backed down from a fight, and she was through with letting people make her feel small.

"So you're the one who let this happen," the mayaka said, eyeing her with derision. "If you hadn't done the most foolish thing, I'd be impressed that you managed to get this far." She looked at Vira in a way that reminded

341

her of the way Amma would look at her—like she was waiting for some-thing about Vira to impress her, and knew nothing would.

"Vira was only looking for the quarries," Amrit said, stepping in defend her. "If the lore of the key wasn't tied so much to the sealing of the qu—"

The warrior raised his hand. He looked surprised that Amrit had spo-ken and defended her. "It doesn't matter now, does it?"

"Yes," the historian agreed, pushing up the spectacles on the bridge of his nose. "What's happened has happened. And now Niveda will kill us all and destroy Ashoka."

"We can fix it," Vira said, shocked at how quickly they'd given up. "We have a plan."

Kaleb had told her what he and the Lyrians had discovered: there was a way to remove magic from an object. They could use it against Niveda, remove her immortality and then break the seal.

"There's no fixing this, child," the historian said.

"Your job is to protect the country," Vira reminded them.

"Our job was to protect a secret," the mayaka corrected. "And we've failed at that, so we have nothing more to say. This meeting is over." She rose and walked out without a glance back. A moment later, the historian followed her with a regretful look at Vira and Amrit.

"Times have changed, Rani," the warrior said as he, too, stood. She remembered him. The long hair, the scars on his face, the way he'd called Amrit *son* when he'd betrayed and abandoned her. This was his father. This was the man who'd killed Amma.

Vira wanted to say something, maybe stab *him* in the heart. But she just stood frozen.

"We don't have the numbers we once did," the warrior contin-ued. "We've done what we can for all these years, protecting the Ivory

Key—something we're not even sure is a noble cause anymore. We can't help you." He looked at Amrit. "But you are, as always, free to make your own choices."

"I've made my decision," Amrit said, looking at Vira. It felt like he was talking about more than just the key.

"Then I wish you well," he said, and then he was gone too.

"Where's the gemstone?" Vira asked. Amrit had said they would need permission to remove it. She wasn't sure if they had it, but she also didn't think anyone was going to stop them.

"Through here," Amrit said, leading her down a corridor and then inside a small room with shelves of books. It was small and intimate with a plush chair and a lamp for reading, as though this was someone's personal library. He reached up to remove one of the books, carefully pulling it off the shelf. He reached for a second book—and then paused as he realized something was amiss. He tugged at one of the shelves. It moved easily, like it had already been opened, revealing a secret passage in the wall.

Amrit pressed a finger to his lips as he disappeared down the hall. Vira followed him. The corridor was short, made entirely of stone, and it opened into a chamber with a column of yellow light in the center, a sword and a scroll suspended in midair.

"It's gone," Amrit said. "The lotus."

The lotus would have been in the center—the sword and scroll crossed over it. The original Kamala Society crest.

"We have to go," Amrit said. He rushed back out the way they'd come—and stopped short at the sight of a figure standing at the entrance to the library.

"Looking for this?" Surya asked, holding up a crystal lotus with a glowing magical gemstone at the base. Amrit took a step toward him. "Stay where you are," Surya warned, waving the sword he held in his other hand. He had a cut along his cheek that looked fresh. It made his grin look even more feral.

"How dare you show up back here after what you did," Amrit snarled. Vira had never seen him so angry. "Father—"

"He's not my father," Surya said coldly, all traces of amusement gone from his face. "And you're not my brother." He looked at Vira. "Why am I not surprised to find you here? All that talk of revenge and rage, but you're just as weak as everyone said you were."

"You don't know what you're talking about," Vira said, hating that her voice shook.

"Don't do this," Amrit said. "The lotus belongs to us."

"It belongs to the goddess," Surya said. "If you really wanted it, you should have gotten here earlier. Goodbye, Amrit." And then he shut the door, trapping them inside.

"Surya!" Amrit struggled with the latch until the door opened again. He yanked it open and ran outside.

But the hallway was empty. Surya was already gone. And so was the gemstone.

CHAPTER THIRTY-EIGHT

— RIYA —

THE CARRIAGE WASN'T the ideal place in which to train her magic, but Riya sat cross-legged on one of the seats, mirroring Varun's posture. Ronak had gone to meet Ekta, and the space felt a little bit too small with just the two of them, especially when Varun had the entirety of his attention fixed on her.

Varun had sent word to Kavita, asking the Ravens to go to Adhura and get Chandrika's sword from Sharadha, so they were waiting for the Ravens to meet them. The carriage was parked at the edge of the forest, shielded from the crowds, but Riya had still insisted they practice inside rather than out in the fresh air where anyone might see them.

And by anyone, Riya was mainly concerned about the other Ravens. Varun had responded well to all this, but she still remembered the fear in Vira's eyes. The mere thought of seeing that same look mirrored on the Ravens' faces terrified her.

"Just talk to her. Be honest," Varun had told her, accurately sensing the source of her apprehension.

"What if she doesn't understand?" Riya had allowed herself to admit in a moment of weakness.

"I understood."

It was different, Riya wanted to say. Kavita was her best friend. She couldn't bear to lose her.

"Relax," Varun said, his voice smooth and soft. "You're thinking too much again."

"I'm not," Riya responded on instinct. She was used to disagreeing with Varun on everything. But when he gave her a knowing look, she took a deep breath and let go of her pride.

"Just focus on my voice," Varun said, glancing at the book in his hand—Papa's book, which Ronak had given her before leaving the palace. They'd been working through some of the exercises together. "I'll guide you through a short meditation, and then we'll try some visualization, all right?"

"All right." She rolled her shoulders back and let her eyes flutter closed.

"Focus on your breathing. Don't control it, just simply observe it."

It was the same thing Papa would tell her when he tried unsuccessfully to train her as a mayaka. She'd never been particularly good at it. It was strange that she'd spent so long resisting his teachings; meditation was too boring, too difficult for her constantly racing mind. She felt a twinge of regret that she hadn't taken him more seriously.

"You're thinking too much again," Varun observed. "Bring your focus back to your breath."

Riya huffed in irritation that he was able to read her so easily, but she did as he said, centering her attention on the rise and fall of her chest, her shoulders, her stomach, feeling the way the air moved in and out of her body.

After a few minutes, Varun spoke again. "Keep your eyes closed," he said. "But this time imagine that there is a ball of light between your feet. Slowly lift it up through your body, all the way from the soles of your feet to the top of your head. Now move that ball of light back down."

It took Riya several minutes to get the rhythm of visualizing this light moving throughout her body and how to sync it with her breath. But slowly, as she grew accustomed to the exercise, she felt something change within her. When the ball of light passed over her chest, there was a spark—subtle at first, and then more and more insistent, the way magic felt within her.

"Magic," she breathed. "I feel it."

"Where?" Varun asked.

"Near my heart," she said.

"Now let go of it," Varun said.

Riya slowly eased the ball of light away, letting it fade into nothingness. The magic too disappeared. She opened her eyes. "How did you know that would work?" she asked.

"I didn't. I was just going to have you keep trying things until you found something that worked."

Riya put a hand over her chest. Ronak had showed her a book the emperor had. According to that there were six centers of power within the body where magic could bind.

"Almost all magic is channeled through your hands, but that's all it is: a way of controlling and directing the power," he'd explained. "It's the centers of power that are most important to identify, because each does something different."

"Can you train yourself to use any of the centers?" Riya had asked, curious.

"In theory, yes, though according to this, people have affinities for one of them usually," Ronak had said. "And it seems like you can only use one at a time."

Riya had studied the drawings in the book and then pointed to one that explained the focus point located near the heart. "That's what I've done," she said. "Healing things. Breaking things apart."

"So maybe try to focus on that," Ronak had said.

It took Riya dozens of attempts at meditating and visualizing before she was able to consistently summon the spark of magic within her.

"You did really well," Varun said, giving her a small smile. "Let's take a break. The Ravens will be here soon."

He pushed open the door and disembarked first—then held out his hand to help her down. He'd done this every time, but she still felt a strange sensation of warmth fill her as his fingers closed around hers.

"Thank you," she said, looking at him sincerely. "I could only do this because of you."

Varun shook his head. "I just gave you some guidance, that's all."

It wasn't just that. He put her at ease, made her feel comfortable enough to relax, but he knew her well enough to know when she was overthinking. His knowing her that well should have been an annoyance, especially when she felt like she couldn't read him at all most of the time. But it wasn't. It made her feel . . . seen.

Riya realized too late that he was still holding her hand. And then his eyes dipped down to her mouth for just a second.

Riya's breath hitched. Somehow all she could do was stare at him, locked in his dark gaze.

We're going to kiss, she thought.

It suddenly felt inevitable, as if they'd been moving toward this moment all along, and now that they were here—

A twig snapped.

The two of them leapt apart. Riya's heart was still beating fast, and she was all too aware of Varun's presence beside her, of the lingering scent of tulsi that washed over her as she twisted toward the sound.

Kavita and Yash walked toward them. Kavita held a sword in her hand, and Riya exhaled in relief. They'd managed to get it from Sharadha.

For the first time, Yash didn't look happy. His brows were knit together as he scowled at Varun. "Do you want to tell me why you ran off without a single word and then had us travel hours and give *all the money we had* to a woman for a sword?"

"I didn't mean to just leave," Varun said. "I was just—"

"You just ran after her," Kavita said, gesturing at Riya. She looked just as displeased. "So what's your excuse?"

Riya swallowed. "I'm sorry," she said. "There was something I had to do."

"Something," Kavita echoed. "You're not even going to tell me what it is?"

"I'll explain later," Riya promised. "I just need to take care of this first." She owed Kavita that much—and the Ravens.

Yash looked at Varun expectantly, as though he might share. Varun cleared his throat. "It's not my story to tell," he said, his eyes sliding to Riya's.

Riya held a hand out to Kavita for the sword. "Thank you," she said. There was so much more she wanted to say to them, but they didn't have much time. Ronak would be back soon, and they had to get to the Crimson Fortress before Niveda.

There was rustling in the trees, and all four of them realized that they weren't alone.

When Riya turned, Tarini stood there, along with several other members of the Order of the Mayura. They were armed with bows, arrows aimed at all of them.

"Tarini?" Yash looked at her confused. "What are you doing?"

"Thank you so much for finding the sword for us," Tarini said with a smirk. "It saved us a lot of trouble."

Riya instinctively stepped forward, holding the sword behind her back. "You're a fool if you think I'm giving this up."

"Then we shoot you all," Tarini said easily. "The arrows are poisoned with something that I'm not even sure has an antidote. It's far worse than what I used on your shoulder. You'll be lucky if you survive an hour."

Riya's magic hummed beneath her skin. She could use it to escape. She lifted her hands up, but Tarini wagged a finger at her.

"Don't even think about it," she said. "There's too many of us, and we're all *very* good shots. Do you really think you could take us all down before at least one of them gets hit?"

Riya hesitated. She didn't know that she could. And she didn't know if she could heal them if they were hurt—or if they'd even survive long enough for her to try.

Kavita, Yash, Varun—they were her family. Her saviors. She couldn't do it.

Slowly Riya dropped the sword to the ground and kicked it over toward Tarini.

CHAPTER THIRTY-NINE

— VIRA —

VIRA STOOD LOOKING up at the Crimson Fortress. It was massive and ancient, and though it looked eerily abandoned, walls crawling with vines and plants, it was a formidable structure. The buildings hadn't crumbled into ruin. The outer walls at least were still intact, protecting the palace in its midst, the stones still an unnatural pristine white.

"Why is this called the Crimson Fortress?" Riya asked.

"Because under the light of the full moon, the magic in the stone turns it as red as blood," Amrit said. "Or it did, once."

Two pillars held up a large metal gate that was wrapped with a tangle of heavy chains to keep it shut. It now hung open, the chains snapped in half, presumably by Niveda.

The seal would be in the heart of the labyrinth. But unlike what Vira had initially thought, Amrit had explained that the labyrinth was merely the easiest way to describe the series of interconnected rooms full of obstacles and traps that they would all have to get through to find the seal.

They'd lost the sword and one of the gemstones. If Niveda managed to get the ring as well, she'd have enough power to destroy the seal. But Kaleb thought there was a chance they'd be able to kill her before that—to use Niveda's own magic against her. He'd created a device that would force the magic in her to run its course in a matter of minutes instead of centuries.

She would come after them looking for the ring, and when she did, they would use it to stop her.

"We don't know if it'll work on a person," Kaleb had admitted to Vira as they left the monastery with Amrit to meet up with Ronak, Riya, and the two Ravens she'd returned with. Dayana and Lukas had left to join the remaining Lyrian soldiers, but they'd helped Kaleb figure this out. "Or what the side effects might be."

"How many chances do we have?" Amrit asked.

"One," Kaleb said. "That's all we could make with the amount of magic we had."

It wasn't a great plan, but it was the only plan they had, so they had no choice but to risk it. They had a shot at stopping her before she got too powerful.

They had a shot at surviving.

"There's three sets of walls," Amrit said. "And then we'll have to enter the labyrinth underground. The outer wall will be easy to get past." He pointed it out. "We just need to find the right door, which might take a while. There wasn't too much information I could find about the other traps inside."

"Great," Ronak said under his breath.

Vira didn't like it either, but they'd survived the temple at Ritsar. They'd solved the Kamala Society's puzzles before. They could do it again.

"We'd better get moving," Riya said, looking at Varun and Kavita. Vira hadn't wanted to take more people she didn't know or trust inside the labyrinth, but they'd insisted on joining, and Riya thought that they'd be helpful.

They're on our side, Riya had assured her. Amrit seemed to respect Varun, and Kavita was protective of Riya, so Vira hoped it was true—that they were truly there to help and not for their own agenda.

The walkway wasn't paved, and it was covered with scraggly bushes that snatched at Vira's kurta like angry claws. It was nearly impossible to stay silent. Twigs and gravel crunched beneath their feet as they walked the circular path.

"Has anyone successfully broken in?" Riya asked, looking up at the large walls that blocked their view of the interior of the fort complex.

"Once," Amrit said. "Niveda did."

Vira looked at him in surprise. She'd assumed Niveda had constructed it.

"This was built before the founding of Ashoka, back when individual lords controlled the provinces," he explained. "The lord who constructed it made it impossible for other provinces to attack this fort, even with a large army. Niveda bribed one of his guards who was familiar with the defenses and was able to capture it."

The wasn't very reassuring, but Vira didn't say anything as they approached the door. They stopped in front of it, and Kaleb put his hand out to touch it.

"There's no magic," he said.

"I don't think it's the right one," Riya said. "It would be foolish for the first door anyone encountered to work."

"Or it could be a misdirection," Varun pointed out. "We have to try every door."

There were a dozen or so wooden doors that led to the next set of walls that encircled the palace. Supposedly some of them were trapped. Some of them were dead ends. Only one led inside, and they had to find it.

Ronak sighed and opened the door a tiny sliver. And then he immediately slammed it shut. "Pit of snakes," he said, his face turning pale. "Let's keep going."

The second door was locked, and despite Kaleb not finding any magic in it and Riya and Kavita spending nearly twenty minutes trying to pick the lock, it didn't budge.

"It might be a false door," Ronak suggested as they walked away from it. "Made to appear like one to waste someone's time or resources and give the defenders a chance to launch an attack."

Riya glared at him. "You couldn't have thought of that earlier?"

The third one opened far too easily. Vira pulled it open and peered inside. It looked normal, leading to another similar corridor. "Wait here," she said. "Let me investigate a little."

Ronak came with her, and as they walked for a few minutes, they realized that it led to a dead end that curved around the corner. They walked back the way they'd come.

"There's nothing here," Vira said, trying to open the door they'd come through. Except it didn't move.

Ronak gave her an odd look and then tried as well. And then he banged on the door. "We're trapped in here," he called. "Can you let us out?"

There was no response. Vira felt her heart rate quicken. "Do you think they're all right?"

"We were gone for less than a minute," Ronak pointed out. "What could have happened in that time?"

They took turns calling through the door and knocking on it, trying to get someone to let them out, until their voices were hoarse—and then the door finally opened, revealing a started Riya.

"What are you doing?" she demanded. "We've been waiting for ages. I thought something terrible had happened."

"We've been shouting for ages," Vira said. "The door locked behind us. It was a dead end."

Kaleb looked concerned. "We didn't hear anything," he said.

"Let's keep going," Ronak said, brushing past Vira. He looked around, then back toward the way they'd come. "Maybe we should try the other direction. We're getting farther away from the palace."

"We should go in only one direction," Riya insisted.

It took a long time to reach the next door. It looked the same as the others that they'd crossed, but this one was narrower, able to fit only one person at time. Vira cautiously opened it. And then she exhaled in relief.

"I think this is it," she said, throwing it open so that the others could see through it. She stepped in first, onto the banks of a moat. And on the other side was the second wall they had to cross before they could enter the fort.

CHAPTER FORTY

— RONAK —

RONAK LED THE way as they walked around the edge of the moat, following the curve of the outer wall. Ronak could see more doors embedded in the wall on the other side. All they had to do was cross the water and they'd be able to access the labyrinth that was hidden beneath the fort.

But Ronak was worried about how easy it looked. They were missing something. And then he realized what it was.

The water was a clear blue—an impossibility, given how long it had been open to the elements. There was a tangle of dark vines that obscured their view of the bottom, but the moat wasn't covered in debris or algae. There were hardly any ripples as it lay as still as a sheet of glass. And yet it hadn't attracted droves of mosquitoes.

"I think there's something magical about the water," Ronak said. "I don't know if we should touch it."

"I agree," Kaleb said. "It looks *too* clean."

Ronak glanced at his brother, but Kaleb wasn't looking his way. In fact, Kaleb had barely spoken to Ronak since they'd argued about the compass. He knew he'd done what he'd needed to do in order to get Ekta's ring, but he'd lied to Kaleb, and a part of him couldn't help but feel guilty about that.

"Maybe there's a walkway underwater," Riya suggested. "It might be like that invisible maze we found. It could be hidden."

At Vira's suggestion, they gathered pebbles lying around on the ground and dropped them into the water as they walked, hoping one of them would stay suspended on the surface or otherwise indicate that there was something special about the water. But they had no luck. Every single one sank.

"Wait—look—" Kaleb said, pointing to what looked to be a wooden raft cleverly disguised as a door. Riya went to help him dislodge it from the wall.

"There's magic in it," Riya said as she tugged it down and laid it flat on the ground. "I think it'll float."

They pushed it into the water, and it did float, but there were no oars, and the plank could only reasonably fit one person at a time.

"I'll go first," Vira volunteered, gingerly stepping onto it.

"Crouch down," Riya instructed. "It'll be easier for you to keep your balance."

Vira did as she was told as they shoved her forward. The distance wasn't very large, but they all watched with bated breath as the raft began to slow before reaching the far bank. But when it did come to a stop, it was close enough to the other side that Vira could simply leap off onto the ground.

"I wasn't entirely sure that would work," Amrit muttered, exhaling in relief as Vira pushed the raft back toward them.

It was painfully slow as one by one, Amrit, Kavita, Varun, and Kaleb all crossed the moat after Vira, until only Riya and Ronak were left.

"You go before me," Ronak told Riya. Riya looked like she wanted to protest, but she reluctantly agreed.

There was less momentum with only Ronak pushing and the raft didn't go as far, but the two Ravens managed to get hold of the very edge and tug her to safety.

And then it was just Ronak. He took a deep breath and pushed the raft into the water, then leapt onto it. It wasn't a clean jump—his foot touched the water. He tugged it up immediately.

But it was clear that touching the water had an effect. The still water began to move, and Ronak could see something that looked like tendrils moving beneath the surface. Terror gripped Ronak. He was still in the middle of the water, too far from either shore.

The vines broke the surface, sending up a spray of freezing cold water that crashed over him. They began to snake around the raft, around Ronak, dragging them both down into the depths.

"Ronak!" Kaleb shouted as Ronak gasped for breath, struggling to break free.

"I have rope," Varun said, digging through his pack. "Hold on to it."

Varun threw one end to him. Ronak lunged for it—but the vines were pulling him down. There was a sickening crack as the wooden raft snapped in half. Ronak was sinking. He held his breath, trying to fight back. He couldn't see anything under the surface of the water, and his eyes burned. The tangle of plants was everywhere, ensnaring his arms and legs and torso and mouth.

He couldn't hold his breath for that much longer. He was going to have to let go, succumb to the water.

Suddenly the vines around him went slack, and a hand reached down and tugged him up.

Ronak gasped as he broke the surface, coughing up the water he'd swallowed. Kaleb was on what remained of the raft, holding one end of the rope in his hand and dragging Ronak up. Behind him, Ronak could see Amrit and Vira slashing at the plants with their talwars while Riya used her magic to burn them.

"I've got him," Kaleb said. Kavita and Varun began to tug on the rope, pulling the two of them toward the shore. Amrit slashed at the vines one last time before he, Vira, and Riya ran back too.

Ronak collapsed on the ground.

"Are you all right?" Vira was staring down at him, eyes wide with fear. Kaleb was behind her, looking just as pale.

Ronak nodded. "I'm fine." He pushed himself up. His lungs burned and his clothes were soaking wet, weighing him down and making him shiver from the cold, but he was alive.

They were all on the other side now, and there was only one way to proceed: underground. The next door in the wall led to a set of dark stairs, and it was open.

Niveda and her acolytes were already there.

CHAPTER FORTY-ONE

— KALEB —

THE STAIRS LEADING down into the labyrinth were steeper than Kaleb had expected. It was quiet, nothing but the sound of their breathing and the soft padding of their footsteps as they descended into the darkness. They all had glowing stones, but their light was feeble—almost like the dark was suffocating them, trying to stifle any bit of light that managed to enter this space.

The stairs ended abruptly, depositing them in a stone room of sorts. They were under the fort now, where it was cool from the lack of sunlight and life. Kaleb wished he'd brought one of the coats from Lyria as he felt goose bumps ripple over the exposed skin of his arms.

"The labyrinth isn't really a maze," Amrit reminded them. "But we need to make our way toward the center where the seal is kept. There are many paths to getting there, some harder than others, and our success will depend as much on luck as it will on our skill."

Kaleb didn't like that. He preferred not to have to rely on chance, but there was not much they could do about it. No one spoke as they walked forward as a group, nervous energy palpable between them. They knew they'd have to split up soon, but for now, Kaleb was glad the seven of them were together.

The fork in the road came far sooner than any of them expected—or maybe it was just their perception. Kaleb didn't really know how long they'd been walking through the dark. The tunnel led to a cavern that branched off in two different directions.

"I'll go this way," Riya said, pointing to the left. Varun and Kavita—the two Ravens Riya had returned with—nodded in agreement.

"I'll join you," Kaleb said. He'd given Ronak his spare set of clothes, and he was glad that his brother was safe. But Kaleb wasn't sure he was ready to be around him like before just yet.

Vira looked at Amrit and Ronak, the only two others remaining, and nodded toward the right. "Stay safe," she said. She hesitated, and then handed Kaleb a dagger. "Just in case."

Kaleb had refused a weapon earlier, but everyone else was armed so he reluctantly took it, nodding as Vira, Amrit, and Ronak walked away from him. He wasn't used to having a weapon, and the thought of using it made him feel a little queasy.

"It's good to have it, just as a precaution," Riya said.

"It's not that," he muttered. "I don't like that we might have to kill anyone at all."

She and the Ravens were armed, and they'd been doing this for a long time. Kaleb trusted that he was safe with them. Not to mention that Riya's magical power had grown considerably stronger now. She could control and manipulate her magic in a way that still left him awestruck. He was proud of her, but it was a little bittersweet. He'd gone to Lyria thinking he had to get answers for her, but in the end she hadn't really needed him. He wasn't sure if any of his siblings really needed him. Once, that would have made him panic, made him question his place within his family. But now it brought him some comfort. They'd be all right even if he wasn't around. But it didn't stop him from worrying.

There was a chance that none of them would make it out of here. Even if they succeeded, Kaleb wasn't sure that the magic Niveda used to power her immortality wouldn't just explode the way the raw magic in Lyria had and destroy everyone and anyone in the way.

Lukas and Dayana had returned to the surviving Lyrian troops, who were still in the safe house Amrit had found for them. They were going to see if they could remove magic from the people—and from Shiv, who had still been unconscious when Kaleb last saw him.

But before they left, Dayana had pulled Kaleb aside and given him a tight hug.

"This isn't goodbye," she'd said. "Promise that you'll come back to Lyria with me."

"I promise," Kaleb said, even though they both knew it wasn't really a promise he could make. "It'll be all right," he'd added, for his own benefit as much as hers. "We'll stick to Vira's plan."

Dayana had looked at him out of the corner of her eye. "Vira's plan," she said mildly.

"They're my family," Kaleb said quietly.

"But you get to be your own person first," she'd said. "You don't think this is unfair? Having to put your life, your wants and dreams, on hold for their sake?"

He'd noticed Dayana—and Lukas too, if he was being honest—watching him closely whenever he was with Vira. He hadn't been sure what to make of what they saw, and for some reason, Kaleb had felt a little uncomfortable being on display like that. They weren't the most functional family, he knew, but he was almost embarrassed. For the first time, he was seeing them through the eyes of outsiders.

He'd known that he had let them treat him this way, that he'd internalized Amma's teachings that as the oldest sibling, it was his job to maintain peace between them. To ensure that they were safe and healthy and taken care of. To ensure that he wasn't a burden on anyone.

But somewhere along the way, he'd lost sense of who he was. And it was only now that he was starting to find his way back to the person he was meant to be.

The tunnel curved, and when they carefully followed the path, they found themselves facing a wall. Kaleb held the lamp higher, letting it wash over symbols that were carved into the stone. They weren't letters, but shapes, triangles and squares and circles, some with dots in the center, some without. And when Kaleb ran his hand over the carvings, he realized that they weren't actually etched into the stone but—

"They're tiles," Kaleb said.

They began to pull them off the wall, grouping them by shape and laying them on the ground. There were fifteen in total. They couldn't actually move the first three symbols on the wall.

"It's a pattern puzzle," Riya said, looking at the wall and then down at the ground. "We have to figure out the right order of elements."

It took them some time to figure this out: a square, a circle with dots, a triangle, a square with dots, a circle, then a triangle with dots. This was repeated three times, so they carefully began to replace the tiles in the wall. When the last one was place, the entire string of symbols began to glow blue and then dissolved into the wall. When the last of the light faded, a door appeared in the wall.

Kaleb carefully pulled it open.

The next room was large—the size of a ballroom—and entirely empty. There was an open doorway on the other side, leading toward whatever the next room was.

"This is odd," Kaleb said. It looked like there should be a trap somewhere that they had to evade, but he couldn't see anything in the limited light.

"Maybe Niveda or her acolytes already triggered the trap," Varun suggested, walking inside.

But as soon as he said that, there was a soft click. He froze, looking down at his feet in horror. There was a small metal plate on the ground—and by putting his weight on it, he'd triggered it. Thick white smoke filled the room, flooding in from unseen vents.

"We should stick together," Kaleb started to say, but by the time he turned back, he couldn't see Riya or the Ravens.

He was completely alone.

CHAPTER FORTY-TWO

— VIRA —

VIRA SET OFF down the corridor with Amrit and Ronak. Ronak was being uncharacteristically quiet and Amrit unnaturally talkative as they walked.

"We only have one chance to do this," Amrit reminded her. "If we fail—"

"Amrit," Vira interrupted him. "I know."

She knew he was only being cautious, but she was on edge—they all were. The fact that Amrit had repeated this multiple times reminded her too much of Amma, of the Council, the way they didn't trust her to remember, to know how to behave in dire situations.

He didn't say anything else, but as he turned away, she caught a flicker of emotion passing over his face and realized with surprise that Amrit was nervous. It worried her because even after everything, she looked to him for reassurance. She didn't know where they stood—if things would ever go back to normal between them. But she'd chosen to trust him, to trust all her siblings.

"What kind of traps can we expect?" Ronak asked.

"Logic puzzles. Magical traps. Physical tests." It would be similar to what they'd found in the temple, except harder on every level. Amrit looked back at Ronak. "Do you know the history of this fort?"

"A little," Ronak said. "It was the only fort that was never captured by any of the maharanis. Historians never knew why, but now we know it's because of the Kamala Society's traps."

"The traps were added by us," Amrit said. "But the labyrinth existed even before. It was why Niveda wanted it in the first place."

"Has anyone made it out alive?" Vira asked. She had to hold on to some bit of hope that they would escape.

"Members of the Kamala Society have," Amrit said.

"Great," Ronak said sarcastically.

Vira didn't know what she'd expected, but it was a little odd that the path wasn't that narrow. She'd never loved enclosed spaces, and she'd expected the labyrinth to feel that way—as though the walls were closing in on her, suffocating her.

Ahead of them, Vira could see that the tunnel was ending, depositing them in a room. Amrit abruptly put a hand out to stop her. He pressed a finger to his lips and crept forward, pressing himself against the wall as he peered around the corner.

He bit the inside of his cheek and then dragged Vira and Ronak back away from the room before he spoke. "Niveda's minions are in there," he said unhappily. "I counted four."

"What are they doing?" Vira asked.

"Waiting for us, I think," Amrit said. "I couldn't hear much." He looked at the bag Vira had slung over her shoulder. "You have the gemstone?"

Vira nodded. Shockingly, Ronak had given her the ring after his fall into the moat. Vira didn't know how well she could protect it, but for the first time Ronak had trusted her with something.

"What's your plan?" Ronak asked.

"Fight them," Amrit said plainly, taking a deep breath and rolling his shoulders back.

"I'm hardly proficient with this," Ronak said, gesturing at the talwar he'd taken at everyone's insistence.

"No," Amrit said. "I meant *I'm* going to fight them." He pierced Vira with his stare. "You two are going to run."

"What?" Vira asked, alarmed. "You just said there's four of—"

"I can handle it," Amrit said. "Stay focused on the plan. There's a path through that room. As soon as I distract them, you both make a run for it." He looked at her a little sorrowfully. "It's the only way."

Vira's heart beat a little too fast at the thought of losing Amrit again. There was so much unsaid between them, so much unresolved. But he was right. This was the only way. Amrit squeezed her hand. It was the briefest of touches—there and gone before Vira could fully curl her fingers around his. And that was the only goodbye they got before Amrit charged into the room.

There was a flurry of steel as Amrit ducked and weaved between the acolytes while Vira and Ronak ran for the door. The iron gate on the opposite side of the room was held open by a rope that connected to the ceiling somewhere. She could hear one of the acolytes chasing after them as they ran through the doorway. Vira started to draw her talwar, but there was a loud crash as Amrit slashed the rope that held the door open. The gate came crashing down.

"Run!" Amrit shouted.

Vira didn't hesitate. She grabbed her brother's arm and dragged him forward down another corridor. They slowed when they could no longer hear the sounds of fighting. Vira pressed a hand to her racing heart as they tried to catch their breath.

"We have to keep moving," Ronak reminded her, looking warily over his shoulder as though he expected something to jump out at them.

"I know." Vira panted as she surveyed the area they were in. This passage was different from the tunnel they'd used earlier. It was more open, brighter, almost like there was light coming from somewhere, but Vira couldn't see any source. At the end was another iron-gated door like the one they'd come through.

"It seems too easy," Ronak murmured.

Vira nodded. "There might be a trap of some kind here."

"I think we just have to keep moving," Ronak said. "If we trigger a trap, so be it. We'll deal with it then."

As soon as he said that, Vira caught movement out of the corner of her eye. "Watch out!"

A stone statue stepped out of the wall of the passage, wielding a club. The statue turned toward them, and Vira could see that it had eyes made of gold.

"The eyes," Ronak said weakly. "They're like the archers from the temple in Ritsar." They'd shot Ronak with a poisoned arrow that had nearly killed him.

The statue raised its club.

"Move!" Vira screamed. She shoved Ronak out of the way and dove to the other side just as the club crashed on the ground where they'd been. A spray of stone and dust erupted around them as the club chipped.

"It doesn't look very sturdy," Ronak said.

He wasn't wrong. The club was already chipped. But Vira still thought it could kill them with one or two blows.

"I'll distract it," Vira said, drawing her talwar. "Get to the gate and figure out how to open it."

The statue wasn't moving too quickly, but it blocked the width of the path toward the exit. Vira charged at the stone, hitting it in the knee. The statue brought the club down again, this time against one of the walls. More stone rained down on Vira as the club broke again. She dodged out of the way to avoid a large rock, but she couldn't avoid several smaller pieces that pelted one side of her arm.

"Run," she directed Ronak as she spun around, attacking the statue's knee again. It crumbled, and Vira took advantage of the distraction to hit its other knee. It collapsed to the ground, and Vira barely managed to get out of the way.

She could see that the statue was rising again, training its golden eyes on her once more.

"Attack the eyes," Ronak said. "I think they're the source of its magic."

Vira charged forward. The statue's arm came out to grab her as Ronak dove to the gate. She ducked out of reach and lunged forward to spear the statue's eye. As soon as she shattered the stone, whatever magic was powering it disappeared. The statue stopped moving and simply dropped to the ground in a pile of rubble.

Vira leaned against one of the walls, breathing heavily. "That was terrible," she said. She watched from a distance as Ronak pulled the gate open easily, using a manual crank. Vira ducked in through the door he held open—and then closed carefully behind them.

Vira was injured, separated from Amrit and her family, but she had to keep pressing forward toward the center of the labyrinth. She only hoped the others were doing better than this.

CHAPTER FORTY-THREE

— KALEB —

WITH THE SMOKE around him, Kaleb couldn't see anything. He squinted and moved his arms about, flailing them to try to get the smoke to dissipate. It made no difference.

"Riya?" he called into the void. "Riya?"

"Kaleb?" Riya's voice sounded like it was coming from the other end of the room.

"I'm over here," another voice said from a distance.

It had been just a few seconds, and they'd all been standing so close to one another right before the smoke filled the room. They couldn't have moved so far away. This was some kind of magical illusion, Kaleb thought as he felt a faint prickle of magic in the air. The Kamala Society had wanted to ensure that their own members would be able to navigate this labyrinth—which meant there had to be a way to shut the smoke off somehow.

"I'm going to move around slowly," Kaleb shouted.

He wanted to walk backwards, try to find the wall, and then use that to guide himself to the exit. But he'd turned around when the smoke had filled the room, moving in circles as he tried to find Riya and the Ravens. He had no idea what direction he'd come from.

Kaleb swore under his breath. It had been foolish of him to do that. For all that he was considered the scholar of the family, the bookish, studious one, he was the most useless when it came to practical applications of that knowledge.

Why do you talk to yourself like that? The voice in his head sounded suspiciously like Dayana. She'd been the one to push back against the way he thought of himself, pointing out that he was skilled and reassuring him in a way that he hadn't fully realized he needed to hear.

He was doing his best, and this was a stressful situation. Kaleb took a deep breath, trying to clear his mind and come up with a solution.

"Let's try to find each other," he said. There was no response. The smoke was clearly making it difficult to communicate—but he'd heard two of them earlier. They must have moved away from him while searching for each other and the exit.

Kaleb began to walk. He had no idea where he was going, but he held his arm out in front, feeling through the smoke for anything he might run into.

He moved slowly, carefully, calling out every few steps in case the others were nearby. But he heard nothing. He had no idea how long he was walking through the smoke, how long he was trapped there, without any sense of direction or sight. Finally, his fingers brushed against something.

He leapt back in surprise and then approached more cautiously. It was a wall. He sighed in relief. He had a way out. Except he didn't know which wall he'd found and which direction he needed to be going in. After a moment, he decided to go to the right, carefully trailing his fingers over the wall to stay connected.

It proved to be a lucky guess because minutes later he found the gateway that led outside. The smoke was harmless, but he still found himself gasping for air as he tumbled out. He looked around the area, searching for a lever or another pressure plate that would diffuse the smoke and help him find his friends, but he couldn't find anything.

He was rifling through his bag, trying to find rope so he could wade back into the smoke to get them, when a sound made him jump. He hadn't properly examined his surroundings, but he knew it was coming from somewhere behind him.

He carefully peered around the doorway. He was in a corridor of sorts that connected several different rooms. And coming out of one of the doorways was an armed acolyte. And worse, the acolyte caught sight of Kaleb, lifted his bow, and aimed an arrow directly at him.

Kaleb had less than a second to make a decision. He could go back into the smoke, but if the acolyte fired arrows without visibility, there was a chance that any of them could get hurt. And worse, they'd be trapped in there without a way of getting to Niveda. He had no choice but to keep moving forward and give Riya, Varun, and Kavita a chance to escape the smoke on their own.

He leapt forward, barely dodging an arrow as he sprinted toward one of the other rooms. It turned out to be full of mirrors. Everywhere he turned, he saw his own terrified face staring back at him, his curly hair disheveled. It was a maze—or maybe it only felt that way, because it was nearly impossible to find a path through the room. Each time Kaleb was sure he had a way through, he ended up crashing into a mirror.

There was a cackle behind him as the acolyte approached the space. "I know you're in here," he called out in a singsong voice that sent shivers down Kaleb's back.

Kaleb hurriedly changed direction, trying to push past some of the mirrors. He could sense a shadow approaching, and though he didn't know where the acolyte was, he could hear footsteps. He threw himself flat against one of the mirrors to try to hide, but to his surprise, it gave way under his weight. He staggered back, barely avoiding falling as he realized belatedly that the puzzle wasn't figuring out a way *through* the maze of mirrors: it was adjusting the mirrors in such a way that . . . he wasn't sure. He tilted the mirror back and forth until he saw a golden line right at the center. He had no idea what it was reflecting, but he knew what it meant. He had to connect the golden lines, and perhaps it would lead him out.

He hastily darted around the room, quickly testing which mirrors were movable and carefully angling and positioning them as he tried to avoid the acolyte, who was closing in on him.

"I know you're close," the acolyte said, his voice echoing eerily through the room.

Kaleb held his breath as he approached the very last mirror, tiptoeing toward it. He adjusted the mirror, tilting it forward to reveal the golden line.

And behind it the acolyte.

Kaleb gasped in shock as the figure in the mirror lifted his bow once more. But the mirrors were all in place. The golden thread glowed bright, and one of the mirrors against the wall dislodged and swung forward, revealing a passageway.

The arrow flew just as Kaleb leapt for the passage. It pierced him in the arm, throwing off his balance, and he crashed into the wall of the passage, landing on his bag. He heard something snap beneath him as he hurriedly slammed the mirror shut behind him.

His left arm was bleeding where the arrow had pierced it, but his right shoulder hurt even more. With trembling fingers, Kaleb slid his bag off the shoulder, pulling it down. But even before he opened it, using the glowing stone to illuminate the contents, he knew what the breaking sound had been.

The device he'd built to try to expel Niveda's magic was broken into three irreparable pieces.

CHAPTER FORTY-FOUR

— RIYA —

RIYA COULDN'T SEE anything. Smoke, thick and heavy, clouded her eyes, and though she'd spent what felt like hours moving around, she couldn't find the others.

And then all at once, the smoke vanished.

Riya blinked in surprise, looking around the room as Varun and Kavita materialized. Varun was standing by the exit.

"I found the trigger to turn it off," he said, pointing to another plate he'd stepped on.

"Where's your brother?" Kavita asked.

"Kaleb?" Riya called, rushing toward the way they'd come. But where there had been a door was only a wall. There was no way for them to go back. Riya slammed her fist against the wall in frustration.

"He must have made it out," Varun said rationally.

She had no idea how long they'd been wandering through the smoke, but that was a possibility. But Riya didn't like the idea of Kaleb being alone.

When they left the room, there was no one outside. "Kaleb?" Riya called again. It wasn't smart to draw attention to the fact that they were there, but she had to chance it in case he was hurt.

There was no response. They walked down the hallway and then stopped when they realized they were at another fork. They didn't know which path he might have taken.

"We shouldn't split up," Kavita said as Riya bit her lip in consideration.

She hoped Kaleb would be all right as they picked the center path. Riya knew that Niveda would have had to go through the same labyrinth and navigate the same puzzles. They didn't know which path she'd taken or how she'd fared, so they had to move quickly.

They'd worked together for years, knew how to act as one unit, but something was off. Maybe it was just that it had been so long since Riya felt she was a part of the Ravens, but the silence between them felt too heavy.

"I'm glad you're here," Riya had told Kavita on their journey from Dvar, and she'd meant it.

They'd talked a bit, cleared the air between them. Riya had told her about the magic, about why she'd left. Kavita had forgiven her for it, just like Varun had said she would. But there was still a bit of tension that lingered. It wasn't back to normal yet, but it felt like maybe they could get there someday.

She missed her best friend.

And then there was Varun, who kept sneaking glances at her, beside her the entire time, giving her reassuring smiles that made her stomach flip.

Varun, who'd spent every waking moment helping her control her magic, making sure that she rested her mind, and talking to her about anything and everything under the sun when she was too overwhelmed and cranky from pushing herself too hard.

She didn't know what to make of things between them now, but she liked hearing about the way he saw the world, the way he thought about everything. He had never been the talkative sort, and that he wanted to talk to *her* made her feel warm from the inside out.

Later, she'd promised herself. *After this is done, we'll talk.*

She hoped she'd get the chance, because she really wanted that.

"If it isn't the Ravens," a cold voice sounded from somewhere up ahead of them. "Ashoka's saviors."

Riya was immediately on edge as Tarini stepped out from the shadows. She looked the same as she had when she was with the Ravens, but now she was openly wearing the ruby pendant signifying that she was a member of the Order of the Mayura.

"I didn't expect to see you here," Tarini said to Kavita tauntingly, eyeing the three of them. She pulled out two swords as she walked toward them.

Kavita drew her own weapon. "I guess it's time for a rematch," she snarled.

Riya had been friendly with Tarini, but Kavita and Varun had spent more time with her. This was personal between them. Kavita had been furious that they'd let Tarini get away with the sword when they'd paid Sharadha so much money for it. Kavita wanted revenge. And if Riya was being honest, so did she.

Tarini only smiled wider. "Three on one?" she asked. "That's not fair, is it." She whistled, and two more of Niveda's acolytes stepped out of the shadows with their own weapons.

Riya didn't recognize either of them.

Next to her she heard the clash of metal as Kavita charged at Tarini, who deftly spun out of the way. But this time Riya was prepared.

You're just practicing with Varun, she told herself as she took a deep breath and called on the power within her.

Push, she commanded. It worked—one of the acolytes went flying into the wall. She did it again. A second one also flew back.

But she was so preoccupied, she didn't notice that Tarini had drawn closer to her.

"Riya!" Varun warned.

Riya whirled around just in time to see Tarini raise one of her swords. She instinctively threw her hands up to defend herself. Fear and adrenaline were coursing through her veins, and before she even registered what happened, there was a flash of light and an agonizing cry.

Tarini crumpled to the ground, her eyes glassy and vacant as she stared up at nothing, a bloody gash in her stomach from where the sword had pierced her own skin.

Riya pressed a hand to her mouth as she stared down in horror. She'd just wanted to push her away, like the others. But she'd lost focus, let her anger and desire for vengeance control her, and she'd paid the price for it.

Some marks—like taking a life—leave a mark on your soul.

And those never disappear.

CHAPTER FORTY-FIVE

— VIRA —

IT WAS TOO quiet.

After Vira and Ronak fought the stone statue, they'd walked in a straight line, following the winding path as it led them deeper and deeper into the heart of the labyrinth. But they hadn't come across anything— no traps, no obstacles, no acolytes, not even another door that signaled a way out.

"Maybe we're going the wrong way," Vira said. She couldn't shake the feeling that she was being pulled even farther away from her siblings, from where she needed to be.

"We're going deeper underground," Ronak said. He pointed back toward where they'd come, and sure enough, they'd been walking down a gentle slope.

"Amrit said there were no dead ends," Ronak said. "Just—"

"Harder paths. I remember." She huffed. He was right. They would be wasting time retreading the paths Riya or Kaleb were already on. "I just . . . I thought Amrit would be able to catch up to us by now," she admitted.

But no one was following them, and part of her was afraid that the reason Amrit hadn't followed was because he wasn't alive. The thought made her feel so sick to her stomach that Ronak had to wait for her until the nausea passed and she could walk again.

"Maybe he found a different path," Ronak suggested. He was being uncharacteristically optimistic. He was trying, she realized. He was trusting her, supporting her. She didn't know what to make of it, but for the first time in years, she felt a spark of hope that things might be better between them someday.

"Maybe," Vira agreed, because she couldn't dwell on the alternatives.

They walked for what felt like another hour before the path abruptly ended. Vira turned in a shocked circle.

"You're telling me all this was for nothing?" Vira asked. Her voice was too high-pitched, on the edge of hysterical.

But Ronak was calm. "We're missing something," he said thoughtfully, looking around again. He tilted his head, eyeing the high ceiling. And then he snapped his fingers, rushing over to one of the walls.

"What are you doing?" Vira asked, confused as he jumped up in the air as though reaching for something. It took him three tries before he managed to get it loose, and a rope ladder tumbled down the side of the wall. "How did you know that was there?" Vira asked.

Ronak shrugged. "Just saw it from the right angle, I suppose. Want me to go first?"

Vira shook her head. "No, let me."

She began to climb carefully. The ladder moved as she did, the rope rough against the skin of her palm as she tried to keep her balance and not look down. The ladder led up to a ledge that opened into a small cave with a door on the other end.

This is clever, she thought as she waited for Ronak to join her. It would have never occurred to her to look above to continue the path. She would have given up and then walked back the way they'd come. She found that she was grateful that she was with Ronak, who approached things so differently, literally saw things from a different perspective.

"Is there another trap?" Ronak asked when he reached the ledge.

"I don't think so," Vira said. The door looked more or less like a normal door. It had a handle on the outside, so she pulled it open.

A spray of mist hit her directly in the face. She stumbled back and wiped her skin, grimacing as she realized it was in her mouth.

"Are you all right?" Ronak asked, alarmed. "Is your face—"

"It's fine," Vira said, using the edge of her dupatta to wipe it off. It didn't feel like poison—or at least her face wasn't melting yet. In fact it felt more or less like water. "I'm fine," Vira said, mostly trying to reassure herself. "Let's just keep moving."

She stepped inside the room.

It was dark at first, but as she kept walking, she began to see more of the space. It was a beautiful room, decadently decorated with plush sofas and a large mahogany desk that reminded her so much of the one that was in Amma's office.

She blinked. It *was* the one from Amma's office. When she drew closer to examine it, she could see Amma sitting there. Her hair was pulled back in a long braid adorned with jasmine flowers. She wore a heavy silk sari and layers of gold jewelry, and when she caught sight of Vira, she expelled a long, arduous sigh of disappointment.

"Have I not told you enough times, Vira," Amma said, "a maharani must always dress to impress and intimidate." She raked an exacting eye over her. "What are you wearing exactly?"

Vira looked down at her simple kurta. "I'm trying to blend in," she said, her voice quiet. It had been so long since she'd seen Amma, since she'd heard her voice or spoken to her, that the flash of pain she felt caught her off guard.

"Blend in." Amma frowned. "That's not your job. A maharani should stand out—deserves to stand out."

Vira swallowed. "Maybe I want to be a different kind of maharani." She lifted her chin defiantly as Amma's eyes narrowed. She'd rarely spoken back to her mother, and even now, it felt strangely out of line. Vira blinked as the odd thought struck her that Amma was gone, that she'd been gone a long time. But she wasn't gone—she was sitting right there.

"A different kind of maharani. How's that working out for you?" Amma looked at her expectantly. It wasn't a rhetorical question. She actually wanted an answer.

Vira swallowed, feeling small as she hung her head. "Not so great." She'd unleashed Niveda on the world, all because she wanted magic, because she thought she was special somehow and deserved to find the Ivory Key. Because she wanted to be the maharani who saved Ashoka, who brought magic back to its lands.

"Look at me," Amma instructed. "Tradition exists for a reason, Vira. Honoring the path of those who came before, upholding a legacy that has prevailed for centuries isn't something to sneer at."

Vira stared at her. "But if we can do things differently, do them better, isn't that worth changing tradition for?"

After all, Niveda was a part of their legacy, wasn't she?

"And who is to say what's better?" Amma countered.

Vira didn't know how to answer. It wasn't that she wanted to reject every aspect of the past. She just didn't want to stick to things simply because that's the way it had been done. There were things to learn from the past—and she wouldn't ever forget or take for granted the work done by those who'd come before her. But she couldn't agree with Amma.

"I'm my own maharani," Vira said finally, looking at her. "I might make mistakes, but they're my mistakes and I will own them. I don't want to be the kind of ruler who hides behind tradition, who uses that to excuse my decisions."

"So you've made up your mind," Amma said.

"I have," Vira said, meeting her gaze head-on. "I know what kind of ruler I want to be. And I'm sorry if that disappoints you or doesn't align with the vision you had for my life. But you don't get to control my life. Not anymore."

And with that, Vira stepped away from her mother and kept walking through the room.

CHAPTER FORTY-SIX

— RONAK —

RONAK FELT A deep sense of terror as Vira fainted.

"Vira? Vira!" He shook her shoulder, patted her on the cheek, trying to wake her up, but whatever mist had hit her face was too potent. She was knocked out. But she was breathing.

He examined the room. There was nothing inside, not even any puzzles or traps—at least not ones he could see. Whatever the mist had done, it had to be the only thing in this room.

Ronak crouched beside Vira again. She didn't stir. He didn't know if the effect would end once they left the room or if she'd wake up after a certain amount of time, but he knew that he had no choice but to keep going. He reached for Vira's fallen bag, slung it over his shoulder, and then picked up his sister, carrying her to the other end of the room.

The door here was unlocked too. Ronak carefully pulled it open, jumping away in case it triggered another spray of the magical mist.

Nothing happened.

But when he peered outside, his stomach plummeted. Niveda's acolytes were milling around. And with Vira unconscious, his options for escape were limited. They were looking for the gemstone, and he knew that Niveda and her acolytes would stop at nothing to get it.

Protect the ring, Amrit had told them, but Ronak knew that if it was a choice between the gemstone and Vira, he would pick his sister. They didn't always get along, but she was still his family.

Ronak rummaged through her bag until he found the ring. He slipped it into his pocket and hoisted Vira up. He could see a room next door. He would make a run for it.

But he had taken no more than two steps when the acolytes turned around, drawing their weapons.

"I have the gemstone," Ronak blurted out. "Let me pass, and I'll toss it to you."

"Or we could just take it after we kill you," one of them responded, advancing on them.

Ronak pulled the ring out of his pocket and flung it into the room he'd just exited, hoping it was enough of a distraction. And the moment they began looking for it, he bolted for the next room, slamming the door shut and depositing Vira on the floor.

He tried again to wake her up, and slowly, she stirred.

"Ronak?" She blinked, confused. "What happened? Where are we?"

Ronak exhaled in relief. "Thank the goddesses you're all right," he said. And then his stomach sank as he realized he had to admit what he'd done. "But I lost the gemstone. Niveda has everything she needs to break the seal."

CHAPTER FORTY-SEVEN

— RIYA —

RIYA, VARUN, AND Kavita were getting close to the heart of the labyrinth.

Riya could feel the presence of a massively powerful object growing closer, almost as if the magic within her were serving as a compass, guiding her toward the seal.

They'd left Tarini's body behind, and Riya was still feeling the dread and regret and pain knotting her stomach as Kavita and Varun had pulled her away.

"She would have killed you," Varun said over and over. But it didn't make her feel any better. It wouldn't undo what she'd done.

But they had to keep going, so that's what Riya did, pushing the feelings aside to focus on what was in front of her.

"This way," Riya said, pulling them left as they encountered a fork.

They hurried down the hallway, if only to put distance between them and the unconscious acolytes—but as they kept moving, Riya heard footsteps coming in the opposite direction. The three of them froze, hands on their weapons as they waited for whoever it was to draw near.

Riya exhaled a sigh of relief as she caught sight of Kaleb's familiar figure. "Oh, thank the goddesses it's you," Riya breathed.

Kaleb looked just as relieved to see her. "Are you all right?"

Riya nodded. "I'm fine." She scanned her brother. He was injured, a wound on his arm that was bleeding. "What happened?"

He waved her off. "It doesn't matter. I broke the device."

"What?"

"The trap for Niveda," Kaleb said urgently. "It broke while I was trying to run from one of the acolytes."

Riya felt the blood drain from her face. "Really?" So they were doomed.

"Can you make it again?" Varun asked.

"We don't have enough magic," Kaleb said. He looked at Riya. "Do you trust me?"

Riya looked at him sharply. "Of course," she said at once. There was no one she trusted more.

"I have an idea," he said. "It's . . . a little . . ." He laughed breathlessly, like he couldn't believe he was admitting it.

"What is it?" Riya asked, worried.

"I think you could re-create it," he said. "With your magic."

Riya stopped walking. "What?" She turned to face him. "Are you serious?"

Kaleb nodded. "I can help you," he said. "It's just like forging objects, but you'd be able to create matter out of nothing." He paused. "Well, not nothing. It would be out of magic."

The very thought of using her magic made her stomach twist. She'd been so afraid it would lead to death and destruction, and now she had proof.

"I can't," she said, looking down. "Kaleb. It's—I can barely control it. What if I do something that hurts people?"

"You won't," Varun said. "You've controlled it before."

"Yes, but that was because—" *of you.* Riya felt her cheeks heat. "I don't know if I can do it again." Making matter required mastery of a different kind of magic that worked at a different point in her body. She didn't even know if she had an affinity for another type of magic. It would be one thing if she'd practiced for hours, but they didn't have that—they had minutes.

"Try," Kaleb said. "That's all I'm asking. And I'll be right here beside you."

Riya exhaled and then nodded. "I need a quiet place," she said.

"We need to find somewhere we can guard," Kavita said. "Varun and I can keep watch while you do this."

They found an alcove that granted them enough privacy, with enough vantage points that they'd be able to see anyone approaching.

Riya sat cross-legged on the floor, Kaleb in front of her, closing her eyes as she tried to summon her magic. She did the visualization exercise Varun had taught her, moving the ball of light through her body. But instead of letting it linger by her chest, where she was used to it, she moved it lower, toward her solar plexus.

It wasn't as easy to hold the power there, but after several attempts she was able to get a wisp of magic. It wasn't as strong a connection, not as insistent as what she was used to, but it *was* there, and it was better than nothing.

"What do I do now?" Riya asked.

Kaleb walked her through it step by step, telling her exactly what the device would look like and what intention she would imbue it with to get the magic to leave Niveda.

The first attempt failed, the magic withering away in her hands as soon as she conjured any image. The next ten attempts also failed. Frustration flooded her, but then she remembered what Varun had told her every time. She was thinking too much. She let go of her fears, her worries, and suddenly she could feel the magic speaking back to her again.

The next time, she was able to make a proper orb.

She looked at it, amazed—and then her smile fell as it fizzled out of existence.

"Very good," Kaleb said, relief clearly evident in his voice. "Do it again, but this time you're going to channel intention, like you're putting magic into an object."

She closed her eyes and concentrated on it again, listening to Kaleb's words. But moments later Kavita's voice cut through her focus.

"We have to move," Kavita said. "There's too many of them, we can't fight." They were being approached by acolytes.

Riya and Kaleb rose. The half-formed orb in her hand fell, disappearing into nothingness before it even hit the ground.

"Which direction?" Kavita asked as they ran through the tunnels, approaching another fork.

"Right," Riya said.

Kavita began to turn right, but Varun stopped her. "We should split up," he said, looking at Riya. "Kavita and I will go left, mislead them."

"Wait," she said.

Varun turned back to her, and before Riya could think too much or talk herself out of it, she flung her arms around his neck. His hands instinctively came up to settle on her waist as she stood on her tiptoes and kissed him. It was a soft brush of lips, barely a kiss if she was being honest, but Riya had the oddest feeling that she would regret it for the rest of her life if she walked away from him without doing that.

"Thank you," she breathed. "For everything. For just . . . For being you." She pulled back, her lips tingling. She held his gaze for a long moment, and then she turned and took off down the corridor.

But she couldn't resist sparing a glance over her shoulder. The last thing she saw was Kavita staring at her in shock and Varun standing beside her, dazed, his fingers pressed against his lips.

CHAPTER FORTY-EIGHT

— RONAK —

THEY WERE CLOSE to the seal. Ronak could feel the powerful magic of it washing over him in waves. And just as he and Vira rounded the corner, they crashed almost literally into Riya and Kaleb.

"What's wrong?" Ronak asked, taking in their flushed faces and heavy breathing.

"Order members," Kaleb breathed.

"I think we lost them," Riya said, glancing over her shoulder. The corridor remained empty.

"We're nearly there," Vira said. "But Niveda has the sword and the gemstones. She's going to break the seal at any moment."

There was only one path forward now, so they walked until they reached a room with a high ceiling. Ronak had a feeling this was the last thing that separated them from Niveda.

The obstacle looked deceptively simple. Just a series of moving blocks they had to use to climb up to the level where the seal was. The blocks were made of stone, and they moved either left to right, back and forth, or up and down.

"We have to get there," Kaleb said, pointing up and to the left, where there was a small glow of something bright.

They had to figure out which blocks to take—and in what order—to get to the ledges in the middle and eventually to where they needed to go.

Ronak swallowed as he looked up. He'd never liked heights, and it was a long way to fall if they missed any of the blocks. It was about timing and luck just as much as it was about physical abilities.

"I'll go first," Riya said. She climbed up the small ledge, waiting patiently for the first stone slab to move in her direction. She stepped onto it easily and let it carry her to the ledge on the other side.

It looked easy, but Ronak knew it wouldn't be. He went next as Vira stayed on the ground, directing Riya toward the subsequent block. There was one beside her that went up and another that moved to the far side of the room.

The stones weren't wide, and Ronak felt his stomach leap into his throat as he stepped on the first one. The journey looked smooth from the ground, but it was shakier than Ronak expected, the sudden shift in momentum making it difficult to maintain his balance.

He stepped onto the ledge—and then followed Riya, taking the stone that moved up and down.

"Crouch down," Riya called as Ronak stepped onto the second slab.

He felt a little nauseated as he was transported up through the air. He crouched down as Riya had instructed—but he didn't stand up quickly enough as he approached the next ledge.

With a sickening lurch of his stomach, he found himself moving down again, the speed of the stone a lot faster than it had seemed from afar.

"Ronak! Give me your hand," Riya said as the stone rushed up again. He reached for her and half climbed and half collapsed onto her just as the stone began to move away from the ledge again.

There wasn't a lot of room, but he leaned against the wall heavily as below them, Vira and Kaleb began their climb.

"We have to do one more," Riya said, looking up at the last stone slab that would take them to the opposite side.

Ronak could hear Vira telling herself not to look down. She didn't like heights either. She also looked sick to her stomach as she clambered off the first stone and waited for Kaleb.

"We can't both stay here," Riya said. When Vira came up, there wouldn't be enough room for all three of them.

"I'll go first," Ronak said, terrified that if he thought about it too much, he simply wouldn't leave.

It was a long way to the other side, but he took a deep breath and stepped onto the stone. It wobbled beneath his feet, and he instinctively threw his arms out to maintain his balance.

Don't look down, he told himself.

But there was a problem. The stone slab didn't go to the very edge of the final ledge. There was a gap.

A gap that Ronak would have to clear by jumping. He braced himself, crouching and counting down until he reached what he thought was the closest point.

And then he leapt.

He crashed against the ledge, the impact sending pain rippling through his knees.

"Ronak?"

"I'm all right," he called back, even as his heart raced. He pulled himself to his feet and waited, watching his siblings scale the stones and finally cross the final step to the ledge.

The four of them leaned heavily against the wall of the corridor, catching their breath. Until they heard a loud crash.

"Niveda," Vira breathed.

"She's breaking the seal," Ronak said.

CHAPTER FORTY-NINE

— KALEB —

THE SEAL DIDN'T look like what Kaleb had expected. It was large and crystalline, its octagonal shape taking up most of the stone podium it had been left on. But now there was a crack down the middle.

And standing in front of it, Niveda held a sword. She was alone there— no acolytes. They were all down in the labyrinth. That was good, Kaleb thought. It meant they would only have to deal with her.

The sword in Niveda's hand was glowing with power, crackling with magic that Kaleb could feel against his skin like a gust of hot air. But that wasn't her only source of power.

Vira had told him about it, but it was different seeing it—black veins spreading over Niveda's neck and shoulders from the power she was exerting. The power of the gemstone she'd embedded in her skin at the base of her neck. The source of her magical strength. And what they would need to target to end her immortality.

Kaleb stared at it from afar, a little awestruck. He could feel its power overwhelming him.

But more than just the physical response, emotionally, Kaleb could hardly believe they were there. After all of Papa's years of endless searching, of believing that the Ivory Key would lead them here, all that stood in the way of the lost quarries was this one seal.

There were three gemstones nestled within the hilt of the sword, shimmering as Niveda lifted it over her head and brought it down on the seal again.

There was another crack in the crystal surface.

"We don't have much time," Vira whispered, panicked. "What's our plan?"

Kaleb glanced over at Riya, who hadn't managed to create the orb they needed. And he had no idea how long it would take her. "I can do it," Riya said.

"I'll distract her," Vira said. Her voice shook, but she stood up, looking every bit as regal as if she were in her formal clothes. A maharani, a leader through and through.

"I'll go with you," Ronak said.

"Be careful," Kaleb said. "We have one shot at this."

CHAPTER FIFTY

— RIYA —

CREATING THE DEVICE was harder than Riya expected. Her hands shook, her mind was too loud and busy. But she had to try. They were all counting on her, and everything that had happened had to be worth it.

She had to do this.

"We need to amplify the power," Kaleb said. "So that's what you have to concentrate on. The intention is to get the magic to do what it wants, just faster. The gemstone has a source of magic contained within it, not used up until Niveda draws on it. What we want to do is get it to simply release all the magic it's holding, so that it floods her. She won't be able to handle that amount of power."

Riya stared at him, confused. "What words do I use for the intention?" she asked.

Kaleb shook his head. "Not words. The feeling. The sensation. Let go of everything except what I told you—it doesn't matter what the words you think or say. Everyone's way of thinking is different. As long as you know what you're trying to get the magic to do, it'll follow your command."

"Do what it wants to do, but faster," Riya repeated to herself.

Almost unconsciously she reached for the tulsi she'd stashed in the pocket of her kurta. She bit into one of the leaves, letting the flavor wash over her as she again pretended she was with Varun, sitting in the carriage, practicing like they'd done so many times. She wasn't afraid of herself anymore—of what she could do. She wasn't resisting her power.

And then she began to summon the magic and create a crystal orb. She could feel it coming to life from her fingers—and she could feel the magic listening to her.

And when she finally opened her eyes, it was complete. And this time, she knew it would be stable, not fading out of existence like the last time.

"I think I did it," Riya said. She felt exhausted. She knew she'd been pushing herself and exerting more magic than she was used to. She had a feeling that it was waning out of her system, almost at a point where she could no longer summon it.

And to her immense surprise, that felt a little like grief. She hadn't wanted it, had tried everything she could to distance herself from it. But it was only now, when she felt it leaving her, that she realized how it had become a part of her.

There was another crash as Niveda slammed her sword into the seal yet again.

"We don't have time to make another one," Kaleb said, picking up the orb. "We just have to hope it works."

CHAPTER FIFTY-ONE

— VIRA —

VIRA HELD HER breath as she and Ronak crept through the room, using the pillars in the space to hide from view as long as possible.

They hadn't made it halfway through the room when Niveda's voice stopped them.

"You shouldn't have come here, little girl."

"You don't have to do this," Vira said. "I know you have your reasons."

Niveda's eyes flashed. "And what reasons are those exactly?"

Vira faltered. Out of the corner of her eye she could see Kaleb and Riya moving around the room toward Niveda. Vira just needed to buy them a few more minutes. "Your sister."

Niveda went completely still. "Excuse me?"

"You didn't want to become like her. Lying to people. Keeping secrets."

"I didn't become my sister. I'm *better than her,*" Niveda snapped.

The black veins of her neck were growing as magic from the gemstone seeped into her veins.

"You were right," Vira said, walking toward her. "You were right that I should have listened to you better. You were right that magic couldn't be hidden like it was. And you were right that you're the true maharani. It should have been your blood, not Savitri's."

"You're too late," Niveda said. "Whatever clever ruse you think you have to try and trap me won't work."

"I can't let you break that seal," Vira said. She tried to walk forward, but she was suddenly frozen in place. She could feel phantom fingers digging into the skin of her neck, digging into the existing bruises there, keeping her from breathing. And no matter how much she struggled, she couldn't break loose.

"You thought you could stop me?" Niveda asked. "You thought you children were clever enough to do what hundreds of people couldn't do five hundred years ago?"

Her grip tightened around Vira's neck. There was no more air. Vira could feel her body begin to shut down as she stopped inhaling.

Then, abruptly, Niveda dropped her to the ground. Vira coughed as she gulped down air.

"You are nothing," Niveda said in that same angry voice. "And you will all pay the price."

Her eyes flashed again, and that was the only warning Vira had before magic punched her through the chest and sent her crashing into a wall. She winced as she hit the stone and crumpled to the ground. Excruciating pain spiraled out from the point of impact.

Niveda raised her hand again, but before it could hit Vira, Riya was standing in front of her, throwing her hands out, and now there was a protective barrier of magic between them and Niveda.

"Kaleb has the orb," Riya said, her voice strained as she struggled to hold on to the barrier. "Go!"

Niveda pelted fire toward her—and it simply dissipated against Riya's shield, which flickered with each attack.

"Clever girl," Niveda said. "Let's see how long it lasts, shall we?"

Vira took a raspy breath, but it did little to quell the panic rising within her. Riya was keeping Niveda occupied with a defensive field as

Vira struggled to her feet. She pressed a hand against her side, wincing in pain. She thought her ribs might be broken. She could barely stand but she limped toward Kaleb. He pressed the crystal orb into her hand.

Vira's legs trembled with every step, but she kept walking. Her heart was racing as she inched toward Niveda.

I hope I've made you proud, Amma and Papa.

CHAPTER FIFTY-TWO

— RONAK —

OUT OF THE corner of his eye, Ronak saw Vira move.

Niveda was using her magic against Riya, but she still had the sword. It was a powerful weapon, and he could see that Riya's power was waning. She couldn't hold on for too much longer.

Vira was hurt and weak. And the moment she approached, Niveda would turn around and attack her. He and Vira hadn't seen eye to eye in many years, and they'd both made mistakes, but as he looked at her, Ronak finally understood just how much she'd given up to be the maharani. Just how much she was willing to sacrifice to protect their country—their family.

And Kaleb, too, had lost so much, had traded his life for their family multiple times over. He'd asked Ronak again and again to let him make his own choices—to live his life the way he wanted to.

And then there was him—Ronak, who'd lost everything and everyone he cared about. Who wanted so desperately to have people in his life who were loyal, who cared about him—but all he'd ever done was push them away, not listen to what they wanted, because he was too focused on himself.

There wasn't a lot of time to act, and Ronak found himself moving before his brain fully understood what he was doing.

Kaleb had dropped the dagger Vira had given him, and it skittered across the floor. Ronak picked it up with one hand and rushed toward Niveda just as Vira reached her.

Niveda swung around, lifting her hand to attack Vira, but Ronak slid between them, swinging the dagger. Niveda had seen him coming. She whirled toward him, grabbing his arm and twisting it so that the dagger went through his stomach instead of Niveda's.

Ronak gasped in pain; his hands were covered in his own blood. His last thought as pain erupted and he lost consciousness was that he hoped he'd bought Vira enough time.

CHAPTER FIFTY-THREE

— VIRA —

ALL VIRA SAW was a blur of movement and a glint of metal—and then Ronak was on the floor, covered in blood.

"Ronak!" she screamed.

He'd created a distraction for her, sacrificing himself, and Vira used the moment to reach up with the orb Kaleb had given her, pressing it against the back of Niveda's neck—holding it in place over the gemstone.

For a moment it seemed like nothing had happened. But then Niveda staggered back, confused, reaching behind her neck. The orb was stuck to the gemstone, glowing bright as magic began to be siphoned out of her.

"What did you do?" Niveda asked, horrified. "You'll—"

But she couldn't draw on her magic. The sword in her arm fell to the ground, and Vira picked it up. It was heavy, full of power so overwhelming it almost burned her fingers.

And then she slid it right through the gemstone on Niveda's back. Niveda let out a guttural scream—clutching her chest as the stone began to glow, pouring more and more magic into Niveda, flooding her nerves and skin and her entire being. Overwhelming her, consuming her. Destroying her.

Until all that was left was the hilt of the sword, clattering to the ground.

Niveda was gone.

Vira dropped to Ronak's side. "Ronak?"

He'd lost a lot of blood. It was seeping out of him onto the floor, and he was unconscious.

Kaleb and Riya were beside them in seconds.

"Can you help him?" Vira asked.

Riya pressed her hands to Ronak's stomach, trying to channel the magic. It took several minutes for it to work. But the bleeding stopped. Ronak's breathing evened out.

And then the magic simply stopped. Riya looked at her hands and then down at Ronak. The wound wasn't fully healed.

"It's gone," Riya said. "The magic. It's—" She looked up at Vira, wide-eyed.

"He's fine," Kaleb said. "You did great. He'll be fine."

Ronak would need medical attention, but it was enough for now. He was stable.

"Vira, look," Kaleb said, pointing at the seal on the podium. It was shrinking before their very eyes—slowly, but it was obvious what was happening.

Soon, the seal would disappear entirely. The quarries would be unlocked.

They'd done it.

They'd found more magic.

They'd saved Ashoka.

CHAPTER FIFTY-FOUR

— KALEB —

KALEB WAS NERVOUS on his way to talk to Vira. He'd mentally run through everything he wanted to say in the week since they returned from the Crimson Fortress, he'd carefully prepared his words and sentiments, but historically he'd never been good at sticking to his intentions. But he felt different this time, a sense of peace with his decision—with his emotions.

Still, when he sat in front of Vira, he felt his will waver.

"I'm angry," Kaleb said before he could talk himself out of the admission. There was something satisfying about saying the words aloud—saying them specifically to his sister.

Vira looked at him in surprise. "Angry?"

"With you," he clarified.

"Oh." Vira didn't say anything for a long moment. "I . . . I regret everything," she said. "I should have protected you. I should have made sure our family stayed together. I . . . I'm sorry." And when Vira met his gaze, he could see that she meant every word.

Kaleb nodded. "I know."

"Can you forgive me?"

"Yes," Kaleb said. "One day." And he would.

"But not today," Vira said.

Her shoulders slumped in resignation, in sorrow. Once, he would have seen that as his responsibility—to take on the burden of her pain so she wouldn't have to suffer. It was strange to hold himself back like this, to not retract his words or rush to assure her that it was all right. That he *did* in fact forgive her.

But if he'd learned one thing, it was that the only way forward for them as a family was to be honest with each other. If they trusted each other, not just with secrets, but with their true emotions. If they didn't hide what they felt.

Vira had made the decision to imprison him back then, but Kaleb had never told her how he felt about it. He'd never even protested, simply accepted his fate. He'd expected her—and perhaps even Ronak—to know what he needed without ever verbalizing it. He'd mistakenly thought it a sign of love, that if they cared enough, they'd have been able to see his struggles and pick up on them and address them. He was learning now the importance of communicating his thoughts.

"How's Shiv?" he asked. He'd heard that the boy had woken up. He was in the palace infirmary with everyone else who'd been injured at Shantha Mahal. The Lyrian soldiers had been there for a few days too before leaving with Lukas and Dayana.

"His magic is gone," Vira said. "He seems happy. He's been asking for his sister. Neha sent some guards she trusted to get her from Ritsar. She'll be here tomorrow."

Kaleb exhaled. "That's good." He was glad they could reunite them. He chewed on his lower lip, wondering how to bring up the other topic that had been on his mind. "I'm thinking of going back to Lyria," Kaleb admitted.

This time he would do what he'd originally intended: he'd explore Lyrian culture, get to know his family, and learn more about Papa's time there.

Vira didn't look surprised at all. "You'll come back?" she asked.

"Eventually," Kaleb promised. He hesitated and then added, "If you need anything, you can write."

"And Lukas?" Vira asked. "Can I trust him?"

Lukas would be crowned the new emperor soon. And before he returned to Lyria, he'd sat down with Vira to negotiate new trade agreements and a new peace treaty—one that Kaleb was sure he would honor. He'd also promised to send over everything they had on liquid magic so that Ashoka could decide what to do with that knowledge. The magic had left all of the emperor's soldiers, too, before they'd returned to Lyria, and now there would be no way for them to get any more.

"I can't answer that for you," Kaleb admitted. "But I trust him."

Kaleb had no idea what the future held for him and Lukas. He was sure it would be messy and complicated. They had to work through the secrets and lies, the death of the emperor, the implications of a romantic entanglement between their two countries.

But those were problems for the future, to be solved another day. They had time.

He was going to live his own life, on his own terms. Finally, Kaleb felt free.

CHAPTER FIFTY-FIVE

— RONAK —

RONAK LAY IN his bed, staring up at the ceiling.

It was strange to think that just three weeks earlier he'd been in this exact same place, contemplating the exact same things: the future, his family, and his friendships. He had answers now. They weren't what he wanted, but for the first time in his life, Ronak felt like he didn't have to run anymore—that he wasn't trying to outrun his fears, his deepest worries.

He sat up at the sound of a knock at the door. Once, the only visitor he'd have had was Jay. But true to his word, Jay had left the palace even before Ronak and his siblings had returned.

"Come in," Ronak called.

Kaleb opened the door. His brother looked as he always did but at the same time different. He was dressed once again in Ashokan clothing— the rich silks of a rajkumaara that mirrored the clothes in Ronak's own almirah.

"I wasn't sure if you'd come," Ronak admitted. He'd written Kaleb a note, but his brother had been keeping his distance the past week.

"When have I not, Ronak?" Kaleb asked. He sounded tired—looked it, too, judging by the dark circles under his eyes.

"How are you?" Ronak asked. It was a strange question. He couldn't ever remember asking Kaleb that. Once, he'd simply have known.

"Riya told me what you did," Kaleb said finally. "You gave Ekta the compass."

Ronak looked away, unable to take the disappointment in his brother's gaze. "I did what I thought was right."

"You lied to me," Kaleb said plainly. "You told me you didn't have it."

Ronak hung his head. He wished he could deny it, but he couldn't lie to Kaleb anymore. "I know. I'm sorry." He didn't know what Ekta was going to do with it—and he had a bad feeling it might come back to haunt him. But what's done was done. He hadn't heard from Ekta since that day. It seemed that she was keeping her word, at least for now.

And if she reached out to him again . . . well, he'd deal with that then.

"I'm going to Lyria," Kaleb said.

Silence hung between them.

"I see," Ronak said. "For how long?"

Kaleb shrugged. "I don't know." He exhaled. "You're my brother, Ronak. You always will be, and I love you. But I just need . . . time? I guess. Space. I need to figure out who I am on my own and get to live my life and make my own mistakes." He ran a hand through his hair. "But this is my home. You're all my family. And I'll be back eventually."

Ronak felt his heart ache at the thought of losing his brother yet again. But this time he was prepared—this time he understood, and he wouldn't interfere in Kaleb's decision. "I hope you find what you're looking for there," he said honestly.

Kaleb nodded. He hesitated and then asked, "And what of your plans to leave?"

Ronak sighed. "I don't know. I was thinking of maybe staying here."

Kaleb looked surprised. "Really?"

Ronak shrugged. It felt strange to admit it, but the thought of staying in the palace no longer felt like a burden. It no longer felt like a prison. He and Vira had a lot to figure out, but they wanted the same thing ultimately. They'd been close once, and maybe he could learn to communicate with her again.

"I was thinking of trying my hand at writing," Ronak admitted. "Chronicling our family history. Writing down the truth of what happened with Niveda and the Kamala Society and the lost quarries."

He'd expected Kaleb to react with shock, but he didn't. "I think you'd be a great writer," Kaleb said.

"You think so?" Ronak asked. He'd always loved books, fiction and nonfiction alike, but it had never occurred to him that he could write his own. "I'd never really considered it."

"But somehow it suits you," Kaleb said.

"I just . . . I don't want to keep these secrets anymore. Hiding history never solves problems. The mistakes of the past are best avoided by teaching it truthfully."

Kaleb smiled at that. "That sounds like something Papa would have said."

It was. And it felt right to make that decision here, to follow in Papa's footsteps as a historian in the very room where Papa had worked and taught them about the value of history.

"I think Papa would be proud of us," Ronak said. "All of us."

"I think so too," Kaleb agreed.

CHAPTER FIFTY-SIX

— RIYA —

THE PALACE FELT different to Riya. It still didn't feel quite like home but . . . she also didn't feel like a stranger there anymore—as if the lingering ghosts of her past selves had vanished, leaving her with bittersweet memories and a sense of peace that felt unfamiliar.

She walked down the corridor from her old childhood room toward Vira's. She knocked and then let herself in. Vira was once again dressed in her usual silk clothes, laden with gold jewelry and thick strokes of kaajal— but she carried herself differently. She looked every bit the maharani, but there was a lightness in her that was new.

"You're late," Vira said, frowning.

Riya couldn't help but smile at that. She supposed it was good that not everything was different. "I'm sorry."

She sank into the divan, opposite her sister. She was still exhausted and achy. The magic had left her body, and despite spending so much time wanting to get rid of it, she was surprised to find that she kind of missed it. The magic had become a part of her for a while.

Vira looked at her for a beat. "You're leaving," she guessed.

Riya didn't deny it. "Soon," she admitted. She'd been thinking about it for a while, but she hadn't decided just when she'd leave.

"You could serve on the new Council," Vira offered. She'd disbanded what was left of the original Council and was working on replacing the members with those elected by the people from each province. It wasn't going to fix everything overnight, but it was a change in the right direction.

"I can't stay here, Vira," Riya said gently.

Vira sighed, but she didn't look surprised. "I know."

"You're all right with that?"

"You get to make your own choice," Vira said. "Even if I don't like it and would prefer for you to stay."

Riya raised an eyebrow. "That's very magnanimous of you."

"I'm trying a new thing," Vira said primly, but she smiled a little. "Where are you going? Back to the Ravens?"

Riya shook her head. "I don't think that life is for me anymore." She'd known it for a while, but the last few weeks had only made things clearer. She wanted to find a different way of making a difference, of helping people. But the thought of leaving them behind still hurt. She'd miss Kavita. And she'd miss Varun.

"So what do you do next?"

Riya shrugged. "I don't know. I'm figuring it out."

"And Varun?" Vira prompted. "Will he go with you?"

Riya's heart skipped a beat. "I'm figuring that out too," she admitted. She hadn't seen him in a few days—he'd gone back to the Ravens, but he'd promised to return to the palace.

Vira nodded. "You'll say goodbye before you leave this time?"

"I will," Riya promised.

✺

When Riya returned to her room, Varun was outside waiting for her.

"Hi," she said, feeling oddly shy.

"Hi," he said, smiling widely. "You look well."

"I still feel as though a mountain fell on me," she said. But her energy and strength *had* come back over the last few days.

"So . . ." he said. "We should talk."

She opened the door and waved for him to go inside first. She sat on the divan, and to her surprise, he sat beside her. But before she could speak, he said the only words she'd never expected to hear from him.

"I told Yash I'm leaving the Ravens," Varun said.

Riya looked up at him, shocked. "What?"

"The are other ways to help Ashoka." His gaze bore into hers. "And . . . I had a feeling you weren't going to return."

She shook her head slowly. "That's not my home anymore." She looked away. "I . . . don't really know where my home is," she admitted. "I was thinking of following in my Papa's footsteps."

"As a mayaka?" he asked, raising a brow, as though he couldn't see her in a lab or a workshop.

"As a treasure hunter," she admitted a little shyly. "Seeking out ancient mysteries. Traveling the world. Unearthing lost history. Keeping dangerous artifacts out of people's hands, and selling the rest and giving the money to people who need it." She bit her lip. "I don't know. Maybe it's not that noble a pursuit, but—"

"You don't need to have the entire rest of your life decided today," Varun said, sounding amused. He smiled at her sweetly, and Riya felt her breath catch.

"I guess not." Riya took a deep breath. "But I was thinking I'd leave in a few weeks," she said. "Go to Adhura and see Sharadha again to see if she has any pointers or leads." Papa had worked with her, and though Riya hadn't trusted her, in the end she *had* done the right thing and given up the sword.

"Oh."

She thought of Vira's question—if he'd want to go with her. The Ravens had been his home, and she couldn't possibly ask him to leave. And she didn't know what scared her more—how badly she wanted to ask him, or thinking that he might actually say yes.

"I thought that . . . or I was wondering rather if you . . . I mean I know treasure hunting isn't helping people exactly but if you wanted—"

"Yes," Varun said.

"Yes, what?" she asked, confused.

"I'll come with you. If that's what you're asking."

Riya's heart stopped beating as her eyes flew to his. "Really?"

He tugged her toward him, and she went willingly, sinking against him. "Yes, Riya. Of course."

He was looking down at her with that dark intensity again—one that Riya was sure was mirrored in her own gaze. He tilted her face up, his thumb brushing along the top of her cheek in a way that made her shiver. And then he kissed her for real this time. It was a soft kiss, gentle, full of promise and the future, and she found herself smiling against his lips.

I'm happy, she thought.

Things were changing. But change wasn't a bad thing—it gave Riya hope that the world would be a better place one day. And maybe she could play a small part in creating that future.

CHAPTER FIFTY-SEVEN

— VIRA —

IT WAS STRANGE being the maharani again.

The Council was mostly gone, and the surviving members hadn't objected when Vira had reinstated herself as the ruler. She was creating a Council now, one that she thought would be better suited to the kind of Ashoka Vira wanted to build, and she was looking forward to all the things they were going to accomplish together.

She sat in front of her vanity, looking at her face in the mirror. A stranger looked back at her. She truly felt like a different person from the one she'd been several months ago—the one who'd found Harish's body, the one who'd lost Ritsar, the one who'd watched her mother die.

She looked at the note on her desk. The captives held at Ritsar had been freed finally and reunited with their families. The land, too, had been returned after the Lyrian troops withdrew at Lukas's orders.

Vira had promised to oversee the rebuilding of the city, which had been ravaged by magic and war, and she intended to keep that promise. The border walls had been put up again, and now that she had magic— more magic than she had any idea what to do with—it felt important to ensure that Ritsar would be especially well protected.

It was strange, too, that the concerns that had plagued so much of her reign were just . . . gone. She'd done what she'd meant to do. She'd found the Ivory Key even if it hadn't led to what she'd expected. She'd unlocked the quarries and gotten more magic that would revive Ashoka's economy and protect their borders for centuries.

No one would know the true journey they'd gone on—what they'd actually found, what they'd sacrificed to accomplish this. But maybe that didn't matter. What mattered was that she was the maharani she was meant to be.

And a new era was dawning. She was going to help more people. She was going to protect those who needed it and help those who had been left behind. And she was going to start anew.

She was going to find people who actually cared about the fate of Ashoka and its citizens and heed *their* counsel—not just listen to people who inherited the position and used it simply to further their own agenda.

It felt good. It felt *right*.

The only thing she couldn't reconcile was that after everything, she'd still ended up alone.

The palace already felt emptier, even though Riya and Kaleb were still there. She had to accept that their destinies and futures lay elsewhere. She had to let them leave and trust that they meant it when they promised to return.

There was a knock at her door. "Come in," she said. Neha, no doubt, with updates on the Council and the palace staff.

But it wasn't Neha. It was Amrit.

Her breath caught as his eyes met hers in the mirror. He looked so different, yet the same. It was odd seeing him here, in her room. He'd been here a thousand different times, but without him dressed in his guard uniform, it felt like the first time.

"What are you doing here?" Vira asked self-consciously.

There was a lot between them that needed work. Needed answers. But

Amrit had promised her honesty, and Vira was going to try to trust him again.

"I've briefed Neha about the Kamala Society," Amrit said. "And I've briefed her about Surya too. You're in capable hands now." Surya had vanished without a trace. They hadn't found him among Niveda's acolytes that they'd rounded up and imprisoned, but Vira had a feeling that it wasn't the last they'd see of him.

Vira turned. "So you're leaving too."

Amrit looked at her for a long moment. "Yes. I suppose I am."

"Where will you go next?"

Amrit shrugged, a ghost of a smile on his lips. "Perhaps I'll find another rajkumaari to train somewhere."

The thought of him training anyone else, having what they had, made Vira's heart seize.

"That sounds nice," she said, wishing the words didn't sound so bland.

"It does," he agreed. He glanced toward the door and then back at her. "Or I could stay."

"Stay?"

Amrit fiddled with the edge of his kurta sleeve, a rare show of nerves that Vira had never seen. "With you," he said.

Vira's gaze lifted to his. There was sincerity in his eyes, but she'd seen that before. Believed it. And there was a part of her that hesitated. "As a member of my guard?"

"As your *friend*."

Vira's brows rose as she made her way toward him. "Friends? Is that what we are?"

Amrit was moving toward her too. His hand reached for hers, twisting their fingers together as he lowered his head to rest his forehead on hers. "We are whatever you want us to be." His breath fluttered over her lips—made her stomach flutter too.

"And you'll do whatever I say?"

"Vira, you're my maharani. I'll follow you to the end of the world."

"The world has no end," Vira said. It was nonsensical, but she couldn't think with him so close to her.

"Then I suppose I'll never stop following you," Amrit said.

Vira believed him.

EPILOGUE

Many months had passed before they all gathered again at the Dvar Palace. There was a celebration to commemorate the first anniversary of Vira's formal ascension to the throne. She'd settled into her role well, leading her new Council, embracing the chance to start anew with policies to revive Ashoka's economy. It was hard work, frustrating at times, but rewarding, and Amrit had stayed right beside her for all of it just as he'd promised he would.

Vira, who'd been the most nervous about the reunion, had sat in her room for ages, fiddling with her jewelry and biting her lip as she considered what it would be like to see her siblings all under one roof again. She knew they must have changed, grown into different shapes, and she was afraid that they might not fit together anymore.

After all, they'd been torn apart once before, and they hadn't known how to be with one another. But Ronak had reassured her.

"This time it'll be different," he said. "I have faith."

He'd always been an artist, but he'd traded in one medium for another, his paintbrushes for inkpots. Perhaps *traded* wasn't the right word. He still painted when he couldn't sleep or was inspired by something, but he spent the majority of his time writing, spinning stories with words rather than images.

Amrit had given him access to the old Kamala Society archives, full of books on forgotten lore and hidden pasts, and whenever Riya and Varun came across a rare book on their travels, they sent it to him.

Riya was the hardest one to pin down. She'd taken all of Papa's journals, determined to unearth everything he'd tried to find, tracking them down one by one. She wrote her siblings infrequent letters—including to Kaleb in Lyria—each one sent from a different city as she followed clues and the whims of her muse. She knew she wanted to help people, but she hadn't decided just what form that would take. But she was allowing herself to be patient, giving herself the grace and time to figure it out.

Kaleb's life was the closest to what he'd envisioned. Quiet. Mundane. Calm. And he loved every second of it. He lived in the palace and helped Emperor Lukas manage his staff of artificers, and he spent his spare time with Alena's family, getting to know them. He worked with magic when he wished, but mostly he worked with people, training students to work with magic.

As Vira waited for her siblings to join her at the Dvar Palace, she found herself touching the necklace she'd started wearing again. Twin swords crossed over a lotus. It hadn't meant what she'd believed it had, but it held new meaning now. It was the journey she'd had to take, not only to find herself but to find her family again.

Riya arrived first, her skin sun-kissed and a smile on her lips. And then Ronak, his hair a mess from running his hands through it too often as he worked. And finally Kaleb, who looked happier, less haggard.

And the moment they all sat down together, a decadent Ashokan feast spread out in front of them, catching up over their favorite dishes and bickering about past grievances, Vira knew she had nothing to worry about. They fit together—they always would.

Not perfectly. Not easily. But they were family.

And that was enough.

ACKNOWLEDGMENTS

Second books are hard. I know everyone says this, and now I understand why. I truly could not have done this without the support of so many brilliant and immensely talented people.

Hillary Jacobson: you are the best champion, advocate, and cheerleader I could ever want, and I'm eternally grateful to get to go on this journey with you. Thank you to Will Watkins, Sarah Harvey, Valentina Adarkwa-Afari, and everyone else at CAA for all that you've done for these books. Thank you also to Felicity Blunt for your advocacy in the UK.

Emilia Rhodes: I'm so lucky to have an editor as insightful as you. Thank you for helping me unearth the story I wanted to tell. A million thanks to Clarion Books and HarperCollins for bringing this book to life, especially Briana Wood, Chris Kwon, Trish McGinley, Mary Magrisso, Erika West, Maxine Bartow, Sabrina Abballe, and Anna Ravenelle. I'm very grateful to Ella Whiddett, Tia Albert, Emma Quick, Sophie McDonnell, and the rest of the amazing Hot Key Books team for giving this series a home in the UK. And thank you once again to Doaly and to Jade Deo for the absolutely gorgeous cover illustrations. I'm so blessed to have two more beautiful covers for this series.

Axie Oh and Katy Rose Pool: I don't even know where to begin. I quite literally could not (and probably would not) have finished this book without you both. Thank you for the daily trees, the many pep talks, and the chaotic chats that make me laugh way too hard and reflect on life way too much. Axie, true love is choosing each other's favorite trees before our own, and I wouldn't want to be having five separate simultaneous conversations at all times with anyone else. Katy, thank you for letting me call you about this book once a week for two years straight. The only reason this sequel makes any sense at all is because of your thoughtful perspective and endless encouragement.

Patrice Caldwell: thank you for being so generous with your time and advice. You've earned every "I told you so" because, as much as I hate to admit it, you're always right. Mara Fitzgerald: you did it, and so did I. Here's to many more years of talking craft and exchanging cursed content. Maddy Colis, Erin Rose Kim, and Kat Cho: thanks for being the most wonderful tree friends. Ashley Burdin, Alexis Castellanos, Amanda Foody, Amanda Haas, C. L. Herman, Claribel Ortega, Janella Angeles, Meg Kohlmann, Melody Simpson, and Tara Sim: you are the best writing squad I could have ever asked for. And to the rest of my writer friends, debuts and veterans alike, thank you for your guidance and support. Going on this journey has been one of the hardest things I've had to do, and I'm so fortunate to have you all to lean on.

Megana Roopreddy, Mai Nguyen, and Monika Alem: I can't believe we're coming up on twenty years of friendship. We've watched each other grow and change through so many phases of our lives, and it's an honor to get to experience each new chapter with you all. Avi Love: I'm glad to have found a lifelong friend in you. Priya Muley: thank you for always providing some much-needed perspective.

I dedicated the first book to my grandparents, and I'd be remiss if I didn't thank them once again for introducing me to my first stories. Thank you to my parents for being the most supportive, patient, and unconditionally loving people as I struggled to navigate the ups and downs of publishing, and thank you to my cat for letting me share his favorite heated blanket on late nights of working. Arjhun and Saadhana, the best ever cousins, I can't thank you both enough for letting me drag you to so many forts—or for indulging my stepwell photo shoot dreams. To the rest of my extended family and family friends, thank you for all your support and encouragement over the years. I'm so touched.

I continue to learn and grow from the people around me, and I've been so fortunate to have found an ADHD community that has taught me so much about my neurodivergence and helped me understand and accept the way my brain works. Thank you to every single member who provided me support and solidarity during the long writing process.

Lastly, I am so, so thankful for every single reader, blogger, bookseller, educator, and librarian who has picked up this series and joined the siblings on their quest. On days when the writing was especially hard, it was your enthusiasm and kind words that kept me going, and it's been such a privilege to get to share their story with you.

AKSHAYA RAMAN

Akshaya Raman is a Tamil American writer born in India and raised in California. She fell in love with writing when she wrote her first story at the age of ten. Though she graduated from UC Davis with a degree in biology, she gave up pursuing a career in science to write books. She lives in California with an actual scaredy cat, and in her free time she enjoys baking, travelling and watching too much reality TV. You can find her on Instagram @akshraman.